SPECIAL MESSAGE TO READERS

This book is published under the auspices of

THE ULVERSCROFT FOUNDATION

(registered charity No. 264873 UK)

Established in 1972 to provide funds for research, diagnosis and treatment of eye diseases. Examples of contributions made are: —

A Children's Assessment Unit at Moorfield's Hospital, London.

•

Twin operating theatres at the Western Ophthalmic Hospital, London.

•

A Chair of Ophthalmology at the Royal Australian College of Ophthalmologists.

•

The Ulverscroft Children's Eye Unit at the Great Ormond Street Hospital For Sick Children, London.

You can help further the work of the Foundation by making a donation or leaving a legacy. Every contribution, no matter how small, is received with gratitude. Please write for details to:

THE ULVERSCROFT FOUNDATION,
The Green, Bradgate Road, Anstey,
Leicester LE7 7FU, England.
Telephone: (0116) 236 4325

In Australia write to:

THE ULVERSCROFT FOUNDATION,
c/o The Royal Australian and New Zealand College of Ophthalmologists,
94-98 Chalmers Street, Surry Hills,
N.S.W. 2010, Australia

Sue Welfare was born on the edge of the Fens and is perfectly placed to write about the vagaries of life in East Anglia. In between raising a family, singing in a choir, walking the dog, working in the garden, taking endless photos and cooking, Sue is also a scriptwriter, originating and developing a soap opera for BBC radio, along with a pantomime for the town in which she lives.

For more information on Sue go to:
www.katelawson.co.uk.

THE SURPRISE PARTY

When feuding sisters Suzie and Liz come together to organise a fortieth anniversary party for their parents, they struggle to keep their own personal dramas in check. Suzie is trying to keep her marriage afloat whilst Liz is keen to retain her Queen Bee status. Their mother and aunt are at loggerheads and Suzie's daughters are experiencing the angst of adolescence. As the champagne flows and the drama unfolds, it quickly becomes clear that this is a party that no-one will ever forget — but will there be a happy family left standing?

SUE WELFARE

THE SURPRISE PARTY

Complete and Unabridged

CHARNWOOD
Leicester

First published in Great Britain in 2011 by
HarperCollins*Publishers*
London

First Charnwood Edition
published 2012
by arrangement with
HarperCollins*Publishers*
London

British Library CIP Data

Welfare, Sue.
The surprise party.
1. Families- -Fiction. 2. Domestic fiction.
3. Large type books.
I. Title
823.9′2–dc23

ISBN 978–1–4448–0947–3

Published by
F. A. Thorpe (Publishing)
Anstey, Leicestershire

Set by Words & Graphics Ltd.
Anstey, Leicestershire
Printed and bound in Great Britain by
T. J. International Ltd., Padstow, Cornwall

This book is printed on acid-free paper

With thanks to the wonderful
Maggie Phillips, the brilliant Sammia Rafique
and the fantastic team at Avon.

This book is dedicated to my new husband, my old children and my faithful dog, along with my fabulous friends — you know who you are.

1

'If you could just take the balloons and the rest of your equipment round to the back, please. We don't want anything to give the game away, do we?' Suzie said, pointing the way to the young man who was standing on the front lawn of her parents' house with a helium cylinder and a large cardboard box on a trolley. 'And then if you could just move your van?'

The young man was wearing spotless navy blue overalls and a baseball cap emblazoned with the legend: 'Danny from Cheryl's Party Paradiso — we help you live your fantasy'. His van was topped with big glass-fibre balloons and a trail of lurid candyfloss pink and silver stars.

If acne was your fantasy, Danny was your man. He didn't move.

'It's meant to be a surprise,' Suzie said as brightly as she could manage. It had been a long, long day, and there were still lots of things to do, but there didn't appear to be so much as a flicker of comprehension from Danny.

'For my parents? Rose and Jack? It's their ruby wedding anniversary — it's written on the balloons? We're having a party. Round the back?' she said in desperation.

Still nothing.

'You really can't miss it, there's a great big marquee in the garden.'

Finally Danny smiled. Suzie couldn't help

wondering if he had been sniffing the contents of the gas cylinder in his spare time.

'Is that that woman off the telly?' he said, pointing towards the front door.

'Ah,' said Suzie, groaning inwardly. 'Yes it is. She's my sister.'

'No!' said Danny, eyes wide with amazement. 'Wow, really? That's awesome.'

Suzie stared at him and sighed.

Lizzie was standing on the doorstep of their parents' cottage, perfectly framed by a mass of pink roses climbing up over the porch. She was wearing something artfully casual and horribly expensive and was apparently just taking in the view. She had arrived about half an hour earlier and, to the untrained observer, it might look as if she was standing in the porch by accident, but a lifetime of having Lizzie as a little sister had taught Suzie that she was standing there waiting to be noticed.

Danny reddened as Lizzie apparently noticed *them*. She flicked her hair over her shoulder, beamed in their direction and did one of those little show-bizzy fingertip waves before sashaying over.

'Well, hello there,' she purred, taking in the logo on the young man's overalls as she extended her hand towards him. 'Lovely to see you. You must be Danny.'

The boy, all embarrassment and eagerness, looked as if he might explode. 'That's me,' he said, as they shook hands. 'Danny.'

'And how are you, *Danny*?'

'Oh right, I'm fine — yeah, really great

— thank you,' he spluttered.

'Good, now would you mind awfully taking all this lot round the back of the house and getting rid of the van? This is supposed to be a surprise party and it's a bit of a giveaway.'

'I've already told him that,' Suzie began; not that the boy was listening.

'Right-oh,' he said to Lizzie. 'Course, not a problem. I watch you all the time on *Starmaker*, you know.'

'Really?' Lizzie smiled. 'Well, thank you, Danny, that is so good to know. And you've been enjoying the new series, have you?'

'Oh God, yeah, this last lot was the best one yet — and that Kenny — I mean, who would have thought he'd a won? I was thinking Cassandra . . . ' Danny stopped and reddened up a touch. 'I don't suppose I could have your autograph, could I?' he said, thrusting his clipboard out towards her. 'Only my girlfriend is never going to believe me when I tell her that I've met you. She really likes you as well.'

Lizzie's smile warmed a few degrees more. 'Of course you can, Danny.' She took the pen from between his fingers. 'What would you like me to put?'

'Oh I dunno. I can't think . . . ' he said.

Now there's an understatement, thought Suzie grimly.

Lizzie pressed the pen to her lips, apparently deep in thought. 'How about 'To Danny, thank you for making my party so very special, lots of love, Lizzie Bingham, kiss, kiss, kiss'?' She purred, barely breaking eye contact as she scribbled across what looked like it might be their delivery note. 'Would you like me to put, 'You're the star, that's what you are?''

It was the *Starmaker* reality show's catch-phrase, but on Lizzie's lips it sounded positively erotic.

Danny giggled and blushed the colour of cherryade. 'Oh my God, right, well yeah, that'd be lovely, thanks,' he blustered, waiting to take back the clipboard. Making an effort to compose himself, he said, 'So are there going to be a lot of famous people here tonight then?'

All smiles, Lizzie tipped her head to one side, implying her lips were sealed, while managing to suggest that anything was possible. 'We're just glad that you're here,' she said after a second or two.

Suzie shook her head in disbelief; the woman was a complete master class in innuendo and manipulation. Poor little Danny was putty in Liz's perfectly manicured hands.

'Righty-oh,' said the boy, coming over all macho and protective. 'Well in that case best I'd get a move on then, hadn't I? Get these balloons sorted.'

'Thank you, that would be great. Hope to catch you later,' Lizzie said, all teeth and legs and long, long eyelashes.

'Oh, for God's sake, put him down,' said Suzie under her breath as Danny strode away like John Wayne, dragging his gas bottle behind him. 'Do you have to do that?'

'Oh, come on,' said Lizzie, switching off the glamour like a light bulb. 'You're just jealous and

I was listening, remember — you weren't getting anywhere with him. Besides, he loved it. Did you see his face? It's made his day, probably his decade. You know you always have to remember the little people, darling,' she said in a mock-starry voice, with a big grin. 'They're the ones who can make you or break you; although I have to say it really pisses me off that after ten years of a career in serious journalism, it's two series of that bloody reality TV show that's finally put me on Joe Public's GPS.'

'Come off it, Lizzie, if you're looking for sympathy you've come to the wrong place. You told me you hated roughing it — living out of a knapsack with no toilets, constant helmet hair, and how being embedded with the troops played hell with your skin.'

'Well it does — just look at Kate Adie and that Irish woman — have they never heard of moisturiser?' Lizzie peered myopically at her watch. 'What time did you say Mum and Dad are due back?'

'Still not wearing your glasses?'

'Oh please. It's fine if you're Kate Silverton, all feline and serious, the thinking man's love bunny, but trust me it really hasn't worked in light entertainment since Eric Morecambe.'

'What about contacts — '

'Darling, I've got more contacts than you could wave a wet stick at,' Liz said slyly with a wolfish grin.

'You know what I mean, and don't come over all starry with me, kiddo. Remember I was there with you when you were in your jarmies interviewing Billy the guinea pig and Flopsy rabbit with a hairbrush.'

Liz laughed. 'I'd forgotten all about that.'

'Well, don't worry, I haven't. Anyway, Aunt Fleur says she'll try and keep Mum and Dad out till six if she can.' Suzie checked her own watch. 'She's going to give us a ring when they're on their way back. So that's just on two hours, I reckon, if we're lucky. So can you come and give us a hand? We've got to put out the tables, get the chairs sorted out, then there's the flowers, the banners to be hung, the red carpet, the balloons. After that we need to get the cake sorted, check on the glasses and then there's the fireworks . . . God, actually there's loads more to do, so which do you fancy doing?'

Lizzie pulled a face. 'You know, sweetie, I'm useless at all that sort of thing. I've got some calls to make and I need to get ready. It sounds like you've got it all covered. You won't really be needing me, will you?'

At which point Sam, Suzie's husband, appeared from around the corner of the garage wheeling a great pile of chairs. 'Oh there you are. For God's sake you two, we haven't got time for a girlie chat,' he said, talking and walking and heading for the back garden. 'It's total chaos round the back there. Can you catch up later and get round there and give us a hand?'

Suzie glared at his retreating back: as if she hadn't been working like a dog since the instant her mum and dad pulled out of the drive. Not to mention all the planning and hiring and booking and worrying about whether the party would all come together.

'So what's up with Mr Happy?' asked Lizzie.

'Don't take any notice, he's just a bit stressed, that's all,' Suzie said, wondering why on earth she felt the need to defend him. 'Work and things, and the girls are a bit of handful at the moment — well, Hannah is. Teenagers, you know how it is.'

Lizzie wrinkled her nose. 'Fortunately I don't and to be honest the man's got no idea what real pressure is.'

No, thought Suzie, *but I certainly do*.

The last few months had been a mass of subterfuge, stealth and planning, culminating in today's big event for Jack and Rose's fortieth wedding anniversary — *forty years*. Given Sam's current frustrated and grumpy mood, Suzie was beginning to think that another forty minutes together was starting to look close to impossible.

The wedding anniversary party had grown out of a chance conversation they'd had when Liz came to stay with them for a few days over Christmas, after a trip to the Caribbean with the guy she had been dating had fallen through at the last minute.

One dark winter afternoon, they had all been sitting around in front of the fire, looking through the family photo albums in the sentimental way you do when everyone gets together, and along the way Suzie had realised their parents' fortieth anniversary was approaching. Somewhere between the wine and breaking out the Baileys they had come up with the idea of throwing a party, which had somehow transformed into a surprise party and then snowballed from a small family get-together to a blow-by-blow recreation of their mum and dad's wedding reception.

'It'll be absolutely brilliant,' Liz had said, topping up her glass. 'I can see it now. Masses of flowers, wedding cake, photographer — I know this brilliant guy. And maybe we could sort out a second honeymoon for them? What do you think? Where did they go first time around?'

'Devon, I think,' said Suzie.

'Perfect. I know this lovely little hotel. Do you think there's any way we can get hold of the original guest list?'

At which point Suzie had turned over a group photo that her mum had given one of her daughters for a family history project and said, 'Actually I think quite a lot of the names are on the back here.'

Liz had grinned. 'Fantastic, that's a start and I'm sure between us we can come up with the rest of them. Maybe you could email Aunt Fleur? Wasn't she Mum's chief bridesmaid? The woman's got a memory like an elephant; she's bound to remember. Hang on, I'll grab my diary.' Liz leant over the arm of the sofa and, grabbing it from her bag, had started thumbing through the pages. 'Okay, so their actual anniversary is on the Thursday but that weekend is free — how about we tell Mum and Dad that we're taking everyone out to dinner at Rocco's on the Saturday evening — my treat?'

'You're saying we can't afford to take everyone

to Rocco's?' asked Suzie.

'No, no, of course I'm not, what I'm saying is that we want to make them think we're taking them somewhere really special just in case they come up with a better idea.'

'They don't usually make a lot of fuss about their anniversary,' Suzie pointed out.

'Well, it's high time they did,' said Liz. 'Forty years has got to be worth celebrating. Right, so, now guests . . . ' she said. 'Have you got a piece of paper there? What do you think, a hundred? Hundred and fifty?'

Suzie shrugged.

'Let's say a hundred and fifty to be on the safe side,' Liz said, sliding the photo album she had been looking through over onto Suzie's lap. 'We could have their original wedding cake copied and those table settings don't look like they'd take much and all this bunting. I mean, we've all got the photos, haven't we? It wouldn't be that hard to do. It would be lovely. Mum would love it.'

Suzie turned the album pages and looked down at a picture of the bride and groom outside the church looking impossibly young and happy. Someone had glued a piece of paper to the front and written 'Mr and Mrs Jack and Rose Bingham' on it in a rounded, bubbly hand. The handwriting looked very much like her mum's, bringing tears to Suzie's eyes. All those years ago, all that joy and hope — a life crammed full of possibilities and plans, their gaze fixed on the future they had together.

'We could easily do Mum's bouquet. I mean,

looking at these — ' Suzie said, infected by Liz's enthusiasm. 'Red roses and gypsophila, it's not exactly rocket science.'

Liz pulled a *whatever* face. 'If you say so. Let's face it, flowers are really your thing, not mine.'

'Actually, if you want to be accurate, *vegetables* are my thing and Mum's not going to be too chuffed if she ended up with a bouquet of radicchio and curly endive.'

'Well, you know what I'm saying here,' said Liz, waving the words away. 'You can sort that out. You're the family gardener.'

'And you're the family star?' said Suzie, raising her eyebrows.

'Well, if the cap fits . . . ' said Liz with a wry grin.

Suzie struggled to bite her tongue. Five days of Liz's ego, of her hogging the bathroom, taking all the hot water and constantly being on her phone even during dinner, had worn Suzie's Christmas spirit right down to the canvas, particularly as Liz had invited herself. Her idea of mucking in was — in her own words — to *stay out of the way* when there was any sign of work, whether it was washing up or anything else that might risk chipping her nail polish. Her Christmas present to them all had been tickets to a show in London, which Suzie knew damn well Liz had been given as comps, and which would cost them a mint in train fares to actually use.

'Play nicely, you two,' Sam had said, mellowed by a couple of glasses of Christmas cheer. 'And tell me again how come we didn't throw a big party for Jack and Rose's twenty-fifth?' Up until the party plan had emerged, Sam had been sitting on the sidelines drinking margaritas and watching *Wallace and Gromit*.

'I don't know really,' said Suzie. 'Mum and Dad have really never made that much of a fuss about wedding anniversaries. You know what they're like — no fuss, no frills — and for their twenty-fifth we were probably too young to organise anything.'

'Or to care, come to that,' said Lizzie. 'I must have been at uni and you two were all loved up and getting married.'

'For their thirtieth they went to Rome, I think,' said Suzie, flicking back through the album. 'And our girls were little then and it was Mum's fiftieth the same year. I think their anniversary just got forgotten in the rush. So actually you're right, a big party is well overdue. The only downside if we really do want to recreate their wedding reception from scratch is that the church hall where they held it burnt down years ago.'

'Don't worry about that. It's the spirit of it that counts. I was thinking maybe we could hire a marquee,' said Liz. 'Stick it up in the garden behind their cottage. There's plenty of room on the lawn.'

Suzie raised her eyebrows. 'Have you got any idea how much those things cost?'

'No, but it'll be my treat, instead of picking up the tab at Rocco's,' said Liz.

'Probably work out about the same if you pair have a dessert there,' Sam had said wryly.

* * *

And so here they were, six months, many phone calls, a lot of Googling and a complete logistical nightmare later.

Suzie took another look at her watch. 'I've told the guests to be here by 5:45 p.m. at the latest.

'And they're all going to hide in the cottage?' asked Liz incredulously.

'No, we've asked everyone to go round the back into the marquee so we can keep them in one place. I've also asked people to park down on the recreation ground so we don't give the game away.'

Liz nodded. 'Right, in that case I'm just going to go upstairs and grab the bathroom before everyone else arrives. Grant will probably be getting here at around six. I know he's just dying to meet you all and I'm sure you'll love him. Anyway, I really need to go and get ready. I don't want him to think that I've let myself go just because we're out in the sticks,' she said cheerily.

'Lizzie, wait — ' Suzie began, but too late, her little sister was already heading for the house. 'You've only just arrived and you've been on the bloody phone ever since you got here,' she mumbled.

'Where the hell's she going now?' said Sam in exasperation as he rounded the corner on his way back from the marquee with a chair trolley.

'Apparently she's just going to get ready,' said Suzie as casually as she could manage. 'I'm sure she won't be long.'

Sam stared at her. 'Well, that'll be a first. Just

bloody great, isn't it? Why on earth did you let her go? There are loads of things still to do and we could really do with another pair of hands. Oh, and while I'm on the subject of helping hands, I can't find either of our dear daughters either,' he said, his voice heavy with sarcasm. 'The band have rung up to say they can't find us, the caterers can't find anywhere to plug in their equipment without blowing all the fuses, Liz's fancy photographer just texted to say he's running late and the fireworks have only just shown up. And you know what? I'm getting fed up of being the one who is supposed to have all the answers. We never agreed that we'd do all this on our own, Suzie, and so far it looks to me like we've done the lion's share. I thought madam there said she'd arrive early and give us a hand?'

'I know, you're right — and we have, but Lizzie has paid for a lot of it,' said Suzie, caught in the badlands between agreeing with Sam (which she secretly did) and defending Liz (which she felt some irrational instinctive urge to do), all the while thinking that being caught in the middle was no place to be.

'I know, but that still doesn't mean she can just swan off when we need her. We're not the hired help here, you know — and she was the one who offered, nobody twisted her arm, although I'm sure Lady Bountiful isn't going to let us forget who signed the cheques in a hurry.'

'Please don't be so snappy, Sam, it's not like you. She said she needed to get ready, what could I say?' Suzie said lamely.

'Oh, come off it. Liz always looks like she's just stepped off the front cover of a magazine,' said Sam. 'Never a hair out of place . . . '

He didn't add, 'unlike you,' although Suzie suspected she could hear it in his voice. She glanced down at her outfit — faded, world-weary jeans and an equally faded long sleeve tee-shirt worn with a pair of cowboy boots that had seen far better days. Suzie knew without looking in a mirror that her hair was a bird's nest and there hadn't been time to put on so much as a lick of make-up because the whole day had been manic since the moment she'd opened her eyes.

'To be honest, I don't know how she does it,' Sam said, his gaze fixed on the front door through which Lizzie had so recently vanished.

Suzie stared at him and laughed. 'You *are* joking, aren't you? A professional stylist, twice weekly trips to the beautician, the manicurist and the hairdresser, a personal trainer, Botox and a grooming budget that would make your eyes water. Not to mention the fact that she hasn't got a husband, two children, two dogs, two cats, a rabbit and a business to run, which probably gives her a *bit* of a head start,' growled Suzie sarcastically, snatching up the boxes of table decorations that she had been taking to the marquee before life got in the way.

'Do I detect a modicum of jealousy there?' Sam said as he headed off back towards the car.

Suzie swung round to say something but he was too quick for her.

Jealous of Liz? *As if*, although even as she thought it, Suzie knew that the thought came too quickly to ring completely true. There were days when Liz's life looked like a total breeze in contrast to her own.

2

'My feet are absolutely killing me,' said Rose with a groan, prising off her shoes and wriggling unhappy toes. She and Jack had managed to find a table outside the café in the shade and Rose had no plans to walk a step further. 'That is just so much better,' she sighed, stretching her feet. 'I don't think I can walk another step. What do you think Fleur's up to?'

'She said that she was going to get a pot of tea and some cake,' said Jack, glancing towards the dark interior of the tearooms.

Rose looked at him and laughed. 'That isn't what I meant and you know it,' she said. 'All this — ' she waved a hand to encompass the day — 'out by ten, slap-up breakfast on the way here, God knows how many hours spent trudging around a stately home and gardens. This from a woman who usually wants to stay put and be waited on hand and foot while she's staying with us. Can you remember the fuss she made last time she was over and we suggested a day out at the seaside?'

'Maybe she's had a change of heart.'

Rose sniffed. 'Fleur's never had a heart, Jack, she's got a calculator.'

Jack raised his eyebrows. 'Play nicely. You have to admit she's been all right while she's been over here this time. Maybe she's mellowing in her old age. Maybe she's beginning to realise what she's missing. And like she said, she's only over here for a couple of weeks this time around and the gardens are only open to the public for a month every year.'

'Fleur hates gardening.'

'Yes, but she knows that *you* like it,' said Jack.

Rose looked sceptical. 'That's exactly what I mean. When was the last time Fleur thought about anyone but herself? When she gets back I'm going to ask her what she's done with my sister.'

Jack laughed and then, changing the subject, said, 'Actually it's been a really nice day all round, hasn't it? I'm really looking forward to a pot of tea and some cake.'

'And that's another thing — buying us tea and cakes,' said Rose. 'Fleur's purse is usually welded shut. So far she's insisted on paying for us to get in and fought like a tiger when we offered to buy her lunch.' As she spoke Rose counted the things off on her fingers. 'And now she's gone trotting off to go and get the teas. I don't understand it at all. There's something up. You don't think she's ill, do you?'

'What?'

'There's bound to be something more to this. I've been trying to work it out all day. Maybe she's softening us up so she can break the bad news.'

'What bad news?' asked Jack anxiously.

'Well, I don't know, do I? Maybe she's coming home for good. Maybe she's finally outgrown Australia. Oh my Lord, you don't think she wants to come and live with us, do you?'

Jack shook his head. 'No, of course not. Maybe she's just . . . ' he began, obviously struggling to come up with some explanation, while fiddling with a sugar packet, tipping it end over end so it made a sound like waves breaking on the beach. After the tide had rolled in and out half a dozen times, he shook his head. 'No, actually, Rose, you're right. I have no idea what Fleur's up to, but to be honest it makes a nice change. In all the years I've known her she's never so much as offered to buy a cup of tea, let alone treat us to a day out. And you have to admit she's been really cheerful and good company today. I'm really rather enjoying myself.'

As if to underline the point, Fleur reappeared from inside the teashop carrying a huge tray. Jack leapt to his feet to rescue her. Rose smiled. Jack was always the perfect gentleman even when it came to her grumpy sister.

'Here, let me have that,' he said, taking it out of her hands. 'Bloody hell, that looks amazing, you must have bought half the shop. Are you trying to feed us up?'

'Thanks, Jack,' said Fleur with relief. 'I didn't know what you liked, so I got a selection of little sandwiches and cakes. There's salmon and cucumber, egg and cress, Victoria sponge, and a lemon drizzle cake. Oh, and Danish pastries.'

Rose looked at them in astonishment. 'We haven't long had lunch, we'll never eat this lot.'

'I know, I got the boy behind the counter to give me a box so we could take home what we don't eat. Waste not want not.' Fleur settled herself down at the table. 'So have you enjoyed your day so far?' she said, in a tone that suggested it was a leading question.

'Yes, we were just saying that it's been lovely,' said Rose, watching her sister's face for clues. 'I was going to talk to you about that.'

'The thing is,' said Fleur, leaning forward to unpack the cups and pour the tea. 'Coming here today. To the gardens. It wasn't really my idea.'

'Now there's a surprise,' said Rose, shooting Jack a knowing look.

'Actually it was Suzie's. She said that you'd always wanted to come here and as it's your fortieth wedding anniversary she thought it would be a nice gesture — '

'If you brought us?' asked Rose sceptically. 'Why didn't she bring us herself?'

'Well, the thing is, Liz is taking us all out to dinner tonight and Suzie got you those lovely olive trees and to be perfectly honest I couldn't think of anything else to buy you. So I thought this would be the perfect present — a nice day out. Just the three of us.'

'I don't know why you bothered. You never bought us anything before,' Rose said, the words out before she could stop herself.

'That's hardly fair,' said Fleur. 'I gave you that lovely cut-glass decanter, remember?'

'Which someone gave you,' Rose fired straight back.

'Only because I thought it was more your sort of thing than mine and how was I to know that you knew the man at the garage?'

'They were giving them away with petrol

tokens,' said Rose to a bemused-looking Jack by way of explanation.

'Yes, but the promotion was over,' protested Fleur.

'I know,' said Rose. 'The man in the garage told me they were throwing the rest of them out and asked if I wanted one to match the one I'd already got.'

'You said you liked it.'

'I was being polite,' growled Rose, ignoring the sandwiches and helping herself to the chocolate éclair from the selection of cakes on the plate.

'I was going to have that one,' Fleur said, sounding hurt.

'I know,' said Rose, biting off the end.

Jack, who had been watching the exchange, looked from one sister to the other. 'When did we ever have a cut-glass decanter?' he asked.

'Fleur gave it to us as a wedding present,' said Rose, through a mouthful of éclair. 'I gave it to your mum for Christmas.'

Jack sighed and made a start on the sandwiches.

3

Across the garden of Jack and Rose's cottage, in a secluded spot behind the summerhouse, and as far away from the marquee as it was possible to get without actually being in the neighbour's vegetable patch, Hannah — Suzie and Sam's older daughter — threw herself down on the grass alongside her little sister, Megan. She put her hands behind her head and closed her eyes.

'That's it. If anyone asks me to carry just one more thing round to that bloody marquee I'm seriously going to flip out. Really. And Mum is just *so* stressy about everything at the moment. I mean, I was just getting myself a drink from Grandma Rose's kitchen and she comes in and reckoned I was skiving off. As if. I mean, just how unfair is that? I said to her, I don't *have* to be here you know. We're volunteering, it's not like we're getting paid to help out or anything.'

'It's Grandma and Granddad's party,' said Megan.

'I know that,' said Hannah. 'I'm not totally thick, you know.'

'Well, you don't get paid to go to a party.'

'You do if you help. Those waiters and the people in the kitchen aren't doing it for nothing, are they?'

Megan considered her answer and then after a second or two said, 'That girl was round here looking for you a little while ago.'

Hannah opened her eyes and pushed herself up onto her elbows. 'What girl?'

'You know, the one that came round to tea. The one Mum says is trouble.'

'Sadie Martin.' Hannah rolled her eyes. 'It's only because she dyes her hair. And she's fine. It's Mum and Dad — they are just so narrow-minded about anybody not like them.'

'She took the mickey out of everything, doing that funny voice, all that 'Thank you, Hannah's mum'.'

'She was just being polite,' Hannah grumbled.

'She was *not*,' said Megan. 'And then she did that thing when Mum asked her if having her nose pierced hurt.' Megan mimed an eye-rolling, sarky face. 'And when Mum said about her having her hair streaked and how she'd done hers when she was a teenager and Sadie said, 'I didn't know they had hair dye then.''

'Yeah, yeah, yeah. So what did she want?'

'She's the one who swears a lot?'

Hannah nodded. 'I do *know* who you mean, Megan. She's okay.'

'Mum says she probably takes drugs — '

'Well she probably does but that doesn't make her a bad person. Okay? Or me a bad person for knowing her, come to that. All right?' Hannah snapped.

'Don't have a go at me,' growled Megan. 'I'm just saying.'

'Well, don't,' growled Hannah, closing her eyes again.

There was a moment or two of silence and

then Megan said, 'She came round with some boys.'

'Yeah,' sniffed Hannah, not stirring. 'What boys?'

'I dunno, just boys. One was sort of blond with cut-offs and a hoodie — like a skater, you know — and the other one was tall and thin with spiky hair.'

Hannah pulled a face, feigning nonchalance; it sounded like Simon Faber and Stu Tucker. Tucker had been seeing Sadie on and off for months and Simon . . . well, he was really cute and Sadie had told Hannah that he fancied her, but Hannah was playing it cool because Sadie could be cruel sometimes, and it might just be a joke and then how stupid would Hannah look?

'How long ago were they here?'

Megan considered; time wasn't really her thing. 'I dunno, maybe twenty minutes. Dad sent me over to the summerhouse to find the extension lead for the lights. You were in the house getting a drink — so not that long really.'

'So what did you tell them?'

'I didn't tell them anything. I just said that you were around somewhere and wouldn't be long, but she said they didn't want to hang about.'

'Right, and did you say what I was doing?'

Megan looked at Hannah warily, sensing a trap. 'No, not really, did you want me to say something?'

'You didn't say we were helping out or anything, did you?'

Megan shook her head. 'No. Why would I?'

'Good, only I told her there was a party here tonight.'

'Oh my God. You haven't invited Sadie Martin to Grandma and Granddad's anniversary party, have you?' asked Megan, incredulously.

'No,' Hannah spat contemptuously. 'Don't be such a moron, of course I haven't, Mum and Dad would go ape if Sadie turned up with all the wrinklies and crinklies about. No, I just said there was going to be a party here and that there was going to be booze and food and stuff.'

Megan nodded. 'And what, they came round to see if you were telling the truth?'

It was a possibility that hadn't occurred to Hannah. 'No, course they didn't,' she said angrily. 'They probably just came round to see if the booze was here yet, and see if I wanted to hang out with them this afternoon, that's all. Did they say where they were going?'

'Down the Rec — '

Hannah got to her feet and brushed her clothes down. 'Okay, well, if they come back tell them that's where I'm heading.'

'You're not going down there now, are you?' asked Megan anxiously. 'Only Mum said — '

'I *know* what Mum said,' Hannah snapped. 'And anyway I won't be very long. They've got loads of people to help. They won't miss me if you don't say anything.'

'But what about all the stuff we've got to do?' Megan protested. 'You told Mum you'd help her with the tables and the buffet. You said.'

Hannah dismissed Megan with a wave of her hand. 'Give it a rest, will you? I've just said I'm not going to be that long; besides, we weren't at Grandma's wedding first time round, and the whole point of a buffet is that you help yourself, all right? It'll be fine, just don't let on to Mum that I've gone with Sadie, all right?'

And with that Hannah was off across the grass, heading towards the back gate and the lane beyond.

'Hannah, Megan? Are you there?'

Right on cue, Megan heard her mum calling from the other side of the garden. She turned towards Suzie's voice and then turned back again to see if Hannah had heard her, but her sister had already gone.

* * *

'Oh, there you are,' said Suzie smiling, as she watched Megan skipping over towards the marquee. Both of her daughters were growing up so fast. She looked around to see if she could spot Hannah among the girls working around the marquee. Probably off sulking somewhere, knowing Hannah. Over the last few months it had felt as if someone had stolen her lovely, happy, helpful, funny daughter and left a grumpy, sulky, argumentative troll in her place. Suzie was almost relieved not to see her and have to badger her into pulling her weight.

'I had to go and get Dad an extension lead,' said Megan in reply to Suzie's unspoken question as they headed into the tent. 'I put it round the back with all the rest of the lights and stuff.'

'I wondered where you'd got to. Do you mind giving me a hand with the tablecloths? It's really simple. Big white one on first and then a red one over the top at an angle — I'll show you. And then I've got a box of table centres,' Suzie pointed to the bar that had been set up in one corner of the marquee, alongside which was a stack of cartons. 'They're in those. If you could just put one on each table, then the girls can come and set up. Have you seen Hannah anywhere?' she said, looking past Megan into the little knot of people who were unfolding the long buffet tables.

Megan hesitated for a split second; she didn't like to lie, especially not to her mother, although not for any particularly high moral reason so much as her personal experience of the big, big trouble she could get into if she was found out.

'I saw her a little while ago,' Megan began, deploying the semantic defence of youth. 'In the garden.'

'Right — ' Suzie began, but before she could ask the follow-up question, someone called out to her.

'Suzie?' One of the caterers waved from the prep area. 'I was just wondering if I might have a quick word with you?'

Suzie nodded. 'Of course.' Turning back to Megan, she said, 'Do you mind carrying on on your own? I won't be long, I'll be back in a minute.'

'Sure,' said Megan, flicking the first of the snowy white cloths out over the table. 'I'll be fine.'

'Good girl,' said Suzie warmly.

Megan smiled. She had a strong sense that there might be extra brownie points awarded to those people who actually stayed around long enough to help with the party.

* * *

Jack and Rose's cottage was the last house at the end of the lane, and was bordered by the hedges that the two of them had planted when they had first moved in, a mix of blackthorn and dog rose that filled the gaps between a row of great polled limes. The trees had been there as long as anyone could remember, and today were heady with perfume in the late afternoon sunshine.

In the middle of a sea of summer colours, the low pantiled roof of the cottage swept down to frame sleepy-eyed dormers drowsing in the summer heat, and a heady old rose rambled lazily around the door and up the walls, the faces of its flowers tipped towards the sunshine. And if the cottage looked a little weather-beaten and tired after all these years, then the garden was a glorious homage to the English country garden at its best, set with great drifts of peonies and lush beds of lupins, hollyhocks, delphiniums and foxgloves.

Upstairs in the guest bedroom, Liz had her mobile phone pressed tight to her ear.

'Hello, Grant darling, I was just ringing to see what time you'll be getting here. And I wanted you to know that I'm missing you lots and lots. I've made sure there's some decent champagne tucked away for us, and I've booked us in to a super little boutique hotel — we can grab a cab and head back there after the party. We don't have to stay here obviously, and we can always leave early if it's too dull. I mean, people will understand. Kiss, kiss, darling. I can't wait to see you,' Liz purred, all the while watching herself in the bedroom mirror.

She pushed up her hair on one side to judge the effect; the tumble of hair and a little pout made her look sexy and vulnerable. She made a mental note to try out the look on Grant later at the hotel.

She didn't really want him staying at her parents' place among the faded florals and nasty cranberry colour carpets with no en suite and a bed that squealed like a wounded buffalo when you so much as turned over.

Nothing much had changed in all the years since Liz had left home: downstairs in the hall they still had the chart measuring how much the girls had grown every birthday, now with a new column added for Suzie's two; and on the hallstand, she knew if she dug deep enough into the pile of coats she could probably still find her old school coat in among them.

The whole house was furnished with a mishmash of furniture, some bought second hand, some given, some picked up from the local auction. There was nothing new, nothing matching, with an assortment of chairs around the farmhouse table in the kitchen and a Welsh dresser stacked with odd plates, things Suzie's kids had made at school and cards that went back to God knows when. While in some ways it was deeply comforting, it wasn't the kind of thing she wanted to inflict on Grant.

Suzie's house was not an option either — in lots of ways it was worse, with noisy children, dog hair, cat hair, a hall full of gardening tools and furniture which owed far more to shabby than chic. No, a nice little hotel was the best option.

The place she'd booked into had a really good write-up in the *Telegraph* and had been awarded all kinds of stars and crowns and crossed cutlery for being tiny, hard to find, pernickety about who they let stay and very, very expensive. Grant would adore it.

Liz turned left and right to admire her reflection in the three-paned dressing table mirror. Her new hair extensions really worked. She'd bought a new robe in jade-green silk especially for the weekend — a colour which the girl in the shop had said really brought out the colour of her eyes — although however good it made her look, it was a bit flimsy for Norfolk and Liz wondered if she wouldn't be better off in the old woolly tartan that still hung on the back of the door in the bedroom she used to share with Suzie.

'If you would like to re-record your message . . . ' The high-pitched nasal female whine of Grant's voicemail cut in, breaking her train of thought. Liz frowned and cut off the recording; she didn't like to think of anyone getting between her and Grant, especially not another woman.

Grant — Grant Forbes. She let the name roll over her tongue. Businessman, entrepreneur, man about town, man with more than one house in more than one country, man with several cars. Man who had sent the maître d' across a crowded restaurant in Paris with a single rose to ask if he might join her and then wooed her with champagne cocktails — now that was style.

Just the sound of his name made Lizzie smile. It sounded solid and at the same time sexy in a sort of American, cosmopolitan way — and Elizabeth Bingham-Forbes sounded really, *really* good.

Enjoying the flight of fancy, which had occupied quite a lot of her time over the last few weeks, Liz imagined what it would be like to be Mrs Bingham-Forbes.

'Do come through and let me introduce you to my husband, Grant,' Liz would say at the elegant dinner parties she would host for the great and good in their perfect, perfect townhouse in Hampstead. Or maybe they'd have friends to stay down at their country place — there would be staff obviously, and someone to walk the Labradors while they were away. As one fantasy gave way to another, Lizzie held up her showbiz personality of the year award, very slightly teary but not completely overcome, and through a brave, brave smile said, 'Before I thank anyone else, I want to say a big thank you to my darling husband Grant for believing in me and for always being there for me.'

She could see the pictures in the tabloids now. Their eyes locked in love, lust and utter undying devotion across a crowded room. They'd have to have a table near the stage obviously, or the camera angle wouldn't work. Liz made a mental note to find out *exactly* what it took to get a table right at the front at those things.

Grant was perfect. They had been dating for almost five months now. And okay, so maybe he was just a teensy-weensy bit overweight and his teeth weren't that great, but she had given him the number of a guy who did the most fabulous cosmetic dentistry and sent her dietician his email address. And after Grant had sent the third or fourth bunch of roses Liz had explained to him that the whole red roses thing was a bit tired and sent him the link to the website of a little florist she always used; they knew what she liked.

Grant seemed quite keen too, even though they were both really busy and didn't get that much time together. They'd been to see some new play written by some chap Grant had been to university with, and a private view at Tate Modern of a sculpture exhibition by some foreign woman with big hair who kept going on about how cuttlefish were a metaphor for disappointment, which apparently wasn't a joke, even though Liz was absolutely certain she wasn't the only one who had laughed. They hadn't quite got around to the whole cosy nights in together yet, but she was sure that would come once she'd got *Starmaker*'s new season's preliminary meetings and photo sessions sorted and out of the way.

They had also been to a couple of premieres and been out to dinner a few times, although

Grant had seemed a bit put out when the PR girl from *Starmaker* had rung half way through the first course to see where to send the photographers.

When Liz had suggested Grant drive up to her parents' party and meet the family, he had hesitated for a split second, and then said he would really love to come, and then something else, although Liz hadn't quite caught what he said because the shampoo girl was ready to rinse her off, and Dieter, who looked after her nails, had just brought over the new shade card for her to take a look at.

Liz had emailed Grant the directions and the postcode and then, just in case he still couldn't find it, had popped round to his house while he was at the office and got his Polish cleaner to let her in so she could programme the route into the sat nav in his new 4×4 and the Audi. Grant had taken the Aston to work, which was a real shame because she had been hoping that that was the one he'd come up to Norfolk in.

Mrs Elizabeth Bingham-Forbes. *Lizzie Bingham-Forbes*. It sounded so good, so natural, it just rolled off the tongue.

Liz glanced down at her newly manicured hands; obviously it was a way off yet but she was thinking maybe a big solitaire might be nice, with something really special inscribed inside the band. Or maybe there was something antique and elegant in Grant's family that had been passed down from generation to generation. That would be nice. It would probably need remodelling but people with taste understood that.

If the ratings for *Starmaker* carried on as they were then they could probably swing a deal with *Hello!* or *OK* for the rights to the wedding. It had crossed her mind on the drive up to Norfolk that maybe she should get her agent onto it now — or at least dip a toe in the waters to see if they would be in with a chance.

Lizzie wriggled her fingers in anticipation, then leant forward to look more closely at her face in the magnifying mirror she'd brought with her, turning her head one way and then the other, gently pulling the skin of her cheeks up a little with her fingertips, wondering whether the time had come for a little lift.

One of the make-up artists on the show had recommended she try a new Russian cosmetic dermatologist called Gregor who had been working on a radical new treatment to deal with lip lines, crow's feet and loss of elasticity. Not that Lizzie had any of those problems yet of course, but Gregor said he was always keen to start early — better to preserve rather than repair — and that she had the most wonderful skin tone and quality for someone of her age.

Lizzie had managed a smile: someone of her age — for God's sake, she was thirty-four not sixty-four. Anyway, apparently she was an ideal candidate for Gregor's new treatment, needing just six initial diagnostic consultations and then twelve holistic in-house therapy sessions, followed by a regular regime which he promised Lizzie would help restore, retain, and maintain that springy dewy look that teenagers took for granted.

Lizzie leant in close to the mirror and screwed up her eyes, trying to judge how the new regime was coming along. Her glasses were in her bag but there was no way she was going to use them if she could manage without.

In an ideal world Gregor recommended four applications of his patent skin cream a day, although he understood most people (the implication being the lesser mortals) could manage only two. Gregor had looked a little disappointed when he'd said it. There were two little tablets to be taken with Gregor's specially electro-neuro-something-ed mineral water, at fourteen quid a bottle, followed by an intensive facewash night and morning, bi-weekly face-packs, and then daily sessions with a strange silver machine with a long handle that you passed over the skin on your face, neck, hands and bosom before you went to bed.

Bosom was a very Gregor-esque word. He had lovingly lingered over the sound of it, extending the first syllable so that it sounded like something warm and liquid in his mouth, while his assistant had demonstrated the technique on a medical mannequin, pointing out the layers of deep tissue that the machine's special rays reached and improved.

Apparently it did something really impressive with oxygen and magnets and ions . . . or maybe it was crystals and ozone and crushed rocks from Tibet. Liz couldn't remember which now. Anyway, it puffed out air, smelt a bit like a mixture of cloves and seaweed and cost about the same as a really good holiday.

Slipping off her robe, Liz plugged in the machine and set the dial to high; after all, she wanted to look her fabulous best for Grant.

4

In the marquee it was getting warm. Suzie was showing a copy of one of the original wedding photos taken at her parents' reception to Matt Holman, whose company she had hired to do the catering.

'God, it's so romantic all this, isn't it?' he said with a smile, his gaze moving backwards and forwards between the photo and her face and then around the inside of the marquee. He took another long hard look at the photo. 'I reckon we've just about got the look right. What do you think they'll say?'

Suzie shrugged. 'I genuinely don't know. Mum and Dad are both a bit low key. I'm just hoping they're going to be pleased with it. Actually I'm sure they will be, they'll love everyone being together, having a good time. They've always had a lot of friends and most of them are going to be here tonight, but they're not too keen on big displays and big fusses if you know what I mean.'

He raised his eyebrows. 'So a buffet supper for half of Norfolk?'

'Might be a bridge too far, but it seemed like a good idea at the time and I'm sure they'll be okay. I mean, how often are you married for forty years?'

He smiled and moved in a little closer. 'You know, you look fabulous. I can't wait to see you in your new outfit.'

Suzie reddened and hastily stepped back. 'Stop it,' she said in an undertone. 'People will see us.'

He grinned. 'I don't care.'

'Well, I do,' she hissed. 'Let's get back to the arrangements, shall we? We're going to put giant-sized copies of the original photos up on the display boards on the screens in front of your prep area,' she said, pointing over to the far corner of the tent. 'I thought people might like to see how everyone's changed over the years and I'm hoping it'll break the ice a bit.'

Matt nodded. 'Great idea — you know this is a lovely photo. Has anyone ever told you, you look just like your mum?'

Suzie raised her eyebrows, warning him off.

'Don't look at me like that, It was meant as a compliment,' said Matt defensively. 'Good bones. Anyway we're more or less bang on schedule; all tables in all the right places, garlands and swags look great. The top table is a picture,' he continued. 'Food's all under control. Champagne's chilling. So all we need now are the guests and the happy couple.'

Suzie nodded. 'And we've still got the banners to put up.'

'The banners?'

'Uh-huh. Ten feet long, three feet high — 'Happy Fortieth Wedding Anniversary to Rose and Jack'. I know it sounds a bit tacky and it probably is, but I was persuaded into buying them by the woman I bought the flowers from — '

'Conned more like, you mean,' Matt said with

a grin. 'Come on, before we break out the step-ladders, how about we grab a little drink? The outside bar is up and ready to roll. Steady the old nerves — or do you fancy road-testing a bottle of champagne?'

'Nice idea, Matt, but I really need to be stone cold sober for the next couple of hours.'

'Don't be such a control freak, Suzie, relax. One little glass isn't going to hurt anyone.' Matt moved in closer and slipped his arm around her shoulders. 'And besides I want to have a quiet word with you,' he murmured. 'Have you had a chance to talk to Sam about us yet?'

'Will you stop it? This is a family party. There isn't any *us*,' Suzie hissed, pushing him away as she glanced nervously towards the open door of the marquee where she could see Sam pacing up and down, talking into his mobile. 'No *us* — all right? The last thing we want is anyone seeing us and jumping to conclusions.'

'Come on, you know what I mean. You'll have to say something to him sooner or later. And he's going to be hurt if he finds out from someone else.'

'Don't,' said Suzie, raising a hand to silence him. 'It's just really difficult to know where to start,' Suzie began, stepping away from him.

Matt looked heavenwards. 'Come on, Suzie, this isn't on. You are going to have to tell him. We can't go on like this, all this creeping around. I mean, for God's sake, it's ridiculous. This is such a good thing for both of us. It's a match made in heaven — you know that.'

Suzie bit her lip. 'I do know, Matt. I *do*, but

I've got no idea how he'll take it. You know how he's been recently. I can barely talk to him, and when we do talk it seems to end up in a row. You're not seeing the best of him. I'm not sure what the problem is; we used to talk about everything, which makes all this worse. I'm worried about him. I don't want to upset him any more than he already is. I just need to pick my moment.'

'You are such a softy. You know that's what I love about you, don't you?' purred Matt, leaning in to kiss her on the top of her head. 'Trouble is, the longer you leave it to pick the moment, the harder it's going to be to say anything to him, and the more upset Sam's going to be when he finds out what you've been up to behind his back. Now, if you're not going to have a drink with me I am going to get on, unless of course you want your guests sending out for pizza? See you later. Here, you'll be needing this,' he said, handing her the wedding photo.

Suzie sighed and glanced down at it. It was one of her favourites — the one where her mum and dad were cutting the cake, while on either side of them family and friends looked on with delight.

Suzie's mum, Rose, was looking up at her dad with a grin, her eyes bright with mischief and warmth and the promise of things to come, while her dad, Jack, looked down at his new wife with such love and tenderness that, even forty years on, it was impossible not to be moved by his expression.

There was so much love in their faces, so

much hope and joy and optimism caught in that single glance. Even now, after all these years, Suzie sometimes caught her dad looking at her mum in the same tender way and the look still tugged at her heart strings. How the hell had they managed to keep it like that, so fresh, so tangible and so alive after all those years together? She had always been aware that there was something really special between them, and for an instant Suzie felt envious and tired.

For years she and Sam had been best friends, best of everything to each other but recently it felt like she was running a marathon with him, all work and no reward, struggling to keep something going that felt battered and heavy and dead in the water. While she loved Sam dearly, at the moment it felt like their love, their marriage, was a bit dog-eared and beaten down by life. It was a real shame because in lots of ways the rest of their lives had got better and better over the last few years.

Once Hannah and Megan had started school, Suzie had gone back to college to take a horticultural course. After a few years of odd jobs and scrabbling around for work, a chance conversation in the local shop had led to the local estate owner offering to let her take over the running of a dilapidated Victorian walled kitchen garden, which belonged to the manor house just up the road from where Suzie, Sam and the girls lived.

'Take over' had proved to be a bit of a joke; there had been nothing to take over besides the lovely old brick walls covered in ivy, with buddleia and elder growing out of them, a dilapidated row of greenhouses, a few crumbling sheds and a cluster of outbuildings in various states of disrepair. Suzie had spent months clearing out brambles and nettles, bed frames, bicycles and broken glass.

But now, five years on, with the help of a start-up grant from the local council, Suzie had it up and running, selling vegetables and fruit and opening to the public for a few weekends over the course of the year. Then there had been the newspaper column and a regular slot on local radio, garden design work and various commissions to help other people set up productive gardens. Unknowingly she had stepped into the vegetable garden, 'grow your own' business at just the right moment.

Now, Suzie had kids coming from local schools and students to help out, as well as half a dozen dedicated volunteers, and so she had been able to turn her passion into a full-time job.

Meanwhile Sam had been busy working as an IT manager in a local electronics company, which had fared remarkably well over the last few years despite the recession — a large part of which was down to Sam's management style, and the previous year he had been offered the job of Managing Director.

In some ways their lives couldn't be better. They should have been happy — except that hadn't proved to be the case. The last couple of years or so, Sam had seemed increasingly distant and cool and a long, long way from the warm, happy, relaxed man she had married.

And now of course there was Matt, and all the potential trouble that he brought with him. Having read a feature about the walled garden in the local paper he had turned up one day to take a look around. Six foot three in his expensive hand-tooled brogues, dressed in designer jeans and a white shirt open at the neck to reveal a light natural tan and just the merest hint of chest hair, he was a feast for the eye. And from the first moment she had clapped eyes on him Suzie had had no doubt that he was trouble. Trouble with a capital T.

'You know what you need, don't you?' he'd purred as she showed him around one of the newly restored greenhouses. Suzie had looked up at him, not daring to ask.

That had been just over a year ago. Suzie glanced across to the servery area where Matt was helping one of the girls sorting out champagne glasses. As if sensing her looking at him, he looked up and smiled and then winked at her. Suzie felt herself redden. This was madness; she really needed to talk to Sam about him before someone else did.

'Suzie?' At the sound of her name, Suzie swung round.

'You made me jump,' she said, flustered, wondering if her face betrayed her thoughts.

'Are you all right?' Sam asked, looking concerned.

'Yes, I'm fine, just thinking,' she said, waving the words away and pasting on a smile. 'There's just so much to do. How's it going out there?'

'Well, the good news is the band are on their

way here, they shouldn't be long.' He looked across the marquee towards their daughter Megan, who was still valiantly shaking out tablecloths. 'I see you've found Megan. Do you have any idea where Hannah is? She said she'd help me put up the fairy lights and pin up the photos on the boards.'

'I haven't seen her for a while,' said Suzie, glancing over her shoulder in a lame attempt to track her down. 'Megan said she was around earlier.'

'We know that,' Sam said, sounding exasperated. 'I was hoping you might know where she is now.'

'Hannah did promise she'd be here,' said Suzie.

Sam sighed. 'Yes, well we all know what Hannah's famous promises are like at the moment, don't we? You know, you're way too soft on her, Suzie — always making excuses. You're going to have to make it plain that you're not going to put up with this kind of behaviour. She knows tonight is important to you and that you need her to be here.'

'*We*,' said Suzie, feeling a flare of indignation.

'What?'

'*We* need her here, Sam. She promised both of us. You make it sound as if she is nothing to do with you.'

'There are days . . . ' he said grimly, before turning to Megan and yelling, 'Megan!' Their younger daughter swung around as if she had been bitten.

'Oh, that's right,' said Suzie. 'Have a go at the

one who did show up and is helping, that'll really help things go with a swing.'

'I wasn't going to have a go at her, I was just going to ask her if she knew where Hannah was,' protested Sam. 'Is that all right with you?'

Suzie stared at him not knowing what to say. Exactly how had things got this bad between them? They never used to be snippy and sharp with each other; they had always been not just lovers but best friends. Yet now all they seemed to do was snap at each other.

Tablecloth in hand, caught like a rabbit blinking in the headlights, Megan was standing very still as she watched the two of them.

'I've already asked Megan — she doesn't know where Hannah is either, do you, honey?' said Suzie. Megan, still rooted to the spot, swallowed hard. 'It's all right, don't look so worried, you're fine,' Suzie said with a wave. 'You're doing a great job. And the tables look great, don't they?'

It wasn't hard to see where Megan had been; each table had been neatly laid with a white linen table and a ruby red linen top cover and in the centre of each table a cut-glass bowl of roses, greenery and a froth of gypsophila.

'Yes, but it doesn't really help us find Hannah, does it?' said Sam with a frustrated sigh.

Megan smiled at her mum and dad and said not a word.

5

Hannah made a point of staying off the main road, instead cutting between the houses and cottages, along the back lanes and down the footpath to the Rec, just in case her mum and dad were looking for her. The last thing she wanted was a lecture on how irresponsible she was and how everyone had to pull their weight. When she got to the gate of the playing field Hannah slowed down; it wouldn't be cool to look as if she had hurried.

The Rec was on a slight incline, flanked on two sides by the church yard, with a footpath cutting through it, the neatly clipped grass rolling down past sandpits and swings, a roundabout and slides, to the village hall, and beyond that the football pitch, the pavilion, the bowling green and then the road.

Sadie was sitting on the swings, all alone in the play park.

'You took your time,' said Sadie as Hannah, with forced nonchalance, ambled over to where Sadie was sitting. Sadie was chewing gum. 'We didn't think you were going to show up. Me and the lads were just thinking about going down the river, maybe having a swim or something.'

'I'd got stuff to do,' said Hannah.

'Right, yeah. For the party,' said Sadie, more statement than question.

'Yeah, for the party.'

'So, did you bring any booze with you then?' Sadie asked as Hannah sat down alongside her. Sadie had her heels buried in the bark chippings, her legs braced and arms at full stretch so it looked as if at any second she might launch herself into space. There was no sign of either Simon or Tucker.

'No,' said Hannah, starting to swing backwards and forwards. 'No one said anything about bringing any booze.'

'Oh come on, you could have brought something,' Sadie said. 'Least you could do, seeing as we weren't invited to your stupid party.'

'I told you, it's not my party,' replied Hannah. 'If it had been mine you could have come. It's more like a family do, you know.'

'Right and so, what? You couldn't invite any of your friends? Nice family you've got,' said Sadie, lighting up a cigarette and taking a long pull on it. 'Or is it just your *nice* friends who can come?'

Hannah didn't know what to say, because the truth was that her mum had said she could invite anyone she liked, although Hannah knew that what her mum really meant was anyone *she* liked, and Suzie definitely didn't like Sadie. So Hannah hadn't even bothered to ask if she could come. Her mum didn't think Sadie was a good influence, and Hannah knew without a shadow of a doubt that Suzie was right.

'Yeah well, you know what my mum's like,' she said. 'Like really straight, anything out of left field like you lot showing up and she'd go mental.'

Sadie sniggered. Hannah joined her.

Sadie was different and funny and *her* mum let her stay out as late as she liked and treated her like an adult, and she didn't check up on her all the time. Sadie's mum treated Sadie like she was a proper person with her own opinions and everything. Sadie came and went as she liked, wore what she liked, ate what she liked — and her mother trusted her, at least that's what Sadie said. 'She doesn't treat me like I'm a baby — it's always been like that. I live my life, she lives hers. It's the way things should be.'

They had been listening to music up in Sadie's bedroom when Sadie had been telling Hannah this, and ironically enough, just at that moment, Hannah's mum had sent her a text to tell her that supper was ready and to remind her that she had homework to do — just like she was a little kid or something.

And Sadie had grabbed the phone and said, 'Oh for God's sake. There is no way my mum would do that to me. She knows the boundaries. That is just *so* out of order. Do you want me to text her back for you?'

Hannah had shaken her head and grabbed the phone because she had seen some of the text messages Sadie sent.

'So you going back?' Sadie had asked, taking a pull on her cigarette and flicking the ash out of the bedroom window.

'No,' Hannah had said. 'No way.' She pretended to be offended at the very suggestion, all the while wondering if there was any way she could secretly text her mum to let her know she was all right, that she would be back later and to save her some supper.

Suzie had made chilli, which was Hannah's favourite, and she was cooking it because Hannah had asked her to. They had been talking about it over breakfast, planning to have tortilla chips and salsa, nacho cheese and guacamole and sour cream, the whole works, because Hannah had asked if they could. When she got home Suzie had saved her some of everything and Hannah had felt guilty and sorry, although she hadn't said so.

Suzie hadn't told her off for being late, simply saying, 'Oh hello, honey, glad you're back. Megan and I made a trifle too if you want some. You know what your dad's like — I've been trying to keep him from eating it all. Have you had a good time?'

And Hannah had just shrugged.

'Did you go out with Sadie?' Suzie asked.

What could she say?

As she handed her the chilli, Suzie had said, 'I don't like to criticise your friends, Hannah, but be careful, won't you? We trust you but we don't want to see you hurt or in trouble, darling.'

Hannah had considered storming out in a huff but decided on balance that she was too hungry and the chilli smelt too delicious to miss. 'You don't know anything about Sadie,' she'd said instead. 'Not really. Not what she's really like.'

'You're right,' said Suzie, 'but I have known people like her. I'm just saying, be careful.'

'I'm going to eat this upstairs,' Hannah had said, expecting her mum would protest.

'Okay,' said Suzie, putting a bowl of tortilla

chips alongside a little bowl of sour cream. 'Can you just make sure you bring the tray down when you're done, please?'

Hannah had rolled her eyes and sighed. God, it was just so annoying to have a mum who was so understanding and so nice.

* * *

Today, sitting on the swings, Sadie looked as if she might have slept in her clothes. Her make-up was thick and as subtle as a car crash, and she was dressed in a long white vest top belted at the waist over black leggings and ballet pumps, teamed with a battered and oversized leather biker jacket. Her bleached and blue-streaked hair was bundled up into a messy pile on top of her head, held in place with a scrunchie and wrapped around with a bit of lace.

The thing was, Hannah knew it wasn't just how Sadie looked or even how she behaved that her mum was concerned about. Suzie had said that there was something cruel, something spiteful about Sadie, you could see it in her eyes — and Hannah had known straightaway that her mum was right, although there was no way she would ever say so.

A lot of the things Sadie thought were funny were actually quite cruel, but Sadie was cool and diamond-hard, really mature and right up there with the best of them when it came to attitude, and that was what something Hannah really wished she had more of. Attitude. *Don't mess with me, take me as I am or leave me the hell alone* attitude. If just a little bit of that rubbed off, then it would be worth it.

Ever since Hannah could remember, she had always been the good girl, the nice girl, the one who worked hard and went to after-school clubs and joined the Brownies and the Guides. She had been doing her Duke of Edinburgh's Award until Sadie had shown up.

Teachers and grown-ups liked Hannah, but it was *horrible* always being good. The pretty bitchier girls had never wanted anything to with her and although they didn't exactly bully her, they didn't want her in their gang either. The girls Hannah used to hang around with were never cool; they were the clever, nerdy, ugly, fat ones — at least, that was what Sadie said.

Sadie had blown in at the start of Year 10 and for some reason, completely lost on Hannah, had decided to buddy up with her. Hannah's change of fortunes had been instantaneous. Now she didn't care what the other cliquey girls did or thought or even said, because she and Sadie were in a gang all of their own.

Boys liked Sadie, and she was clever too — clever enough not to get caught doing stuff, and clever enough to ensure she did just enough work to keep out of real trouble. Nonetheless, Hannah sometimes felt that having Sadie for a friend was a bit like sharing your life with a wild animal: she might be exciting to be around but you never quite knew when you were going to get bitten. Sadie could be unpredictable and moody and, although she liked her, Hannah had to admit that she never felt quite at ease with her. It wasn't a warm, friendly, giggly friendship like she used to have with Lena Hall and Caroline Hunt. They didn't go round each other's houses for tea all the time, or camp out in the garden or drink hot chocolate around the kitchen table or laugh with her mum any more; in fact Lena and Caroline hadn't spoken to her since Sadie had told the boys in their class that they were lesbians.

There was still a part of her that thought that maybe Sadie wanting her as a friend was a big joke and that Sadie would turn on her, or worse. But Hannah wasn't planning to tell her mum that.

Sitting beside her on the swings, Hannah realised that Sadie was staring at her, blowing out a long dragon's breath of smoke. She looked disappointed.

Seconds later Simon and Tucker arrived running, whooping and laughing like baboons. Tucker leapt up and swung from the bar between the swings where the two girls were sitting.

'So — what'cha doing, Hannah-the-spanner? Bring me and Sadie any vodka, did you?'

'No,' said Hannah, on the defensive, as Tucker hung one-handed and leered close up at her. 'They hadn't set up the bar before I left.'

'There's going to be a bar? Cool. You didn't tell me there was going to be a bar at your party. How about we go back to your place and suss it out?' said Sadie, slyly.

Tucker grinned as he dropped to the ground. 'Sounds like a blazing idea to me, what do you reckon, Si? Back to Hannah's place, grab us some booze and then — what? Back to your house, Sadie?'

'Yeah, all right, if you like. My mum's going to see her new bloke later on tonight so we should have the place to ourselves.'

Tucker grinned. 'Sweet. I'm thinking party, party, parteee.'

Simon, who was standing beside the swings, nodded. 'Yeah, sounds cool. I've got twenty quid. We could send out for some pizza and stuff.'

Sadie rolled her eyes heavenwards. 'Oh right, mister family man — we've got to eat, haven't we? I can think of a lot of other things we could get with twenty quid . . . '

'Oh yeah,' Tucker whooped.

Simon looked hurt. Hannah glanced up at him, longing to offer support, but at the same time not really wanting the spotlight to fall on her. Although as it happened it was coming her way, like it or not.

'So it looks like back to your place first then, Hannah?' said Sadie, as she hopped off the swing.

Hannah hesitated for a second before nodding.

'Sure, okay,' she said, as casually as she could manage, although as they fell into step alongside her, Hannah wondered how she was going to get round this one. Home to her grandparents' anniversary party really was the last place she wanted to take any of them.

6

'I was thinking we really ought to go and see the folly before we go home,' said Fleur, moving aside cups and tea plates to make enough room to spread out a map of the stately home's formal gardens on the picnic table. 'I reckon if we go down that way — ' she pointed towards an impressive row of topiary arches, 'and then turn right, that takes us down past the lake and out through the woods.'

'Are you completely out of your mind?' said Rose, finishing off a Danish pastry. 'The bloody thing is miles away. When in heaven's name did you ever want to see a garden folly?'

'But you like gardens,' protested Fleur. 'That's why we came.'

'I know and I've had a really lovely time looking round this one, but my feet are killing me. We've been here all day. I'm dog-tired and to be honest I just want to go home now,' said Rose.

'Oh right, that's it, it's always what *you* want, isn't it?' snapped Fleur. 'I'm only over here for a couple of weeks.'

'So you keep telling everyone,' said Rose with a theatrical sigh.

'And it wasn't cheap to get in.'

'If it's about value for money,' said Rose, opening up her handbag and pulling out her purse, 'please let me pay for me and Jack — that way you won't feel as if you've been robbed.'

'I don't want your money,' protested Fleur, holding up her hand. 'It's my treat.' She said it with no grace whatsoever, making it sound more like a threat than a gift. 'As I said, we don't see each other that often and I've only got a few more days left before I go back and I didn't know what else to buy you.'

'And you're telling me that your trip back to England won't be complete without a walk down to this folly?'

'It was built by the late fourth Earl and is designed to represent the ruins of a gothic fairy-tale tower,' said Fleur, reading from the description on the map. 'Complete with a spiral staircase, and one remaining stained glass window showing the slaying of the dragon by St George, it is considered one of the finest examples of architect Cornelius E. Fletcher's early work.'

'Really? Well, in that case you'd better go,' said Rose sarcastically, waving her away. 'We're all right here, aren't we, Jack? We'll get ourselves another pot of tea and have a crack at the rest of the cakes. Don't you worry about us. We'll be fine. We'll wait for you here. Knock yourself out . . . '

Fleur stared at her open-mouthed. 'What?'

'Well, you want to go and see it, don't you? We'll wait for you here,' said Rose, glancing at her watch. 'You'd better get a move on if you want to get a good look at it before closing time.'

Very slowly, Fleur got to her feet.

Meanwhile Jack picked up the map and began

to fold it up for her. He folded it carefully so that the route to the folly was uppermost. 'There we are,' he said smiling benignly. 'You'll be needing this . . . '

* * *

After checking her watch for what seemed like the thousandth time that day, Suzie made her way across the garden towards the house. The guests should begin arriving soon. She had been hoping that Liz would have reappeared by now, all buffed and puffed and oh-so-beautiful, to act as the chief meeter and greeter for their guests. Suzie's baby sister Lizzie had always had a natural gift for the kind of social handshaking and air kissing that made people feel as if they were the centre of the universe. And who wouldn't want to be met by Lizzie Bingham, the golden girl off the TV? So far, however, there was no sign of her.

Suzie glanced around: there were drinks on standby, canapés . . . Mentally she ran through the checklist, working out what else needed to be done.

She glanced at her watch again; all this clock-watching was getting to be a nervous tic. She really wanted to hand over responsibility to Liz for a while so that she and Sam could nip home, grab a shower and get changed. While she was there she'd have a chance to see if Hannah had sneaked home, she could feed the animals, let the dogs out, check the phone in case anyone had rung to say they were on their way or were lost or God knows what else. Even as she thought it, Suzie smiled to herself: actually, maybe going home wasn't such a bright idea. There were almost as many jobs to do at home as there were at her parents' house.

Pushing open the kitchen door of her parents' cottage, she made for the hallway and called up from the bottom of the stairs. 'Hello? Liz? Are you going to be much longer?'

Not a sound.

'Lizzie, are you up there? How much longer are you going to be? Only Sam and I would really like to go home and get changed. Liz?'

There was still nothing.

Suzie climbed the stairs two at a time and knocked on Lizzie's bedroom door. There was no answer.

'Lizzie? You're not still in the shower, are you? Liz!' She knocked harder and then finally pushed the door open. Inside, her younger sister was lying spreadeagled on top of the bed wearing nothing but the skimpiest pair of knickers, basking under some kind of lamp. Her eyes were firmly closed, her head tipped up towards the light, with her iPod on and earplugs in.

The sound of the door as Suzie slammed it shut made Liz jump, her eyes snapping open. She leapt off the bed and snatched up her robe.

'What the hell!' she shouted furiously, pulling it on. 'What are you doing? Why didn't you knock?'

'I did. I knocked and I called and then I knocked some more. What are *you* doing?'

'It's my new holistic body therapy, it energises

and revitalises your skin from the cellular level. I need to — '

Suzie held up a hand to stop her. 'What you need to do is to come downstairs and hold the fort while Sam and I go home and get changed. People will be arriving soon.'

'Don't be ridiculous. Look at me, I can't go down like this, I haven't done my hair or my make-up yet.' Liz protested, tying up her robe. 'I'm not ready — '

'For God's sake, Liz, you've been up here for ages. And don't look at me like that. Sam and I haven't stopped all day. You've had plenty of time to get ready, you swanned in and spread a little star dust around the place and basically you've done nothing else since.'

Liz squared her shoulders indignantly. 'That's not true. I've paid for all — '

Suzie spoke over the top of her. 'I know exactly what you've paid for, Liz, we've chipped in too and we've done the lion's share of the work, so please can you come downstairs and give me and Sam a hand?' Suzie could feel her frustration bubbling over.

'I'll be down in half an hour,' said Liz, sitting down at the dressing table.

'But people could start arriving in half an hour,' protested Suzie.

'Well in that case it'll be perfect timing then, won't it?' Liz snapped. As she was speaking, Liz opened up a Pandora's box of potions, lotions and creams and started to unpack a selection of brushes.

'I need to go home and get ready,'

'Well, off you go then,' said Liz, waving her away. 'I'm not stopping you, am I?'

'But — ' Suzie began.

'But what? Oh for God's sake, Suzie, stop being such a bloody martyr.' Liz said furiously, spinning around to glare at her. 'You're not indispensable, you know. The whole world isn't going to fall apart just because you're not there to sort it all out. People can manage perfectly well without you. *We* can manage without you — now just go. It'll be fine. Go!'

Suzie was about to protest and then stopped and stared at Liz, all the words jammed up in her throat in a tight and angry knot. Finally, not trusting herself to say anything civil, Suzie stalked out of the room, down the stairs and out of the front door. Pulling her keys from the pocket of her jeans, she headed for her car.

* * *

In the grounds of the stately home, Fleur, who was hurrying along one of the gravelled side avenues, glanced back over her shoulder to see if Rose had had a fit of conscience and decided to come with her after all. When she saw nothing, and was out of sight, Fleur sank gratefully onto a stone bench beside a bubbling rill. She wondered if anyone would complain if she slipped off her shoes and stuck her tired, aching feet in the glittering tumbling water.

The irony of today's day trip wasn't lost on Fleur. Ill-named, Fleur loathed everything to do with gardening and flowers — although it wasn't just that that was worming away at her. Being a confirmed singleton, there was something rather grisly about being asked to help celebrate forty years of someone else's happy marriage. Talk about rubbing it in.

Fleur opened her handbag, took out her cigarettes and lit up — her last guilty pleasure. She blew out a long plume of smoke into the warm afternoon air and contemplated the present turn of events.

Forty years; it seemed impossible that it had been forty years ago since her little sister Rose's wedding. She remembered it as if it had been yesterday. She had been chief bridesmaid in a blue and white Laura Ashley print dress with puff sleeves and a floppy hat. After the wedding, a few hours after the happy couple had driven off for their week's honeymoon in Devon, Fleur had boarded a train to Heathrow to catch a flight to Australia.

Although Fleur had never said anything to anyone else, Rose getting married to Jack had been one of the factors that had finally convinced her to take the job in Australia.

Her little sister Rose had always seemed to have life so easy. Whereas Fleur was big and clumsy, Rose had always been petite and pretty, with those great big blue eyes and a mass of curls. Unlike Fleur, who had a gift for telling it as it was, Rose was more circumspect about what she said and how she said it. Rose had always been sweet and obliging, always laughing and kind, the apple of her parents' and everyone else's eye.

While Fleur had had to struggle every step of the way and work like a dog to succeed, things just seemed to drop into Rose's lap. It all felt so unfair and it was difficult — even though she loved Rose with all her heart — not to be envious.

So while Fleur had slaved away at college, and spent all her money on books and cookery courses, no one had been at all surprised that it was Rose who managed to bag Jack, tall, dark, handsome Jack. Jack who owned his own business, Jack with money and prospects, a house of his own and a car.

Fleur sniffed; *prospects* — what an old-fashioned idea that was. While she had been working her fingers to the bone, no one would ever had said Fleur had prospects.

Fleur had studied and worked all the hours that God sent, taking poorly-paid jobs in good kitchens, and made herself comfortable up there on the shelf. Rose made jewellery and painted things and sold hand-decorated bowls of bulbs on a market stall, and always got on with her parents, while Fleur didn't. Sadly, they were both gone now, which meant that she had never had a chance to heal all those rucks and scrapes and scratches that they'd had over the years. She had known deep down that they were proud of her, always pleased to see her when she came home, but there was a part of her that always believed they were even more pleased when she left.

Oh yes, Rose was most definitely their blue-eyed girl, but even so Fleur was expecting — hoping — that, when she announced she was considering going to Australia to take a job managing a restaurant, there would be someone in the family who would beg her to reconsider, tell her not to go, tell her it was a step too far, that they wanted her to stay. But — all caught up in plans for Rose's wedding — no one had raised a single word of protest, not a single solitary word. Looking back at her younger self, Fleur knew she had come across as independent and bolshie, and that the lack of attention her family had showed was a matter of poor timing, not indifference. Nevertheless, even after all these years, it still hurt.

Fleur backhanded away an unexpected flurry of tears. They had let her leave, just like that, all those years ago when she had wanted everyone to tell her to stay, wanted them to tell her that they loved her too much to let her go. They had said nothing.

But pride is a strange thing. When no one had spoken up, Fleur had gone to work in a diner in Sydney, cutting off her nose to spite her face. Forty years on, she had ended up in Queensland, single, successful and still — despite plenty of relationships along the way — all alone, a wealthy woman with a chain of restaurants and enough money to do more or less anything she wanted. If only she could decide exactly what that was.

Forty years. Fleur sniffed back a fresh crop of tears. Where had all the time gone? And here were Rose and Jack, still up there in the spotlight with their perfect bloody marriage.

And now, just when she thought it was over,

Fleur had finally met someone, Frank. Not that she had told Jack or Rose — or anyone else come to that. The trouble with relationships was all that love nonsense didn't get any easier as you got older.

They'd been seeing each other for months now but she still couldn't work out how he felt. What if he didn't care after all? When she'd mentioned the idea that he might come with her to England he'd said he couldn't get away.

'Well okay, that's fine,' she had snapped. 'Maybe that's a good thing. It wasn't going anywhere anyway, was it?'

And with that Fleur had left Frank sitting in the restaurant with his coffee, her dessert and the bill, and not so much as a backward glance.

She stubbed out her cigarette in an ornamental urn. God, there were times when she wished she had learnt how to keep her mouth shut.

* * *

Back at Jack and Rose's house, Suzie was heading for the car.

'Where the hell are you going now?' shouted Sam, hurrying to catch up with her.

'I'm going home to get changed and so are you. If anyone wants anything, just tell them to talk to Lady Bloody Bountiful upstairs.'

Sam stalled and came to a halt. 'So *now* what's happened?' he said.

'What do you mean 'So now what's happened'? You make it sound like I'm about three. I just want to nip home and get changed out of my jeans and put something nice on and Liz is upstairs being her usual self. When I asked her to come down and help she told me to go. Apparently you can manage without me.'

'I can?' said Sam, looking confused.

'Not just you — everyone. I'm not indispensable, you know.'

'Is that what she said? Oh come on, Suzie, you're over-reacting.'

'Oh right, so take her side why don't you? *I'm* over-reacting? Oh, so it's my fault that Liz is a lazy, selfish, spoilt, self-centred . . . ' Suzie ran out of air and words. 'You know what she's like. She thinks the whole world revolves around her. She drives me mad.'

Sam raised his eyebrows and, for the first time in weeks, laughed. 'You don't say.'

'It's not funny. She said that everything would be just fine here without me, without us.'

'She's probably right — come on, let's go.'

Suzie stared at him. 'But we can't do that, you know she won't do a thing. She'll be upstairs painting her face and doing her hair and not taking a blind bit of notice of what's going on out here. After all the planning and arranging and trying to keep it all secret that we've been through I want everything to be perfect — '

'And it will be. I'll go and pin a notice up on the marquee to say Liz is in charge and inside, and let everyone else know that if they've got any queries they just ask Liz. Oh and I'll fetch Megan while I'm at it and leave a message with Matt just in case Hannah shows up. It'll be fine.'

'How will it be fine?' Suzie protested.

'Because when it comes down to it, these things always are. Why don't you go and get the car. I'll only be a couple of minutes.'

Suzie watched him go. He was right of course. They'd hired good people, and had already done most of the donkeywork themselves — the whole thing wouldn't crumble and fail if they took half an hour out. Would it?

The trouble was that Suzie couldn't help thinking that if they were going home, there really ought to be someone in charge. She had wanted to hand the baton over, not have it thrown back in her face. Liz always had a knack of getting out of things, as well as getting under her skin. Although Suzie had no doubt at all that when it came to handing out medals for who did the most on the day, Liz would be right up there, elbowing her way to the front to take the applause.

By the time Suzie had unlocked the car and moved a pile of boxes and bags off the seats, Sam was hurrying back across the grass.

'Okay, let's hit the road. I've told everyone that if they want anything Liz is in the house, and Megan said she wants to stay and get the rest of the tables done. I said we'd bring her dress and shoes back with us. Okay?'

Suzie was about to protest and then nodded. 'Okay.'

Sam looked at her, eyebrows raised in surprise. '*Okay?* Really? You're not going to say it can't be done, and that we can't go and that we should hang around until Madam decides to put in an appearance?'

'I'm not really like that, am I? Liz said that I was a control freak.'

Sam tipped his head to one side. 'If the cap fits. You know as well as I do that someone's got to take charge of things and you're just naturally good at it. If that's control freakery — who cares?'

Suzie glared at him and then gave in and sighed, 'Actually you're right and to be perfectly honest I'm way too knackered to argue. I just want to get home, grab a shower, have a cup of tea and put my frock on. Although at this rate I'm going to be too tired to enjoy the party.'

'You'll be fine,' Sam said, which Suzie realised was pretty much his answer to everything.

* * *

'Just how much longer do you think Fleur's going to be?' said Rose, peering off into the middle distance beyond the topiary arches and the rose beds and the great borders of perennials and expertly trimmed shrubs. 'She's been gone ages. I want to have a shower and get changed before we go out to dinner. What time did she say Liz had booked the table for?'

Jack glanced at his watch. 'Seven, I think. I'm sure Fleur won't be much longer. I mean how long does it take to look around a ruin? Maybe we should go and look for her?'

7

'My parents don't really like people smoking,' said Hannah apologetically as Sadie, Tucker and Simon arrived at the back gate of her grandparents' cottage.

Sadie pulled a face and then peered down at the cigarette she was holding between her fingers as if it had appeared by magic. 'They are just so bloody straight, aren't they, your parents?' she grumbled, bending down to tap it out on the sole of her shoe. 'I mean, you know, it's not like I'm asking them to smoke it for me or anything.'

'Yeah, like it's a free country,' said Tucker, making a meal of putting his out.

Hannah hesitated, hand on the gate. Taking the three of them in with her would be a recipe for potential disaster. She could almost hear her mum now, putting down whatever she was doing, putting on her cheery face and waving them over, while giving Hannah one of those sideways looks that she did. The one that said, 'I'm not going to make a fuss now but we'll talk about this later.' And then Suzie would smile and say, 'Come on in,' to Sadie and Tucker and Simon. 'Would you like some juice? I think we've got some Pepsi here somewhere. If you want to hang around that would be great, there'll be food later on. Oh and maybe while you're here you could give Hannah a hand? I know her dad needs some help with the fairy lights — you look nice and tall, Simon.' And then Suzie would laugh and smile and be nice to Sadie even though she didn't like her, and find them all a glass or a can and some crisps or something.

Hannah cringed; just how bad would *that* be? Sadie would never let her forget it. Sadie had told her how much she hated all that being treated like a baby stuff. Hannah could already picture Sadie pulling sarky faces, mouthing 'Mummy's little girl', while rolling her eyes and making chatty mouth mimes with her fingers behind Suzie's back, swearing under her breath while Suzie was nice to her. She knew it would happen because that was just what Sadie had done when Suzie had suggested Sadie come round for tea. God, what a mistake that had been.

And this would be worse, because however much trouble Hannah got into from her mum for hanging out with Sadie, it would be *nothing* compared to the stick she would get from Sadie for them being treated like they were babies. Hannah looked from face to face. Sadie was chewing gum; Tucker was fishing something out of his ear. Simon looked as if he was waiting to see what happened next.

'Actually, you could stay out here if you liked. I mean, I could just nip in and get something. It would probably be easier that way, you know, in and out,' Hannah said, making it sound all very casual. 'Lot less chance of us getting caught, and way less hassle than us all going in together.'

Sadie let out a long theatrical sigh. 'Great, so now you tell us. We could have stayed down the

Rec and sent you all on your own,' she said, retrieving the dog end from behind her ear. 'All right then, we'll wait out here, but don't be too long, will you — or we might just have to come in and find you,' she added with a sly knowing wink.

'I'll come with you if you like,' volunteered Simon. 'You know, give you a hand with stuff.'

Sadie raised her eyebrows and grinned at him. 'How much booze are you thinking of getting?' she asked. Simon ignored her and, catching hold of the gate, held it open for Hannah.

'Oooooo, get you,' said Sadie, grinning. 'Real knight in shining armour, aren't we?'

Tucker suppressed a snort of laughter while Hannah felt herself reddening furiously; she daren't even look at Simon.

Sadie settled herself up against the garden wall, one leg cocked so that her foot sat flat against the old bricks; closing her eyes, she tipped her face towards the sun.

'Go on then, don't hang about,' she said, waving them away. 'We haven't got all bloody day, you know. See if they've got any vodka, or if not vodka then get some gin or something. Not whisky though. I hate whisky.' Reaching into her jacket she pulled out a lighter and relit her cigarette. 'What about you, Tucker? Want to order anything from the bar, do you?'

'If they've got any cider — ' he began.

Sadie snorted. 'Yeah right, it looks like just the sort of do where they'd have laid on a shedload of White Lightning for head-bangers like you, doesn't it? You can be so dense sometimes

— they're more likely to have champagne than cider, you pillock.'

Tucker looked hurt. 'Yeah, all right in that case I'll have a bottle of that then,' he said self-consciously, stuffing his hands into his pockets. Hannah stared at him, thinking about how things were very slowly shifting, how she used to be really pleased that Sadie was her friend and how it was that now, all this time down the line, she had ended up being as intimidated and nervous of her as she had been of any of the cliques in school.

Hannah glanced up at Simon. He shrugged and then winked, which made her smile.

'C'mon then,' he said. 'Let's get this show on the road.'

They went through the gate, circling around the back of the summerhouse before stepping out onto the lawn. Hannah made a show of nonchalance. There was a buzz of activity behind the big marquee and nobody appeared to notice them as they wandered in among the hired help. There were girls dressed in black and white checked chef's trousers with snowy white jackets carrying in trays of food, and boys dressed all in black, with waistcoats and slicked back hair chatting in a corner. A trail of older men were ferrying musical instruments, speakers and all sorts of other paraphernalia from the front of the house around into the big tent. Hannah looked left and right, wary as a feral cat. There was no sign of her mum and dad, or in fact of anyone else that Hannah recognised.

'This way,' she said to Simon. 'We need to be

quick, while there's no one about. The bar's in here.'

Without another word, Simon followed her into the marquee. Away from Tucker and Sadie, he looked more normal, the kind of boy her mum would think was fun and nice to have around and would smile at and mean it.

'Are you sure you want to do this?' he said, loping along beside her. 'You know, getting the booze and stuff?'

Hannah sighed. 'I can't see I've got a lot of choice really. If I don't Sadie's going to come bowling in here causing trouble.'

'So you're okay with it?'

Hannah sighed. 'Yeah, well, kind of . . . You know, yes and no. It'll be all right as long as my mum and dad don't catch us. They don't like me hanging out with Sadie very much. But it'll be cool.'

'So what are you going to say?' he said. '"Hello. I want some booze for my mates?"'

Hannah hesitated, considering her options. Lying really wasn't her forte, better to tell the truth. 'More or less. I was just going say someone sent me to get a bottle of vodka and a bottle of champagne,' she said looking up at him with a grin.

He grinned right back at her, which made something tingle inside her. 'And you think that's going to work?'

'Dunno,' said Hannah with a shrug. 'It's worth a shot though I reckon.'

Inside the tent, despite the activity, the air was flat and hot and heavy, muffling the sounds from outside. A couple of waitresses were busy setting up the tables with cutlery and glasses. On a dais to the left of the door was a long table with a screen hanging behind it, and behind that was an area being used to organise the food for the party. To the right, in the corner, was the bar, while in the far corner the band were setting up their instruments. A large man with a beard and glasses was putting together a drum kit, and another was running wires out for the various guitars and amplifiers.

'Looks like it's going to be a good do,' said Simon, nodding towards the group.

'Yeah.'

'Shame we can't stay really,' Simon said.

Hannah glanced at him. 'Really?'

He nodded. 'Yeah, food, drink and a band — it'd be great.'

Hannah tried to work out whether he was being serious or not. 'We could maybe come back later if you like,' she said, testing the waters.

'Okay, sounds good,' he said. 'But not with Sadie. I mean — well, you know . . . ' Simon hesitated, as if waiting to see if Hannah was going to protest and then, when she didn't, he smiled and added, 'It's not exactly her kind of thing, is it?'

'No — I suppose not. Not enough thrash metal and swearing.'

Simon laughed and then shifted his weight. 'You know my mum won't let her and Tucker come round ours any more. Did I tell you that?'

Hannah shook her head and was about to ask why when she saw Megan hurrying across the marquee towards them.

'Where on earth have you been? Mum's looking all over for you,' Megan said indignantly, casting a cool appraising eye over Simon. 'Dad's going leery because you said you were going to be here to help him with the lights and the photos and stuff. It's not fair, I'm not going to cover for you — you're in big trouble, they're really annoyed that you cleared off.'

'All right, all right, I know, I know,' said Hannah, not wanting to be shown up by Megan in front of Simon. 'Did you tell them where I was?'

'No, of course I didn't,' snapped Megan. 'But what if they ask me again?'

Hannah shot a sharp look at Simon who took the hint and wandered off.

'It's all cool, okay? I've just been hanging out with Sadie for a bit and now I've come back to pick up a couple of things,' she hissed angrily.

Megan eyed her suspiciously before taking another look at Simon. 'What do you mean, like running an errand or something?'

Hannah nodded. 'Yeah, like running an errand or something.'

Megan didn't look convinced. 'Who for? I thought you just said that you were hanging out with Sadie — '

'I was,' said Hannah ignoring the question. 'But I've come back to get this stuff sorted out. All right? So where did you say Mum and Dad are?'

'They've gone home to get changed. They shouldn't be very long. Dad said if we want anything before they come back then we've got to go in and ask Liz.'

'And where's Liz now?' asked Hannah, glancing around the marquee.

'Still upstairs getting ready as far as I know. So are you going to stay and help now?'

Hannah looked over towards the bar, where a woman with big earrings was busy fitting bottles up into the optics. 'No, not at the minute. I just told you, I've got to get stuff.' Hannah was hoping that if she said it forcefully enough that Megan would assume it was one of the grown-ups who had sent her.

Megan looked as if she was about to argue and then said, 'Well, all right, but you'd better hurry up and get back. Mum said they were only going to be gone for half an hour and they're expecting you to be here to help.'

'I know, I know, now just get off my case, will you?' snapped Hannah. 'I just need to do this first, *all right*?'

'Can I come?'

Hannah stared at her in amazement. 'What? What do you mean, can you come?'

'With you. It's going to be so boring here.'

'I don't think so,' said Hannah.

'You're going to do something, aren't you? You're up to something.'

Hannah sighed. 'What's it got to do with you what I get up to?'

'Why don't you just let me tag along? I won't be any trouble, I promise. *Please*.'

Hannah rolled her eyes. 'Why would I want to drag you along?'

Megan flinched. 'I'll tell them you were here.'

'Tell them what you like.'

'You know Mum's really worried about you going around with Sadie, she thinks you're going to get into drugs or get pregnant or — '

Hannah swung round. Stepping in close to her little sister, she loomed over her. 'Why don't you just shut up? What I do is my business, *all right*?'

'You used to like it when we did stuff together.'

'Uh-huh, and I used to think there was a tooth fairy too,' snapped Hannah.

'I miss you,' said Megan miserably as Hannah turned away. The words caught hold of her heart and made her wince but Hannah didn't turn back.

Instead Megan sniffed and went back to her job while Hannah made her way to the bar with a certain determination in her step.

'You okay?' asked Simon, hurrying across to catch up with her.

Hannah nodded. 'I'm fine.'

The barmaid had just put up a bottle of gin on the bar.

Hannah hesitated for a second or two and then, putting on her most helpful-child-on-an-errand face, said politely, 'Excuse me?'

The woman turned round and smiled. 'Hi there, honey. You all right? What do you want?'

Hannah took a deep breath and, pretending that she was reciting a list, said, 'I've got to come and get a bottle of vodka and a bottle of champagne, please.'

The woman laughed. 'Really? What sort of

cocktail is that for then? Do you need any mixers? Orange juice or something?' She indicated the rest of the bottles stacked up in crates.

Hannah glanced up at Simon who pulled a face. 'I don't know,' she said, looking back at the barmaid. 'I don't think so. I just had to come and get vodka and champagne.'

'Righty-oh, well, if you want anything else you'll have to come back and I'll sort you out. Hang on.' The barmaid reached in under the bar. 'There we go, me dear,' she said, sliding a bottle of vodka across the counter. 'You're not planning a little party of your own somewhere, are you?' she added, although it didn't sound as if she was expecting an answer. 'I just need to book it out. It's not a problem. I can get the boss to bring me down another bottle when he comes. I'm not in charge of champagne though, you'll have to go and ask one of the catering staff for that.' As she spoke the woman took a pad of paper off the bar and began to write. Hannah could feel her colour and her heart rate rising and waited anxiously for the hammer to fall. Instead the woman looked up at her. 'Was there anything else you wanted, pet?' she said. 'Orange juice? Maybe a lemonade or a Coke for you and your friend?'

Hannah realised with a start that it had worked and said hastily. 'No, no that's everything. Thank you.' And grabbing the bottle, she headed off towards the caterers.

'Bloody hell,' hissed Simon, stepping up alongside her. 'That was easy.'

Hannah looked up at him. 'You think so?' she said between gritted teeth. 'I thought she was going to make me sign for it. Here, you can carry it.'

He grinned. 'Fair enough.'

With Simon holding onto the vodka, Hannah decided to try the same tactic on one of the waitresses, who was busy unpacking a box of glasses. 'Hello, we've come to pick up a bottle of champagne,' Hannah said brightly, with a confidence that she didn't feel.

The girl half turned to check her out and then yelled at the top of her voice, 'Matt, can you come out here and sort this out, please? Someone wants champagne.' At which point Hannah felt a great rush of panic and willed the ground to open up and swallow her whole, but instead her mum's friend Matthew, who was busy in the prep area, looked up and smiled at Hannah.

'Hi there,' he said, 'Yeah, that's okay, it's Suzie's daughter. For Liz, is it? It'll be fine.' And with that he went back to whatever it was he was doing.

The girl disappeared out into the kitchen area and returned seconds later carrying a chilled bottle of champagne, which she handed to Hannah with a wink. 'Don't go drinking it all at once now, will you?' she said.

'Course not. Thank you,' said Hannah, turning away and letting out a long slow breath as she and Simon made their way towards the door.

'Whatever you do, don't run,' said Hannah out of the corner of her mouth.

8

'So where exactly are you at the moment, Fleur?' said Suzie, pressing the mobile phone tight to her ear. 'The signal's absolutely terrible. It's really crackly.'

'That's probably the twigs,' said Fleur. 'I'm hiding.'

'What?' said Suzie in surprise. 'What do you mean you're hiding?'

'In a shrubbery, near the lake.'

'What on earth are you hiding from?' asked Suzie.

'Your mother and father. I thought I just saw them coming down this way. I'm supposed to be looking at some folly in the woods but my feet are killing me and it's bloody miles away. I don't want the two of them to catch me.'

'Right . . . ' said Suzie, deciding that whatever the explanation was she could do without hearing any more of it; but Fleur was on a roll.

'This is all your fault, you know. I've been trying to keep them out of your way as long as possible. Your mother's been really rude to me.'

Suzie considered for a split second whether she should carry on with the family tradition. She had wet hair, was naked except for a bath towel, couldn't find the new shoes that went with the new dress she'd bought for the party and would still be in the shower if Fleur hadn't rung and insisted that she really needed to speak to

Suzie *now*. Sam had assumed it was some sort of emergency and had practically dragged her out of the bathroom.

'So how long do you think it's going to be before you get home?' Suzie asked, taking a long hard look under the dressing table as she spoke. Her new shoes had got to be somewhere.

'I'm just going to go back and find your mum and dad. It'll be a least another half hour before we leave.'

'Okay. Perfect. Fleur, I'm really sorry but I've got to go — '

'Oh that's right. It's all right for you, I don't know why you couldn't have taken them out for the day and come here with them instead of me. You know I hate all this garden lark,' said Fleur miserably. 'It's been my idea of hell dragging them round this place all day.'

'You're doing a brilliant job,' said Suzie as brightly as she could. 'We couldn't have managed to do it without you.'

But Fleur was in no mood to be interrupted, or flattered, come to that. 'My place, I've got gravel, couple of strips of Astroturf, bit of paving and some plastic trees. You just hose the whole lot down once in a while to wash the dust off. I don't hold with all this weeding, cutting and pruning palaver. Talk about a waste of time. You know your mother knows the name of all the plants, don't you? *In Latin*. I've never been so bored in my entire life — red flowers, yellow flowers, why would anyone get excited over a bush, for God's sake?'

Sam, who had leapt into the shower as soon as he had dragged Suzie out, walked into the bedroom wrapped in a towel. He looked at her anxiously. 'Everything all right?' he mouthed, indicating the phone.

Suzie nodded and gave him the thumbs up as she continued the conversation with Fleur. 'Well, you can come home as soon as you like now, we're more or less ready here.'

'Thank God for that,' sighed Fleur. 'I'm totally petunia-ed out.'

* * *

Meanwhile, up on the terrace outside the stately home's tearooms, having decided not to go looking for Fleur, and having finished off a pot of tea and the best of the cakes, Rose had left Jack sitting in the sunshine reading the guidebook, while she went off to wander around the gift shop. She had intended to go looking for plants, but what caught her eye instead was a large notice standing slap bang in the middle of the main aisle that read: 'Unfortunately our fairy tale folly will be closed this summer for refurbishment. We apologise for any inconvenience to our visitors and invite you along next year for the grand gala opening. Special rate tickets are available at the counter.'

Rose raised her eyebrows; it looked as if Fleur was going to be disappointed after all.

* * *

Back at Rose and Jack's cottage Liz was becoming increasingly flustered and annoyed. She hated to be rushed: it made her feel uneasy. Usually she allowed herself at least two hours to get ready, that was the absolute bare minimum; and as far as she was concerned it was two hours well spent.

Suzie's daily regime appeared to involve slapping on a bit of moisturiser, some mascara and an old pair of jeans. But then again there was nothing in Suzie's precious organic vegetable patch that was going to think she'd let herself go just because she wasn't in full make-up at six in the morning for some stupid promotional do in a park in the middle of nowhere. No cabbage, courgette or cauliflower was ever going to suggest Suzie needed to lose a few pounds, no leek would ever mention in a meeting that they had seen this *fantastic* new girl on some obscure cable show who was really hot and *incredibly* talented and only twenty-bloody-three.

Oh no, in her line of work Suzie could go on till she had a face like a badly worn moccasin, whereas in Liz's profession one slip, one slide, one filler session gone wrong, and you could find yourself hosting an afternoon car boot show. Once you reached a certain age it was easy to glide from golden girl to Granny's collectibles in one short step, and while Lizzie actually felt that she was at her peak and had several good years ahead of her yet, it was important to be ever watchful, to keep herself in shape, keep up with those facials and not let time get the upper hand.

The gym, Botox, fillers, Gregor and his

diabolical machines were going to be an occupational hazard for as long as she wanted a face and figure that fitted on prime-time TV.

For her parents' party, Liz was planning to go with a subtle but sexy local-girl-made-good-comes-home look. Dewy, bright, natural-looking skin, pink, pearly lips, bright but subtle eyes, her hair lightly styled and looking very slightly windswept.

Laid out on the dressing table was a palette and selection of brushes that wouldn't have looked out of place in an artist's studio. Liz leant in a little closer to check how she was doing — looking natural and girl-next-doorsy was the toughest look of all to pull off.

Her stylist at *Starmaker* had sorted out three possible outfits for the party: a little Victoria Beckham number with its trademark full-length zip, a Hervé Léger bandage dress and something from Burberry that Emma Watson had worn to some daytime thing, although this one was in jade not grape. While the outfits had looked just fine in London, looking at them now on their hangers with the shoes standing underneath, Liz suspected that they were all too dressy for West Norfolk. For the girl who styled her at *Starmaker*, Camden was probably her idea of rural.

It all looked way too show-bizzy — and those Louboutins were going to be a complete nightmare on the grass. Liz took a deep breath and tried not to let Suzie unsettle her. 'Calm, calm,' she murmured. 'Deep breaths, inner strength. Do not let her get to you.'

Just why the hell should she be expected to rush when she'd paid for almost all of the party?

Liz picked up a make-up brush, closed her eyes and took another calming breath. Breathing; for the last six weeks Liz had been paying her yoga teacher a small fortune to teach her something she had been doing all her life without giving it a moment's thought. She tried to visualise being at one with the open plain, the rolling woodlands, the mighty ocean, the whole of creation — but all she could think about was getting one over on Suzie.

Bloody woman, bursting in her telling her what to do. Had she any idea how much a marquee cost? *Half an hour, my arse*, Liz thought furiously. It was going to take her that long to get her foundation right. And no one was going to show up this early, surely?

Breathe.

Anyway, Suzie was such a control freak, Liz couldn't see her being away for very long. After all, how long did it take to have a shower and towel-dry an unstructured bob for God's sake?

Liz made the effort to concentrate on her breathing and inner peace and radiant beauty, imagining her body was light as a butterfly and suffused with joy and contentment, at one with the universe.

From somewhere downstairs Liz heard the doorbell ringing.

'Bugger it,' she spat as her eyes snapped open.

* * *

'My new shoes have *got* to be here somewhere,' said Suzie, coming up for air after a prolonged hunt under her side of the bed. 'This is absolutely ridiculous. Where the hell are they? They can't just have disappeared. I put them in the bottom of the wardrobe, I know I did.'

'So why are you looking under the bed?' asked Sam, who was busy towelling his hair dry.

'Because they're not in the wardrobe, I've looked.'

'Are you sure?'

'Of course I'm sure. I've had everything out,' she said, pointing to a jumble of things piled up on the bedroom floor. 'They've got to be here somewhere; shoes just don't vanish.'

The family cats sat on the bed and watched with considerable interest as Suzie folded back the duvet and dived under the bed again. So far she'd found a stray trainer, a vacuum cleaner attachment, a sprinkling of coat hangers, some spilt cotton buds, enough fluff to re-carpet the sitting room — but no shoes. Still wrapped in her towel, Suzie sat back on her heels.

'They're brand new, they're in a box, they're peacock-blue silk. I mean, where the hell could they have got to?'

'Well, don't look at me,' said Sam, busy sorting out his own clothes. 'I'm not into high heels.'

'They're not that high,' she said, not bothering with the joke. 'They're just gorgeous and I bought them specially and I haven't got anything else that goes with my new dress.'

He looked at her sceptically. 'You must have something else you can wear . . . '

'Well, I haven't. All I've got are flip-flops, sensible dog-walking shoes, gardening boots and wellies. The only other pair of going-out shoes I own are the ones I wore with my going-away dress, and how many years ago was that? They're so out of fashion I'm expecting a call from the V&A any day now.'

'Don't have a go at me, I was just saying,' Sam said, sounding hurt as he headed back towards the bathroom, making Suzie feel guilty that she had snapped at him. She sighed; if she was honest, it wasn't only Sam's fault that things weren't great between them. She had too many secrets to make life easy for either of them.

Suzie also knew that if she had worn her old shoes to the party, Sam wouldn't have said a word, and even after all these years she couldn't decide whether that was because he just didn't notice or he just didn't care. He always used to say that he loved her just the way she was, which in one way was wonderful, but as time had gone on — and particularly at the moment, when things between them were so tense — Suzie had begun to feel less certain. There was a very fine line between acceptance and indifference.

Giving up on the shoes, she took her new outfit out of the wardrobe and held it up against herself. It was a rich Persian blue, beautifully slimming, beautifully cut, column dress, with a little matching jacket that had cost a small fortune even though it had been in the sale. She ran her fingers over the fabric. With her job and the girls growing up it had been so long since Suzie had bought anything really nice for herself. She turned to look in the mirror to gauge the effect. The colour brought out the deep blue of her eyes and looked lovely against her lightly tanned skin. It had been a great choice.

And okay, so it was more than twice what Suzie had ever paid for an outfit before, but she had needed something new, something special for tonight and Sam could hardly complain — she was earning her own money these days, proper money, not peanuts. Now that she was more successful it was time she started to make more of an effort, that was what Matt had said. 'Dress for success,' he had said, and if this dress was anything to go by, success was a foregone conclusion.

Seeing her sister Lizzie, even when she was dressed down, had made Suzie feel dowdy and plain, so she was even more pleased that she had made the effort to find something special to wear for the party.

She and Sam had been together so long that she wondered if he still really noticed that she was a woman. Not that Suzie had ever been a girlie girl and these days working in the garden all day meant that she had a lot of checked shirts and jeans and hands that said more about manual labour than manicures.

But all that was going to change if Matt had his way.

Matt. She sighed.

Matt had insisted on going to Cambridge with her to help choose the dress for the party, and when — after half a dozen outfits — she came out of the changing room in the blue outfit, he had given her a round of applause, saying she looked lovely, really gorgeous. For the first time in years, as she did a little twirl for him and the shop assistant, that was exactly how she felt.

Hidden away in the back of the wardrobe were the other outfits Matt had insisted she should buy. When she had protested that they were far too expensive and she couldn't justify spending that much money on anything, let alone clothes, Matt had insisted on buying them for her as a treat. An *investment* was what he had actually said, as he had had them wrapped, and after a token stand-off she had let him settle the bill. And now they were yet another guilty secret that she was keeping from Sam. How had things gone this far?

Out on the landing Sam was pulling on the crisp white shirt she'd ironed for him. Watching him doing up the buttons, she felt a pang of sadness. It used to be that he said thank you when she did those things for him. It used to be that he thought she was lovely, and said so.

Just when exactly had they started to take each other for granted? There was a time when he used to come up behind her and slide his hands around her waist while she was at the ironing board, snuggling up, kissing her neck and making her giggle, till she had to push him away, afraid of burning herself or the thing she was ironing. Sometimes just recently it felt as if she was remembering a different lifetime, with two different people.

'Penny for them,' Sam said, as he caught her staring.

Suzie managed a smile, not knowing how to start the conversation that she needed to have with him.

'No, it's fine, nothing important,' she said. 'I was just thinking.'

'Well, we haven't got time for any of that,' said Sam, buttoning his cuffs. 'We need to be out of here.'

* * *

'All right, all right — I'm coming, I'm coming, take your finger off the bloody bell,' growled Liz as she hurried across the landing and down the stairs of Rose and Jack's cottage. The bell kept on ringing and ringing until finally Liz threw open the front door.

'Yes?' she barked. 'What is it?

'Oh hello, love, I'm sorry, we're not too early, are we?' said the woman on the step, as she looked Liz up and down, all smiles and a big hat. 'Have we got the right place? Only I wasn't sure if there was anyone home. We didn't want to arrive late and miss the big surprise. I'm Beryl and this is Charlie — Charlie and Beryl? Here for the party, Jack and Rose's wedding anniversary?' She waved an invitation under Liz's nose. 'We were there first time around, weren't we, Charlie? I used to work with Rose years ago. And I wore this hat for their wedding. I thought it would be a nice touch to wear it again. What do you think?' She turned left and right so that Liz could get the full benefit of all those chins in profile.

'Charlie nearly gave it to Scouts for their Guy on Bonfire Night, cheeky monkey, but I'm glad I hung onto it now. Although I can't get into my dress these days and we gave Charlie's suit to the local amateur dramatics for some kiddies' thing they were doing, didn't we, Charlie? Are we the first?' she said, peering past Liz into the confines of the hall. 'Where have you got Rose and Jack hidden then?'

Liz was about to reply when a noise from the road made the woman look back over her shoulder.

'Oh my God,' she squealed, clapping her hands together. 'Look at that, there's June and Roger Bell — I haven't seen them for donkey's years. Always among the front-runners, those two. We were always the first to arrive everywhere, me and Charlie, June and Roger. Do you remember, Charlie?' And with that she scuttled off back down the path to embrace the new arrivals.

'You're early,' said Liz grimly to Charlie, who was standing on the doorstep holding a card and a present.

'I know, Beryl always likes to be early, doesn't like to miss anything. All the clocks in our house are set fifteen minutes fast, just in case,' he said, eyes slowly taking in Liz's tanned legs, bare feet and skimpy little robe. 'Anything I can help you with, is there?'

'No, thank you,' she said briskly. 'Everything is under control.'

'Righty-oh. So, where would you like us then?'

Liz hesitated. Trust Suzie to be somewhere else when Liz needed her. Typical.

'If you'd like to go round into the back garden,' said Liz, managing a thin smile. 'The marquee, on the lawn, you can't miss it if you just go round the side, through the gate.' She pointed to make sure he'd got it. 'My sister will be back soon. She's actually the one doing all the hands-on stuff. She shouldn't be very long.'

He grinned. 'Righty-oh, well in that case we'll go round there then and wait,' said Charlie, although he didn't move. Instead he looked slightly sheepish and shifted his weight from one foot to the other as if working up the courage to speak.

'Was there something else?' asked Liz.

'I was just going to say that you don't look anything like your photo in the paper. It doesn't do you justice — you're not how I imagined at all.'

Liz's smile broadened a little, wishing that she had been a bit more gracious; after all, it wasn't every day you met a real-life celebrity. Dressed in her robe all fresh from the shower, she must be a fantasy come true for someone as old and wrinkled as Charlie. Famous TV star opens the door half naked; she could almost hear him telling his friends down at the bowls club or wherever it was people like Charlie hung out. '*Ohhh she was so nice, lovely legs — and so natural*.'

From the path they could both hear Beryl and

the other new arrivals giggling and whooping with delight.

'And fancy you being one of Rose and Jack's girls,' Charlie said, beaming now. 'They must be very proud of you.'

Liz nodded, making a good show of looking modest.

'You're really famous round here, you know.'

'Well, I don't know about that,' she began, all smiles and self-effacing charm.

Seeing her response, Charlie had brightened visibly. 'You're a lot smaller than I thought you'd be. I was saying to Beryl on the way here that I was hoping we'd see you. You know, I read your gardening column in the *Gazette* religiously every week, never miss it. I keep meaning to write in and tell you about how good that tip was about the hot manure bed under the melons. Last year I had four real beauties. Absolute crackers. And this year I reckon there's going to be even more. You ask Beryl. We call it Suzie's Magic manure — '

Liz managed to hold the smile. 'Really, well gosh . . . fancy that — that's lovely, marvellous,' she said. 'Now why don't you and Beryl go round to the back and hide just in case Jack and Rose show up early too? I'm sure someone round there will find you a glass of champagne and some canapés.'

'All organic I expect?' said Charlie with a big stagy pantomime wink. 'If we get the chance while we're here I'd really like to have a quick chat with you about my brassicas.'

Liz smiled. 'I can hardly wait,' she murmured.

At which point a minibus pulled up in the driveway and people started clambering out, laughing and waving, bearing presents and outrageous hats and calling hello. From the shrieks of joy and squeals of laughter it seemed there was a good chance that Beryl knew them all.

9

'Oh for goodness' sake, why couldn't you have gone while we were at the tearooms?' said Rose testily, as Fleur bundled out of the car and headed for the toilets behind the service station.

Ungrateful bugger, thought Fleur, as she scurried across the tarmac, rooting through her handbag as she went. Fleur wanted to let Suzie know they were on their way home and couldn't think of any other way of doing it without drawing attention to herself. She had planned to text as soon as they left the gardens, and then half way through had started to worry that if she did there was a chance Suzie might not pick up the text if she was still busy getting everything else ready. Phoning seemed like the only sensible option.

Fleur scrolled down to find Suzie's mobile number and pressed 'call'. The phone began to ring just as she pulled open the door to the lavatory.

The service station toilet smelt like a monkey cage. It was the kind of place where you'd feel dirtier after washing your hands, if you could bring yourself to use the hand basin. Liquid soap had formed a slimy grey stalagmite on the splashback and damp paper towels and crumpled tissue littered the scuffed, dirt-caked floor. The toilet seat was up, but there was no way Fleur was going close enough to even think about lowering it. Above a pitted and stained mirror a chipped yellowing sign read: 'These facilities are inspected regularly.' Fleur wondered by whom — trolls?

She let the door swing shut. On her mobile someone had answered.

'Suzie?' she said in a hoarse whisper, 'Are you there? I just wanted to let you know that we're on our way back, we're — '

'Who are you ringing?' said Rose from behind her.

Fleur almost jumped out of her skin. 'You frightened the life out of me,' Fleur stammered.

'I was worried about you. I thought you said you wanted to go to the loo?'

'I did, I mean, I do. There's a queue,' said Fleur lamely.

'No, there's not; look the thing's on green,' said Rose, pulling open the door. 'Are you sure you're feeling all right?'

'Oh, I'm just tickety-boo,' said Fleur, phone still clamped to her ear as she stepped inside.

* * *

'That was Fleur again, she said she couldn't talk for long — they're now on their way home,' said Sam, handing Suzie her phone. 'They've just stopped at the service station at Hunter's Cross. What on earth are you doing in Hannah's room?'

'Looking for these.' Suzie, on her knees and still wrapped in a towel, triumphantly held up her new shoes. The family cats, Sid and Harry, had padded in behind her to watch the rest of the show. 'They were under Hannah's bed, although I've got no idea what she's done with the box. She must have been trying them on. I just can't believe her sometimes,' Suzie sighed. 'She knows they're mine and they're new and that I bought them especially for the party. I don't take *her* clothes. She would be furious if she thought I was going through her things.'

'You should take it as a compliment.'

Suzie pulled a face. 'Well, excuse me if I don't. I wouldn't mind if she asked but she just helps herself — my shoes, my perfume, my make-up. Last week I caught her sloping off in my boots and the jacket Mum and Dad got me for Christmas. I'm going to have to say something.'

She looked around the bedroom. Vampire posters and right-on, edgy, slightly grungy slogans had taken the place of Hannah's pony posters. Her teddies and toys were stuffed into a box on top of the wardrobe. The room was a tip, despite Suzie's constant efforts and pleas for Hannah to clear it up. You couldn't see the bedroom floor for clothes and crumbs and books and magazines, and every flat surface was covered in mugs, empty packets, make-up and hair paraphernalia.

In one corner a pile of freshly ironed clothes lay alongside a black plastic sack spilling out crumpled papers and rubbish, abandoned half way through an enforced clear up.

Suzie sighed; she longed for the old Hannah to come home: the one who used to giggle with her in the kitchen; the one who couldn't wait to get home from school to tell her how the day had gone; the one who enjoyed helping her cook; the one who didn't sulk and who would have loved tonight's party. The old Hannah would have joined in and had fun with everyone, not crept off somewhere to moan and feel all grumpy and hard-done-by.

'We really need to be getting going,' Sam was saying.

'I can hardly go anywhere like this, can I?' said Suzie pointing to her towel. 'And I need to put a face on.'

Sam rolled his eyes. 'No, you don't, you know you look gorgeous just the way you are. Come on, just put your frock on — it'll be fine. I'll go downstairs and let the dogs back in.'

'Can you leave the dogs in the kitchen, I don't want muddy pawprints all over my dress,' said Suzie, hurrying into the bedroom. 'Just give me ten minutes.'

'You're the one who was worrying about it all going wrong if we weren't there,' called Sam, shucking his jacket off the hanger and pulling it on. 'I won't be a minute.'

Suzie didn't reply. At least she had found her shoes. She took a quick look at the clock beside the bed and made a start — towel off, underwear on. Then she slipped the dress off the hanger and slithered into it, tugging it on over damp shoulders, before pulling on the jacket. She sat down at the dressing table, dragged a brush through her hair, added a slick of kohl pencil around her eyes, a little lipstick and a dab of perfume — and was all done and ready to go with time to spare.

Checking her reflection, Suzie grinned. Matt had been right — despite getting ready in a rush, her new outfit was absolutely perfect, fitting her like a dream and making her both look and feel wonderful.

'Are you ready? I'm just going to go and start the car,' Sam was saying as he opened the bedroom door. Suzie was in the last-minute throes of getting ready, stepping into her new shoes, putting in her earrings, picking up the little clutch bag she had bought to finish off the outfit. For an instant as he caught sight of her, Sam stopped in his tracks and stood stock-still in the doorway, taking in the view.

'Wow,' he said after a second or two. 'You scrub up well. Anyone taking you home tonight?'

Suzie smiled. 'Well eventually, yes, let's hope so. As long as he's not blind drunk; I'm not sure how far I can walk in these shoes.'

He nodded. 'Okay. So, you ready now? I've given the dogs some water and a few biscuits.'

'Yup,' she said, taking one last look in the bedroom mirror before pulling the bedroom door closed behind her.

Sam stopped in the hallway, waiting for her, eyes bright. 'You look . . . '

'What?'

'You know . . . ' he said.

Suzie waited.

'Nice,' Sam said after a moment or two more. 'Really nice.'

Suzie smiled to herself. It was the closest thing

she had had to a gushing compliment from Sam in years.

'Best we get back to the party and make sure everyone is hidden away and ready for the off,' he said. 'Be a shame to spoil it now.'

'Did Fleur say how long it would be before they get here?' Suzie asked as she locked the front door.

Sam shrugged. 'No, but not long. Hunter's Cross is, what, twenty minutes from here?'

Suzie nodded. 'Half an hour if my dad's driving.'

'That outfit, it's new, isn't it?' he said, looking her up and down as they got to the car.

'Yes, it's been ages since I had anything new and I wanted to have something nice for tonight,' she said defensively.

'I wasn't complaining. That colour is good — really suits you.'

Suzie smiled self-consciously. 'Thank you.'

'No really, it's nice. Reminds me of the colour me and my brother sprayed his BMX when we were kids,' he said, unlocking the car door.

Suzie laughed. And there she was, thinking romance was dead.

* * *

When they pulled up outside her parents' house the front garden was already full of people milling about, saying their hellos and chatting to each other, all busy socialising, while Liz, still in her bathrobe, appeared to be desperately trying to direct guests around to the backyard. When she spotted Suzie and Sam, her expression changed from starry self-effacing welcome to something cooler and far less convivial.

'I'll just drop you off here and go and park the car,' said Sam, peering out at the crowd.

'Well, thanks for that,' said Suzie. 'You know Liz is going to kill me, don't you?'

'You did tell her we were off and she told you to go.'

'That isn't going to help one little bit and you know it,' sighed Suzie, as she got out of the car.

Liz, on an intercept course with Suzie, didn't bother with anything in the way of social niceties and certainly didn't compliment Suzie on her new outfit.

'Where the hell have you been? You did this on purpose, didn't you?' Liz growled through gritted teeth. 'You knew people would be turning up, didn't you? How could you leave me here on my own? After all I've done to help pay for this party? I'm nowhere near ready and Grant is going to be here any minute now. It's so unfair. What on earth is he going to think? The bloody doorbell just keeps on ringing. I was going to put up a sign with directions on it but I didn't get the chance. Look at me — just look at me,' she said furiously. 'Thank God the press aren't here, they'd have had a field day. I can see it now, '*Starmaker*'s little Miss Perfect cavorts around half naked at family party.' They're just waiting to catch me out, you know. Did you see the headline in the redtops? 'Lizzie Bingham's the head girl of reality TV.' It wasn't meant as a compliment, you know. They can't wait for me to fall flat on my arse. They'll assume I'm drunk or on drugs, you know — is that what you want? Is that it?'

Suzie held up her hands in surrender to stem the tide. 'Whoa there, just calm down. Of course it isn't what I want, you know that — you're over-reacting. Besides, you told me to go, remember? Wasn't it you who told me less than an hour ago that I wasn't indispensable?' said Suzie as evenly as she could manage.

'Oh, very clever,' snapped Liz.

'I don't suppose you checked all these people off against the guest list, did you?'

Liz glared at her. 'Do I look like a bloody doorman?' she snapped. 'Of course I haven't checked them off, I haven't even had time to get my bloody dress on yet.'

At which point another car with the next wave of guests pulled up in the drive.

'Oh, I think that's Peter Hudson, Mum and Dad's best man.'

'I don't care if it's the Pope.'

'What I mean is, I'm sure he'll give us a hand. Why don't you go inside and finish getting ready?' said Suzie. 'I'll sort this lot out.' Turning her attention to the new arrivals, she smiled and, ignoring the grumbling from behind her, said, 'Hi, Peter and Mary. How lovely to see you. How are you?'

Liz meanwhile looked as if she might just explode with fury.

Peter smiled. 'We're just fine, aren't we, Mary? All ready for the off, are you?' he said, as they shook hands and said their hellos.

Suzie nodded. 'I think we're more or less there now. It's been a really hectic day. We haven't stopped yet.'

'I can imagine. Many people arrived?' Peter asked, glancing around.

'Quite a few, we're asking everyone to stay round the back in the marquee till Mum and Dad get here. I'm so pleased that you could both make it, and that you've agreed to do the speech, Peter. You're still okay with that?'

Before he could do more than nod, his wife Mary raised her eyebrows and laughed. 'Just you try stopping him, he loves to be the centre of attention, don't you, Peter?'

He grinned and patted his top pocket. 'It's all in hand. Don't you worry, all done and dusted. Anyway I'm just going to park the car. See you in a few minutes.'

'Right,' said Suzie, turning her attention back to Mary. 'Well in that case let me take you round to the marquee.'

Behind them, Liz had turned on her heel and stalked back into the house.

10

'Who on earth are you texting *now*?' snapped Rose from the front passenger seat of the car. Although she hadn't pressed the matter, Rose was getting increasingly worried about Fleur's behaviour. It certainly wasn't like her to be so furtive; normally she was brutally direct.

Fleur grunted.

'Are you going to tell me what's going on?' Rose asked.

'Colin,' said Fleur, without looking up from her phone.

'The man who manages your restaurant?'

'Uh-huh. That's right. And Frank.'

'Frank?'

'Frank.'

'Frank who?' pressed Rose.

'He's a friend of mine. He's feeding my cat while I'm away.'

'I didn't know you had a cat,' said Jack with surprise.

'I didn't know you had any friends,' murmured Rose under her breath.

Jack shot her a killer look.

'I didn't think you liked animals,' continued Rose.

'I don't, and anyway it's not exactly mine. It's a stray really, a skanky flea-ridden one-eyed thing — you know how it is with cats. Waltzes in to your house as bold as brass, eats and then waltzes out, they're a law unto themselves, cats. How long do you think it'll be before we get home?'

'About a quarter of an hour,' said Jack from the driver's seat.

'You could ring them then if you like when we get back. Colin and this Frank. See how things are, if you're worried,' said Rose, glancing across at Jack, who shrugged.

'No, you're all right. It's much easier this way,' said Fleur, fiddling for a second or two longer. 'Fewer details to worry about. And besides I tried to ring back at the service station and I couldn't get through.'

'But I thought you were talking to someone?' said Rose.

'It was just Frank's answer machine,' said Fleur, after what appeared to be a second or two of hesitation. Rose still wasn't at all convinced. There was something going on and she wanted to know what it was.

'So who's this Frank then?' she asked, determined that if she pushed hard enough something had to give.

'No one in particular,' Fleur answered casually.

'But he's feeding your cat — got a key, has he?'

'Oh, for goodness' sake, stop fishing,' snapped Fleur, dropping her phone back into her handbag. 'Of course he's got a bloody key. He couldn't get in to feed the cat if he didn't have a key, could he? He's not Spiderman. He's just a friend, all right?'

'If you say so,' said Rose, struggling to suppress a yawn.

'Sorry,' said Fleur. 'Am I boring you?'

'No, of course you're not, I'm just tired, that's all. It's been a long day.' She glanced at her watch. 'I'm hoping Liz will have arrived by now. She said she'd give me a ring as soon as she got to the house. It's weeks since we've seen her. She rings at least once a week but she's always so busy these days — talking on the phone's not the same. She seems very keen for us to meet this new man of hers, doesn't she?'

'Maybe she's finally found Mr Right,' said Jack, eyes fixed firmly on the road ahead.

'Well, let's hope so,' said Rose. 'I'm beginning to worry about her.'

'You mean in case she turns out like me,' said Fleur.

'Of course that isn't what I meant,' said Rose. 'She's just so picky, that's all.'

'Nothing wrong with being picky,' sniffed Fleur.

'Well no, I know that, but let's face it, no one is perfect. I just keep hoping she'll find someone nice and settle down. I'm worried about her ending up on her own.'

From the back seat Fleur sighed. 'Oh for God's sake. It's not as bad as you make out, in fact there's a lot to recommend it — all the bed to yourself, no one doing foul things in the bathroom.'

'What about company?'

'She can always buy herself a budgie.'

'I was being serious,' snapped Rose.

'So was I.'

'I'd like her to find someone normal, someone ordinary.'

'I can't see Liz settling for ordinary,' interrupted Jack.

'You know what I mean, someone sensible with their feet on the ground who'll love her for who she is — '

Fleur snorted. 'You are such a bloody romantic, Rose.'

'I can't help it, I know people do it all later these days but I'd really like her to be happy and settled.' Rose yawned again. 'Sorry, I'm totally worn out, I'm not really sure I can manage a night out on the tiles. I was thinking, how about if we just order a takeaway and stayed in tonight? Or Jack could do a barbie — there's plenty of food in the freezer. Do you think the girls would mind? I mean, we could always do something another night.'

Sitting in the back of the car, Fleur decided to say nothing.

* * *

'They should be here soon,' said Suzie to Sam as he arrived back at the cottage after parking the car. 'I just got a text from Fleur — Mum and Dad are about ten minutes away. I'm going back to make sure that everyone stays out of sight.'

Sam nodded. 'Okay, I'll send any stray guests round. Tell you what, can you send Megan round if she's about? She can keep an eye out for them.'

‘Good idea,’ said Suzie. ‘If I go round to the marquee, can you pop into the house and let Liz know Mum and Dad will be here soon? Only I’m not sure what sort of reception I’m likely to get if I go and tell her.’

He nodded. ‘Okay. Do you reckon I’ve got time to put up that other banner on the front of the house before they get here? I was thinking of hanging it from the trellis above the door.’

Suzie stared at him. ‘Are you serious?’

‘Why not? It shouldn’t take more than a few minutes — ’

‘If you want to but you’ll have to get a move on. Where is it?’

‘Still in the hall I think, in a box — I took the other one into the marquee.’

‘Okay, do you need someone to give you a hand?’

‘Yeah that would be great. Matt maybe?’ suggested Sam.

Suzie stared at him, wondering why he had asked for Matt of all people. Did he suspect something? ‘Matt?’ she asked.

Sam grinned. ‘Yep, like he hasn’t got enough to do already. Last time I saw him in the marquee they were all running around like headless chickens trying to get everything done in time.’ He paused. ‘It was a great idea getting him in to do the food.’

Suzie forced a laugh, aware that her heart was beating like a drum. ‘Good, I’m glad you approve. So?’ she said. ‘Do you want me to ask him or not?’

‘No, I think I can probably manage. I’ll ask Liz

if she's not too busy.'

This time Suzie really did laugh. 'Well, good luck with that,' she said as she made her way around to the marquee.

* * *

As Suzie rounded the corner of the house, the noise from the tent hit her like a tidal wave. It was even louder as she stepped in through the open flap to be greeted by the voices and faces of friends and family, neighbours and people from the village all standing around drinking champagne, nibbling on canapés and deep in conversation. There was a real buzz of anticipation in the air. It was going to be tricky to hide all this lot for very long . . .

Matt was standing just inside the doorway with Megan, welcoming the new arrivals while waiters handed out the drinks.

'Well, thank God for that, the cavalry have finally arrived,' said Matt with a grin as their eyes met. 'And not before time, eh, Megan? I was beginning to think the whole family had abandoned me — except for Megan here obviously. She's been an absolute star.'

Megan beamed under Matt's approval.

'And you look gorgeous, Suzie, doesn't she, Megan? That's the most amazing outfit — new, is it?'

Suzie blushed as Matt looked her up and down, making Megan giggle.

'I'm so sorry about leaving you on your own,' said Suzie, trying to ignore the mischievous look in his eyes. 'I was hoping Liz would be helping out with the meeting and greeting. She should be here any minute now . . . ' She glanced across the crowded tent. 'People started showing up earlier than we thought . . . which is good — I'm not complaining. I mean, it'll be nice for Mum and Dad, bigger surprise.' Then Suzie smiled at Megan. 'Well done you, do you think you could just pop round and give your dad a hand?'

Megan looked crestfallen. 'But I like it in here,' she complained.

'I know you do, sweetie, but we need someone to spot Grandma and Granddad, and you can come straight back just as soon as they get here. All right?'

Matt nodded. 'Actually, Meg, letting us know when they're about to arrive is probably the most important job of the evening.'

'Go on — off you go,' said Suzie, shooing her away.

'Do I have to?' Megan whined, dragging her feet.

'Yes, your dad's expecting you — and hurry,' said Suzie. 'You don't want to miss them. He's in the house.'

'So where did you say your sister Liz has got to?' asked Matt, smiling at another new arrival as Megan scurried across the lawn.

Suzie rolled her eyes. 'Don't ask. Sulking probably. Actually I need to make an announcement.'

'Sure thing,' he said and, stepping forward, he clapped his hands. 'Ladies and gentlemen, if we could have a little hush, please . . . ' Matt called in his deep dark brown voice. 'Suzie would like to make an announcement.'

Nothing like stating the obvious, she thought, aware that all eyes were now on her.

'Good evening. I just wanted to say that it's great to see everyone . . . As you know, this is a very special evening for my mum and dad and I want to thank you all for being here to share it and also, and more importantly, for managing to keep the cat firmly in the bag. As far as we know, Mum and Dad have absolutely no idea what's going on. My mum's sister, Fleur, who probably most of you know, has kept them out of the way all day so that we could get everything ready. And apparently they're on their way back here now. We've been told that they should be arriving very soon, so could I ask that you find your seats, please? We'll try and give you as much warning as we can when Mum and Dad get closer so that we can all be quiet. Meanwhile, there is plenty of champagne and lots of gorgeous nibbles courtesy of Matt here. So until they arrive — eat drink and be merry. Thank you.'

There was a murmur of approval and then people returned to their conversations.

Matt smiled. 'Well done you, you're a natural, you know that, don't you?' he said and, catching hold of her elbow, he kissed her on the cheek. Suzie felt herself light up like a Christmas tree, colour flooding her cheeks. 'Please . . . ' she whispered, pushing him away. 'Do you mind? I've already told you to stop that. What if anyone sees you? What will people think?' She rubbed her cheek just in case there was some great big indelible neon sign plastered on it that announced she had been kissed.

'What?' he said, aping offence. 'What's the matter? Can't a friend give another friend a little kiss?'

'No,' said Suzie firmly. 'No, he can't.'

'Have you said anything to Sam yet?' Matt said, in an undertone. 'You haven't, have you, I can tell by that look on your face.'

'I've hardly had the time, have I?' said Suzie. 'And now isn't exactly the ideal moment, is it?'

'If you don't tell him, then I'm going to,' said Matt.

Suzie stared at him. 'You wouldn't.'

Matt raised his eyebrows. 'Just try me,' he said, smiling as he handed her a glass of champagne.

* * *

Upstairs in the guest room, Liz was struggling to regain her calm, carefully rubbing a dab of serum into her hair to make sure there would be no last-minute outbreaks of frizz. Slipping off her robe, she took a long hard look at her body in the mirror. She was wearing sheer jade-green silk underwear that perfectly matched her robe over a light spray tan (it was just so passé to be orange), she had smooth bare legs, pink painted fingernails and matching toenails. The whole creation was a real work of art.

Pulling her glasses out from under a towel and holding them up like a pince-nez, she looked again with a more critical and focused eye. The effect was uncannily like before and after airbrushing. There were a few uneven patches of skin tone on her legs and a broken vein or two on her thighs, and despite all the work with her personal trainer Liz was still undeniably pear-shaped. In the unflattering light from the bedroom windows, and with the benefit of 20/20 vision, she could pick out the beginnings of cellulite on her thighs. She made a mental note that it would most definitely be lamplight when she and Grant got back to the hotel. Lamplight and that little wisp of a négligée that she had picked up in Paris when she had been guest presenter on the *Travel Programme*. It was such a shame that you couldn't be airbrushed while you were on the move.

Tucking away her glasses, she pulled the jade-green dress off the hanger and wriggled into it oh so carefully, so as not to mess up her hair or make-up. The stylist at *Starmaker* was right, the colour really did wonders for her complexion and eyes, and it went beautifully with her underwear. Pouting, she admired herself in the mirror, letting the straps slip seductively off her shoulders.

She imagined Grant undressing her later and smiled to herself; it would be just like unwrapping a beautiful parcel, one which he really ought to be very, very grateful to be getting his hands on. Lizzie Bingham didn't come with any kind of dodgy reputation or rumours of a tacky past. She had carefully cultivated the whole gorgeous-girl-next-door image, and was very scrupulous about who she associated with in public. So, despite all the media interest in the show, no one had ever caught her falling out of a nightclub half cut and half naked in the arms of a footballer or someone else's husband. Not for her the charms of some hairy-arsed Neanderthal, oh no. Lizzie Bingham wanted, no . . . demanded, something all together more stylish and upmarket.

The idea of seeing Grant gave her a little frisson of expectation. After all, before all the unwrapping, he was just bound to bring her a present. Presents were Grant's thing — well, actually they were *her* thing, but Liz had explained to him how those little tokens of affection always made her feel special. Grant had laughed and suggested that they should really make her feel grateful (and that he knew just the way she could show him how grateful she was, which Liz thought was a little sordid, but anyway). Earrings, diamonds, perfume, silk stockings, weekends in spa hotels and far-flung luxury villas — she'd given him a list of all her favourites and made it clear that anything else he might come up with was acceptable — just as long as it wasn't roses.

Deep in thought, the sound of knocking followed by a man's voice made her jump; for an instant she thought it might be Grant and wondered if there was time to draw the curtains.

'Liz? Lizzie, are you in there? It's me, Sam.'

Liz took a second or two to regain her composure and push her glasses firmly back under a towel before painting on a wolfish smile and opening the bedroom door. There was still the little matter of getting even with Suzie.

'Well, hi there — come in,' she said, all smiles and smouldering eyes. 'Actually I'm so glad you're here. Can you help me?'

Sam looked confused. 'Sure, what's the problem?'

'Could you do me up? I'm really struggling here,' she lied. Before he could reply Liz turned around, presenting him with her bare back. 'Can you just do the zip for me?'

Sam hesitated. 'Sorry, Liz, I'm not really qualified — ' he began, obviously uncomfortable.

'What?' Liz laughed. 'Oh come on, Sam, don't tell me you don't know how to do up a dress?' she said, tugging at the straps of her dress in a contrived effort to keep it from slipping off. 'Please, Sam.' Her voice dropped to a seductive purr. 'I don't bite. I just can't reach the zip.'

'Actually I'm not sure I've got time. I'm going to hang up the banner . . . ' Sam said, holding a roll of fabric out in front of him like a shield. 'Suzie just wanted me to let you know that your mum and dad are on their way and should be here any time.'

'Okay, fair enough,' she said. 'Well, in that case you'd better get a move on, hadn't you? Put the banner down and help me with the zip, will you? I can hardly go downstairs with my dress undone now, can I?'

There was a split second when Liz really wasn't sure what Sam was going to do. She felt his eyes on her, and then felt him moving closer and smiled triumphantly. He wasn't a man who was often wrong-footed but she could sense just how uncomfortable he felt and her first thought was 'good'. Liz wanted to teach Suzie a lesson for leaving her on her own when she had to get ready, and somehow it felt like this was the perfect way.

Sam had big capable hands and long fingers but he fumbled nervously as he caught hold of the tiny catch, mumbling an apology as he carefully pulled the zipper closed. The dress was made of silk as fine as cobweb over a heavier inner sheath, so he had to work the zip quite slowly, so as not to snag the fabric, which Liz found rather sweet considering how he had been bullied into doing it.

'There we are,' he said, stepping away. The relief in his voice was audible.

'That's great. Can you just do up the hook at the top please?' she purred.

'No, I can't, I can't see it,' he snapped gruffly. Liz could feel the warmth of his breath on her bare shoulder and, sensing Sam's increasing unease, her smile broadened. As his fingertips accidentally brushed her skin, she giggled and Sam leapt away from her like a scalded cat.

'Whoa there, cowboy. It's all right,' she said. 'It just tickled a bit, that's all — they can't hang you for it.' But he had already snatched up the banner and was backing out of the door as if she was a crazed gunman. The sense of power gave her a nice little buzz.

'You'll have to ask Suzie to do up the hook when you get downstairs,' he was saying. 'I'm going to sort this banner out. Suzie just wanted me to let you know that we haven't got long before your mum and dad arrive.'

'So you said,' said Liz, turning to look up at him from under long, perfectly mascaraed lashes. 'Thanks for that. You know you've got a lovely touch.' Was it her imagination or was Sam blushing? 'See you later,' she said, but he was already gone.

Liz leant close to the mirror to paint on a little more lipgloss and add a spray of perfume. As she looked into the eyes of her reflection she grinned and licked her lips; that had felt like a victory.

Poor Sam, he had looked absolutely terrified. She hadn't been able to help herself, there was a bit of her that wanted to show him exactly what he was missing. After all, she was a real woman, a woman who liked to take care of herself. A glamorous woman who knew exactly how to treat her man. She pressed her lips together and then ran her tongue over her teeth.

And yes, okay, so Sam *was* her sister's husband and quite *obviously* off-limits but he was still gorgeous and quite sexy in a lived-in, slightly crinkled way. If she was honest with herself, she had always thought that he was wasted on Suzie. Not that she would ever say anything or do anything about it, but it was just nice to flex a bit of muscle from time to time, show the world exactly who was boss.

Sam had been with Suzie for donkey's years, since Suzie had been a gangly teenager and Sam was all elbows and knees and long curly blond hair, and there had always been a teensy-weensy bit of Liz that was jealous of

Suzie. And yes, she had fancied Sam, even though she had never done anything about it. Even when he was teasing her about her braces and her love life and her clothes, she had always thought he was cute. And of course he noticed her, which had always made Liz think that maybe he might be just a little bit interested too.

* * *

'I think there must be something going on at the community centre tonight,' said Rose conversationally as they drove into the village. 'There are a lot of cars parked over on the Rec. Must be something special — it's absolutely jam-packed. I haven't seen any posters up, have you?'

'Probably some sort of private function,' said Jack, slowing down for the junction.

'You think? Oh look, over there, Jack, isn't that Peter Hudson?' said Rose, pointing to a man getting out of a parked car close to the community centre. She craned around to get a better look. 'Yes, you know I'm sure that is him. He's all dressed up. I wonder what he's doing in Crowbridge? We haven't seen him and Mary for ages.'

'You're right,' said Jack. 'Would you mind if we stopped and had a quick word with him, Fleur? I mean, there's nothing spoiling at home, is there? I'm surprised Peter or Mary didn't give us a ring, they usually do if they know they're coming out this way.'

'I feel sick,' said Fleur in a pitiful little voice from the back seat.

'What?' said Rose, swinging round.

'Sick,' muttered Fleur miserably. 'Really sick — I feel awful. I think it might be because I'm sitting in the back of the car. Would you mind if we just went home?'

She sounded so pathetic that Rose didn't feel she could refuse. Turning to Jack, Rose said, 'We'd better go home. We can always ring Peter tomorrow — or do you want Jack to stop the car?'

Fleur shook her head. 'No, no, I just need to get home.'

'He's nipped through the cut anyway,' said Jack. 'In a hurry to get somewhere obviously. Maybe he's popping round to see if we're in.'

Rose glanced at Fleur. 'Is it your stomach?'

From the back seat Fleur groaned theatrically. 'I don't know. I just don't feel right. Have you got any milk of magnesia in the house?' she whimpered.

Rose craned round to take a good hard look at her sister. 'I don't think we have actually. You do look a bit flushed. Do you think it was something you ate?'

'I don't know.'

'We all ate more or less the same,' said Jack. 'Are you going to be sick? Only if you are, give me a shout and I'll stop.'

'Maybe you're coming down with something. You can pick bugs up anywhere, could have been that fresh cream in the cakes,' said Rose conversationally. 'Or on the door of that toilet.

What are those people thinking? I mean, for goodness, sake, how much does a bottle of bleach cost?'

'Would you mind if we just stopped off at the shop? They're bound to have some milk of magnesia there,' said Fleur.

'Maybe if you're not feeling well we should cancel going out this evening? I've already said I really don't mind not going out, especially if you'd prefer to stay in. We could pick up a DVD from the shop, they have a good selection in there — unless you want to go to bed? Everyone would understand. And I don't suppose Liz would mind going out with Grant without us there to cramp her style. I mean, Rocco's is a bit upmarket, not to mention pricey.'

'We can't call it off, Rose. She wants us to meet him,' said Jack.

'Well, we can always meet him, and then after he's said hello they can go off and eat. You know how she feels about our house. Mind you, she was like that when she was at school, always trying to smarten us up — '

'Don't say that,' said Jack. 'She loves coming home, you know she does. Liz just worries too much about what other people think, that's all.'

'She'll get over that,' said Fleur.

'Well, all I'm saying is that I don't mind staying in if you want to,' said Rose. 'It's been a long day, and we can't drag Fleur out if she's feeling poorly now, can we?'

Fleur sighed. 'Let's see how I feel later, shall we? After I've had something to help settle my stomach. I mean, I wouldn't want to spoil the evening for the rest of you.'

Rose laughed. 'You won't, you brave little soldier. Come on, let's get you home. I'll make you a nice cup of tea just as soon as we get in.'

In the back seat Fleur lay back and closed her eyes.

11

'They're on their way, Peter Hudson just saw them passing the Rec,' Sam called to Suzie as he dashed into the marquee, clapping his hands together to attract everyone's attention.

'Hello? Hello!' he called. 'Can I have your attention please? Just to let you know that Rose and Jack are on their way. It'll just be a few more minutes before they get here — they've just been seen on Low Road near the recreation ground by one of the guests. So if we can ask everyone to be really quiet now and make sure you've got a glass in your hand. And no one leaves the marquee, please, until after they get here. It shouldn't be more than a few minutes before they arrive — okay? And please keep as quiet as you can. Suzie, are you coming round the front to meet them?'

Suzie nodded and followed him outside. He was walking fast, looking horribly flustered and she struggled to keep up.

'Hang on, Sam, wait for me. I can't run in these shoes. Have you told Liz that they're nearly here?' said Suzie, trying to keep pace with him.

'I'm not totally brainless, you know. I've just sent Megan,' he said brusquely.

'Sorry, I was just saying,' said Suzie. 'Liz will be livid if she gets left out. You know what she's like.'

'I wasn't thinking of leaving her out,' he

snapped. 'I just said Megan's going to get her.' They were almost at the kerbside now. 'If she can't be bothered to get herself downstairs it's hardly my fault, is it?'

'The banner looks good,' Suzie said in an attempt to placate him.

'Yeah, right.'

Suzie stared at Sam. 'What on earth is the matter?'

'Nothing,' he said.

'Has Liz upset you?' she said. 'I didn't think that she'd give you a hand with it.' She couldn't imagine Megan would have made him so angry, and he wasn't usually the kind of person who would get this annoyed over hanging a banner up over the front door. And then Suzie's heart lurched; maybe he had heard something about her and Matt . . .

'What makes you say that?' he said.

'What?' said Suzie, struggling to regain her cool. 'About Liz? Well, like you just said, we all know what she's like. You know how much she gets under my skin. I love her dearly but she can be the most irritating bloody woman on earth when she's in one of her moods, and from what I've seen so far she's in a beauty today. I think she's nervous; she's probably worried about us meeting this new man of hers. I'm sure she didn't mean to — '

But Sam was way ahead of her. 'Oh yes she did, Suzie. You know, that is the trouble — people are always making excuses for her. She is completely self-obsessed. The only person Liz ever worries about is Liz,' Sam said with real venom. Suzie stared at him; she couldn't remember seeing him so angry.

'What did she do?' said Suzie anxiously. 'Sam, talk to me. What did she do?'

'What's that?' said a familiar voice from behind them. 'Talking about me again, are we?'

'I was just saying that you would hate to miss Mum and Dad arriving,' lied Suzie, her eyes still on Sam, who had a face like thunder.

'I'd have made them drive round till I was ready,' Liz said wryly, giving them a wink, while running a finger over her eyebrows. 'I was wondering, Suzie, do you think you could do up the hook on the top of my dress for me?'

Sam grunted furiously.

'Sure,' said Suzie, but before she could move Megan began yelling from her vantage point upstairs at one of the bedroom windows.

'Mum, Dad — they're here, they're here,' she squealed. 'Their car's at the end of the lane.'

'Come on down then, love,' said Suzie.

'Where's Hannah?' asked Sam, glancing over his shoulder, his tone prickly.

'I don't know. I haven't seen her for ages. I'm sure she'll turn up sooner or later. Short of chaining her to the marquee I don't know how I could have kept her here — '

'She said she would help,' Sam snapped back.

'Play nicely, you two,' said Liz.

'Is she with that girl? You know, what's-her-name?' Sam continued, completely blanking Liz.

'Sadie? I don't know, but if I was asked to have a guess I'd say yes. Don't you remember when your parents said keep away from something, anything at all, just how attractive it made whatever it was — drink, drugs, or in my case *you*,' Suzie said with a smile, trying hard to lighten the mood.

'Yes, but — '

'But nothing. Look, here are Mum and Dad.'

Which was exactly when Suzie spotted Peter Hudson and Mary wandering across the grass from the back garden. She groaned.

'Please can you go around the back to the marquee?' Suzie said, shooing them away, but they seemed totally oblivious, and it was too late to stop them now.

Megan ran across the lawn. Wide-eyed and giggling, she was practically jumping up and down with excitement. 'They're here, they're here,' she shrieked, as her grandparents' car pulled up into the driveway.

There was a moment, a split second, when nobody moved and Suzie watched her mum reading the banner above the door and saw the surprise register on her face. Rose was barely out of the car before Megan had thrown her arms around her and whooped, 'Grandma, Grandma, we've been waiting for you for ages — happy anniversary.'

Meanwhile Jack was taking his time climbing out of the car. He stood on the driveway, hands on hips, a big smile on his face as Peter Hudson and Mary came over to join in the group hug.

'Well, well, well,' Jack said, looking from face to face and then at the huge sign above the doorway as Megan rushed around to hug him too. 'Will you just look at that,' he said. ' 'Happy

Fortieth Wedding Anniversary to Rose and Jack.' You and your mum and dad and Auntie Liz have been busy, Megan. Haven't they, Rose?' He grinned at Peter and extended a hand that turned into a hug. 'Peter, wonderful to see you. We wondered where you were off to in such a hurry all dolled up to the nines.'

Peter laughed. 'Mary and I wouldn't have missed it for the world, you know that,' he said. 'Congratulations, mate. Well done.'

Rose said nothing as Fleur got out of the car to join them on the driveway.

'Well, what do you think?' Fleur said with a smile.

'Is that what today was all about?' said Jack. 'The trip out and everything.'

Fleur didn't say a word.

'So you're not feeling sick then?'

'No, I'm just fine, Jack. Just fine.'

Alongside them Rose remained silent, while Megan skipped around the garden like a spring lamb.

'Happy anniversary, Mum and Dad,' said Suzie, her voice crackling with emotion as she hugged first one and then the other. 'Congratulations.'

'You really shouldn't have,' Rose finally began, and then turned to confront Fleur. 'Did you know anything about this?' she said, but before Fleur could answer Liz stepped forward and caught hold of Rose by the hands.

'Mum, you can't blame Fleur. I thought, I mean we *all* thought this was just too important an occasion to let slip by, didn't we?' said Liz looking from face to face. 'And we've got such a surprise for you,' she said.

'I'm with the ladies on this,' Peter Hudson interrupted. 'Although just between you me and the gatepost, we were a bit surprised really, weren't we, Mary, you calling it your fortieth wedding anniversary on the invitations.'

'Invitations,' said Rose. 'What invitations?'

But Peter was pressing on full steam ahead.

'Bit of artistic licence there, eh? Papering over the cracks and all that. But who am I to say anything?' Peter said with a wink. 'I don't suppose anyone minds these days, do they? Any excuse for a bit of a booze up, eh, Jack? Forty years of wedded bliss? That's certainly gilding the rose a bit, eh? Geddit — *gilding the Rose?*' he laughed. 'You know, like lily?'

Mary shot him a killer look. 'Peter,' she said sharply. 'You said you wouldn't say anything.'

Jack reddened. Rose's face was a blank canvas.

Suzie stared at Peter, trying to work out exactly what he meant.

'Well, not to anyone else, *obviously*,' said Peter with a big cheesy grin. 'But this is family and good friends, we all know the score.'

'Actually we don't, I'm not with you,' said Suzie, aware of the tension now on her mum's face.

'Peter,' Rose cautioned, holding up a hand to silence him, but he simply laughed.

'Oh come off it, Rose, you don't have to pretend with us, love.' And then, turning to Suzie, he continued, 'We've known Jack and Rose for donkey's years. Since well before they got hitched and I'm just saying that a lot of people haven't got a clue that your mum and dad got divorced, and those who do won't mind you being a little bit economical with the truth, will they? I mean, does it really matter these days if you're married or not?'

There was a split second when the world went hot and still; Suzie felt her mouth fall open. 'What?' she managed in a gasp.

'I mean, nobody bats an eyelid these days, do they?' Mary said. 'Not really, although I did say you weren't to make a big thing about it, Peter, not today of all days.' She looked around the stunned faces, 'I did tell him he had to behave himself but you know what he's like.'

Suzie's gaze fixed on her parents' faces. '*You're not married?*' she said.

Rose and Jack glanced at each other.

'Not exactly,' said Jack sheepishly.

'*Not exactly?*' Liz snarled at him before Suzie could respond. 'What the hell is that supposed to mean?' she said. 'How can you not be married? You are joking, aren't you? Please tell me you're joking.'

'We can explain,' Rose began, but Peter Hudson was on a roll.

'We were really surprised the girls asked us round tonight — pleased though, obviously. I mean, your mum and dad are both fantastic people, we love 'em, don't we, Mary? We both thought it was great that you were brushing over all that other business,' he said.

'What other business?' Suzie said, looking from face to face, feeling as if someone had knocked all the breath out of her.

'You don't have to worry, pet. I'll be brushing over it in the speech too, nudge nudge, wink wink, say no more . . . ' Peter said with a sly grin, tapping the side of his nose.

There was a moment of absolute stunned silence while everyone considered what Peter had said and Megan, oblivious to the tension between the adults, skipped by them.

'I feel like I've woken up inside a bad dream. I don't understand. Can you please explain what the hell is going on here? How can you *not* be married?' Liz snapped. 'It's ridiculous. We've got the photos. I've made a film about the two of you and your life together. About *us*. I've had your wedding certificate blown up. Have you got any idea how much it costs to have something blown up to twelve feet long?'

'Well yes, it is true, we did get married,' said Rose looking increasingly uncomfortable. 'We did get married but we also got divorced — it's years ago now . . . ' She glanced at Jack for support.

Jack was nodding. 'Years ago,' he echoed. 'I mean, does it matter in this day and age? Lots of people live together. Other people do it all the time.'

Liz stared at him. 'This isn't about *other* people, Dad, this is about us. About me. How could you not have said something?'

'Well, it was a long time ago, now. It must be, what? Probably thirty-two? Maybe thirty-three years,' Rose said, biting her lip and trying to work it out on her fingers. 'I can't remember exactly now.'

'Probably closer to thirty-six,' said Peter Hudson helpfully.

'No, it can't be thirty-six, Liz is thirty-four,' said Rose.

'I said that,' said Mary, eager to chip in with her two-penn'orth.

The four of them were so caught up working out the maths that they seemed completely unaware of the impact the news had had. Suzie could see her dad also trying to work it out.

'What year *was* it?' he asked lightly, almost conversationally.

'Do you mind? What do you mean, what year? How come you don't remember?' wailed Liz. 'And does it matter what bloody year it was — how come you've never said anything? How could you? Why didn't you say something before? When the hell were you going to tell us?'

'All those years,' said Suzie, almost to herself. It seemed amazing, impossible.

'All those anniversary cards . . . ' said Liz.

'But you and Dad went away on your twenty-fifth,' said Suzie.

'That's right, we did. We wanted to avoid anyone throwing us a surprise party,' said Rose wryly.

'And what about the trip to Rome on your thirtieth?' said Liz.

'Same reason,' said Jack.

'I assumed that you both knew,' Peter said to Suzie.

'I told you that I didn't think they knew,' Mary

said to Peter. 'I said, didn't I? I'm so sorry,' said Mary. Turning back to Peter she snapped. 'I told you, you and your big mouth.'

'The thing is, does it really matter?' said Rose gently. 'People live together all the time these days. Let's be honest, it's no big thing. You know your dad and I love each other,' she said, smiling up at Jack. 'I'm sorry — we should have told you, but least said, soonest mended.'

'What the hell is that supposed to mean?' growled Liz.

Peter shrugged haplessly. 'I didn't mean to cause any trouble. I just assumed — ' At which point Megan skipped over and cut him off mid-sentence.

'Are we going to have the surprise now?' she said.

Suzie stared at her younger daughter; she suspected the consensus was that they had probably had enough surprises for one day.

'What surprise, sweetheart?' asked Rose gently.

'I can't tell you. You have to close your eyes, Grandma, and you're not to look. And you too, Granddad.'

'Do I?' said Jack. 'And why's that then?'

Megan giggled. 'We can't tell you — it wouldn't be a surprise then, would it?'

Rose's gaze moved from face to face.

'Oh come on. It's hardly rocket science, Mum. Just close your eyes, the pair of you,' snapped Liz.

'Go on, Mum, it'll be fine,' said Suzie. She glanced up at Sam who just shrugged; after all, what was there to say?

'All right, but just mind this paving — if I fall over . . . ' Rose was saying warily, finally doing as she was told.

'You won't, you won't, I promise,' said Suzie, gently taking hold of her mother's hand while Sam and Megan took hold of Jack's hands. 'We'll lead you, won't we, Liz? Just don't peek. Promise?'

'It's not a barbeque, is it?' asked Rose, as they led her carefully across the lawn and through the side gate. 'Only if it is we've still got those things in the freezer — '

'No, it's not a barbeque, Mum, just mind your step here,' said Suzie as they guided her in through the open flap of the marquee.

'What the hell are we going to do?' hissed Liz in a whisper — as if by closing their eyes, her parents had suddenly been rendered deaf as well as blind.

'I don't know,' said Suzie, through a forced smile. 'We'll sort something out. Let's play it by ear.'

Liz glared at her and shook her head.

Rose tipped her head to one side as if trying to pick out the change in the sound. 'Where are we?' she asked, sounding suspicious.

'You can open your eyes now,' said Suzie as Megan and Sam brought Jack to stand alongside Rose.

As the two of them opened their eyes the whole tent erupted into cheers of 'Surprise!' and 'Happy Anniversary!' There were great whoops of pleasure, with cameras flashing and people clapping and cheering and stomping as the surprise was sprung.

'What a bloody mess,' growled Liz in an undertone as the crowd bayed and clamoured with delight.

Rose's face was a picture. Her mouth dropped open, her eyes widened. 'Oh my goodness,' she began. 'Oh my . . . oh, I don't believe it. I had no idea . . . '

'No, me neither,' grumbled Liz.

Ignoring her sister, Suzie felt her own eyes prickle as she saw Rose's eyes filling with tears. Jack slipped his hand around Rose's waist and, pulling her close, kissed her gently on top of her head.

'Will you just look at all this? Isn't this amazing? Fancy you doing all this. Rose, look at all the photos of the wedding. Oh, and just look at the cake,' he murmured, all joy and smiles.

'Did you know anything about this?' Rose asked, looking up at him.

'No, not a clue,' Jack murmured. 'I can't believe they did all this while we were out. It's fantastic — absolutely amazing. Lovely . . . what a lovely thing to do.'

Suzie could see her father's eyes misting over too.

'I really don't know what to say, girls. How on earth did you sort all this out without us knowing?' he said.

'It's been a real feat,' Suzie said. 'We've tried to invite everyone who was there first time around, and a few more besides, obviously. There are still a few people yet to arrive but a lot of them wanted to be here to surprise you.'

As people started to come over to congratulate them, Rose turned to Fleur. 'So did you know about all this?'

'Yes and no,' says Fleur.

'What sort of answer is that? Why didn't you say something?'

'Because it wouldn't have been a surprise then, would it?' Fleur laughed. 'And besides, I could ask you the same question, couldn't I? Why didn't you tell me you were divorced?'

Rose frowned. 'Not now, I'll tell you later.'

'Well you better had,' said Fleur. 'You've got no idea how hard it's been to keep all this lot quiet I can tell you. Suzie and Liz rang me over Christmas, and said if I was coming over this year, could we work it so I was here for what I *thought* was your anniversary,' she added archly.

'I thought you were ill,' hissed Rose, reddening furiously.

'I certainly was sick to death today — all those bloody plants,' Fleur said looking heavenwards. 'I've never been so bored in all my born days.'

'I was really worried about you,' said Rose.

Fleur sighed. Sisters, eh? Stepping forward, she hugged first Rose and then Jack tight. 'Seems to me there are a lot of things we need to talk about, you and I. To be honest I have no idea how Jack puts up with you.'

At which point Matt stepped forward with a tray of glasses. Sam took one of the glasses of champagne and held it aloft while Matt passed the others around.

'Ladies and gentlemen, friends and family,'

said Sam. 'I'd like to welcome everyone here and thank you once again for joining us tonight. If I could ask you to raise your glasses to propose a toast? To Rose and Jack.'

There was a great wave of noise that rolled towards them as everyone joined in with the toast. 'Rose and Jack'.

The words echoed and hung in the air for an instant, then were followed by a huge cheer as the band struck up with an impromptu burst of 'Congratulations'. The guests flocked forward to offer their good wishes and kind words and marvel at the fact that no one had guessed or let the cat out of the bag and to ask Rose if she had had any idea and to congratulate Jack and pump his hand until finally Jack lifted his hand up and called for silence.

'Thank you, thank you,' he said. 'We're absolutely delighted and totally amazed to see you all here this evening. We really had no idea about the party. Now if you'd just to give us ten minutes to catch our breath, we'll be happy to come and have a chat to everyone and thank you once again for coming.' He turned to Suzie, Liz, Fleur, Sam and Megan and smiled. 'Thank you. This is the most wonderful surprise. Isn't it, Rose? Now if you'll just give us a few minutes I'm sure your mum would like to go and freshen up, put a party frock on, wouldn't you, Rose?'

Before anyone could protest, the two of them hurried out of the marquee, closely followed by Suzie, Liz and Fleur. Sam turned back towards the guests and began encouraging people to top up their drinks and enjoy the canapés.

* * *

'Are you okay?' Suzie asked, as her dad opened the kitchen door.

'Why are you asking *them*, why aren't you asking me?' said Liz. 'You should be asking me. How could the two of them do this? We've been planning this party for months.'

'They didn't know that.'

'Well, it's unreasonable and so unfair. I mean, how does this make us look? We don't even know the truth about our own parents.'

'Getting all het up about it isn't going to help,' said Suzie.

Jack plugged in the kettle. 'Tea, anyone?' he said.

'Bugger the tea, Dad,' said Liz. 'We thought we couldn't let forty years go by without doing something special and all the time you've been living in sin.'

Rose, who was slipping off her shoes, laughed. 'Oh come off it, Liz, no one lives in sin any more. This is the twenty-first century.'

'Not where my family are concerned, it isn't. Have you got any idea how embarrassing this is? We've invited everyone who came to your wedding and all your friends. I've put together a film for later.'

'We found all kinds of things,' said Suzie helpfully.

'Yes, but apparently not the important things,' Liz snapped back. 'We'd got it all planned — anniversary waltz, lovely buffet, speeches, photographer, cutting the cake and everything.

Just like the big day. We managed to track down the ushers, and both your bridesmaids, Fleur obviously, and Janet Fielding — '

Rose looked up. 'Really? Fancy you tracking Janet down. We haven't see her for years, have we, Jack?' she said conversationally as she put her shoes in the cupboard.

' — And Peter Hudson. We obviously knew he was your best man, he helped us with all the names. The bastard, why didn't he say something before tonight?' Liz slumped down into a chair at the kitchen table. 'What on earth are we going to tell people? Why didn't you tell us, Mum?' said Liz.

Rose glanced at Jack. 'I know it sounds silly saying it now, but it didn't seem all that important, to be honest.'

'How can something like that not be important?' whined Liz.

'Because it just wasn't. Before we got divorced, your dad used to work away a lot of the time, and so in lots of ways life wasn't that different after we split up and you were both very little and . . . ' Rose paused, glancing from face to face. 'Obviously if we'd stayed separated, then we would have had to have said something to you eventually, but your dad came home nearly every weekend to see you both and to see me, and we still did lots of things we'd always done together and we went on holiday together all of us. It was all very civilised. You were little, and it was all a very long time ago now.'

Liz rounded on her father. 'How could you leave a woman with two little children?' she said.

'I can't believe you did that, Dad — that's not the man I know at all.'

Jack looked as if she had punched him.

'Liz, don't,' said Rose hastily. 'It wasn't your dad's fault. It was me who asked him to leave.'

'What?' gasped Liz.

Suzie stared at her. 'Oh, Mum,' she whispered.

Rose sighed. 'We were young and these things happen. And then one day I was standing in the kitchen, your dad was walking up the drive and he just looked at me and smiled and my heart did that fluttery-happy-excited thing that hearts do and I realised just how much I'd been looking forward to seeing him. And how much I'd missed him and I realised that I'd made the most awful mistake and that I still loved him and that I didn't want him to go.' As she spoke, Rose looked up at Jack, smiling, her eyes bright with tears. 'And so I asked him to stay, and he did. And that was it really.'

That was it? What an understatement. Suzie stared at the pair of them, seeing the love between them and their obvious joy in being together even after all these years, and was stunned and close to speechless.

'All those years and I had no idea,' she murmured. 'No idea at all.'

'Well, how would you? We didn't need to say anything, because things were back to how they had been,' said her dad apologetically. 'And through it all we always loved you — '

'And besides Mr and Mrs bloody Peter Hudson, just how many people out there know?'

said Liz pointing towards the marquee. Her face was a picture.

'Quite a few of them, probably . . . And there is something else — ' he said, glancing at Rose.

'This is just too bizarre,' Liz stammered, cutting him short. 'And what about Fleur? Did you know?'

So far, Fleur hadn't said a word and now, looking from face to face, she began to laugh, and laugh hard. 'You know, all this is absolutely bloody priceless,' she said, 'There was me thinking you two had got it all worked out. All these years I've thought of you as the golden couple, nothing ever going wrong, roses all the way. All sorted. Bloody hell — I don't believe it.'

Rose looked at Jack and then at Fleur. 'I'm sorry, we owe you an apology too. You were living in Australia at the time and had this whole new life out there. It sounded so different from mine — all high-powered and go-getting — and if you remember, we weren't talking much back then. You always seemed to have your act together and were so successful, I thought you'd think I was being stupid, foolish. It was pride really — I was worried what you might think of me . . . And we'd lost Mum and Dad by then, and it just didn't seem the right time to say anything.'

'So come on then, why did you ask him to leave?' said Fleur. 'Did you meet someone else? What the hell happened?'

Rose shifted uncomfortably under everyone's gaze. 'It wasn't like that, and it was a long time ago now. Do we have to talk about it now? We need to get changed. We can talk about it later.'

'We want to talk about it now, Rose,' said Fleur. 'You can hardly spring that one on us and then not tell us what the hell happened.'

'I think we should,' Jack began. 'I mean, after all, we aren't the only ones involved.'

'Look, I don't like to point this out again,' said Liz. 'But we've got a marquee full of people out there expecting to celebrate your fortieth wedding anniversary. We can't keep them waiting all night. What the hell are we going to say to them?'

'Maybe we could just change it to forty years together,' said Suzie hastily.

'Give or take a few years, you mean?' snapped Liz angrily, prowling round the kitchen. 'How could you do this to me, you two?'

'In some ways it's a lovely story, really romantic. We could just cut out the whole marriage thing — ' suggested Suzie.

'And the wedding cake? And the ruby wedding party favours, and the band that are all primed to play 'Here Comes the Bride'?' snapped Liz, glaring furiously at her mum and dad. 'The more I think about it, the worse it gets. I can't believe you two, I really can't. We've had balloons specially printed and everything. And what about our emotional and mental wellbeing? Do you know what you've done?'

'What do you mean?' asked Rose anxiously.

'Well, we've all been holding you two up as prime examples of good, clean living for years — happily married, weathering life's storms together, kind and good and well behaved. You've been this family's moral compass,' said

Liz. 'God knows what'll happen now.'

'But all those things are still true,' protested Rose. 'Nothing's changed, it's just that we aren't married.'

'They might not have changed for you,' said Liz indignantly. 'But it's a disaster for us. What is Suzie going to tell the girls? How can she have a go at them for behaving badly when their grandparents are living in sin?'

'Oh for goodness sake,' Rose said, reddening furiously. 'We're doing no such thing. You sound like some Victorian patriarch. This is not the Dark Ages, Liz. People do it all the time. Marriage as an institution is on the decline. Lots of people's parents aren't married.'

'Yes, but not *my* parents,' glowered Liz. 'My parents are the height of respectability.'

'Why didn't you just get re-married?' asked Suzie.

'It wasn't that simple,' Rose began, just as the back door flew open and Megan burst into the kitchen, all smiles and joy and noise.

'Grandma, Granddad, why aren't you changed yet? Dad wants to know what's taking so long. And he wanted you to know that the photographer is here to take the photos and Matt said the crowd is getting restless, and that people want to eat, and how much longer are you going to be, only I'm *totally* starving.'

Rose laughed. 'Well, we can't have that now, can we? You go and tell your dad we'll be over in five minutes. Tell him Grandma just needs to change into her glad rags. Come on, Jack, let's get going, we can't keep everyone waiting.'

And with that she turned and headed upstairs leaving Suzie, Liz and Fleur with an awful lot more questions than answers.

For the briefest moment, Suzie thought that her dad was going to say something else, but instead he turned and followed Rose upstairs.

12

Down on the riverbank, a mile or so away from the party, Sadie pursed her lips, screwed up her eyes and very carefully, having slipped the wire cage off the cork, began to ease it out of the champagne bottle with her thumbs.

'Steady, steady,' she murmured to herself.

'Oh bloody hell, just stop messing about, will you?' said Tucker, breaking the tension. 'How long does it take to open a bottle of booze? Just get the bloody cork out, will you? A man could die of thirst around here.'

'We wish,' said Sadie. 'Don't you know anything about anything, Tucker? You have to do it right or it'll go all over everywhere. What's the point of Hannah nicking us a bottle of champagne if it ends up all over the floor?'

'But I thought that was what you did with champagne — you know, shake it up and spray it about like they do on the telly,' Tucker said, miming with his thumbs pressed together.

'Not if you want to get drunk on it, you don't, dingbat,' said Simon, without taking his eyes off Sadie or the bottle.

'Who are you calling a dingbat, moron?' Tucker snarled at him.

'Shut up and cool it, you two. If you shake it up you lose half of it,' said Sadie. 'Nice and easy does it.'

They were hiding out inside a dense stand of

rhododendrons down beyond the golf course that over the years had formed a natural den by killing off the grass and plants beneath it. Overhead the thick evergreen foliage formed a leafy canopy. It was cool under the contorted branches and the spread of dense, shiny, green leaves. Shaded from the late afternoon sun, their makeshift camp was softly dappled, the air heavy with the scents of summer, of loam and barbeques and newly mown grass. Beyond the shelter of the foliage, Hannah could pick out the early evening sound of insects buzzing away and the distant drone of a mower, but inside the air was still and heavy with the smell of cigarette smoke.

The ground beneath the branches was clear except for a few logs, a battered folding chair and an assortment of odds and ends that the four of them had brought there. In the centre of the den were the remains of a campfire that they had had the previous weekend, surrounded by stones that Simon and Tucker had carried up from the river. Beyond the bushes and below the den, the water idled past, glinting in the sunlight, cool, deep, dark and inviting.

Tucker had the patience of a toddler. 'Daft bloody stuff. What's the point of having something when you lose half of it when you open it? That's stupid — why don't we just crack open the vodka instead? I've got half a bottle of Coke in my rucksack, we could just mix the whole thing up. Get on down and parteeeeeeee.' He stood up and waggled his hips, hands above his head.

'And you drank out of the bottle?' asked Sadie, eyes still on the end of the champagne bottle.

Tucker nodded, looking confused. 'Yeah, why wouldn't I? Like I carry a silver goblet around to drink out of — '

'Like we want to drink your spit,' said Sadie, as the cork finally slid from the end of the bottle with an explosive, satisfying thunk. It soared out through the rhododendrons, vanishing in the long tussocky grass further down the riverbank.

As the bubbles erupted, Sadie quickly pressed the bottle to her lips and drank greedily, belching back the gas as she pulled away and wiped her mouth with the back of her hand. The bottle was cloudy with condensation, little rivulets of moisture trickling down the outside of the heavy green glass.

'Oh wow, that is so cold,' she said with a shiver, handing the champagne over to Hannah. 'Ladies first,' she growled, as Tucker tried to make a grab for it in passing.

'Oh come on,' said Tucker. 'Hannah's a total lightweight. She doesn't really want any booze, do you, Hannah? Come on. Gimme a go.'

'She will when she's done,' said Sadie.

Aware that they were all watching her, Hannah held the bottle in both hands and tipped it up, expecting the contents to be sweet and fizzy like lemonade; certainly not sour and tasting vaguely like sick, which was what it did taste like. She spluttered as the taste filled her mouth, and then gasped and choked all in the same instant as the champagne flooded down her throat. She couldn't help but pull a face, grimacing and struggling to stop herself from retching as she pulled the bottle away.

'See. Yeah, you're a real hard drinker, aren't you?' laughed Tucker triumphantly, trying to snatch the bottle away from her. 'Gimme that here. Let me show you how it's done.'

'Shut up,' said Hannah, slapping his hand away. 'It just went up my nose, that's all. I've had loads of champagne at weddings and parties and stuff, it just went down the wrong way. Okay?'

Determined to show him she could do it, Hannah took a great big slurping slug from the bottle before handing it on, trying hard not to gag as she did so.

'Yeah, like you're so hard,' said Tucker as he took a mouthful. Screwing up his nose, he pulled the bottle away to stare at it. 'Yeuk, bloody hell — no wonder you choked, that's horrible, this can't be the stuff all them footballers and that drink. It's foul. I like the blue fizzies. My brother gets them for me, they taste like bubble gum.'

Simon took the bottle from Tucker and drank without comment. Hannah couldn't help but be impressed.

Meanwhile Sadie had got her hands on the vodka. 'You pair should have got some Coke or lemonade or something as well,' she said to Hannah and Simon, cracking the seal on the bottle.

'We would if you'd have said something,' said Simon.

'Well, I didn't think I'd have to,' said Sadie, all sarcasm.

'I've got — ' Tucker began.

'Yeah, yeah, we all know what you've got,' said Sadie waving the words away. 'You already said and if I need it I'll tell you, okay?'

Simon stretched and stood up. 'I could go up to the shop and get a couple of cans if you like. What do you reckon?'

Hannah wondered if she dared offer to go with him. As she was thinking it, Simon said, 'You fancy coming with me, Hannah?'

Sadie caught her eye and grinned. 'Worried you might get lost, are you, Simon?' she said.

Hannah felt her colour rising.

'Yeah right,' he said. 'I was just thinking she could help me carry stuff.'

'Really?' said Sadie.

'I was just thinking we could do with some paper cups or something.'

Sadie laughed. 'You pair will be wanting bloody doilies next.' And then turning to Tucker, she leant over and waggled her fingers at him. 'C'mon on then, hand it over.'

'What?' he said looking bemused.

'The Coke, you moron, give me it here, will you?' she said. 'The alcohol will kill the germs and, let's face it, beggars can't be choosers. We can pick up some cans on the way back to my house.'

Simon was about to say something but Sadie was ahead of him. 'Sit down and relax, Si — it was a lovely offer, sweetie, but let's be honest, we can't wait that long.'

Tucker meanwhile did as he was told and handed the bottle over and, while they all watched, Sadie very carefully decanted a hefty measure of vodka into the half empty bottle. She swirled the contents round a little and then, after wiping the top, took a long, slow, gulping drink. She offered it to Tucker who, grinning like a loon, took a swig.

'Oh yeah. That's better,' he said, wiping his mouth. 'Oh yesssss, very nice, very nice indeed. Loads better than that poxy bloody champagne.' He handed it on to Hannah.

Hannah looked at the contents of the bottle warily, turning it around a few times. There was something that looked suspiciously like a piece of crisp floating around on top of the liquid. Aware that Sadie and Tucker were watching, she took a little sip and then another one. She'd never had vodka before. It didn't taste too bad; in fact it didn't taste that different to Coke, just sort of thicker and with a bit of a warm tang to it, so she had a little more, and then a little more. Tucker was right, it was a lot nicer than the champagne. She took a long slurp and sighed. Drinking wasn't so bad. She took another pull on the bottle.

'Lot better, isn't it?' said Tucker as she came up for air.

Hannah nodded and took another mouthful. On the other side of the clearing, Sadie settled down with her hands behind her head, resting against a log as she lit up a cigarette. 'Don't hog it all, honey, hand it around, let your boyfriend have a blast,' she said, waving the bottle on.

Hannah made an effort not to react to the boyfriend comment and instead tried to stay cool. She knew Sadie was just trying to wind her up and she planned to say nothing, so why could she feel herself going red and hot and giggling instead? Hannah bit her lip but instead of making it stop, it just seemed to make it worse.

Tucker rolled his eyes. 'Told you she was a lightweight,' he said with a sniff.

13

'So what *exactly* are we going to tell people?' Liz murmured to herself, thinking aloud. 'You know this is a disaster. All that planning. What a bloody mess.'

'Oh come on, Liz, like Mum said, this isn't the Dark Ages. In all honesty, once you get past the shock of it, does it really matter?' said Suzie. 'Surely the thing is that they're together now.'

'The thing is,' growled Liz, 'that we've organised a bloody great party to celebrate the fact that they've been married for forty years. We have to say something.'

Suzie stared at her. 'No, we don't.'

'People out there know.'

'People out there came to the party to help them celebrate — no one rang up and complained. No one said, 'Excuse me, we can't come because actually they haven't been married for forty years.' People don't care, Liz.'

'I care,' snapped Liz, eyes filling up with tears. 'I can't believe they've lied to us all these years. You know, if it hadn't been for Peter Hudson dropping them in it they probably wouldn't have said anything — ever.'

'They didn't lie,' said Suzie defensively.

'Well, what did they do then? They didn't exactly tell us the truth, did they?'

Suzie shook her head. 'I don't think it matters as far as the party is concerned. Why don't we just try and enjoy the evening?'

'Easy for you to say,' said Liz.

'Why don't I pour us all a glass of wine?' said Fleur, who had been standing listening on the other side of the kitchen. 'Just a quickie?'

'Just water for me,' said Liz. 'My dermatologist told me that alcohol can be terribly ageing.'

'Well, he sounds like a real bundle of laughs.' Fleur snorted as she took a bottle of white Zinfandel out of the fridge and retrieved a couple of glasses from the cupboard. 'Presumably you didn't invite him along?'

While she was trying to work out where they went from here, Liz pulled out her phone to see if Grant had called. What on earth was she going to tell him? And what would he think? She had held up her parents' marriage like a shining beacon. How many times since they'd started dating had Liz told him that it was the kind of relationship she was looking for — loving, stable, safe, an oasis of sanity in an otherwise chaotic world? Now what the hell could she say? That she'd like to shack up with someone and then lie to their children? Honestly, how could her parents be so selfish?

She peered at the phone's screen. There were no missed calls, no texts, nothing. Liz glanced out of the kitchen window at the marquee, listening to the sounds of the party, the laughter and people chattering. All the money she'd spent, and for what? Eventually her parents would have to say something, surely. People out there were partying under false pretences.

Grant was probably driving, which was why he

hadn't rung her — that had to be it. He had probably left in a hurry, late as usual, and hadn't had a chance to phone.

Since she'd first met him Liz had never known Grant be on time for anything, but then again he had no one at home to organise him, no one to gently chivvy him along to make sure that he made his appointments on time. She smiled, imagining their life in a few years' time, her waving the children off to school, handing Grant his briefcase, him kissing her as he headed off to the office. Her PA hanging around on the periphery waiting to talk to her about the phone call from her production company. Keanu Reeves on line two waiting for a decision on whether he could have the part in her new film. George Clooney on hold.

Grant just needed stability and support and a framework to his life, that was all. He was always telling her that people understood, and that if they wanted to see him they would wait — and there was some girl in his office who seemed to be on permanent standby to apologise for his tardiness — but Liz was confident that, given a little bit of time and the right strategy, she could get him sorted out. After all, it was only polite to turn up when you said you would, good manners cost nothing, and Liz had told Grant several times that she really wanted him there on time.

She glanced up at the clock. It was past seven. He knew how important tonight was to her. Maybe it was a good thing he hadn't turned up on time. Or maybe he had had an accident. She looked up at the ceiling and sniffed back an unexpected little flurry of tears, hoping it was nothing too serious. She couldn't manage if he was maimed and she wouldn't even get to be the grieving widow — after all, who cared about grieving girlfriends unless they lived in and took the rough with the smooth?

This wasn't how she had planned the day going at all. First her mum and dad, and now Grant — God, life was so cruel. Widowed before she was even married.

Then again, maybe he was just stuck in traffic, or had pulled into a layby to take a call, although that wasn't likely. He'd probably be on his hands-free, working away at some business thing, some big deal. Actually, when Liz thought about it, it would be amazing if Grant *wasn't* on his phone — it would certainly be a first.

After the initial flush of madness Liz had soon realised there was always *something* coming up in Grant's life that took him away from her, someone who needed talking to, or something that needed dealing with, some crisis, some conference, some man flying in from Colombia. But then again, Grant had told her more than once, when she had mentioned in passing that taking a business call halfway through supper wasn't very nice, that he was that kind of a guy. Entrepreneur, fingers in lots of pies, always looking for the next big thing. You didn't get as rich as Grant by sitting around on the sofa all day watching Jeremy Kyle and Australian soaps, he had said. But surely even he could see that, sometimes, some things were more important than the next deal. There were limits and there should be boundaries.

Liz, of all people, understood the importance of working hard and focusing on what needed to be done; but if they were going to have a future together, Grant would really have to understand that sometimes she came first. Tonight was one of those times.

On the kitchen clock the seconds were slowly ticking by. Suzie and Fleur were still talking but Liz zoned them out.

He was probably almost there. He'd probably be arriving any minute now. She was getting herself in a state over nothing. Liz took a deep breath and straightened her dress, swallowing back the little squall of self-pity. She needed to get a grip. After all, it didn't do to look anxious or annoyed — men didn't like that, nor did they like it when you glared at them and said things like, *Where the hell have you been?* and *What time do you call this?*, as she had found from previous experience. No, it was far better just to stay calm and concentrate on what the hell they were going to tell a marquee full of wedding guests, family, friends, and hangers-on. Inwardly she groaned. *How could her parents do this to her, tonight of all nights?*

On the other side of the kitchen, Fleur was topping up her wine and was well on her way down the second or maybe it was the third glass. Rose and Jack were still upstairs getting changed.

Suzie got to her feet and said, 'I think I'll just pop out and let everyone know the happy couple will be out in five minutes. Can you go and hurry them up?'

The happy couple. The irony of it; Liz couldn't even *think* the words without pulling a face.

'Trust Suzie to bugger off when the going gets sticky,' Liz said to Fleur, trying not to look at the kitchen clock. 'She should stay here with us and sort this out. We really need to think about how we're going to handle it — manage expectations and all that. Typical of her to leave it to someone else. How could they do this to me?'

Fleur handed her a glass of wine. 'Here, you need one of these.'

Liz sighed and sat down alongside her. 'I think perhaps you're right. Bugger Gregor.'

'Is he your new bloke?'

'My dermatologist.'

Fleur nodded and lifted her glass in toast. 'In that case, bugger Gregor.'

'I can't believe that Mum and Dad lied to us all these years,' said Liz. 'I'm just so shocked. I mean, *really* surprised.'

'Well, it doesn't surprise me one little bit,' said Fleur. 'The thing is we're all the same, the whole family — all of us with our little secrets.'

Liz glanced at her. 'What?'

'I've always thought we're all cut from the same cloth, all the women in this family. I bet you've got all sorts of little things you're keeping to yourself, keeping hidden away — a whole cupboard full of skeletons.'

Liz had a momentary flashback to Bali and the nineteen-year-old surfer dude, all tattoos, teeth and tan. The one with bleached blond dreads and stomach muscles like warm taut leather, the one who had tasted of sea and salt and had made her howl like a bitch on heat for hours. Boy, that guy had some staying power. And he hadn't been the first, although Liz had always been extremely careful and discreet about her little liaisons.

'You, me, your mum, your sister — all naturally secretive. It's just in our blood,' Fleur was saying. 'My mum, your mum's mum, was just the same. Always played our cards very close to our chest. We're very much alike.'

Liz, who felt herself reddening, stared at her aunt. 'Are you serious?'

Fleur's eyes narrowed. 'You and I in particular. Secretive, lousy taste in men?'

Liz snorted. 'Speak for yourself.'

Fleur shrugged. 'I'm only saying.'

The last thing Liz wanted was to dwell on the similarities between her and Fleur. Fleur was wealthy and beautifully preserved for a woman in her sixties but at what cost? No husband, no family, working all hours that God sent. Rich, yes, but surely lonely too? In the middle of the night when she couldn't sleep, Liz could see that it wouldn't take much for her to end up in the same boat. God, she wished Grant would hurry up and get there.

'Look at the evidence,' Fleur was saying. 'There's your mum and dad with this whole divorce thing for a start. Who would ever have guessed that? I had no idea, and I'm her sister, for God's sake. And then there's all this business with Suzie — look at her, she always looks like butter wouldn't melt in her mouth.'

This took a second or two to register. Liz

stared at her. 'What do you mean? *What* business with Suzie?'

Fleur hesitated and then looked flustered. 'I thought you knew? I thought she would have told you. Maybe I shouldn't have said anything. Do you want something to eat with the wine — I'm sure I saw some crisps in the larder.'

'No,' snapped Liz. 'You can't just leave it at that. What do you mean? What about Suzie?'

'I didn't realise you didn't know,' said Fleur defensively. 'See there we go, what did I tell you?'

'Oh come on, Fleur.' Liz frowned, or at least she would have done if the Botox had let her. 'You just said yourself that Mum didn't tell you about this whole divorce thing. Suzie doesn't really confide in me these days — I mean, we used to be very close obviously when we were kids, but we move in different circles these days. We hardly see each other. We're different people. She loves family life and all that stuff — not that I don't, but I've got my career to think about, whereas she's always put the whole family thing first . . . '

Liz knew she was guilty of protesting too much, while across the table Fleur was weighing up the options. Finally, leaning closer, she said, 'Not for much longer, she isn't. And that's the problem.'

'What?' gasped Liz, unable to help herself. 'What do you mean, 'Not for much longer'?'

Fleur glanced over her shoulder as if there was some chance she might be overheard, before she continued in a low voice, 'I'm not sure that I should be telling you this but it's this thing with

Matt, the guy who is doing the food for the party tonight. She's really worried that Sam will find out before she tells him herself. Things have been a bit prickly between them for a while now.'

As Liz stared at Fleur she felt something shifting in her chest. '*Suzie and Sam?*' she whispered.

Fleur nodded and then raised her eyebrows. 'And Matt is very easy on the eye.'

What the hell was going on with those two? Like her mum and dad, Suzie and Sam were rocks in her ocean, landmarks she guided her own ship by. Was there nothing sacred or true or solid any more?

'Are you telling me that Suzie's having an affair with the caterer?' she said haltingly, in a voice barely above a whisper.

In among her feelings of shock and amazement, Liz heard another more petulant voice inside her head — how the hell had Suzie managed to grab herself *two* men, when Liz couldn't reel in one? It was so unfair and so infuriating. Sam was lovely in his own lived-in way and this Matt, whoever he was, was on TV. Okay, so Suzie scrubbed up all right but most of the time she looked like something the cat had finished with. It was so not fair.

'*I* didn't say that,' said Fleur. 'And anyway we should be getting back to the party.' She hesitated. 'And your mum told me not to say anything. I mean, that just tells you how anxious she is, normally she doesn't tell me anything at all.'

'You can't just stop there,' snapped Liz.

At which point Liz's phone rang. Tempted to ignore it, she picked it up and squinted at the screen: it was Grant. Trust him to ring now. Torn, she said to Fleur, 'It's Grant — he's probably lost. He was supposed to be here by half past six.'

Fleur shrugged in a 'suit yourself' way that made Liz think that if Fleur didn't finish telling her about Suzie now she probably never would. The phone rang again. One of the techies had programmed in the ringtone for her — it was the opening bars of the theme tune to *Starmaker*.

The side panels flashed, the phone buzzed frantically under the ringtone, while the words 'Mr Right' pulsed on and off on the screen. She had meant to change it; it had been a bit of joke when they first got together but Grant hadn't thought it was at all funny. Maybe she should change it to Mr Grumpy.

Meanwhile Fleur's attention had wandered away from Liz, back to the counter top and the wine bottle.

'I'll see you outside,' Fleur mouthed, in a glorified stage whisper. 'I don't suppose your mum and dad will be much longer.' She picked up the bottle and headed for the door. 'Tell them I'll see them in the tent.'

'No, wait!' said Liz, jumping to her feet. 'I need to know about Suzie and Matt.'

Fleur looked back over her shoulder. 'What about golden boy?' she said, nodding towards the phone.

'He can wait,' Liz said, decision made. 'I'll ring him back later.' Another ring or two and it would go to voicemail.

Fleur smiled wolfishly. 'Are you sure? I thought you were waiting for him to ring.'

'Yes I am. Just tell me about Suzie and Matt.'

'I'm not that sure there's that much to tell really,' she said.

'Oh purlease, stop playing with me, Fleur,' Liz growled. 'Just spit it out.'

'Apparently it's all very hush-hush at the moment. Matt's planning to open a restaurant in the old dairy on the estate, which is a stone's throw from Suzie's precious garden. She's going to be growing stuff for him. They're supposed to be signing the contract at the end of next week.'

'Is that all?' said Liz, feeling cheated. 'One new restaurant — it's hardly going to change the world, is it?

'Well it might for Suzie. Your mum was saying that there's going to be some sort of TV thing — doing the place up, updating the décor, a step-by-step, fly-on-the-wall thing — you know how these things work. They're planning to cash in on the whole 'grow local, eat local' thing and there'll be a series and a book, obviously.

'Suzie will be doing the gardening and Matt will be cooking the food. Your mum said Suzie is really excited and I'm not surprised. I mean, what a turn up. I'm amazed she hasn't said anything to you. Apparently she's really natural and he's really good fun, very down to earth — '

Liz stared at her. 'Suzie? On TV? Are you sure? Is it some sort of local thing?'

Fleur shook her head. 'Channel 4 I think, although it could be the BBC. Problem is, Suzie doesn't know how to tell Sam. And who can blame her? It's going to mean a lot of work, a lot more hours away from house and home. I don't know all the details but apparently the company Sam works for has been on thin ice for months and according to your mum — and reading between the lines — there's trouble in paradise. It's a great opportunity for her but you can see how Sam might feel she's stepping up a league, leaving him behind — or maybe he doesn't like the idea of her working with someone as slick, good looking and successful as Matt.' Fleur paused for effect. 'You don't have to be a genius to see what's going on there. Long lunches. Working late, the odd weekend away at trade shows . . . ' Fleur let the words hang in the air between them.

'Are you serious?' Liz murmured.

Fleur nodded. 'Oh yes, she's barely at home these days.'

Liz stared at her, finding herself torn between the revelations that Suzie was carrying on with someone and that somehow along the way she had also managed to wangle herself a TV show.

'She can't be on TV,' Liz finally snapped. 'I mean, she just can't. It's not right — it's not fair. How on earth can Suzie just be on TV? *I'm* the one who is on TV. I've done my time. I've paid my dues. I don't suppose it's occurred to her that they're probably only taking her on because she's my sister. It's obvious when you think about it, they're just trying to cash in on the whole *Starmaker* thing. It's disgusting.'

'I suppose they could be, but I don't think

they are,' Fleur said quietly. 'I don't think they even know she's your sister. Suzie uses her married name and I can't imagine she'd use those kind of tactics; she's not like us really, is she?'

Liz stared at her; the implication being that Liz would, presumably. Fleur shrugged. 'Don't look at me like that. You and I are like peas in a pod — driven, businesslike . . . unlucky in love,' she said.

'Speak for yourself,' Liz said.

Fleur continued as if she had not spoken. 'Whereas Suzie and your mum . . . '

Liz waited for whatever was coming next.

'Aren't,' said Fleur, after a second of two of deliberation. 'I mean, they're not very worldly, are they? The TV company approached Suzie after her garden and Matt's restaurant had been on the radio and in the local papers and after all, he's got the contacts. I don't think it's about you at all.'

'Don't be naïve, Fleur, of course it's about me,' sniffed Liz, snatching up her phone from the table; surely there had to be someone she could call about this? Her agent? Probably not — knowing Hector his next call would be to Suzie to see if she wanted him to represent her.

'The whole point about this, Liz, is that Suzie is worried about how Sam is going to take it. But who would have guessed by looking at her? Secretive, that's what I'm saying. The whole bloody lot of us. Shame really. Sam's always seemed such a decent guy.'

Liz stared at her aunt. 'Decent guy,' she

repeated, looking down at her phone. How come she couldn't find herself one of those?

'You'd better ring His Nibs back,' said Fleur. 'You don't really want Mr Right getting himself lost tonight of all nights now, do you?'

'I'm sure he'll be here any minute now,' Liz said with forced casualness as she marched outside. 'That's the trouble living in such a backwater, people always have a hell of a job finding it.'

Out in the garden Liz could barely contain her fury. It was outrageous. How could Suzie possibly end up on TV *and* having an affair? Liz took a deep breath and made an effort to compose herself. Before having a word with Suzie, she'd ring Grant and find out exactly where he was and what was going on. Be calm and nice, although that wasn't what the raging peevish voice inside her head was telling her — oh no, not at all. She wanted to go into that tent and ask Suzie what the hell she thought she was up to. TV, they'd make mincemeat of someone like her. See how Suzie liked it when the tabloids went on and on about how fat she'd got or how thin or how she had let herself go.

Liz sniffed and scrolled down to find Grant's number, peering at the blur of numbers on the screen. But she was unable to bring herself to ring. What she needed now wasn't Grant sounding distracted and busy, gagging to take a business call on the other line, but some moral support, a little emotional *there, there, there*. What she needed was someone to stroke her ego and make a little conversation over a decent bottle of wine, or snuggled up in bed, about her career, how well she had done so far and how very pretty and clever and bright she was.

Unfortunately Liz suspected that that kind of moral support was probably outside Grant's repertoire. He had told her right from the very start that he didn't like clingy, whiny women, although he did like his women feminine and soft, not cold and hard-nosed like his ex-wife. Liz doubted he'd be much use in a crisis unless it involved her tripping over and breaking a heel on her Jimmy Choos and him carrying her back to the car, or maybe needing his jacket draped around her shoulders because she had got chilly at some outdoor jazz thing. She could see that Grant liked to think himself good at the whole 'me Tarzan, you Jane' stuff, but he was probably not the kind of man who would be there for her in a crisis of confidence. And that was another thorn in her flesh, because Liz had no doubt whatsoever that Sam was exactly that kind of man. He would be just perfect in a real crisis. It was so bloody unfair. How come Suzie had managed to get it all?

Which brought her rage full circle. Why hadn't Suzie said anything to Liz about the whole TV thing? Surely Liz would be the most natural choice of confidante? All the years of experience she had, along with the know-how, the contacts . . .

As if Liz's thoughts had summoned her up, Suzie now appeared in the door of the marquee, carrying a champagne flute. Suzie smiled and held it out towards her.

'Okay?' Suzie mouthed. 'Are they coming down? People are beginning to get restless and I'm not sure how much longer we can hold the food.'

Liz was about to speak, but before the words could form, her phone rang again. It was Grant. This time she painted on a broad confident smile and took the call, waving Suzie away.

'Hello, darling, we're missing you already. Where are you?' she said in a voice that carried across the lawn, stopping Suzie in her tracks.

'I'm in the office,' said Grant.

'What? What do you mean you're in the office?' she said, heading across the garden so that Suzie wouldn't be able to hear her. 'Just how late are you going to be? I thought you said you'd be here by half past six.'

'No, *you* said I should be there by half past six,' Grant said.

'My parents are already here; supper's going to be served soon. What time will you be here?'

'I'm not going to be there at all, sweetie, I told you the other day that I couldn't make it tonight.' He sounded quite cheery, which was unnerving.

'What? When did you tell me that? You didn't, I'm sure you didn't — ' hissed Liz.

'Yes, I did, babe, maybe you weren't listening. You were busy making plans and talking to someone else, so no change there. You were having your hair done or something — when you said you wanted me to come I told you I'd love to but I'd got to meet Felipo this evening. Remember?'

Liz stopped dead in her tracks. He *had* said something else, she knew that, but it hadn't occurred to her that he had said *no*.

'Anyway, we've got a table booked at the Ivy. It's a long-standing arrangement, and besides being a good friend, Felipo is a very important man. Not someone you mess around. I did tell you — anyway I was just ringing to say I hope you have a lovely time. Got to go now. Ciao, babe.'

Ciao, babe? That wasn't the answer she was expecting at all.

'No, just wait a minute,' said Liz hastily. 'You knew that this was important to me. I reminded you last week and you said — '

'I said I would think about it, that I'd check my diary and get back to you. And I did — you just didn't listen, sweetie.'

'You had plenty of time to reschedule this meeting. I've been talking about my parents' party for weeks.'

'You're right, I did, but I didn't want to. Look, babe, family things really aren't my scene, and to be honest this is all a bit much — too much, too soon, do you get what I'm saying here?'

'Too much, too soon?' she repeated. 'Are you saying you don't want to meet my parents?'

'Well yes, that's right. I didn't want to make it sound quite so harsh but you haven't really given me much choice, have you? So yeah, exactly. I mean I don't know about you but I'm really not looking for anything too heavy at the moment, and it's all been getting a bit intense recently. Every weekend, meeting the family. I mean, for God's sake, it's not like this is really going anywhere, is it? I'm thinking fun — get together when we're both free, you know, have a good time, have some fun.'

'Fun . . . yes, of course,' Liz said, struggling for breath as she held back tears, trying very hard to keep the pain out of her voice. How could she have got it so wrong? 'Well, we have been having fun, haven't we?' she managed between gritted teeth. 'The last few months. It's been great, you know, nothing too heavy.'

'No, sure, you're right, it's been good but this every weekend thing — '

Somewhere in the background Liz could hear a woman giggling. 'Is there someone with you?' she said.

'Sorry? Oh that, yeah that's Felipo's baby sister Angelique and her friend Martina — couple of crazy, crazy girls. Now they *really* know how to have fun, those two. Martina's twenty-two. She's a lingerie model — six foot two, 38,24,34, all of it one hundred percent natural.'

Liz couldn't believe what she was hearing: just who the hell did he think he was talking to? Did he expect her to be pleased for him? She could practically hear him wiping the drool off his chin. Bastard.

'Well, I hope you all have a lovely evening. Lots of fun,' she said before hanging up.

He was forty-eight, for God's sake. A twenty-two-year-old lingerie model? Liz sniffed.

'I hope he chokes,' she growled as she headed into the marquee and the increasingly restless guests.

14

Down on the riverbank, Sadie, Hannah, Simon and Tucker were all a little the worse for wear.

'I reckon we should go back to your gran's place and grab another couple of bottles of something,' said Sadie, stretching out like a cat in the dappled sunlight.

'Yeah, but not any more of that champagne stuff,' Tucker said, pulling a face. 'That was totally foul.'

'We've still got some drink left,' said Hannah, holding up the bottle of vodka and Coke as evidence.

'Yeah I know, but we might want some more later and you were the one who told us it was a piece of cake last time,' said Sadie, flicking her dog end into the remains of the campfire. Her speech was slurred and thick. 'We'll go and get some more booze and then we'll go back to my place, okay? And then Si here can ring up for take-out pizza or whatever it is he wants,' she giggled.

'I don't know,' said Hannah. 'The party is supposed to have started at seven. Everyone will be there by now.'

'Yeah, but just think about it. That'll be better for us, won't it? Everyone already being there will make it easier to get in and get something without being spotted. You know, slip in under cover of the crowd?' said Sadie, illustrating stealth with a hand gesture.

Hannah considered the sense of what Sadie was saying. Thinking through her plan, it seemed complicated and muddy, which Hannah guessed meant that she was most probably drunk. *Finally*. She tried hard to suppress a big grin. *So this is what it feels like*.

'So what, you mean like all of us go back now?' she said. 'To my Grandma's, or just me and Simon?'

'Oooooo, *just me and Simon*,' Tucker whooped in a horrible imitation of her voice.

Hannah glared at him, or she would have done if she could have focused properly.

'Shut up,' she snapped. 'You're just jealous.' Her bottom lip felt numb and her voice sounded as if it was coming from a long way back in her head and even though she was thinking the words before she said them, when they came out she was surprised by how loud they sounded. This being drunk business was weirder than she had expected.

Between them, Sadie, Tucker, Hannah and Simon had finished off the champagne and drunk quite a lot of the vodka, and when she closed her eyes Hannah was disconcerted to discover that the darkness was busy going around and around.

Up until she had closed her eyes, Hannah had been watching Tucker move slowly across the clearing, approaching Sadie very carefully, like she was one of those insects on the wildlife programmes that bites the heads off the male. Stealthily he had moved closer and closer, watching Sadie's every move until he had finally slipped onto the ground alongside her.

Hannah tried hard not to laugh as Tucker very cautiously slid his arm around Sadie's shoulder and then settled himself back on the log so that she had no choice but to lean up against him. Just when it looked like he might have got it licked, Sadie suddenly stood up, brushed herself off, took another swig from the Coke bottle and then settled herself down again on an upturned milk crate by the remains of their campfire.

'Did you say there was going to be food at the party?' asked Tucker, pretending not to notice that Sadie had moved.

Hannah nodded. 'Yeah, they're going to have a buffet and stuff and a wedding cake.'

'Well, in that case, Simon, trouser your cash, mate. We'll eat when we get there,' said Tucker brightly. 'You think your mum and dad would mind if we crashed your gran's party, Hannah? You know, just like grab some food and that? We don't need to stay for long.'

* * *

Earlier, the thought of them all going to the anniversary party had seemed crazy, but now it didn't seem like such a bad idea. After all, they were her friends, weren't they? And even if her mum didn't really like them, surely she could see that they were cool and she should be allowed to have some of her own friends there. It was only fair.

The trouble was that the thought was slippery

and hard to hold onto, like a fish in her head. The fish idea struck her as really clever and then really funny and then Hannah giggled so much she rolled off the log she'd been sitting on, which made her laugh even more.

'So do you think they'll mind?' asked Tucker.

Hannah did a big panto shrug. 'I don't know. Probably they won't be that happy about it, because it's mostly all their friends and my grandma and granddad's friends, but they're hardly going to chew me out in front of all those people, are they? And it'll be a laugh.' Hannah replayed the words in her head. *Had she really said that?* There was no way to take it back now because the others were getting up and ready to go. And maybe it *would* be a laugh.

'What are you doing?' asked Hannah.

'Well, it sounds like a plan to me,' said Sadie, brushing herself down and twisting her hair back up into a knot. 'And anyway we can't go round my place for a while yet, because my mum will still be there with what's-his-face, all loved up and snogging,' said Sadie, screwing up her face. 'Not that I mind, you know, what she does is her business but you know . . . ' The words faded away.

Hannah stared at her; she couldn't imagine what it would be like to have a mum who brought boyfriends home. But Sadie's thoughts had already moved on.

'So we'll head up to your gran's, see what's going on there, get something to eat, mingle with the wrinklies for a bit, and then we can grab some more drink and bugger off back to my house. Okay?' She paused to see if there was any dissention in the ranks and then said, 'Sounds like a plan to me. Tucker, bring the booze.'

Tucker did as he was told. Hannah, sitting in the dust beside the log, wanted to explain that it probably, *maybe*, wasn't such a good idea after all, but she didn't seem to be able to concentrate on more than one thing at once, and at the moment all her brainpower was focused on trying to stand up. How come she had never had to think about standing up before? Her legs felt very odd. Simon, already on his feet, came over and slipped his arm through hers, carefully helping her to stand.

'Are you okay?' he whispered. He was grinning and looked really cute.

'Yeah, of course she's okay, why wouldn't she be? Leave her alone, you letch,' sniggered Tucker, with a big grin.

Simon coloured crimson. 'I was only — '

'Yeah, we can all see what you were doing, get your hands off her,' teased Sadie. 'Taking advantage of the drunk. It's illegal, you know. You should be ashamed of yourself.'

'I'm okay,' Hannah said aloud, although she was anything but, and then, catching Simon's eye, she smiled. 'Thank you,' she murmured, brushing herself down. 'I don't think I could have made it up without you.' Which for some reason made her giggle all the more. 'Sorry,' she spluttered. 'My legs and my brain have gone weird.'

'Are you sure you're all right?' Simon asked. His anxious expression made her want to laugh all the more but she managed to hold it together and made an effort to straighten her clothes. Hannah felt wrecked and wished she had a hairbrush with her. 'I'm okay. I just feel a bit . . . '

'Drunk,' said Sadie loudly.

'Sick,' Hannah muttered with horror as a great wave of nausea rolled over her. 'Oh my God, I'm going to be — ' and clutching her stomach with one hand and clamping the other over her mouth, Hannah ran headlong out of their den into the rough grass beyond. In her confusion and panic she picked the wrong side of the bushes and a split second later she found herself teetering on the edge of the riverbank, the momentum carrying her over the edge down towards the water. Slipping and sliding, she slithered messily down the slope, down through the dense grass and the brambles and the bushes, down to the very bottom where she threw up all over her new ballet shoes. And then she threw up some more, and then some more, until she was dry heaving and it felt as if she might cough up her whole digestive system along with maybe her lungs.

Finally, after what felt like forever, Hannah slumped down onto the grassy bank, trembling, shaky and cold, her stomach still heaving miserably with little aftershocks.

God, if this is drunk you can keep it, she thought, closing her eyes and wishing the world would stop tilting so violently. Another great wave of nausea rolled through her and she dropped onto her hands and knees, wondering if she was going to die, and just how angry her mum and dad would be with her if she didn't.

* * *

'What on earth is keeping your mum and dad?' said Sam, catching up with Suzie inside the tent.

'They won't be long. They said five minutes.'

Sam raised his eyebrows. 'When was that, ten minutes ago?'

She painted on a smile. 'Something like that. If they're not here in another couple of minutes I'll go and see where they've got to.'

'Everybody is getting a bit tense. What are they doing in there? And what about your sister, where's she? I thought she was supposed to be out here with the hoi polloi, charming everyone with all that starry-eyed thing she does?'

He sounded annoyed and Suzie couldn't work out why. One of the most basic tenets of her relationship with Sam had always been that they were honest with each other: no lies, no secrets, just the bare bald truth and it had always served them well. When had they stopped? She kept trying to work out when truths had become half-truths and the lies of omission, and when secrets had started being hidden away and not shared. Although maybe now wasn't the time.

Suzie had known for months that Sam was unhappy and worried but now realised with a growing sense of unease that she didn't really know any of the details. How long ago was it that they would have sat together in the kitchen with a coffee or a bottle of wine and talked it all through, turning the problem this way and that, holding it up to the light, trying to find an answer?

'I'm sure Liz won't be much longer either,' said Suzie. 'She's outside chatting to her new man. And Mum's probably rushing around trying to find something to wear. You know what she's like.'

'I know what you're all like. While you've been in the house, I've been having a chat with Matt. Apparently there are lots of things you haven't been telling me.'

Suzie felt a rush of heat. What the hell had Matt said now?

Suzie held on tight to the smile. 'Really. And what would those be?' As Suzie spoke she tried to spot Matt in among the throng. People had started to mill around. The sense of expectation and excitement felt close to anti-climax and disappointment. They couldn't hold off on the buffet for much longer: the waiting staff were busy setting out trays of food on the long trestle tables. But Matt was nowhere in sight.

'He was saying how well the whole walled garden project is doing — saying it might be time to think about expanding, maybe diversifying.'

'Right,' Suzie said, nodding cautiously. 'Well, it might be.'

'I can see where he's coming from but I was a bit worried it was all too much, too soon, and that you'd be outside of your comfort zone. You know — pigs and chickens and God knows what else. That is the idea, isn't it?'

Suzie felt the tension in her stomach easing and nodded. 'The estate manager has been talking about it for a while now; there used to be stables and piggeries and chicken coops attached to the garden and I know they're really keen to get them back into working order. It's really just a natural progression of what we're already doing.'

Sam nodded thoughtfully. 'It used to be that you and I would have talked about it. It seemed really odd to hear it from someone else.'

Suzie swallowed hard; he was echoing her own earlier thoughts. She could see that Sam was waiting for some kind of comment and finally said, 'You're right, but we haven't really had the chance just recently, have we? What with the party and everything, and the girls and you working late or me down at the garden.'

He nodded and then smiled. 'No. You're right. So is there anything else you want to tell me while we're here?'

Suzie bit her lip; just how hard would it be to say, 'Actually there is something else I need to talk to you about'? Instead she hesitated, caught on the brink; surely this was just the right moment to say something about what she and Matt were up to but she just couldn't find the words. Suzie stared at him and then tried out a smile. 'Why, what else has Matt been telling you?' she said, hedging her bets. *God, this was madness, why didn't she just tell him?*

Sam sighed. 'Nothing. Look, why don't you go and see where your mum and dad have got to? We really ought to let people eat.'

* * *

While all this was going on, Jack and Rose were upstairs.

'So what do you think, Jack?' asked Rose, standing in the bedroom doorway of their cottage and striking a pose. Even with the bedroom windows closed she could hear the sounds of the people outside and music from the marquee.

'White linen trousers, grey silk shirt and that gorgeous black and white chunky necklace you bought me in Paris. Nice and stylish and not too wedding-y?' She laughed. 'Come on, you might at least look, Jack. Do you think I should wear a dress instead? Or what about a jacket with this? I suppose I can always nip in and grab a cardigan later if it gets cold.' She did a little twirl. 'Well? What do you reckon?'

Jack was in a world of his own, sitting on the end of their bed looking out of the window, watching the revellers in the garden below.

'My God,' he murmured. 'There's Jonathon Jacobs and Laina, oh and look there's Phil and Rachel — fancy them coming up from St Austell. All that way. You know, I haven't spoken to Phil for years.'

Rose bent down and kissed him. It wasn't like him not to answer her, nor to be so preoccupied.

'Well, you will in a minute. You need to get dressed. We've been up here for ages. You can't spend the whole evening sitting up here people-watching in your underpants. We need to get back down there and say hello to everybody.

I've put a shirt out for you and those nice new trousers. Now what do you want, your cream linen jacket or your navy blazer?'

Jack didn't move.

'What's the matter?' Rose sat down on the bed beside him and took hold of his hand. 'We can't keep everyone waiting. They're our friends and they've come to see us and help us celebrate — and you have to admit that the girls have done a lovely job. They weren't to know about all the other stuff.'

He smiled at her, his handsome face full of love and concern. 'No, I know that, but I was just thinking that Liz is right, that we really should have said something to them before. After all, it isn't just about the divorce, is it?'

She smiled at him reassuringly. Her Jack, usually the strong one of the two of them, looked almost at a loss.

'No, you're right,' said Rose. 'And as soon as tonight's over we can sit them down and explain. It's not like we can turn back the clock and undo what we've done. It wasn't till I started to tell the girls about it that I realised what a big thing it was to them. To be honest, I hadn't really considered it to be that important. Us being together has always been the big thing for me, the important thing.' She caught hold of his hand and entwined her fingers with his. 'And you know I never take that for granted, don't you, not for one moment, not one second. Letting you go was the biggest mistake of my life — and it could have gone so horribly wrong. I could have lost you forever.'

Jack glanced up at her and smiled. 'Come on, you're right, we shouldn't keep people waiting.' He paused. 'You know that Suzie and Liz have invited everyone who came to our wedding, don't you?'

Rose sat down at the dressing table to put on her lipstick, a generous 'O' of dark coral that she had worn all her adult life. She smiled to check the effect; her choice in lipstick was older than her children. 'And?' she said.

'Oh come on, Rose, you know where I'm going with this.'

She blotted her lips on a tissue and dropped it into the bin before glancing back at him over her shoulder. 'Of course I do, but I've no idea whether she'll be here. It's all been a bit of a blur since we got back. And actually, given the circumstances, I think the girls have taken it very well.'

'That isn't what I meant and you know it,' said Jack gently. 'How do you think they're going to take it when they discover that they've invited my second wife to our anniversary party as well?'

15

'Hannah?' Simon called, sounding panicky and anxious, his voice coming from the bushes that seemed to be way above her. 'Hannah? Are you down there? Are you all right? Where are you? Answer me . . . '

A second or two later she heard him slithering down the bank, crashing through the shrubs and scrub, before landing a few feet away from her.

'Oh, there you are,' he said, sounding relieved. 'Bloody hell — are you okay? Did you hurt yourself? I mean, is anything broken? Do you want to ring for an ambulance or something?'

He pulled his mobile out of his pocket.

Hannah, still on all fours on the pebbles, swallowed hard. 'No, don't do that, please. I'll be fine, just stay over there, will you?' As she spoke she retched again and held up a hand to ward him off. 'Please, Simon. I just need a few more minutes, that's all.'

But he took no notice and came over anyway. 'Jesus,' he said, squatting down so that he could give her the once-over. 'You look really awful.'

'Well, thanks for that,' Hannah sniffed, pushing herself up onto her knees.

'Are you going to be all right? Do you want me to do anything?'

Hannah glanced across at him and for one awful moment thought he was going to hug her. She ran her fingers back through her hair, which she just knew was a complete bird's nest.

'No . . . just stay there, will you?' This was hardly the impression anyone would ever want to make on someone they fancied. He must think Hannah was a complete and utter dork. She was covered from head to foot in grass stains and bits of twig and leaves and God alone knows what else from slithering down the bank, had sick on her shoes, a foul taste in her mouth and a horrible suspicion she might have some sick in her hair too.

Great.

Very gently she eased herself onto her feet. 'You haven't got a drink, have you?' she asked, wiping her lips with the back of her hand.

Simon gave her an odd look. 'I don't want to be a killjoy, Hannah, but I reckon you've probably had enough already, don't you?'

'No, not booze, you idiot, like water or something — oh, it doesn't matter,' she said miserably.

He reached into his pocket. 'I've got some mints. Will those do?'

'Yeah, that would be great. Thanks.' Keeping at arm's length, Hannah took the packet from him and slipped a couple of sweets into her mouth. She tip-toed her way out to the water's edge to carefully rinse her shoes and feet, all the time aware that Simon was just a few feet away and watching her every move.

'Stop looking at me,' she snapped over her shoulder, carefully fishing her shoe out of the shallows.

'I'm just worried, that's all. You going to be all

right?' he asked, stuffing his hands into his pockets.

'I already said yes, didn't I?'

'You sure?'

Hannah nodded and instantly regretted it as the whole world lurched sideways and she stumbled. Simon was there in an instant, catching her arm to steady her and grabbing hold of her shoes. She was too grateful and felt too awful to resist.

'Actually I feel horrible,' she said, leaning up against him. 'And I still feel a bit drunk but I think it probably helped being sick. God, why on earth do people like booze? It's crazy — I feel like shit. I suppose Sadie and Tucker are up there laughing themselves stupid, aren't they?'

He grinned. 'Wouldn't take much.'

Hannah looked at him and smiled. Simon really was cute; it was such a shame that the whole world was spinning and that she looked so dreadful.

'Those two were made for each other. Come on, I'll help you back up,' he said, and before she could protest, or fall over, Simon helped her pick between the rocks and the pebbles and rills of mud and gravel, holding onto her every step of the way to steady her. 'I've got a comb if you want.'

She looked up at him, still trembling, and grinned. 'That's the best news I've had all day. Exactly how bad do I look?'

Simon just stared back at her, looking uncomfortable and self-conscious.

'That bad,' she giggled, aware of a funny little

tingle of tension that arced between them as she let go of his hand and took the comb he was offering. As Hannah tried to sort out her hair, Simon shucked off his hoodie and handed it to her.

'Here, put this on,' he said. 'Warm you up. Make you feel a bit better.' He was so close now that she could feel the warmth of his body, could even smell him. For a moment Hannah thought he might be going to kiss her and stepped away, terrified he just might — God, she had just thrown up, how gross would that be?

She guessed that Simon had thought about it too, because she could see it in his eyes. She knew that if she hadn't just been sick, she really wouldn't have minded. Instead Hannah smiled, wrapped his hoodie tightly around her shoulders and said, 'You know, you're a total star, Simon, thank you. I suppose we'de better get back to the others.'

'Sadie and Tucker?'

'Uh-huh,' she laughed. 'Who else did you think I meant?'

'They've already gone.'

'What do you mean *gone*?' asked Hannah.

'They're heading for your gran's place. I said that you'd be all right and that I'd keep an eye on you, so they said they'd get going and that we could catch them up.'

Hannah stared at him. 'Are you mad?' she said, instantly sober. 'Those two let loose at my grandma's party? My mum hates Sadie and they're both drunk. God only knows what they'll get up to.' She grabbed her shoes from him and started to climb up the bank. 'Come on,' she said. 'We need to catch them and quickly.'

Simon hesitated for a second or two longer. 'You know that I really like you, don't you, Hannah?' he said. 'I was wondering if you would be my girlfriend. Go out together and stuff. I could take you out, maybe the pictures or something, or swimming — or we could just hang out together.'

Hannah swung round. It wasn't exactly the perfect moment to be asked out. Simon was grinning and he was standing strangely, all shoulders and elbows and she was about to say something rude and funny, when she saw the look on his face. It had obviously taken a lot of courage to pluck up the nerve to say something to her.

'Si, I'd really like to go out with you but if we don't stop Sadie crashing my grandparents' anniversary party there is a good chance I'll be grounded for the rest of my life. So if you're serious, give me a leg-up the bank, will you?' she said.

His grin held. 'So is that a yes then?'

16

As she opened the hall door of her parents' cottage, Suzie could hear an animated conversation coming from the bedroom upstairs.

'Mum, Dad, are you ready?' she called.

The voices stopped dead.

'Only you've been ages and everyone is beginning to get really restless out there — is everything okay?'

There was a little flurry of whispering and then her mother called, 'We're fine, we're just on our way. Won't be a minute. Your dad's looking for his shoes.'

'Do you want me to come and help you look? I'm good with shoes.' Suzie said, taking the stairs two at a time.

* * *

Out in the garden, Liz had dropped her phone into her handbag. She took a few minutes to compose herself before pulling out a mirror to check on her appearance. If anyone asked she would say she had something in her eyes. At the doorway she painted on a bright, tight smile to cover the mix of emotions she was feeling, and marched into the marquee.

The show must go on, mustn't it? Wasn't that what people said? Liz pulled her shoulders back and plumped her hair up a tad. After all, she had her public to consider and Grant-bloody-Forbes wasn't the only fish in the sea. A man like him ought to think himself lucky that a bright, intelligent, successful woman like her had given him a second look in the first place. Him with his great big hairy white belly and those nasty baggy grey Y-fronts — when was that ever a sexy look? And in all the months they had been seeing each other, while Liz had made all sorts of effort to make sure she looked her best for him, Grant had invariably rolled up on dates looking like he'd slept under a bridge. Well, he had his chance, and he had well and truly blown it.

No, once you got past the cold hard cash, the house in Hampstead, the castle in Scotland, the villa in Capri, the chalet in Switzerland, the apartment in Paris and the pent-house in New York . . . oh yes, and the cars, Grant Forbes really had no style, no grace and a terrible case of halitosis, although she had never summoned up the courage to actually tell him that. Maybe she should have said something — maybe she should ring him back to tell him, or perhaps Miss Twenty-Two with her pneumatic breasts and penchant for mindless fun would be the best one to break it to him that his breath smelt as if he had been sucking on a sewage pipe. No, all in all, Liz was better off out of it.

Inside the marquee the guests had formed into tight little groups, the sound of their chatter and laughter, the clink of glasses and drifts of conversations filling the warm evening air.

As Liz walked in there was a flutter of heads turning to check her out, but tonight for once she wasn't the main event, just part of the scenery. There was a sense too that everyone was eager for the party to get started, and her *not* being Rose and Jack just added to the guests' disappointment.

Fleetingly Liz wondered if anyone would ever arrange a party like this for her. Or would she just end up old and alone, dried up and childless in some little mews cottage somewhere with a couple of cats, a bottle of sherry and a boxful of old photographs for company? Why did she always end up picking Mr Wrong?

Liz sniffed back a little phalanx of tears and blinked furiously to try to stop any renegades sneaking out. Bastard, how could Grant do this to her tonight of all nights? Despite the pain and the embarrassment, Liz was certain that he'd live to regret it. It was his loss — he'd probably come crawling back once the novelty of the whole Little Miss I'm-Crazeeeee-Let's-Have-Fun thing had worn thin, and come knocking on her door, phoning her, begging her to reconsider, begging her to take him back. She sniffed again. How could Grant behave like this, just when she had been thinking about where to have the wedding and everything?

Struggling with a huge heap of self-pity, Liz waved away the waiter with his tray of champagne and headed for the bar instead. Ignoring Gregor's sage advice, she ordered herself a large G&T before gazing around the room to see if she could spot anyone she knew, someone she could impress, someone who would stroke her ego and tell her how pleased they were to meet her at long last, to see her there in the flesh. She tried hard not to squint.

The waiters moved to and fro with canapés and glasses between the guests. There were lots of familiar faces among the crowd, but no one really sparked her interest. Most of the people there were well over fifty, barring a few family friends, the grown-up children of wedding guests and the odd neighbour and work colleague. Most of them were faces from her childhood who remembered her when she was a chubby precocious eight-year-old with braces and lank, mousey hair.

Which was exactly what she was thinking when she spotted Megan, Suzie's younger daughter, who was already sitting at the top table, still dressed in her tee-shirt, cut-off denims and flip-flops, swinging suntanned legs as she watched the to-ing and fro-ing of the adults as they waited for her grandparents to come back.

Liz sighed. There were moments when she wished she could go back to her childhood, relive those days of unselfconscious joy, when the whole of her life was ahead of her, with potential as far as the eye could see in every direction.

'Penny for them?' purred a male voice from behind her.

Liz turned around slowly, adjusting her smile to a slightly warmer version of the one she used for the public at large. Careful not to screw up her eyes, she focused on the man standing next to her at the bar.

'Sorry?' she said.

'For your thoughts. A penny for them. It's a

quaint old country expression. I'm sure you must have come across it before, you being a country girl.'

'My thoughts?' Liz laughed. 'I'm afraid they're not for sale,' she said. 'The tabloids would have a field day.'

He smiled and nodded towards her glass. 'In that case maybe some other time. Would you like another drink instead?'

Liz held her drink up in a mock toast. 'As I've barely touched this one, it's my parents' party and it's a free bar?' she said, raising an eyebrow.

The man laughed. 'Touché. I wondered if you might like a little company and I'm fresh out of new material so I thought I'd re-run a few old favourites.'

'Do I know you?' Liz asked, trying to focus in on the details of his face. After all, she was single now and from this distance the man looked more than presentable. Wouldn't it be fantastic if she found someone this close to home, and when Grant rang begging her to take him back, be able to tell him that actually she had already met someone else? She could almost hear the surprise and indignation in his voice now. Serve him right, he had no idea what he was throwing away and no idea how to treat a real woman. All those bloody red roses. And then, when he started to get upset, she would say, 'But I thought you told me you just wanted a little fun.' God, that would give her such a lot of pleasure.

She moved in a little closer. Her new companion was taller than her by a head at least, which was good, and he was slim — which was even better. He had a rugged, angular face and a mop of shaggy black hair, shot through at the sides with grey, giving him a distinguished, slightly rakish look. He was also wearing good clothes; glasses or no glasses, it didn't take a genius to recognise quality when you saw it. Life was getting better all the time.

'I'm Matt,' he was saying. 'And you are the famous Lizzie Bingham. Star of stage, screen and television.'

Unexpectedly Liz felt herself reddening. 'Hardly stage,' she said lamely.

'I'm sure it's only a matter of time,' Matt said. 'Actually we've spoken several times on the phone over the last few months.'

She peered at him some more. 'We have? Really?'

'I'm doing the catering this evening,' he added after a moment or two, finally putting her out of her misery. 'We've met before briefly when you were down visiting your mum and dad but you probably meet thousands of people in your line of work.'

Liz laughed. 'You're too modest.' She didn't like to tell him that if he was more than about ten feet away he would have been little more than an attractive blur. So this was Matt. Matt who was going to make her big sister famous — damn, he was gorgeous. 'And things have been a bit hectic just recently,' she said.

'So Suzie has been telling me,' he said, and as he spoke he lifted her hand and pressed it to his lips.

'Oh, very smooth,' Liz said, with a sly smile,

trying to work out if there was an edge to him or not. 'So you're the TV chef?'

'Hardly *the* TV chef. More the chef who occasionally turns up on the box when the others are fully booked. My main job is still running restaurants.'

'I thought it was quite a coup, my sister booking you to cater our party.'

He smiled, all self-deprecation and good will. Liz recognised the expression because it was one she frequently used herself. 'Kind of you to say so,' he said.

'Until of course I found out you two are in cahoots,' she added slyly.

Matt threw back his head and laughed. 'Cahoots? Well, that's a new one on me. So she told you, did she? Well, thank God she's finally said something to someone. I was beginning to feel like some dirty dark secret that Suzie's keeping hidden away in the attic.'

'Maybe you're right.' Liz sipped her gin and tonic, swirling the ice around in the bottom of the glass. 'Or maybe she just wants to keep you all to herself,' Liz added mischievously, watching Matt's face for a reaction. 'Or am I way off beam here — is there nothing in it? Maybe Mrs Matt likes to keep you on a tight rein?'

'Here, why don't you let me freshen that up for you,' said Matt, completely ignoring her question as he moved in closer to take her glass. He smelt wonderful.

As she struggled to remember the name of the aftershave he was wearing, Liz tried to get a handle on Matt's body language. He wasn't wearing a wedding ring and she guessed that he was the kind of man who probably would wear one if he was married, but he was being cagey. So, was he telling her that there was something going on between him and her sister, or was he just teasing?

Certainly he was a slick act, and Liz could already sense that there was most definitely a little frisson between them. Playful and flirty — you'd have to have been dead not to warm to those great big brown eyes and that little-boy-lost expression. She smiled at him as he glanced back over his shoulder at her. Broad shoulders, muscular in all the right places. Why on earth should Suzie have all the fun? Liz glanced round the room to see if anyone was watching them.

She could almost see the headline in the tabloids now: *Celebrity chef and TV's golden girl share a quiet drink at family party*.

As the barmaid tinkered with their drinks, Liz couldn't help but notice that Matt chatted to the woman in the same easy way, which was both endearing and at the same time slightly infuriating. Liz wanted him to focus on *her*, wanted him to take notice, be impressed, and make her the centre of his attention.

The woman behind the bar laughed at something Matt said, and he said something else, which made her laugh even louder, and then he thanked her profusely while she positively glowed under his undivided attention. Liz looked away; obviously the man had an ego the size of a house.

'There we are,' he said, handing her the glass.

'Fresh as a daisy. Here's to Rose and Jack,' he continued, lifting his glass in a toast.

'Do you always have that effect on people?' she said, tipping her head towards the barmaid, who was now practically skipping around behind the bar like someone possessed.

Matt laughed. 'It can be a curse. Don't you find?'

Liz gave him a sceptical look.

'I'm not joking,' he said, holding his hands up in defence. 'No one ever takes me seriously. My mother told me to always be nice to women, so I am.'

'And . . . '

'And sometimes they mistake my intentions.'

Liz laughed. 'You don't say.' There was a funny, weighty little silence, and then Liz said, 'Actually I was thinking that maybe I might be able help out in some way.'

Matt, still smiling, tipped his head to one side, implying a question. 'What, with the whole being-nice-to-women thing?'

'With the TV thing.'

'Ah okay, well, that's very generous of you. What had you got in mind?'

Put on the spot and not expecting such a direct question, Liz shrugged. 'I don't know at the moment. I'm sure there must be something though. Maybe we should get together and discuss what you need some time?'

'Really?' Matt smiled and stepped in closer. 'Well, that's great. In that case, perhaps we could talk about it over dinner? Although Suzie has already warned me that your boyfriend will be along later, and I wouldn't want him getting jealous.'

Before Liz could reply, there was a great flurry of activity around the door and then someone yelled, 'They're here, they're here.' An instant later this was followed by a loud burst of voices and excitement, and everyone's attention turned towards the door.

'I'd better be getting back,' said Matt, sliding his glass onto the bar. 'Maybe we can catch up later?'

Liz rippled with delight. 'That would be great. I'd really like that. And about dinner?' she said as he was about to move off; after all, it paid to strike while the iron was hot.

He paused. 'So you'll come then?'

Liz looked up at him coyly from under her perfectly mascared eyelashes. 'I don't see why not. It might be fun,' she purred. 'I scratch your back . . . '

He laughed. 'Sounds like a plan to me. As soon as I get a chance to talk to Suzie I'll ask her when she's free and then I'll get back to you about it. Okay? Presumably I can get in touch with you through her? Are you down here for a few days? Maybe you'd like to come along to my restaurant while you're home? See what we've got to offer.'

Liz stared at him in disbelief. *Ask Suzie when she was free?* That wasn't what she had in mind at all. Liz was so stunned she couldn't reply. How could she possibly have got it so wrong?

'And it's been great to meet you at long last,' he said, shaking her hand as he turned to make his way back to the kitchen. 'I've heard a lot about you.'

Was he mad? Liz felt a knot of fury curling in her stomach. *Ask Suzie?* For God's sake, had the man no idea what he had just passed over? She watched him as he made his way across the marquee, watched him share a joke with one of the girls who was finishing off the buffet, watched him wave to someone else, all smiles. Arrogant, conceited — her mind conveniently provided a whole rack of adjectives, while mentally she scratched a line through Matt.

Shame though, he was very tasty.

Meanwhile, at long last, her parents were making their way through the crowd towards the top table, stopping briefly to say their hellos and shake hands with friends on the way.

* * *

'Hello, hello,' called Rose, waving like the Queen as she and Jack pressed the flesh and waved to those people they couldn't reach. Jack, dressed in an open-neck shirt, linen jacket and jeans, cut a real dash as he gallantly helped her up the steps of the little dais so they could take their place at the top table, centre stage.

Liz made her way over to catch up with Suzie, Sam and Fleur.

'The seating plan on the top table is a disaster,' she said under her breath as they scurried up the steps on the other side. 'There are going to be gaps. Grant has been delayed and where on earth has Hannah got to?'

'I don't know,' Suzie whispered. 'I'm sure she'll be here soon. Is Grant all right?'

'Yes, yes,' Liz lied glibly. 'He's got caught up with something. But he and Hannah are going to leave a gap, aren't they?'

'It'll be fine if we just move everyone up and then when they turn up they can sit on the end.'

Liz sniffed. 'I had it all planned. Mum and Dad flanked by Fleur as chief bridesmaid on one side, with Peter Hudson as their best man on the other. Then you and Sam on Dad's side, with me and Grant on the other, and Hannah with you and Megan with us. A really nice symmetry.'

'Well, nobody is going to know that if we don't tell them, are they?' said Suzie. 'Why don't you go and ask Peter to bring his wife up instead? Or what about Mum's other bridesmaid — '

'It's a bit late now,' Liz hissed as she pulled out her chair. 'And to be honest, after his little revelation earlier, I'm not sure I want Peter sitting next to anybody. I mean, God knows what he's going to say next.'

Suzie smiled. 'Don't worry, it'll be okay.'

Liz stared at her. *Oh really*, she thought as she sat down. *Oh bloody really*.

After much whooping and cheering, Jack lifted his hands for silence, and the noise faded away. Liz glanced up at him, wondering if he had any cats he planned to let out of the bag.

'Apologies for keeping you all waiting so long but you know what Rose is like — so many clothes, so little time.'

There was a ripple of laughter.

'I'd like to welcome you all here this evening.

It is such a pleasure to see so many of you coming to help us celebrate all the years Rose and I have shared together. Peter, our best man, Fleur, chief bridesmaid — it's lovely to see you all.

'I'm sure I'm not alone in wondering where all the years have gone. I won't say very much because my family informs me that everyone is starving. According to the itinerary Suzie's given me, there will be a buffet supper followed by speeches, toasts and a short film show of all our adventures over the years, followed by dancing. I'm sure Peter here has got a corker of a speech if the first one is anything to go by . . . '

To his left Peter grinned and patted his top pocket.

'So, before the festivities begin, I'd just like to say how much I admire your fortitude and stamina for volunteering to be here at all if you saw this list before you agreed to come. Many of you here have been friends since Rose and I were courting, one or two friends even before then — and I just want to say how wonderful it is to see you all. Old friends, new friends — it's a privilege to be able to share tonight with you.' His rich, strong voice crackled, tight with emotion. 'Anyway before I make a complete fool of myself, enough of all that — let's eat, drink and be merry, shall we?'

And with that he took Rose's hand and, raising it to his lips, kissed it. 'I love you,' he murmured, and then he sat down while the waitresses whipped the covers off the food. As the room filled with the rich aroma of the hot buffet, the staff moved around as if on oiled rails, some guiding people to the servery queues, while others brought out bottles of wine and jugs of water.

Liz sighed with relief — at least her dad hadn't let everyone know they were all there under false pretences. She glanced along the top table; it looked like a row of teeth with a few crucial ones missing. Maybe Suzie had been right and they should have closed up the gaps.

'So,' she said to Megan, trying to take her mind off the great raft of things that had gone wrong so far. Sitting alongside her, Megan was busy trying to persuade her paper napkin to become an origami frog and didn't look up. 'Are you having a lovely time?'

Megan sighed. 'No, not really. It's all a bit boring, isn't it? And I've eaten all the breadsticks and I'm still hungry and the lady said I couldn't have anything else until everyone else has theirs. You'd think they'd let us go and get ours first, wouldn't you? I mean, you and Mum organised all this. *And* I had to help do all the tables.'

Liz nodded. She couldn't have put it better herself. It was hard being a hero, as Liz knew only too well; people just never fully appreciated you or what you did. 'It shouldn't be long now,' she said, patting Megan on the leg. 'I thought you'd got a new dress for tonight?'

'I have but there's just been so much to do that I haven't had time to put it on. Mum said she'd bring it back from our house, but I haven't had a chance to change,' Megan said, turning her attention to a small crusty scab on the back of her hand. 'Maybe I'll put in on later. When everyone starts dancing.'

'And what about Hannah? Do you know where she is?'

Megan looked up at Liz with the world-weary expression of a nine-year-old who has seen it all before. 'Up shit creek I reckon,' she said grimly. 'Mum and Dad are going to kill her when she finally shows up.'

One of the waitresses was approaching their table. 'Would you like to come and make your selection from the buffet?' she said.

'And not before time,' sighed Megan, pushing away her chair.

17

Simon and Hannah were half way across the recreation ground, almost at the swings, trying hard to catch Sadie and Tucker, when Hannah had to call a halt. Panting hard, she bent over double, hands on hips, desperately trying to catch her breath and ease the stitch in her side. Truth was, she was in no shape to run anywhere.

Simon looked at her anxiously. 'You look awful, do you want to sit down?' he said, crouching down alongside her. She wished he wouldn't keep doing that.

'No, I don't. I'll be fine,' she snapped between snatched gasping breaths. 'They can't be that far ahead of us, surely?'

Simon looked around. 'I don't know. I would have thought we'd have caught up with them by now. Maybe they went a different way.'

Hannah ran her hand over her face, which was clammy. She still felt cold and shivery despite the run, and, as she straightened up, her stomach tried out another spasm, just to let her know she wasn't quite off the hook yet.

'We're talking about Sadie and Tucker, not a herd of gazelle,' she said miserably. 'They've got to be around here somewhere.'

'We know where they're going,' said Simon.

'Yes, I know that, but I was hoping we could catch up with them *before* they get to my grandma's rather than after,' growled Hannah.

'Whoa there, keep your head on. I was only saying,' Simon said, as Hannah straightened up and headed off across the grass.

'I know, I'm sorry. I'm just cranky — I feel like shit, my head aches, I still feel sick and, even as we speak, two drunken people who my mum like totally hates are about to gatecrash her big-night-out, no-expense-spared family party. Talk about a bloody disaster . . . '

'She hates Tucker?' said Simon in surprise. 'I didn't know that.'

'No, well, not really, not Tucker so much, but she really doesn't like Sadie and if he's Sadie's friend, and he's with her — well, you get my drift. Come on, let's get a move on. We might still be able to catch them up.'

Simon dropped into an easy loping jog while Hannah struggled to keep going at any pace at all. They headed over the football pitch, up between the swings, and out onto the footpath which eventually led up to the lane that wound its way back to her grandparents' house. It felt as if they had been going for hours by the time they rounded the final corner before home. And as they did, Hannah spotted Tucker and Sadie way up ahead of them, letting themselves into the garden through back gate. Surely they should have waited for her so they could all go in together, hadn't that been the plan? Hannah called out but evidently they didn't hear.

'Come on, we've got to try to catch them up before my mum sees them,' Hannah yelled to Simon, breaking into a run which made her body scream in complaint.

Not that she needed to encourage him; Simon took off at a gallop. Hannah sighed; if only she could move that fast.

* * *

Fabulous food, was the general consensus as the party inside the marquee started to warm up. People began to settle down now that Jack and Rose had finally appeared and everyone was eating. Music played and conversation flowed while obliging and cheery young waiters and waitresses moved among the tables carrying great platters of vegetables and salads to top up anyone who felt they had missed out on anything. More staff circulated, checking on the state of play vis-à-vis the wine, and generally everyone seemed to be having a fine old time.

'It was an absolute masterstroke you booking Matt,' said Rose, popping a sliver of smoked salmon into her mouth, as Sam reached across to top up their wine with the last of the white.

'Having a good time?' Suzie asked.

Rose nodded. 'Oh yes, you know we like a party. Although it was such a surprise. You've done wonders between you. I mean, just look at it.' She held up her hands to encompass the marquee, their guests and all that went with it. 'You know, your dad and me had no idea, no idea at all.' Rose had already polished off a couple of glasses of wine and it was starting to show. 'I don't think I've ever had buffet food quite as nice as this before. It's absolutely amazing — he's very good, isn't he?'

'Who, Matt?'

Rose nodded. Her mum leant in a little closer. 'And I'm so sorry about all the other stuff.' The words weren't quite slurred but near as damn it.

'Sorry?'

'You know, the divorce and everything. We really should have said something sooner.'

Suzie touched her arm. 'It's all right, Mum, and maybe now isn't the moment. We can talk about it later.' She glanced up at the banner announcing their forty years together.

Rose, following her gaze, smiled. 'You're most probably right — but this food is still fantastic.'

Meanwhile, Sam was trying to attract the attention of one of the waitresses to get another bottle of wine.

'I can absolutely understand why you want to do some more work with Matt, Suzie. I mean, he's such a nice man, so charming, and his staff are just lovely. And this new project of yours, you and him — it's just so exciting. I've been thinking about it and I know it's all very hush-hush but — '

Before she could say anything else, Suzie said hurriedly, 'Have you tried one of these little chicken parcels? They're fantastic. The chickens are all free range and raised by a friend of Matt's on the other side of Swaffham. We're hoping to have some of them down at the walled garden. I'll get you one.'

Rose giggled; she was no drinker. 'A chicken?'

'No, not a chicken, Mum, a chicken parcel,' Suzie said with a laugh as she got to her feet. 'Do you want to come with me? See if there is any more of that smoked salmon?'

'Oh good idea,' said Rose, pushing herself to her feet, her mind sliding gracefully away from hush-hush projects.

* * *

Outside in the garden, Hannah had almost caught up with Sadie and Tucker. She and Simon hurried across the grass to where Sadie and Tucker were hovering out the back of the marquee.

In the seconds since they had let themselves in, Sadie had managed to light up a cigarette and Tucker was lying flat on his belly, trying to peer in under the canvas of the marquee. Hannah couldn't work out whether they were waiting for her to show up or trying to work out what to do next.

'What kept you?' said Sadie, through a great curl of cigarette smoke. She had the remains of the bottle of vodka and Coke tucked under her arm.

'I thought you were going to wait for me.'

'Well, we were but we didn't. You know how it is. Lover-boy here said you'd be fine and besides,' Sadie added with a salacious grin, 'I didn't know how long you two were going to be, if you get my drift.'

Hannah was too out of breath and too annoyed to think before she spoke. '*What?* Oh right. Are you totally nuts? I'd just thrown up, do you think Simon is some kind of animal? You said we'd all come back together. I thought that was the plan.'

Sadie pulled a face. 'Whoa there, Rambo, just calm yourself, we're all here now, aren't we?'

'Only because we ran after you. What were you planning to do, gatecrash my grandparents' party on your own?'

'Look, just chill, will you? It's no big thing. You said so yourself.'

'I was drunk,' said Hannah.

'Exactly, but we're here now and it's going to be fine,' said Sadie, acting as if she was the reasonable one in the gang. Glancing down, she said, 'So what can you see Tucker?'

Tucker's attention was focused on the gap under the canvas, but, at the sound of his name, he glanced back over his shoulder to give a report, like a soldier on forward patrol. 'Looks like everyone's eating at the moment. Getting their plates, going up to the buffet. This bit behind here where we are is the kitchen — and there's no one about in there at the moment that I can see. They're all serving and those who aren't are having a fag out the back round the other side,' said Tucker, now addressing Hannah. 'We saw them go out a minute or two ago, and some bloke taking them a cooler of beer.'

'What about booze? Can you see any booze?' snapped Sadie, apparently not wanting him to lose sight of why they were there.

'Nah — I think it must be over there in the main bit where all the people are.'

'Yeah,' said Hannah. 'The bar's over on the other side of the tent, near the door.'

Sadie nodded. 'Right, so what do you reckon then, Hannah?'

Hannah looked at her incredulously. 'What do you mean, what do *I* reckon?'

'Well, they're your family. How do you think we should play this? I was thinking that maybe we should walk in, pick up a plate, nice and calm, join the queue for the buffet? Get ourselves a little chow. What do you reckon?'

'*Are you totally mad?*' said Hannah. 'None of you three are invited. None of us is dressed for a party. People are going to notice us walking in, and my mum is going to go totally *apeshit*.'

'Joke, joking,' Sadie said with a nasty little laugh. 'Or did you lose your sense of humour along with the booze when you threw up?'

Hannah glared at her, fury making her far bolder than she would normally dare to be where Sadie was concerned. 'No, I just don't want to get into any more trouble than I'm already in.'

'Back in the woods you said it would be fine.'

'Well I was wrong. It won't be fine, trust me,' Hannah snapped.

'Well get you, little goodie-two-shoes,' Sadie laughed. 'The worm's turning. See, I knew you'd shape up if you hung around with me long enough. So are we walking in then?'

'Or alternatively,' said Tucker, rolling over onto his back and then flipping up onto his feet. 'How about I slide in there under the canvas and walk across to the other side of the kitchen, man on a mission, you know, looking as if I know exactly what I'm doing and where I'm going — people don't challenge you if you do that — then I'll swing round the corner of the bar and get us some more booze. I'll just say I've been sent to fetch some drinks, just like Hannah did last time. Why not?'

Hannah stared at him in disbelief. 'Because no one is going to believe *you*. You don't look like you should be here. No one shows up for a fortieth wedding anniversary party like this dressed like that — everyone else is in their best clothes and you're in cut-offs and skate boots.'

Tucker looked hurt and zipped up his hoodie, dusting off the last of the grass before setting about straightening his hair by slicking it back with his palms.

'And besides,' Hannah continued, ignoring his clean-up efforts. 'I can't see it working twice. Everyone is in there now. Last time the woman at the bar thought the vodka was for someone outside — same with the champagne. They thought it was for my aunt.'

'May be worth another shot though,' said Tucker.

Hannah shook her head. 'Don't be so stupid.'

At these words, Tucker, grinning like a loon, dropped down onto the grass, lay flat on his back and rolled in under the side wall of the marquee like something out of the SAS.

'Oh my God,' shrieked Hannah, dropping to her hands and knees. 'Will you come back? Tucker — Tucker, get out of there, get out now!' she shouted into the void. But it was too late. He had already gone.

What on earth would her parents say? God, if he got caught she could see her dad calling the police. They'd never let her out again.

Frantically Hannah tried to crawl in after

Tucker but the canvas was far too tightly pegged and so she ended up wedged in a crouch, half in, half out of the marquee, with her shoulders through and tightly wedged inside the tent while her bottom stuck up in the air outside — and how great must that look from Simon and Sadie's point of view? Tucker had the right idea, it was flat or nothing — so after a split second's hesitation, Hannah dropped down onto her stomach and dragged herself into the marquee by her fingertips.

Tucker had been right about there being nobody about in this part of the marquee, which made things easier. Hastily, Hannah got to her feet and brushed the dust and grime from her front. At one end of the kitchen, a flap had been raised in the tent wall and, just as Tucker had said, she could see a group of young men in chef's whites outside enjoying a cigarette. Which surely must mean supper was more or less over or they'd have been on standby.

Hannah picked her way past the trestle tables and the bain-maries. Where the hell had Tucker got to? He was a lot quicker on his feet than he looked. This was complete madness. If he got caught, her parents would kill her. Slowly.

From where she was standing, Hannah could just about see into the main marquee, where all the people were sitting at their tables, eating and drinking, others at the buffet filling their plates. Some of them must have seen her and Tucker roll in under the canvas. What if someone said something and blew the whistle? Hannah could feel her pulse rate lifting; she was going to be in such trouble. She was no more than a few feet away from the top table, although fortunately there was a screen between her and her family, and they were facing the other way but how long would it be before they were spotted? She really needed to find Tucker and get the hell out of there.

Hannah took a deep breath. Getting into a flat-out panic wasn't going to help at all, so she made the effort to look as if she was meant to be there. She let the tension ease in her shoulders and then, composed, she strode purposefully across the grass behind the screen towards the back of the bar, all the while keeping an eye out in case anyone spotted her. She was barely half way across the marquee when, glancing back, Hannah spotted Sadie roll in under the canvas, elbows tightly tucked in, followed closely by Simon.

Oh, for God's sake. This was going from bad to worse.

'Go back, go back,' she hissed, waving her arms at them. 'What the hell do you think you're doing?' But they kept on coming and no flapping of arms or frantic eye rolling and face pulling was going to stop them.

At that exact moment, Matt walked around the side of the screen, deep in conversation with one of the girls who had been working the buffet. They were both carrying empty serving dishes and were obviously on a mission to restock. Hannah froze.

There was a moment when Matt spotted the two teenagers — Sadie scrambling to her feet,

Simon still on the floor — and then, obviously trying to put the pieces together, Matt looked around the rest of the tent and spotted Hannah, who was trying very hard to look nonchalant. As their eyes met, Hannah felt her heart sink.

'Well, hello there. Something to do with you, are they?' he asked dryly, tipping his chin towards Sadie and Simon, who were now both standing and busily dusting themselves down.

Hannah nodded, not daring to speak.

'You've got to be pretty desperate to crash a fortieth wedding anniversary party. You know your mum and dad have been looking all over for you, don't you?' continued Matt.

Hannah nodded again and did her best to look contrite, which made Matt laugh. Sadie and Simon had the good sense to stay silent.

'So what are you doing round the back here?' asked Matt. 'Trying to avoid your parents? We're still serving supper if you're hungry. I'm sure we can find somewhere to squeeze your friends in.'

At this point Tucker reappeared around the side of the panel at the far end of the room. Spotting the three of them apparently waiting for him, and oblivious to Matt, he said, 'The bloody bar staff are all standing around behind the bar, there's not a chance in hell of us getting any more booze — unless . . . ' And then he clocked Matt, and shut up like a clam.

Matt raised his eyebrows and looked at Hannah. 'Well, hello to you,' said Matt. 'And who have we got here, then? Another of your friends?'

' 'Lo,' said Tucker, stuffing his hand in his

pockets. 'I was just — '

'I heard what you were just doing. There's not a chance in hell of us getting any booze — unless *what*?' prompted Matt.

Tucker stared at him as if he didn't quite understand what Matt was saying. Matt's eyebrows remained raised. 'Well?' he asked again. 'Anyone here want to say anything before I march you all round to see Hannah's parents?'

Hannah could see that Sadie was about to say something but she was ahead of her. The last thing they needed now was Sadie getting all smart arsed and lippy.

'Unless we can get someone to get some for us,' Hannah said hastily, deciding the truth was going to be easier to swallow than any number of lies. 'We just wanted some booze, you know. Have a bit of a party of our own.' She squirmed under his unflinching gaze. 'This is so . . . '

'Dull?' suggested Matt.

Hannah nodded. 'Yeah. It's not exactly cool, is it?'

She could see by his expression that Matt would probably concede the point.

'Look, I know what you're saying, but I can't get you any booze — and getting your mates to gatecrash your grandparents' party isn't the brightest idea I've ever come across. I can get you some soft drinks, some food and maybe a couple of cans of beer, if you fancy some, but that's it. Okay?'

Hannah eyed him suspiciously; surely it couldn't be that easy? 'Are you going to tell my mum I was here?'

'Not unless she asks but I really think you ought to at least put in an appearance. Go and eat with them and then slope off later. Take a tip from one who knows — it's going to get you into a lot less trouble if you roll up a bit late rather than not show up at all. Meanwhile if you three want to go round the back of the marquee I'll get the guys to sort you out some food.'

There was silence.

Matt held up his hands. 'Okay. It's up to you. It's not an open-ended offer, now take it or leave it. I've got a lot of other things to do.'

Hannah glanced from face to face, trying to gauge the reaction of the others.

Finally it was Sadie who said, 'Yeah, all right then. Sounds good to me. I'm starving.'

Which might have been the end of it if Suzie hadn't popped her head around the edge of the screen at that very moment. 'Are there any more of those — ' she began but whatever it was she planned to say was blown out of the water when she spotted Hannah.

'What are you doing round here?' she asked, sounding surprised. 'We've been looking for you — and what on earth's happened to your clothes? Did you fall over? Your father is beside himself, you said you would stay and give us a hand. You promised, Hannah.'

Hannah stared at her, desperately trying to come up with something to say. Suzie's attention moved on to Sadie, Tucker and Simon. 'Ah,' she said. 'I might have guessed.'

Only Simon tried out a smile. 'Hello?' he said brightly.

Suzie ignored him. Hannah closed her eyes as her mother came round the screen and into the kitchen. Coming right up to her, Suzie said in a very even voice that chilled Hannah to the bone. 'I think it might be better if we talked about this later, Hannah, don't you? And you . . . ' Suzie said, turning to glance at the others. 'I think it would be better if you went home now. This is a family party and I'm afraid Hannah is going to be busy for the rest of the evening.' Returning her attention to Hannah, Suzie continued, 'Now if you'd like to go and get yourself some supper . . . '

Hannah looked up at her.

'*Now*,' said Suzie.

Any smart arsed answers died on her lips and Hannah, heart beating like a drum, did as she was told. She didn't see Sadie, Tucker and Simon leave because she was frogmarched by Suzie to the buffet queue, where she was handed a plate and fell into line.

'You knew we needed you here tonight,' said Suzie, through a tight smile.

'I'm sorry,' Hannah began.

Suzie glared at her. 'No, you're not, you're just sorry you got caught, that's all. Going off with your friends before the party was a deliberate choice. I'm really disappointed in you, Hannah. You knew that there was lots to do — we were depending on you to give us a hand.'

Hannah sniffed, hating the way her mother's words made her feel.

'If you had wanted to have some friends here, you could have invited them, but you said no, you didn't want anyone to come. And you've been drinking — and before you deny it, Hannah, I can smell it.'

'I was sick,' said Hannah miserably.

'Good,' said Suzie and then she paused, her expression softening. 'I do understand that tonight might not be your idea of a good time, Hannah, but sometimes in life we have to do things we don't want to do. It's one of the big shocks of growing up, and helping out with a family party for a few hours is hardly hard labour, is it? Grandma and Granddad were really concerned that you weren't here, and I'm hurt that you couldn't make the effort after all the things they do for you.'

Hannah felt her eyes filling up with tears. 'I *am* sorry,' she said.

Suzie nodded. 'Good, but I'm still angry, Hannah. Now get yourself something to eat to soak up the alcohol, and the first thing I want you to do is apologise to your dad and to Grandma and Granddad for being late.'

When Hannah glanced up, she could see her grandma at the front of the queue, talking to one of the girls who was serving. As their eyes met, her Grandma Rose smiled.

'Hello, sweetie,' she mouthed, doing a little wave. 'Are you all right?'

Hannah nodded, even though she didn't feel all right at all, and her grandma's pleased-to-see-you, so-glad-you're-here, completely non-judgemental smile certainly didn't make her feel any better.

The smell of the food made Hannah realise how just hungry she was, although it also made her stomach do a nasty backflip. Suzie stayed close by, as if to ensure that Hannah didn't make a break for it.

Still trying to regain some lost ground, Hannah said, 'I am sorry, Mum, really. You look really nice, and your dress looks great.'

'And what about my shoes?' asked Suzie with a little edge to her voice.

Hannah reddened, knowing exactly where that conversation was leading. It was going to be a long, long supper.

18

'Right, if you'd like to move in a little closer. Closer . . . That's lovely,' said the photographer, waving Jack and Rose into the centre of the frame. 'Hold it there, great. And everyone *smile* . . . That's fantastic, now let's just have another one, shall we? Okay? If you just hold the knife a little bit higher? *Higher* . . . Great, and now, *big smiles*. You two have got to be experts at all this marriage and cake-cutting lark by now.' The man babbled on, all *faux* joviality and bonhomie as he snapped away. 'Lovely, lovely . . . And *smile* . . . '

With supper over and done with, he was making a start on the formal photos. He had been moving from table to table all evening, like a benign hitman, picking off people one by one, couple by couple, group by group, till now there was just the top table left to shoot, a few more formal family shots and obviously the cutting of the anniversary cake, so that the whole evening would be recorded for posterity.

Matt, who was standing on the sidelines as the photographer captured yet another 'magic moment' — Matt's words, not Suzie's — grinned and murmured, 'When David Bailey here's finished, I'll get the cake taken away and cut up or we'll be here all bloody night.'

'The sooner the better as far as I'm concerned,' Suzie said grimly, through teeth clenched in a rictus grin. Just how many more photos did they need?

If the photographer had heard them, he didn't show it. Instead he and his assistant carried on tinkering with the arrangement of couples, cake and confetti.

'If you could just look this way . . . lovely, lovely . . . and hold it. Say 'cheese', that's fabulous,' said the man, as the motor drive clicked away furiously. 'Now if we could have all the original wedding party over here by the flowers?' He pulled a piece of paper from his pocket and read out the names, mumbling very slightly as if the read-through was more for his own benefit than theirs. 'Right, so, we've got the bride and groom, the best man, Peter Hudson, the bridesmaids Fleur and Janet Fielding . . . '

Rose shot a glance at Jack.

Looking up, the photographer smiled and said, raising a hand in invitation, 'Come on, folks, you know who you are. Let's get you all over here and make a start, shall we? The sooner we start, the sooner we're finished.'

'I haven't seen Janet, is she here?' Rose said in passing, as the photographer's assistant started to move them all across the dais, and Matt and a couple of waitresses slid in like an SAS snatch squad and grabbed the cake from the table.

'I don't know. I haven't seen her,' Jack said, his eyes working across the faces of the guests. 'I'm certain if she was here she would have come over and said hello.' He turned to Suzie. 'Do you know if Janet is here?'

'Janet?' It was one name in a sea of others as

far as Suzie was concerned.

'Janet Fielding — she used to work with your mother. Janet and Fleur were our bridesmaids.'

'Right.' Suzie glanced across at the original photos mounted on the boards behind the top table, trying to put a face to the name. 'To be honest, Dad, I'm not sure. Do I know her?'

Rose and Jack glanced at each other and shrugged. 'I don't know. It's been years since me and your mum have seen her. She moved away, so probably not — we didn't see a lot of them, did we, Rose?' said Jack.

Suzie nodded. It must be strange for them having kept everything under wraps so long; were they worried that someone was going to come along and ask them what the hell they thought they were up to?

'I'm sure you met her when you were little,' Rose was saying. 'You probably don't remember. We always exchange Christmas cards,' she continued, as if that might explain everything. 'She moved to Edinburgh, she's got two girls.'

Suzie nodded; somewhere down in the vaults of childhood memory, Edinburgh rang a bell. 'Actually I think she is here, with her husband. Do you want me to go and check the list?'

Rose shook her head. 'No, don't worry about it, it's all right. We'll catch up with her later, I'm sure. I'd like you to meet her.'

'What do you mean it's *all right?* What about the photographs?' said Liz indignantly, who had been listening in to the conversation. 'Surely the whole point of all having them done is that we try and get everyone in them who was there first time around?'

'Well yes, but it doesn't really matter, does it?' asked Rose. The expression on Liz's face suggested that that was the wrong answer.

'Do you want me to send one of the girls to see if we can find her? I mean, if she's here it shouldn't take much to track her down.' Suzie interjected.

Liz shook her head. 'No,' she said, sounding exasperated. 'It's all right, you stay here. I'll do it myself. The seating plan is on the board.'

'Well, don't be too long, will you?' said Rose. 'He's going to be wanting you two in the photos too, you know.'

Liz caught Suzie's gaze and rolled her eyes heavenwards. *Parents*.

'We could have the ushers as well if you like,' Jack was saying, glancing around the tent. 'Colin's just over there and I'm sure I saw Richard heading for the bar a few minutes ago.'

'No change there then,' said Rose wryly.

'How about I go and get them?' said Jack, breaking ranks and heading for the bar, much to the photographer's frustration.

'Chicken,' Rose called after him, laughing. 'See if you can find Janet while you're at it.'

Jack glanced back at Rose and smiled.

Before Liz could head off into the crowd too, Suzie caught hold of her arm. 'Can I have a quick word with you?'

'Can't it wait? We need to find what's-her-name.'

'This won't take a second.' Suzie glanced over

her shoulder to make sure she wouldn't be overheard, and then whispered, 'I've been thinking that maybe we should pull the plug on the speeches.'

'You mean the ones about forty years of wedded bliss and never a cross word?' said Liz grimly.

Suzie nodded. 'Those'd be the ones. I'll grab Peter Hudson and have a quick word with him. I know he's been working on his best-man-forty-years-on speech for weeks, but I think I'll ask him if he can just say a few words of thanks instead and leave it at that.'

'Yes, you're probably right, although at least we can be sure he knows.'

Suzie nodded. 'That's what worries me.'

Liz sighed. 'Maybe you're right. In that case maybe the film show might develop a technical hitch . . . ' said Liz. 'I wish we'd known, you've got no idea how long it took me to put that film together.'

'While we're waiting I thought we'd have one of just the girls,' the photographer interrupted. 'Three generations of sisters — okay? Is everyone here?'

'Lovely idea, I won't be a minute,' said Liz, hurrying off down the steps. 'I just need to find someone.'

'*Do you mind?*' groused the photographer.

'I'll be back in a second,' Liz said over her shoulder.

'Has Grant arrived yet?' Suzie called after her.

'No, not yet,' said Liz, avoiding her eye.

The photographer sighed and turned his

attention back to the gaggle of stragglers left behind.

* * *

On the far side of the marquee, the band had started to get itself together. Those guests who had finished their suppers were beginning to break ranks and go feral, heading for the bar or outside for a smoke. Looking from face to face, Suzie had the impression that after a shaky start everyone really was having a great time.

At what remained of the top table, Megan was getting ready for her big moment in front of the camera, busying herself with tidying her hair, pushing a tangle over to one side, and straightening up her tee-shirt, tugging it down over her stomach. Suzie watched her affectionately and couldn't help smiling at her younger daughter's attempts at scrubbing up fast under pressure.

'Do you want to borrow my hairbrush?' she said, opening her bag.

Megan grinned. 'Yeah, that would be great, Mum.'

She still had the slightly plump and puppyish look of childhood, her long unruly hair streaked by days spent playing outside and helping Suzie in the garden, her skin tinted the very lightest shade of gold from the early summer sun. Megan looked like an advert for healthy, happy living, and Suzie found herself hoping that somehow her younger daughter would be spared the transformation into a grumpy, unhappy, confrontational teenager that her elder sister had undergone . . . and instantly hated herself for thinking it.

Talking of which, Suzie glanced across at Hannah, who was still sitting toying with her food, a picture of discontent, and sighed. She really missed the girl Hannah had been and struggled constantly with the sullen creature that had been left in her place.

Hannah looked up, as if she knew she was being watched. 'What?' she asked.

'We're going to do some photos in a minute with you and Megan, me and Liz, Grandma and Fleur — all the girls together.'

'God, and just how naff is that? Do we have to?' Hannah complained. Suzie stared at her. Where had 'sorry' gone? Between getting caught in the kitchen with her friends and sitting down and eating supper, any hint of remorse appeared to have well and truly evaporated.

'Yes, we do,' Suzie said. 'It won't take long.'

'But I haven't finished eating yet and I've still got my old clothes on,' Hannah whined.

'Whose fault is that? And before you say anything else, don't forget you're on very slippery ground here, young lady. You would have had plenty of time to do both if you'd have stayed here and helped.'

Hannah gave her the full benefit of the dead-eyed, hundred-yard-stare she had been perfecting over the last few months.

'There,' said Suzie to Megan, handing over her

hairbrush, refusing to be fazed by Hannah's expression.

As if to emphasise the contrast with Hannah, Megan turned and beamed at her. 'Thanks, Mum. Have I got time to go and put my party dress on?'

'Yes, if you want to and you're really quick. It's hanging up in the car.' Suzie had barely finished the sentence before Megan was on her way. 'Come straight back, won't you?' Suzie called after her.

Megan's response was to look back with a great big sunny grin on her face.

'How come you brought her dress and didn't bring mine?' grumbled Hannah.

'Because *she* was helping us get the tables finished, like you said you would, remember? And because she didn't have time to go home and change, and because she asked me to. Hannah's lip curled up into a little moue of displeasure and she took a long breath as if she was about to say something, but Suzie was way ahead of her. 'And don't you dare tell me it's not fair, Hannah. You're the one who cleared off and left Megan here on her own. You know I would have done the same for you — '

'Yeah, but you didn't, did you? And whatever you say, it's just not fair. Not fair at all. You like her better than me, don't you? *Don't you?*' Hannah demanded, her face contorted into an ugly sneer.

Suzie sighed and considered her answer for a second or two. It would be so easy for the sake of keeping the peace to say something conciliatory and placating, but why should she be nice when Hannah was being anything but? There was a time, surely, when Hannah had to understand that she didn't operate in a vacuum, and that there were consequences to the way you behaved and the things that you said.

'Do you know what?' Suzie said evenly, after a moment or two more. 'You're absolutely right. At the moment you're behaving badly — you're grumpy and you're selfish and you're making yourself very hard to like, but I want you to know that whatever you do and however you behave, and whether I like you or not, I love you very much and always will. But I don't like the way you're behaving at all . . . and I miss you. Now let's get this photo done, shall we?'

* * *

Hannah glared at her, blinking away a flurry of unexpected tears and a great flare of hurt. Suzie had just confirmed her worst suspicions.

Since her mum had found her in the back of the marquee with Sadie, Tucker and Simon she had been trying to make herself as close to invisible as possible during supper. Grandma and Granddad had been really pleased to see her but her dad and mum had both given her that steely-faced look that said, 'You are in big trouble. Just wait till we get you home.'

'Where the hell have you been?' had been her dad's opening words as Hannah had slipped into her seat, but before she could reply Suzie had reached across them both to get the jug of water and murmured, 'Do you think we can talk about this later, please?'

'Oh yes, that's right,' her dad had growled. 'You know you're always taking her side. Hannah promised us that she would stay here and help get everything ready and she clears off, how can that be right?'

'I'm not saying it's right, Sam, and I'm not taking anyone's side,' hissed Suzie. 'I'm just saying that now isn't the right time to talk about it.'

'Oh right, and so when exactly *is* the right time?' Sam had snapped right back. 'When are we going to find time to sort this out when we can barely find time to talk about what's going on in the rest of our lives as it is?'

Hannah had glanced from one to the other before starting on her food. The two of them sniping at each other like that made her feel sick and uneasy. This wasn't how her parents usually behaved towards each other; God, was this all her fault too?

'Please don't argue,' Hannah said in a tiny voice. 'I said I'm really sorry — and I know I should have been here — ' she began.

'Too bloody right you should have,' Sam had said, getting to his feet. 'I'm going to go outside and get a bit of fresh air and you — ' he had continued, pointing at Hannah. 'Don't think you're off the hook yet.'

And now, just because she didn't want to be in the stupid family photos, her mum had started on her too. How unfair was that? *And* they liked Megan better than her. Feeling her bottom lip start to quiver, Hannah pushed her plate away, got to her feet and sloped across to where the photographer was taking pictures of Grandma holding a champagne glass, feeling as if she was on her way to the scaffold.

'Right, if you could just hold that a little bit . . . There, there we are, that's just perfect,' the photographer was saying. Grandma looked radiant.

Hannah stuffed her hands in her pockets, dropped her shoulders and sighed. How come everyone was being so nasty to *her*? It was just *so* unfair. She tucked an unruly strand of hair back behind her ears and, from under her fringe, scanned the crowd to see if she could spot anyone she knew. Just how dire would it be to be spotted being chewed out and shown up by your mum? And how come her mum was being so unreasonable and so mean to her anyway? It wasn't like Hannah had done anything serious, like murdering someone or something. And God, like, she was *here* now, wasn't she? And she was playing happy families and queuing up like a nice girl to have her photo taken with the rest of the gene pool, said the sarcastic little voice in her head, which sounded a lot like Sadie. What else did they want? Blood?

Except of course, as soon as she'd thought it, Hannah also caught a glimpse of how right her mum and dad were. She struggled to keep the thought buried but it kept pushing its way to the surface. She *had* promised to help them out with the party and she *had* let them down, and her mum wouldn't have thought twice about bringing her outfit over for her if Hannah had asked. Suzie would have washed and ironed it and probably bought her something new if she had really wanted, and of course tonight was about her grandparents, not Hannah. Although the bit about liking Megan more than her had come as a real shock.

Surely that wasn't right, was it? It shouldn't be allowed. Parents were not supposed to have favourites, were they? Nevertheless, it finally confirmed what Hannah had always feared. Her parents really did like Megan better than they liked her. Actually, she thought miserably, they probably *loved* Megan more and *hated* Hannah. In fact she could see now that she was probably adopted, or had been left with them by somebody who couldn't look after her, and her mum and dad had felt that they couldn't just give her away, so they'd kept her, not so much a child as a burden and a duty.

Awash with melodrama, after reworking and editing what her mum had said to her, Hannah felt a completely fabricated, self-induced wave of self-pity roll over her, so powerful it almost made her cry. God, why hadn't someone said something to her before? Hannah had never been able to work out where she got her funny ears from, and the way her little toes curled in bore no resemblance to anything the rest of the family had, and now she knew the reason — they came from some passing stranger who had left her on the doorstep, probably in a basket with a note pinned to her blanket, which explained why she had nothing in common with her parents, nothing at all.

Hannah sniffed back a great wave of misery and wished she could be anywhere else but here, in this bloody tent with all these people who *obviously* couldn't stand the sight of her, certainly didn't understand her, and who probably all knew she was adopted. Thinking back to slights past, Christmas presents that had missed the mark by miles, old arguments and differences of opinion, when Hannah looked at it from a distance, it was awful, and just *so* obvious when you knew the truth.

How come no one had said anything before?

Magnanimously she decided it wasn't really Megan's fault that they loved her and not Hannah, not really. After all, technically Megan should be an only child, so no wonder she sometimes stole Hannah's make-up and hair scrunchies and went through her things when Hannah was out. It was amazing she wasn't really screwed up.

Hannah continued scanning the room, wondering if there was a chance she could slip away as soon as the photo session was over. After all, they didn't really want her there, did they? The foundling with the peculiar ears and dodgy toes.

Sadie, Tucker and Simon would probably have got back to Sadie's house by now. They were probably watching a DVD or listening to music or on the Playstation. Having a great time. Tonight was one of those nights that convinced her that Sadie was right about her family.

She glanced over at the bar, wondering if maybe she could sneak another bottle of booze before she left. It was the kind of behaviour you'd expect from a crazy, mixed-up, abandoned orphan kid.

While Hannah was jamming on the whole neglect/abandonment/not-being-loved riff, she started thinking about what Simon had said to her down on the riverbank. That was weird and when she let the thoughts replay they gave her a funny warm sensation in the pit of her stomach. She'd never really had a proper boyfriend before, not a real one, certainly not one who took her out to places and hung out with her, and who she did stuff with. *A real boyfriend*. She let the idea roll around for a moment or two longer to see how it felt. Despite everything, it made her smile.

Simon had a Saturday job in a DIY shop in town and earned proper money. He was saving up so he could travel in his gap year before going to university and was thinking about maybe going to Mexico. He had some really cool plans about the way he wanted his life to shape up, besides wanting to travel and things, which was good because she didn't want to get stuck in Crowbridge or anywhere else with some loser.

The thought of having a proper boyfriend made Hannah feel funny and slightly uneasy. She wasn't really sure what she was supposed to do. Oh, she knew the theory — you'd have to be dead not to catch all the gossip at school about who fancied who, and what they had and hadn't done, and with whom. But this was different. This was her and Simon and it was really real — not someone else, not a flight of fantasy like

Hayleigh Cornwall and that boy in Wilkinsons. No, this was real. She tried very hard not to grin, as grinning didn't sit well alongside feeling hard done by and unloved and an orphan. But a proper boyfriend . . . wow, just how cool was that?

She glanced at her watch, wondering just how much longer she had to hang around with these weirdo baby finders before she could find a way to slide off and find Simon.

* * *

Liz meanwhile had picked up a copy of the seating plan from behind the bar and, having checked the whereabouts of the missing bridesmaid, was making her way over to table six, which was at the back towards the middle. She eased her way between the guests, smiling graciously, moving around the chairs and tables, smiling and nodding. It was turning into something resembling a royal progress and hardly the quick dash she had hoped for. People wanted to say hello and have their photographs taken with her, or were asking for autographs, which was usually extremely flattering but tonight was just a nuisance.

By the time Liz finally got to the table, the twelve guests who should have been on table six had been whittled down to half a dozen, although there were signs that it had been full earlier — there was a muddle of discarded napkins, half full glasses and chairs pushed awry.

'Excuse me,' she said to an elderly couple still

seated at the table, who she recognised as the people who had lived next door to them when she and Suzie were little. 'Mrs Roberts, isn't it?'

'Oh yes, Elizabeth, it is you, isn't it?' said the woman, looking up at her with delight. 'How lovely to see you. Gosh, look at you, all grown-up and so gorgeous. I think you must have been about twelve the last time I saw you. You know we always watch you on TV. Every week. Your mum and dad must be very proud of how well you've done.' She beamed and caught hold of Liz's hand in hers. 'Graham is going a bit deaf, dear, but I always say, 'Look, there's our little Lizzie, Graham'; you know we're all very proud of you, dear, even if you're only ours by association.'

Liz reddened. 'Thank you,' she said, genuinely touched. 'Actually I'm looking for someone called Janet Fielding and her husband — they were sitting on your table. I don't know if you know her? She was my mum's bridesmaid. They should have been sitting there — ' Liz indicated the seats the Fieldings had been allocated.

The woman pulled a face and then shook her head. 'No, I don't think so, dear. At least they weren't sitting there. There were two young women in those seats. Helen and Nina — they seemed very nice, the pair of them.'

'Any other older couples on the table?' said Liz, glancing round to see if she could find the place markers.

The woman laughed. 'Well, there are lots of older couples, dear, but none of us are called Janet as far as I know.'

Liz smiled to hide her frustration. She wished that people could just stick to the damned seating plan; it had taken her ages to work out who to sit where, and with whom. Why couldn't they just sit where they'd been told?

'Maybe she's on another table?' Mrs Roberts suggested.

Liz stared at her — presumably she had come to the conclusion that Liz couldn't work that out on her own. 'Yes, probably,' said Liz, adding a little chill to her voice, not that Mrs Roberts noticed.

'It's been lovely to see you, dear,' Mrs Roberts was saying. 'I'm hoping to catch up with your mum and dad later on when the formalities are out of the way. I suppose the next big celebration will be yours, eh?' she continued, all smiles. 'Your mum was telling us last time I saw her in the hairdresser's that you'd got yourself a nice man. I said to Graham, I said, that girl really deserves someone nice. And what are you now, dear, mid thirties? It's about time you settled down, isn't it? Old enough to know what you want, and young enough to take full advantage, eh? Don't want to leave it too late, do you? I know you've got your career but I often say to Graham, these young people think they can hold back time, but if you want to settle down and you want a family, in my opinion you should have them when you're young and healthy, that's what I say. Isn't it, Graham?'

So, life according to Mrs Roberts there, then, thought Liz grimly, as she watched the old lady craning around like a tortoise to try and pick out Liz's Mr Right among a sea of faces. Though why she imagined giving Liz and Suzie a couple of chocolate digestives and the odd glass of Ribena over the hedge gave her the right to an opinion on how Liz lived her life, God alone knew.

'And you'll be able to afford a nanny, I expect, and someone to clean the house,' Mrs Roberts continued gleefully. 'Here, is he?'

'Actually he's not, no,' said Liz, keeping the smile tacked on, reflecting on whether there should be some sort of bylaw introduced to prevent the elderly from having an opinion on everything. 'He's got other commitments tonight unfortunately.' Liz didn't venture any information as to what those commitments might be exactly.

'Oh, what a shame, and it's such a lovely evening too. But I suppose in your line of work things come up all the time. Famous, is he?'

'No — ' Liz began but Mrs Roberts was ahead of her.

'Probably best that way, just having the one star in the family. Well, my advice would be hurry up and get him down the aisle, dear,' said the old lady brightly. 'I can just see you in *Hello!* magazine. 'At home with the lovely Lizzie Bingham.' Will you keep you name or are you going to change it to his?'

Smile set to stun, Liz turned away. *Bloody old people*.

Diverted from her quest to find Janet, and not quite ready to go back and face the family yet,

Liz made for the door. How many other people were expecting Mr Right to show up tonight, and just exactly how many people had her mother told?

* * *

The bar was now doing a steady trade, the band had started to warm things up with something soft, swinging and easy, and the cake had just come out from the kitchen cut into finger-sized slices. Fleur, still waiting to take her place in the sisters' group picture, pulled out her compact to check on her lipstick and hair. If she was going to have her photo taken, she didn't want to look like a startled wildebeest.

She glanced across at Rose, who looked radiant. Jack looked on, eyes bright with love and affection. It made something dark and sad throb deep inside her. How was it that she had never had anything that wonderful, that warm, that constant? Fleur turned away, choking back a great wave of loss and self-pity. Bloody happy families. She sniffed and made an effort to pull herself together.

Thanks to all the to-ing and fro-ing, she hadn't had the chance to change out of her garden trip outfit since they'd got home, although the cream jacket and trousers and pale blue tee-shirt she'd worn all day didn't look too bad. The blue brought out the colour of her eyes; it was just a shame she hadn't had a chance to have a quick shower and put on a bit of jewellery and some extra slap. Never mind.

The guy with the camera was still focusing his

attention on Rose. Fleur sighed; some things never changed.

Megan, meanwhile, was hurrying back towards them. It looked like she had finally put on her party dress. She waved at Fleur as their eyes met. Her great niece now looked all windswept and winsome in a pale blue sundress, looking as if she'd just come back from a day at the beach. At least Megan was smiling and seemed to be enjoying herself, unlike Hannah, who was watching Rose and the photographer while fingering a lank strand of hair into a tight coil. She'd looked as if she was chewing on lemons in between grinning inanely for the camera. She certainly didn't envy Hannah being a teenager. It had all been so much simpler when she and Rose had been girls. You went from school and childhood into work and adulthood, often over the course of a weekend when school finished and you started earning your living first thing the next Monday morning. Now it seemed as if childhood lasted until you were in your thirties.

Megan bounced up onto the dais alongside her and seconds later the photographer was waving her and Hannah in front of the camera.

'Come on, girls, let's get this show on the road,' he cajoled, as his assistant steered them into position. 'Get the younger generation in there with Granny, one either side . . . That's brilliant . . . Lovely, lovely.' He glanced at Fleur and smiled. 'Won't be a minute, sweetheart,' he said before his gaze moved back to his viewfinder. 'Now, let's see some happy faces.'

Sweetheart indeed. Cheeky beggar. Fleur

shifted her attention back to the compact mirror. It would soon be her happy face under the lens. She added a little dash of lipstick, pressed her lips together and took another look to see how she was doing before dropping the compact back in her bag.

'You don't need to worry about all that, you look just grand,' said a voice from behind her. Fleur recognised it but couldn't quite put a name to it. She glanced over her shoulder and laughed. 'Peter Hudson? Well, fancy seeing you again,' she said, heavy on the sarcasm. 'I suppose you mean for a woman of my age?'

'Did I say that?' Peter said with a big grin, just as her phone started to ring in her handbag. 'Curse of the modern age, those bloody things. Do you want to get it? Your man, is it?'

Fleur glanced at the screen. How very prescient of Peter. It was Frank, the man she had left behind in Australia, the man she had walked out on. The man she had said there was no future with. Fleur smiled at Peter, not altogether sure she was ready to hear what Frank had to say. She shook her head. 'It'll keep.'

Peter raised his eyebrows. 'Not playing hard to get, are you?'

Fleur smiled.

'That's the Fleur we all know and love. Always in demand, always with some good-looking guy chasing hard on her heels — nothing changes, eh?' He held out a hand as if to shake it and as she took it, Peter pulled her in close for a hug. 'I was just thinking how good you looked.'

'You know, you dropped a bombshell this

afternoon,' she said *sotto voce*. When he looked confused, she elaborated, 'Jack and Rose . . . '

Peter reddened and put his finger to his lips. 'Oh God, yes, sorry about that. I had no idea — '

Fleur laughed. 'No, me neither.'

He shook his head. 'Amazing. Actually I've been trying to have a word with you all evening,' he said, moving in closer.

'I've only been at the other end of the table.'

'I know but I wanted to pick my moment,' he purred. 'I didn't want to pounce too fast and frighten you away.'

Fleur rolled her eyes. 'Always the flirt. So how are you doing?'

'Me? I'm just fine. It's nice to see you again, lovely party, isn't it? In spite of everything . . . ' He paused, his expression all jokes and cheekiness, as he eyed her up and down appreciatively. 'You know, you're looking really good.'

Fleur smiled. 'You don't look so bad yourself, and Mary looks fantastic too. Obviously married life suits you. How is Mary?'

Peter mimed a comedy wince. 'Touché,' he said and then tipped his chin towards the main body of the tent. 'She's over there somewhere on a table with a whole gang of people she hasn't seen for ages. You know what Mary's like — likes nothing better than to talk. Knowing her she'll be having a whale of a time catching up with all the gossip and digging up the dirt.'

Fleur raised her eyebrows with amusement. 'I seem to remember you saying something very similar last time we were doing this.'

Peter's voice dropped down to a conspiratorial

murmur. 'Well, fancy you remembering that.'

Fleur laughed. 'I'm just older, Peter, I've not gone completely gaga.'

'Crowbridge's village hall was a lot less salubrious than this place, remember?' he said, glancing around. 'Crumbling plaster and the smell of damp.'

Fleur laughed. 'And the playgroup pictures pinned up to the notice board behind the wedding cake.'

'And that toilet block across the yard? God, those were the days, eh? You still look fabulous, you know, and you always were sexy as hell. I love what you've done with your hair.'

'Oh *please*,' Fleur said, although it did give her a nice little fillip to think that he had noticed and bothered to comment. 'You always were such a terrible flirt.'

'Still am,' he said, eyes sparkling with mischief, 'if given half a chance. Although I seem to remember you always gave as good as you got.'

'True. So how are things with you?'

'Going really well. I'm still incredibly busy. Mary would probably tell you I'm a workaholic. I took early retirement last year and to be honest I haven't stopped since. Every day something new — new projects, new hobbies, new adventures. I've bought myself a boat, taken up golf.' He paused, his tone dropping still further away from banter down to something all together more intimate. 'And what about you?' He nodded towards the phone. 'Got yourself a good man?'

Unexpectedly Fleur felt herself reddening.

God, how many years had it been since that happened?

Peter grinned. 'So what are we saying here?'

Fleur forced a smile. 'You know me; I prefer mine bad — and besides I like to keep my options open. Treat 'em mean, keep 'em keen.'

He raised his eyebrows. 'Same old Fleur.'

But even as she was saying it, Fleur was thinking what a lie that was. That mask had fooled so many people but the problem was that after so long she didn't know how to be any different. Fleur sighed; she had been waiting her whole life for someone who could see beyond the prickly exterior and, for the briefest of instants, she had thought Frank might have been that man. The memory made her smile. If there was a man she thought might have the measure of her, Frank had been it.

When he'd first asked her out, Fleur had left the choice of destination up to him; they had ended up at a crocodile farm watching some mad man feeding snappers with dead chickens. Second date — and not wanting to be outdone — she'd taken him on a riverboat up the Trinity Inlet, where for a few dollars you got a reel, line and a pile of fish heads, and they'd spent the morning catching and boiling crabs, pulling off their legs and eating them, in the company of a great flurry of Japanese tourists who had a photographic record of every second from the instant they had embarked, and, for once, just for once, Fleur had begun to think that maybe, just maybe she had got it right. And now he was gone and it was her own fault. Her mouth hardened into a thin line. Shows that even after all these years you could still get it wrong.

Alongside her Peter was still smiling. 'It really is great to see you again, Fleur. I've often thought about you over the years, you know. You and me and all those might-have-beens.'

Genuinely surprised, Fleur stared at him. 'What? What do you mean? What might-have-beens?'

'Oh come on, don't play coy with me, Fleur. You know exactly what I'm talking about. That night at Rose and Jack's wedding reception — don't tell me you've forgotten? I've often wondered what might have been if we'd just . . . ' The words dried up and he looked deep into her eyes. 'Well, you know. Me and you . . . if we'd just carried on from where we left off. Or maybe not left off at all.'

Fleur felt her heart lurch. 'Jesus, Pete, it's forty years ago. That's a hell of a lot of might-have-beens that we could have crammed in there if we'd wanted to. It was only one night — '

He smiled. 'Don't you think I've thought about that too? I've often wondered if we didn't make a terrible mistake just walking away from each other like that. Didn't you ever think about me?'

She frowned and considered what he was saying. 'Well, I suppose so, once or twice,' she began. Fleur didn't like to add that Peter hadn't crossed her mind for donkey's years and that one quick, guilty, drunken fumble behind the church hall while their respective partners danced the night away to local musical legend,

Billy Michael and the Mikettes, hardly counted as the greatest romantic encounter of her life. Looking back over all those years, Fleur couldn't even remember the name of the boy she had been going out with at the time, although she seemed to vaguely recollect that he was ginger.

While she had been deep in thought, Peter had moved in a little closer. 'You know, I kicked myself for years for not asking you to stay, or for not having the guts to come out to Australia and track you down. See if we could make a go of it. I've always wondered what might have happened.'

'Why are you telling me this now?' asked Fleur, stepping back to give herself a bit of breathing space.

'I suppose seeing everyone here tonight I suddenly got this sense of how fast the years had gone by. Seemed like we had all the time in the world back then — and now, well, it made me think what little time we have and how little we've got left.'

Fleur laughed. 'Jesus, Peter, you sure know how to charm a girl — there's nothing like looking on the bright side,' she said, and then she looked at him and realised he was serious. His eyes were bright with emotion. She took a deep breath. This was ridiculous. It was time to put a stop to this and put him out of his misery.

'Pete, you know as well as I do that the grass is always greener. Fantasy is always so much better than the real thing — you might have come out, found me and it could have turned out to have been a disaster, we could have fought like cat and dog and hated the sight of each other by now. And it was only one night a long, long time ago,' she said. 'One night and — '

'How can you say that? It was so much more than that,' Peter insisted.

'For you maybe,' she said evenly.

'Oh come on now,' said Peter. 'Don't tell me it meant nothing to you? We'd been circling round each other for months before the wedding reception. And don't tell me you don't remember either, Fleur. All those little looks and snippy, flirty little comments every time we met up. I'd have made a move earlier except that I always got the impression that you were afraid of getting involved with me — '

'Because you were engaged to someone else,' growled Fleur.

There was a little pause. A few feet away the photographer was still trying raise a smile from Hannah who looked as if she was in pain.

Apparently deciding on a different tack, Peter said, 'I've always kept up to date with all your news, for all these years. Where you were, what you were doing, I heard about your restaurants. I've got the whole chain bookmarked on my computer at home. I regularly dip into your website to take a quick look at the new menus and read the reviews. See how things are going — '

Fleur held up a hand to quieten him. 'Stop it, Peter, you're really weirding me out here.'

He smiled. 'I don't mean to. One thing that has always struck me is that after all these years you've never got married. I kept thinking over the years that maybe that was my fault. Maybe . . . well, you get my drift. What I'm saying is that I didn't mean to hurt you, you know, not now, not ever.'

Fleur stared at him, stunned, and finding herself trying hard not to laugh. What an ego the man had on him. 'Whoa there, cowboy, you really need to get over yourself,' she said briskly. 'Let's just wind this one back, shall we? You think the reason that I didn't get married was because I've been pining for you all these years?'

'Well, maybe not pining exactly, but what we had was special, wasn't it?'

Fleur couldn't hold back the laughter. 'What we had was non-existent, Peter. One night spent fumbling around in your brother's Ford Capri really isn't my idea of a great romance. And I certainly didn't put my life on hold waiting for you to come along on your white charger and rescue me, if that's what you think.'

Apparently oblivious, Peter closed the gap between them. 'Stop fighting it. There's no need to be so defensive, Fleur. I know you, remember, and I respect you for being a strong, independent woman. I've been thinking a lot about us just recently. It's not too late, we could still make something of it. I mean, why deny what we feel?'

'What?' Fleur spat. 'Are you nuts? What we feel?'

'You and me, Fleur, think about it. How long have we waited for this moment? Mary and I, we haven't been getting on for years. We go our own ways these days, living totally separate lives. It was a mistake staying together really after I had a glimpse of what I could have had with you. We've got our own friends, our own interests. I can't remember the last time we slept together.'

'And that's supposed to *encourage* me?' said Fleur, incredulous at the nerve of the man. 'I really don't think so, Pete . . . '

Peter's smile held, but she caught a glimpse of something all together crueller and darker in his eyes. It obviously hadn't occurred to him that she might have the audacity to reject him.

'Oh come off it, Fleur, what have you got to lose?' he pressed. 'Let's be honest, at your age you won't be getting a better offer.'

Fleur stared at him, speechless.

'Right,' the photographer said, unwittingly breaking into the conversation. 'If we can have you over here, Fleur . . . That's lovely. If you'd like to stand with Rose at the back and you two young ones, just stay where you are. Now we'll just get a few of you four. Have you got any idea where Suzie and Liz have got to?'

* * *

Having escaped from the unwittingly painful comments of her parent's ex-neighbour, Liz wished she had had the foresight to grab a drink on her way out of the marquee. She planned to just take a minute to compose herself; this wasn't how she had planned the evening going at all.

The area around the entrance to the tent was circled by smokers and people taking some evening air before the dancing really got started — or maybe, it occurred to her, they were waiting for the speeches. Liz made a mental note to sort that out just as soon as she got back inside.

Maybe it was a good thing Grant *hadn't* turned up. How much worse it would have been if he'd shown up, met everyone and *then* dumped her. She wasn't sure if she could cope with Suzie's little look of pity and another re-run of her, 'Don't worry, there is someone special out there for you, you are an amazing woman, the man is a complete arsehole,' pep talk. 'We know the big softie that you are behind that mask,' Suzie would say. 'The *you* with a heart as big as a house and lots of love to give. It'll happen. You see.'

Lizzie wiped away a tear and made an effort to pull herself together. That mask had fooled so many people, the problem was that she was getting more and more afraid to step out from behind it. Truth was that she had the most terrible taste in men. Lizzie sighed; she had been hanging on hoping that eventually she would find someone who could see beyond the prickly exterior and, at least for a while, she had thought Grant might have been that man. If there was someone she thought might have the measure of her, Grant had been it.

Liz looked around wondering if Janet, the escapee bridesmaid, was outside. She had to be somewhere, for heaven's sake, guests didn't just vanish into thin air.

A little knot of teenagers had congregated

around the garage, looking as if they wanted to be anywhere but here. Liz suspected they were something to do with Hannah. They all had the same unkempt, sullen look. It occurred to Liz as she watched them that Suzie had probably invited them so that Hannah had someone to talk to. After all, hanging out with your parents' and grandparents' friends couldn't be most teenagers' idea of a good time. The girl in the group appeared to be busy bumming cigarettes off one of the older men, not to mention flirting outrageously. Liz would have a word with Suzie about *that* when she went inside; it wasn't something she wanted to encourage.

Meanwhile, over by the pergola, Sam appeared to be in conversation with people she vaguely recognised as something to do with the local village shop. As she looked across at him, Sam looked up and caught her eye. Liz smiled, remembering how he had blushed when he had been zipping up her dress, not to mention the sensation of his fingertips brushing against her skin. Maybe, she thought as he hastily looked away, catching his gaze now was an omen. She made her way over.

'Well, hello there,' she said, offering her hand to Mr and Mrs Whatever-Their-Names-Were, who seemed slightly overwhelmed to have her make a beeline for them. 'How lovely to see you. Are you enjoying the party?' she asked, shaking each hand in turn. She was using the voice and manner she imagined the Queen used — neutral but warm, interested but not gushing.

The two shop owners smiled and made polite

deferential noises. Liz offered up a few more social pleasantries in the name of good manners before finally the woman said, 'We wondered if you'd be here. I thought you might be jetting off somewhere glamorous now the show's finished for the summer. You know, this being Norfolk — hardly St Tropez, is it?'

Liz smiled graciously. 'No, you're right, but I wouldn't miss this for the world. My family is really important to me.'

The woman murmured her approval as Liz continued, 'It's so important to have people around you who you can trust — people who knew you before you were famous. People not taken in by all the hype. Isn't that right, Sam?'

Sam took a long pull on his drink and didn't say a word, but Liz could see that the woman was impressed.

'We always watch you on the TV. Never miss,' she was saying. 'Although I'm sure you must get sick of people saying things like that . . . '

Liz laughed, a little light-hearted laugh she had perfected after much practice. 'No, not at all — I'm always pleased to meet people who enjoy the show and appreciate what we do. It's a real privilege to be able to help give talented people the chance to shine. And we're just so lucky to have such a great team. And let's be honest, without people watching us, we'd all be out of a job, wouldn't we?' she continued magnanimously.

Alongside her she could almost hear Sam groaning, particularly when the woman pulled a piece of paper and a pen out of her handbag and asked Liz for her autograph.

'Oh course, my pleasure,' said Liz.

The woman beamed. 'Thank you.'

Sam rolled his eyes. Still smiling, Liz turned to him and, leaning in close, picked an imaginary piece of lint off his jacket. As she did she looked up at him from under her beautifully painted and subtly enhanced lashes. 'There we are,' she purred. 'Can't have you looking untidy now, can we?'

She knew she was in his space, right in his face, and sensed a little victory as she saw him colour just a shade or two. Outside the intimate little circle they had created, Mr and Mrs Shopkeeper smiled, looked slightly uncomfortable, and then made their excuses and left.

'Did you have to do that?' he said, slapping her hand away.

'Do what?' asked Liz, with feigned innocence.

'You know exactly what I mean, the whole *I'm just the girl next door made good* act.'

'But that's exactly what I am,' Liz laughed. 'Oh come on, relax, it makes me a lot of money,' she said. Taking the glass he was holding, she took a swig. 'Oh my God, vodka and Coke?' she said screwing up her nose. 'Bit slummy for you, Sam. I'd have had you down as a single malt man.'

Retrieving his glass, Sam said, 'I see your man's not shown up yet then?' in a voice Liz suspected was meant to be the opening salvo fired across her bows. Fortunately she wasn't that easily rattled, at least not by Sam.

She had been planning to answer, but at that

moment, by some twist of fate, as Liz glanced across towards the open door of the marquee she spotted Suzie standing just inside, caught in the soft early evening light. She was deep in conversation with Matt who, as they watched, fed her a sliver of wedding cake from the tray he was carrying. Matt leant in close, Suzie seemed to be listening intently and then, shaking her head, smiled at something he said. It all looked very intimate and oh-so-cosy. Liz couldn't have planned it better if she had scripted it. She knew that Sam's gaze had followed hers and she purred, 'Not yet but I see your wife's new man has', in a voice full of mischief and malice.

Sam's expression changed and he stared at her. 'What?' he gasped. 'What do you mean?' She enjoyed seeing her oh-so-perfect brother-in-law a little rattled. Liz feigned innocence. God, it was almost too easy.

As Sam spoke, Suzie looked up and waved, while behind her Matt slipped away, back into the shadows.

'There you are,' Suzie mouthed, all smiles, as she beckoned them over. 'I've been looking for you everywhere. The photographer is starting to froth at the gills. Come on — he's waiting.'

Liz did exactly as she was told, while alongside her Sam didn't move. Liz smiled to herself as she sashayed across the lawn; she could almost hear Sam's imagination revving into overdrive.

'Did you find the missing bridesmaid?' asked Suzie conversationally, as Liz stepped inside the tent.

'No, couldn't see hide nor hair of her,' said

Liz. 'Talking of which, how does my hair look?'

Suzie gave it a cursory glance. 'It looks fine to me. What was Sam doing? He doesn't seem himself at all . . . '

Liz raised her eyebrows. 'I don't know. What about my hair?'

Suzie took a slightly closer look. 'Looks great. It always looks great.'

Liz sighed. 'I don't know why I'm asking you, as long as it's not up on end you probably wouldn't notice.'

Suzie laughed. 'True. Is there something the matter, you look flushed?'

'No, I'm fine — just chatting with Sam, that's all.' She paused and took a second or two to compose herself; after all, it wouldn't do to gloat. 'It's just all the trouble we went to sorting out the table plans and whats-her-name wasn't in her seat — two girls there apparently. Someone's probably playing fast and loose with the place names. She could be anywhere.' Liz craned her head around the room.

'But she's definitely somewhere?'

'Apparently.' Liz unfolded the guest list and handed it to Suzie. 'There we are — name's there on the guest list, RSVP'd and everything. I was thinking of getting the band to ask over the PA.'

'Everyone here now?' asked the photographer.

'I can't find Janet Fielding,' said Liz, stepping up alongside Fleur. 'The other bridesmaid.'

'Right,' said the photographer. 'Well, don't worry, we'll do two or three with all the girls together, and then we'll have the happy couple and the best man and hopefully by that time she will have turned up. Now if you can all just come over here alongside the flowers.'

Smiling, Liz looked back out into the garden. Sam hadn't moved an inch and had been watching them every step of the way. She nodded in his direction, but if he noticed her he gave no sign.

19

Rose, still cradling a champagne glass in her hand, was feeling warm and sentimental as she gazed around the inside of the marquee, taking in the faces of her family and dearest friends. It was such a lovely party, and unlike the first time around when she and Jack had got married, tonight they hadn't had to worry about whether or not people would turn up or whether her mum and dad could afford to pay for the catering or if they were going to run out of beer before the boys ran out of steam.

The photographer, who hadn't stopped all evening, was busy rearranging them into a group so that the six girls could get into shot together. Rose and Fleur, Suzie and Liz, Hannah and Megan. It was such a lovely idea. All her lovely girls together. Three generations. Rose glanced around at her female clan and beamed. She was so proud of them all, even Fleur, who, despite their prickly relationship, and even though she would never have described their relationship as close, Rose loved fiercely. Although neither would admit it, they both knew they enjoyed their bickering.

The booze was making her feel all sentimental, but she had to admit to herself that even after all these years she hadn't quite got over the shock of Fleur moving to Australia. There was a part of her that missed having her sister around, missed the bickering and the bitching and big belly laughs that they had shared as children and young teenagers. Where had all those years gone?

'Right, if you two could sit there . . . and then Liz and Suzie behind and could you two go either side? Fantastic, we're nearly there . . . '

Standing alongside Rose, Megan was practically bursting with excitement, although poor Hannah looked as if she would prefer to be anywhere but there with the family. Being a teenager seemed to be such a terrible trial these days. Perhaps life had been easier when you had to go out to work at fifteen and all that angst could be directed into packing shelves or serving customers or doing the filing. You'd never have got away with being so temperamental when she was in her teens because life simply wouldn't let you.

As soon as she got a few moments alone with her, Rose planned to suggest that Hannah went off and spent the rest of the evening with her friends. Fleur meanwhile was tinkering with her hair. She looked a little preoccupied, but then again it had been a long, hard day. Maybe she was just tired — after all, neither of them were teenagers any more.

Suzie was smiling, but she almost always was. It was nice to see she had made an effort to dress up rather than turn up in her usual jeans and a shirt — her outfit really was stunning. Blue suited her. Despite the smiles and the dress, if you knew her well — which Rose obviously did — Suzie looked stressed, but then Rose knew she had a lot on her mind. Suzie was one of those people who got on with life just as it was, whereas Liz, who looked as if she had just stepped out of a beauty parlour, liked things just so — her way or not at all. Beauty parlour or not, tonight Liz looked positively radiant, almost triumphant. It was amazing what a little romance could do for the soul.

Rose wondered what time Liz's new man would be turning up; from the expression on her face it surely couldn't be that much longer now. She looked like the cat that got the cream. As the man finally gave them the thumbs up, Liz struck a pose, all eyes and teeth. Rose laughed; she'd been doing the same thing ever since she was a toddler.

The camera clicked. 'That's fabulous,' the man purred. 'I think that's the money shot — lovely — thank you, ladies, now if we could just have the happy couple and the best man and the bridesmaids and I think that's us more or less done, don't you?' He waved Peter Hudson and Jack over. 'If you'd like to come this way, gentlemen.'

'I haven't been able to find Janet,' Liz said to her mum.

'It's all right,' said Rose lightly. 'We can always catch up with her later.'

'But Mum . . . ' Liz began, but the photographer was already shepherding his next victims into position. 'I was saying that we could ask the band to ask her to come to the stage.'

'I wouldn't. She'd hate the fuss,' Rose said, her attention on Hannah, who was very slowly working her way over to the steps. 'Honestly, I'm sure she won't mind.'

'She hasn't had the chance.' Liz said.

The photographer topped up Rose's champagne glass and handed out glasses to the others.

'Right, now we can just get the bride and groom sitting on the chairs in the centre and if you two, Fleur, Peter, it would be lovely if you two could stand at the back . . . And if you'd like to put your arms around each other . . . That's lovely. Fleur, if you could just manage a smile . . . '

Rose's only real regret about the whole evening was they hadn't said anything sooner to the girls about the divorce, but then if they had they wouldn't be having the party now, would they? And it was such a nice night.

'Smile,' said the man.

'As if I could do anything else with my arm round a beautiful woman,' said Peter from behind her. Trust Peter Hudson to drop them in it. She glanced up at his smug expression. She had always liked Mary, but Peter was a different matter entirely.

She lifted her glass as the photographer waved them higher.

So lovely to see so many familiar faces. She could tell by the look on Jack's face that he was having a lovely time too. He was such a good man, and Rose guessed from the notes he'd been making on his napkin during supper that he was trying to work out exactly what he was going to say when it came to making a speech, although surely no one was expecting one — not really. He'd said his thank yous before they started to eat and Peter was bound to have something prepared.

'That's lovely, thank you very much, I think that's all, folks,' the photographer was saying.

'Well, thank God for that,' said Jack with a grin, leaning closer. 'I thought he was never going to bloody finish.'

Among the murmurs of agreement, Rose noticed Hannah slipping away into the crowd.

* * *

As soon as the group broke up, Peter Hudson took it upon himself to jump down off the dais and make a beeline for the stage. Taking a microphone from one of the band members, he began calling the marquee to order.

'Ladies and gentlemen, if you'd like to take your seats please. I reckon it's time we got this show on the road and — if you remember what a great time we all had first time around, those of us who were here — it's time we got this party started. So make sure you've something in your glasses for the toasts. I think the plan is speeches, toasts, then a film and outside for the fireworks before the dancing really gets going. So if you'd like to take your seats.'

Suzie hurried across to intercept him. 'Peter, can I have a quick word?' she said, as people began to drift back to their tables.

'You didn't mind me doing that, did you?' he said, as they made their way across to the top table. 'Only you know what your dad's like, just letting things ride. I thought we'd better make a start before people get too drunk,' he continued, pulling his notes out of his jacket pocket. 'Mind you, I suppose there's probably a better chance of my jokes getting a decent laugh if the audience is well oiled.'

'I'm sure they're great, Peter, but there's been a slight change of plan.' Suzie looked around to see if she could spot Liz, but she seemed to have vanished just at the moment when Suzie could do with a little moral support. 'We won't be running the film. Bit of a technical hitch. We've been chatting and I know you've done a lot of work on your speech but we were thinking that maybe we could cut them back a bit. Perhaps you could just do a bit of a thank you for coming kind of thing? Make it a bit more informal.'

Peter looked puzzled. 'I thought the whole idea was to make it just like their wedding reception. I've been working on my speech for weeks,' he said, and then he laughed. 'I promise you it's not long and it's not dull if that's what you're worried about, and people are expecting it. Forty years of marriage is not something to be sniffed at, you know.' And then he grinned slyly and tapped the side of his nose again, which was just the kind of thing Suzie had been worried about.

'You should see your face, pet,' he said. 'Relax, I'm not going to let the cat out of the bag if that's what you're thinking. Let's be honest, in this day and age your mum and dad still being together after all these years is something to be proud of. It'll be fine. Trust me.'

She stared at him and hoped he was right.

* * *

Behind the screens in the kitchen area, the staff were busily clearing up and packing away. Matt was helping one of the waitresses to finish off wrapping and boxing up little slices of anniversary cake for people to take home and for Suzie to post out to those guests who couldn't make it.

'Can I have a word with you?' said a male voice.

Matt looked up. 'Sure, how can I help?'

Sam was standing on the other side of the table with a face like thunder. 'I want to know exactly what's going on between you and my wife,' he growled.

Matt's expression remained firmly neutral. 'I'm not sure what you mean,' he said.

Sam leant in a little closer. 'Oh I think you do. I saw you earlier, all over her like a bloody rash.'

'I'm not with you,' said Matt.

'All that crap about expanding the business and the bloody animals is a smokescreen, isn't it?' Sam's tone was icy cold and held a barely concealed threat. 'I saw you out there, feeding my wife cake. Do you think I'm a complete moron?'

'Look, Sam, I don't know what's going on here, but I think you really ought to talk to Suzie about this,' Matt said, calmly and evenly. He was used to dealing with leery customers and he had promised Suzie that he wouldn't say anything about the TV show. 'She — '

'Is my fucking wife,' roared Sam, launching himself around the table and grabbing Matt by the throat. 'You bastard. How long has this been going on? Have you been sleeping with her? Of course you have — it's bloody obvious — how could I be so stupid?'

Matt was so stunned he didn't resist. '*What?*' he said incredulously, smelling the booze on Sam's breath.

'You heard me,' Sam snorted.

'Come off it, mate, don't be so ridiculous. I don't know what the hell you're talking about.'

'Don't take me for an idiot, Matt — all those bloody meetings and long business lunches. I know exactly what's going on,' he snarled.

Matt held up his hands in surrender. 'I don't think you do. You're making a huge mistake here, Sam — it's not like that at all . . . Please go and talk to Suzie about this, will you?'

'Oh, I will, don't you worry,' growled Sam, pulling him closer so that his face was just inches away from Matt's. 'I just wanted to hear your side of the story first. So what is it you're *not* telling me that you think will be better coming from her? Not man enough to own up yourself, are you? Slimy little bastard. I should have bloody known.' He pushed Matt away. 'What sort of man are you?'

'I'm Suzie's friend, that's what I am, Sam,' Matt said, rubbing his neck. 'And you should know she's better than that.'

Sam squared up again, red faced and tensing for a fight. 'Oh right. 'Friends', eh? So that's what they call it, is it?'

'Look, you're drunk, please go and talk to Suzie — '

Just then there was a disturbance behind them and a woman ran around the end screen of the kitchen yelling his name. 'Matt, Matt, please can you come out and help sort this out! Some kids have nicked a load of booze from the bar. Come quick, quick!'

* * *

Fleur topped up her glass and headed back to the table to take her seat. Hannah had vanished, Sam too, and Megan was hanging around on the edge of the stage looking like she was going to make a break for it at any time. Liz looked smug, Suzie looked distracted — only Rose and Jack looked at all themselves, although surely they had to be wondering if someone would let the cat out of the bag about their not being married at all.

Happy families my arse, she thought. And the cheek of Peter-Bloody-Hudson, just who did he think he was? She took a sip of wine. Bastard.

Somewhere deep in the confines of her handbag, her phone started to ring again. She pulled it out and took a look at the name on the caller display. It was Frank. She sighed. He was a great guy with a sense of humour that matched her own and she had played it all wrong. Their first real date — when she had warned him that he'd better watch out because she could be snappy — was to a crocodile farm, where even she couldn't compete with the snap on show there.

And Frank was kind — the manky cat she had

found out the back of her house that she been nursing hadn't fazed him one bit, and he'd been there with the gardening gloves and a blanket to grab and wrap the bloody thing every time she needed to give it tablets or clean up its latest scrape. She looked heavenwards and blinked back a little flurry of tears; all those years she had been waiting for someone to see her tender side and finally, when someone did, she had driven him away.

The phone rang on.

She considered whether to ignore him but on balance thought it would be better to get whatever it was out of the way; after all, how much worse could things get?

'Hello?' she said, finger in one ear to cut out the background noise.

'Hello, Fleur, Fleur, is that you?' said Frank.

'Certainly is,' she said, watching Peter making his way across to Mary, presumably before heading back to the top table. She could have sworn he was looking her way to see if she was looking at him.

'Where are you?' Frank was saying. The line was bad and full of crackles, pings and breaks in the flow.

'Good question,' she murmured miserably, and then said, in a louder voice. 'At my sister's. You knew that — I'm at their surprise party. Why?'

'I've got a surprise for you too,' he said.

'Oh really — what's that then? Managed to find yourself a little surf babe while I've been away, have you? Don't tell me, you're taking her to Bali for a holiday.'

Frank laughed, his good humour not at all pricked by her sharp tongue, or perhaps the signal was so bad he couldn't hear how miserable she sounded. 'Not exactly. How's the party going?'

Peter was kissing Mary now; bloody hypocrite.

'Fine,' she sighed. 'Just fine.'

'You sound a bit down.'

Peter was heading back towards the dais now and as he caught her eye he winked.

'Oh don't mind me,' she said, suddenly full of tears. 'It's been a long day and I'm tired and . . . ' Fleur stopped speaking. 'Oh, I'm so sorry, Frank — look, I've really got to go. They're just about to do the speeches.' And before he could reply she hung up.

* * *

Hannah had managed to get outside and into the garden without being noticed by anyone. Having slipped around the back of the marquee, she was heading for the back gate and freedom when she heard a commotion behind her. Glancing back over her shoulder, she was amazed to see Sadie bearing down on her, whooping and squealing like a banshee, her hair streaming out behind her, Tucker following hot on her heels. Both were carrying a bottle in each hand and had their arms outstretched as if pretending to be aeroplanes, and both were roaring with laughter. She had assumed they had left for Sadie's house ages ago but apparently not. Simon was nowhere in sight.

'Come on, come on,' shrieked Sadie, giggling madly. 'Quick, quick. Run! They're right behind us. Come on — run!'

'What?' yelled Hannah, bemused and still in shock at seeing them there.

'Look what we got, in and out. We'd have been all right if it hadn't been for bloody Tucker here, telling the barmaid we'd be coming back for more. Look, party-time,' she said, waving the bottles. 'Oh my God, here they come. Run . . . run!'

Hannah looked back across the lawn to see Matt and a barmaid heading towards them. Sadie's panic and excitement was contagious and, without really thinking about the consequences, Hannah found herself throwing open the back gate and running through it, followed close behind by Sadie and Tucker.

'Keep going, don't stop, don't stop . . . ' squealed Sadie in a ragged, hysterical voice. 'They're catching up, they're catching up,'

Hannah did as she was told.

* * *

When he got to the corner of the lane, Matt stopped and bent double, hands on his knees as he dragged in a great lungful air.

'I thought you said you worked out,' said the barmaid, as she came trotting up behind him.

'I do,' gasped Matt.

'You could have fooled me. They're getting

away,' she said, somewhat unnecessarily.

'I know that,' said Matt, still panting hard. 'But I'm not going to kill myself chasing kids a third my age to get back a couple of bottles of booze — they're on a mission and I'm not.'

'You want me to go and get a couple of the lads out of the kitchen?' asked the girl. 'I reckon they could catch them.'

Matt shook his head. 'No. I know exactly who it is. What was it they took?'

'A bottle of Avoca, half a bottle of cherry brandy and two big bottles of that blue alcopop stuff — I reckon they just grabbed the first things they came to.'

Matt laughed. 'Jesus, that's going to be one hell of a cocktail.'

'You think they're going to drink it?' asked the girl.

Matt looked at her. 'Well, they didn't nick it to pour in the bath, did they?'

* * *

Megan had been watching everyone with interest all evening. Mum and Dad were bickering, Grandma and Granddad kept whispering to each other, but not like they usually did, Liz kept hurrying off, and Hannah had vanished. You didn't have to be a genius to know that something was up. But was it all the same thing or different things?

She was just about to sneak off and find Hannah, to see if she could find out, when Grandpa Jack came over and sat down alongside her.

'All right?' he asked. 'Having a good time, are you?'

'It's a bit boring.'

He nodded. 'That's grown-ups for you. Do you want anything? A drink or something?'

'I was thinking of maybe going outside for a while.'

'Okay, I'm sure your mum wouldn't mind. You could go into the cottage and watch a DVD later if you like; we're just going to do the speeches now.'

'Do I have to stay for them?' asked Megan.

He smiled. 'I think your mum would like you to, why don't you ask her?'

Megan and Grandpa Jack got on really well. He'd taught her how to tie her shoelaces and mend a puncture in her bike and read the plans to put together her desk. He could mend anything but he didn't talk much and she liked that about him. When they were doing things together, he treated her like she knew things and was already somebody, not just a little kid, and he didn't try to fill the spaces up with noise and words that meant nothing like some grown-ups did. As far as she knew he'd never ever told her anything but the truth.

Megan glanced up at him. He had nice eyes that were always bright and full of fun and life. She knew that, of all the adults there, if she could just find the right question, Grandpa Jack would be the one to tell her what was going on. If only she could just find the right question. They sat in silence for a few seconds while Megan thought it through and then finally she said, 'Grandpa, what exactly is the matter with everyone tonight?'

He didn't rush to answer, which she knew he would, and after a few seconds more he said, 'Everyone has just got too many secrets.'

Megan nodded thoughtfully. She didn't quite understand what he meant but she had no doubt that it was the truth. 'What secrets?' she said.

He smiled and, bending down, gently kissed the top of her head. 'They wouldn't be secrets if I could just tell you now, would they?'

Megan sighed; apparently there was a lot of difference between telling the truth and knowing what was going on.

'Come on, it's time for the speeches.'

Megan nodded. 'Okay, I'm just nipping outside.'

Grandpa Jack lifted an eyebrow but said nothing.

Outside people were chatting and drinking and no one noticed her slipping into Grandma's cottage. She wondered if maybe Hannah had gone inside to watch TV too. But she wasn't there. While she had the chance, Megan changed back into her shorts and tee-shirt and picked up a fleece from the porch. She needed to get to the bottom of all this.

* * *

Thanks to Peter's announcement, the marquee was filling up nicely. People were filing back to their seats and there was a little buzz of anticipation in the air. Which was unfortunate,

Suzie thought, as there wasn't going to be the planned round of speeches, bad jokes, reminiscences or a film show. Hopefully a couple of toasts and a few words of thanks would be enough to satisfy them and then everyone could pile outside to watch the fireworks.

Waitresses were busy topping up glasses for the toast and Liz had settled herself down at the top table and was sipping a glass of mineral water.

'What did you say to Peter?' she asked.

'I just told him to cut it right back, just say a few thank yous,' she said, although what was actually holding Suzie's attention was Sam, who was now standing over by the bar, being served with what looked like vodka. This struck her as out of character — he was no drinker. As she looked, he glanced up at her, his expression fixed and unreadable.

'I'm just going to go and have a word with Sam,' she said. 'Won't be a minute.'

Liz smiled noncommittally.

'Are you going to come and sit down?' Suzie said as she came up behind Sam. 'We're about to start the speeches.' As her husband turned round, she realised just how drunk he was. 'Are you okay?' she asked anxiously.

'You tell me,' he snapped right back.

Suzie stared at him. 'What on earth is the matter, Sam?'

He snorted. 'I have to tell you?'

On stage, Peter Hudson was tapping a glass. 'Come along, come along, ladies and gentlemen,' he was saying. 'Let's get those bums on seats and glasses in hand, shall we?'

Suzie glanced at Sam, trying to work out what the problem was. He surely couldn't still be angry with Hannah. The thought made her look around to see where she had got to — at the moment Hannah certainly had a knack of winding everyone up. Maybe she had said something else to her dad. Suzie wasn't altogether surprised to find Hannah was nowhere in sight. Megan either, come to that. Maybe they had gone off somewhere together. A couple of years ago, Suzie knew she would probably have been right, but these days — well, Lord only knew where Hannah had got to. Megan was probably around somewhere. Her eyes worked the crowd.

'Can we talk about this when we get home?' she said. 'I need to get back up there with Mum and Dad and then go and tell the firework guys that we're nearly ready — ' But when Suzie looked back, Sam had already walked off, something else which was completely out of character. She didn't like the way that felt.

On stage Peter Hudson had picked up a microphone and Suzie hurried across to join her parents on the dais.

* * *

'Right,' said Jack, settling himself down alongside Rose. 'Well, I've worked out what I'm going to say once Peter's done his bit.'

Rose smiled. 'Are you sure you really want to do this?'

Jack nodded. 'It'll be fine. Don't look so worried.'

'You know that I love you, don't you?' Rose said.

He grinned and leant forward to kiss her. 'Yes, and at the end of the day, whatever else happens, that's the main thing, isn't it?'

Rose raised her eyebrows, as Peter welcomed everyone to his speech. Hopefully Peter would have the good sense to keep away from the *other* main thing.

* * *

Further along the table Suzie caught the look that passed between Rose and Jack. They were holding hands, fingers loosely knitted together on the tabletop. As Peter launched into his speech, she saw her father's fingers tighten around her mother's, and she hoped that Peter was as good as his word about cats and bags.

20

'So,' Peter said, lifting his glass. 'In conclusion I'd just like to say what an honour and pleasure it is to be up here, talking to you all again forty years on. I'd ask you all to raise your glasses with me and wish Jack and Rose good health, good luck and happiness and here's hoping that they have another forty happy years together. The toast is *Rose and Jack*.'

To a man, the whole tent lifted its glasses in approval and joined the toast with much stamping and cheering and good humour.

Suzie smiled. Peter's speech had been longer than she had hoped, but generally not too bad at all. He'd made a few risqué jokes and a couple of snappy one-liners but had generally kept it short, sweet and funny as promised, and had steered well away from the topics of divorce, separation and the mathematical shortcomings of celebrating the whole forty years. In fact, to give the man his due, he hadn't dwelt too long on the whole marriage thing at all, concentrating instead on Jack and Rose's life now, though he had given her a big cheesy wink as he drew the speech to its close.

Suzie was just about to get up to invite people to join them outside for the fireworks and give the band the nod, when to her surprise her father got to his feet. He was clutching a paper napkin to his chest. There was much hushing and shushing as he took the microphone from Peter.

'What the hell is he doing?' hissed Liz, leaning around the back of her parents so that she could catch Suzie's eye.

'I don't know,' said Suzie with a pantomime shrug. 'But at least he knows what's going on.'

Liz rolled her eyes. 'You'd like to think so, wouldn't you, but have you seen how much wine he's put away tonight? I'm surprised he can still stand.'

Jack tapped the microphone experimentally. 'One-two, one-two,' he murmured into it, to good humoured laughter and cheering, before unfolding the napkin, clearing his throat and looking out across the sea of faces.

'Just before we all break ranks and get on with the serious business of dancing and drinking and generally being merry, I wanted to say a few words. First of all, a great big thank you from Rose and I to the girls and Sam for this wonderful surprise.' He turned to look at Liz and Suzie as the applause sounded and then, as it died, continued, 'Some of you here know the long and not always smooth road that Rose and I have travelled together over the years to get to this evening. We're deeply touched to see you all here tonight and to be able to share this very special evening with you. You know who you are — our good friends and family, those who have shared the ups and downs, the high days and holidays, the sunshine and the stormy weather and all the things in between.' He was beaming, his eyes bright with joy.

Suzie could hear the emotion in her father's voice and felt her eyes filling with tears.

'One thing that has kept Rose and I coming back for more over the years, above and beyond everything else that has happened, is that we have always loved each other. In the best of times, in the worst of times, right down at the bottom of our hearts there was this little given truth that has kept us going. So tonight, while we're all together, I just want to tell you all how much I love her and how very glad I am that we've shared all these years together and I hope with all my heart that we share many, many more. So before we get this party started, I give you a toast, my beautiful Rose — '

As Jack raised his glass to her mum, Suzie felt a great lump in her throat and tears welling up in her eyes. Her father was a strong man, warm and gentle, but she had had no idea just how deep and intense his feelings ran for her mum. Watching the way he looked at Rose now, Suzie felt a great pang of regret. She had to talk to Sam before it was too late. What they had built was also way too precious to lose and whatever the problem was, surely it wasn't too late to put it right.

As the last of the cheers faded, the band struck up with the opening chords of 'Isn't She Lovely' — which was so much more appropriate than the anniversary waltz — and Jack led Rose down onto the space in front of the band. People cheered and clapped as he guided her expertly around the floor and a few seconds later they were joined by Peter and Mary Hudson, then a handful of others.

* * *

'So, have you thought about it?' Peter whispered in Fleur's ear as she joined the queue at the bar a little later.

'Thought about what? I thought you were going to dance the night away with the long-suffering Mary,' she said.

'Oh come on, surely you haven't forgotten already? You and me. Me and you.' He waved the barmaid over. 'I'll have a gin and tonic and an orange juice — and what about you, what are you having?' he asked, nodding towards Fleur's glass.

'I'm just fine, thank you,' she said, covering the top with her hand.

Peter laughed. 'Oh come on, you weren't queuing up here for your health. At least let an old friend get you a drink. What are you having?'

'I'll have a white wine spritzer, please,' she said to the barmaid, handing her the glass.

While the girl busied herself pouring drinks, Peter leant in closer. 'There, that wasn't so hard now, was it? Feels just like the good old days.'

Fleur smiled. 'I thought that we'd already had this conversation. And to be perfectly honest I'm not so sure that they were that good, Peter. What's to say that if you cheat on one woman that you wouldn't cheat on another?'

'Oh come on, don't be such a prude, Fleur. Last time around we were both playing away. It takes two to tango, you know — and I didn't exactly have to force you, did I?'

Fleur nodded. 'You're right, but you know what? That's not something I'm particularly proud of. People get hurt . . . and I've grown up a lot since then.'

'Grown up or grown old?' he said, with nasty little laugh that she guessed was meant to hurt.

'I would have said wised up, Peter. Anyway,' she continued, in an effort to lighten the mood. 'Let's leave it alone, shall we? There's no need to get heavy about it.'

'Who's getting heavy?' he said, waving the words away and then, just as she thought he was going to take his drinks and go, he leant in closer and whispered, 'You maybe want to consider what exactly it is you're passing up here, honey. There are a lot of women who would like to be in your shoes.'

'You're probably right,' she said, holding on tight to her smile, and deliberately misunderstanding him. 'Successful businesswoman? World traveller, independent, wealthy?' Deep down in her handbag she could hear her phone ringing again.

Peter laughed. 'Come on, sweetie, we both know what I meant. Putting your life on hold, no man, no wedding bells, no kids. All right, professionally you've done all right for yourself — but when it comes to your personal life . . . ' he grinned. 'I mean, honestly . . . '

'*Honestly?*' said Fleur, feeling something cold and dark and furious flare in her chest. Some people just couldn't take a hint.

'An awful lot of women would be grateful I was showing an interest. Let's face it, I'm a real catch,' he purred.

'So's smallpox,' Fleur snapped. 'You wouldn't know what honest meant if it came up and bit you on the arse. And if you're trying to bully me into some kind of sordid little fumble while your wife's back is turned, then boy did you pick the wrong woman . . . *sweetie*.'

Peter's face was a picture.

* * *

They ran and ran, down through the lane, along the footpath and out over the Rec; they ran until all Hannah could hear was the pulse roaring in her ears and she thought her lungs would burst; they ran till her legs felt as if they were on fire. They ran on and on until she didn't think she could run another step and then they ran some more.

Finally Hannah followed Sadie in through a gap in a hedge and into a derelict farmyard beyond. There was a tumbledown barn and a row of sheds in the yard, which formed an angle framing rusting machinery and crumbling oil and water tanks covered in what looked like a hundred years' worth of creepers and dead grass.

Inside one of the barns Sadie finally stopped and, setting the bottles of drink down on the ground, collapsed onto the pile of crumbling straw bales, sucking in air like it was going out of style.

'Oh Jesus, I've got a proper stitch now, bloody

hell . . . What a run — I thought they were going to catch us for sure,' Sadie said, rolling over onto her back and drawing her knees up to her chest. 'Bloody hell. I can barely breathe.'

Tucker threw himself down alongside Sadie, holding the bottles aloft like trophies, while Hannah slumped onto another of the bales.

'Shame Simon chickened out really, eh?' said Sadie, still breathing hard. 'We could have had a proper party then, lit a bonfire, stayed out all night — or you too scared, Han? You wanting to go home already?' She said it in a mocking baby voice.

'No, I'm cool, great idea — he'll be pissed he's missing out, huh?' Hannah said, with feigned indifference. She didn't want to even think about the reception she was going to get when she got home. 'So where *is* Simon, anyone know?'

'Bottled it,' said Sadie, sitting up to inspect their spoils. 'He was worried about getting into trouble, so he buggered off home, I reckon. He's not here anyway and that's the main thing. But we are.' She whooped jubilantly. 'So we get the booze. Come on then, Tucker, let's deal it out, shall we?'

'Lightweight,' said Tucker conversationally, cracking open one of the bottles of blue alcopops and taking a long pull. 'So, you reckon we should stay here or head back to your place, Sadie?' he said, wiping the top of the bottle before passing it on to Sadie. Sadie gulped the booze down, gasping as she pulled the bottle away and wiped her lips.

Before she could reply, they heard the whiz

and crack of a rocket from somewhere not too far away shooting up into the night sky, followed an instant later by a great chrysanthemum of red and gold flashes against the rolling, slate-grey clouds.

'Fireworks,' commented Tucker unnecessarily, as another rocket cracked into the darkness, exploding with a great burst of silver and gold rain in among the stars. 'Wow, they're cool. Are they coming from your gran's place?'

Hannah nodded. She had been looking forward to the fireworks.

'I love fireworks. We should have maybe hung around a bit longer,' said Tucker, eyes fixed on the sky.

'Yeah right, hung around and got caught. Don't be such a dipstick, Tucker.'

He sniffed. 'I was only saying. So are we going to your place then?'

'Dunno,' she said, handing the bottle on to Hannah. Hannah pretended to take a swig and then another. The drink was sweet and sticky on her lips and it was tempting to have some for real.

Above them a turquoise and yellow cascade of twinkling, clattering sparks lit them up like the flare from a Very pistol.

'Come on, don't hog it,' snapped Tucker. 'You're not going to be sick again, are you?'

Hannah shot him a killer look and then licked her lips and passed the bottle back. 'No, *are you?*' she growled and then to Sadie she said, 'So are we staying here?'

'Yeah, that would be a great idea,' said Tucker.

'We could light a fire, like you said. It's getting dark, we could watch the fireworks, it'd be great.'

Sadie laughed. 'Don't tell me you're frightened of the dark, big man.'

Tucker looked hurt. 'Do I look as if I'm frightened of the dark?' he said, which made Hannah suspect that he probably was.

He got to his feet and began grubbing around for paper and sticks, but Sadie stopped him.

'If we light a fire here someone is just bound to spot it. Last thing we want is the law sniffing round. No, we'll give it a minute or two and then head round to my place. We should have the place to ourselves. Give Hannah's family a chance to head on by if they're chasing us, and if not — well, what's the rush?'

Above them a lime-green flash lit up the night like a lurid unhealthy sun.

'Cool,' whispered Tucker.

21

Fleur pulled her phone out of her bag.

'Hello?' she snapped into the mouthpiece, watching Peter Hudson scuttle back through the crowd towards his wife. *Bastard*. Fleur wondered if Mary had any idea what kind of man she was married to. Outside, the fireworks were cracking and rattling and hissing into the night sky. She could hear the 'oohs' and 'ahhs' from the guests from where she was standing inside the tent. Apparently Mary was keen to see them too and was making for the exit.

'We must have got cut off before,' Frank was saying into Fleur's ear. 'The signal's still not great. How's it going?'

Fleur really wasn't in the mood for small talk. 'Look, thanks for ringing, Frank, but now is really not a good time. It's not that I'm not pleased to hear from you,' she began, still with her eye on Peter's back. 'But, like I said, I'm right in the middle of my sister's party and I can barely hear you above the fireworks.'

Right on cue, there was a loud bang from outside.

'I know, that's why I'm calling.'

'Well, it's very kind but — '

'No wait — don't hang up on me. I just wanted to check the address.'

'The address?'

'Yeah. I miss you. I was thinking of surprising

you, maybe sending some flowers or something.'

'Not much of surprise now then.' She smiled and managed to stop herself from telling him that she hated flowers, that this really wasn't the time to send her anything, and that she had left Rose's address on the pad by the phone in the house for him. Because after all, wasn't this what she wanted? Someone who cared about her, someone who did nice things for her? Maybe Frank really did care after all.

'About what I said — ' she began.

He laughed. 'Which bit? Was it when you said bugger off or that you never wanted to see me again?'

She winced. 'Did I really say that?'

'Not exactly but a man can take a hint.'

'Frank . . . ' Her voice softened.

'Don't you worry about me, chook, I've got the skin of a rhino. Now about your sister's address,' he was saying.

'That's really sweet, Frank, but — '

'But nothing, Fleur, just tell me the bloody address, will you?'

'Isaac's Cottage, Mill Lane, Crowbridge.'

'Okay, I've got that.'

'What about the rest of it?' she protested.

'No, that was the bit I wanted to check.' And then it was him who hung up. Fleur shook her head. Maybe he'd lost his nerve. As she looked around her she felt a great wave of homesickness — not for Crowbridge or for the past and all those tangled might-have-beens and old resentments, but for Cairns and the restaurant and the guys she worked with and her house out at Palm

Cove and for Frank, dear old Frank with his big belly laugh and great big heart and the fact that he wasn't taken in by all that woman of the world crap. And for a moment she longed not for the past, but for the future she had been building for herself. All these years she had been pining to come home, and she suddenly realised that she had been home all the time.

⋆ ⋆ ⋆

Megan had made her way around to the front of her grandparents' cottage, trying very hard not to attract attention to herself. She was grateful for the fireworks which seemed to have drawn everyone's attention skywards. While everyone else *ooh*-ed and *aaah*-ed, she wandered casually down the drive and ambled out into the road, as if she was just taking the air and enjoying the crashes and bangs and waterfalls of brightly coloured sparks shooting up into the darkening sky from the bottom of the garden. Most people at the party were around the back of the house, drinking and talking and entranced by the fireworks, so they didn't see her leave, and those who did didn't say a word.

As soon as she was clear of the garden, Megan slipped her hands into her pockets and hurried off towards the village. Above her the streetlights were beginning to glow with a soft yellow light, coronas of brightness in the gloom.

Head down, Megan was on a mission; she didn't really know what was going on with Hannah or her mum and dad, but she felt that her sister was in big trouble and she was worried about her. She had never seen her dad and mum so angry, and although she wasn't exactly sure what she was going to do when she found Hannah, Megan knew that she had to try something. Her plan was to go back to their house first and see if Hannah was there. If not she'd try the recreation ground and then finally Sadie's house.

Beyond the streetlights the darkness was thickening and creeping closer. Megan hated the dark. The fireworks were making it worse, the gaudy flashes lighting up the lane as bright as day before plunging everywhere back deep down into darkness. She wasn't altogether sure exactly where Sadie lived. She knew it was somewhere on Moongate Lane, but she really was hoping that she wouldn't have to go there and find it. If she was lucky Hannah would have crept home by now and be watching TV or be upstairs listening to music; although there was a part of her that intuitively knew that Hannah had gone home with Sadie.

Moongate Lane was on the edge of the village behind the allotments. There weren't that many houses up there, but past the wood yard and the barns was a straggle of cottages, inhabited by hippies and people with big hairy dogs and lots of babies. There weren't many streetlights, Megan knew, because once she and her mum had gone up there to collect some wicker cloches for the walled garden from a man who made them. He lived at the far end of the lane where it petered out into a single unmade track.

He had had dreadlocks and said that he recycled everything, which Megan knew was supposed to be a really good idea, but he hadn't struck her as really good at all, just dirty with funny clothes and a kitchen full of jam jars and plastic bottles. He had given her mum a mug of tea made with leaves out of the garden — which didn't seem right at all.

There had been kittens in his hedge but not the kind you could pick up and love, even if they did look cute. They were the kind that hissed and bit and clawed you if you came too close, only he hadn't told her that until it was too late and a ginger one had scratched her and bitten her arm. She had had to go to the doctor and have an injection.

Megan put her head down and carried on walking, trying hard not to think about the man or the kittens or the big dogs or how much she hated the dark.

But, just as she got to the corner, someone further up the road called out her name.

Startled, Megan was about to run back to the cottage when she recognised the loping gait of Hannah's friend, Simon, whom she had seen with Sadie and Tucker earlier. He hurried across the road to meet her.

'Hi,' he said, breathlessly. 'I don't suppose you've seen Hannah about, have you?'

Megan shook her head. 'No. I thought she was probably with you and Sadie and that other boy.'

'Is she with Sadie?' he asked, sounding surprised.

'How would I know?' snapped Megan. 'I was

just coming out to look for her.'

Simon laughed. 'Whoa there, I was only asking. She's not at the party then?'

Megan looked him up and down; boys could be such drips at times. 'No . . . ' she said slowly in case there was some chance that he couldn't keep up. 'That's why I'm going to look for her.'

He nodded but didn't move.

'You can come and look for her with me if you like, I'm going back to our house and then the Rec and then Sadie's house,' she said with a confidence that she didn't feel, as if the plan was rock solid, all the while thinking about the dark shadows, high hedges and wild cats up on Moongate Lane.

She could see Simon weighing the options and after a few more seconds of waiting, she sighed and said, 'Please yourself.' And with that, Megan stuffed her hands back in her pockets and started off up the street, hoping that Simon might follow her.

'So they're definitely not at the party then?' he said to her back.

'What?'

'Sadie and Tucker; they were going to crash the party and I thought . . . ' The words dried up, and when she turned back, Megan could see even in the half light that Simon was blushing furiously. 'I thought I'd better not, just in case, well, you know . . . '

'No, I *don't know*,' snapped Megan. 'Why do people always say that? I hate people who say *you know*. What is it I'm supposed to know?'

She wondered if Simon was always this drippy

or if it was just because he fancied her sister. He stared at her and then shifted his weight from foot to foot under her gaze. She guessed from his expression that Simon didn't have a little sister or he'd have known they don't take much in the way of crap.

'Okay. The thing is, I really like your sister and I didn't want to crash the party because I didn't want your mum and dad to think I was a total dork.'

Bit late for that, thought Megan. Fancying people obviously did something weird to your brain.

'Well, she's not there now,' said Megan primly, moving off.

'Have you been to Sadie's before?'

Megan shook her head. 'No. Have you?'

He nodded. 'Yeah, a few times.'

'Well, in that case you can show me where it is,' said Megan briskly, job done.

'Do you think they might have gone back to your house?'

Megan shrugged. 'I don't know. I failed my psychic entrance exam for Hogwarts.'

Simon flinched. 'Are you always this prickly?'

Megan looked at him and raised an eyebrow by way of a reply.

'What I mean is, if it were me, I wouldn't take Sadie back to my place if my mum and dad were out — you don't know what she might do.'

Megan sighed. 'Okay, I see what you're saying but I still don't know for sure. There's no one at our house, so they might have gone there. It's worth a look.'

Simon nodded. 'Okay, and if she's not there, then we try the Rec?'

'That was my plan,' said Megan briskly.

At which point Simon nodded. 'Okay,' he said, and fell into step alongside her. Megan wondered if all boys behaved like this when they fancied you and how interesting it might be to have a tame one all of your own.

* * *

In the garden behind the marquee, the night had darkened fast, the navy-black sky a perfect backdrop for the final round of fireworks. God alone knew how much Liz had paid for them, but they were most definitely spectacular. They had drawn almost everyone out of the marquee and onto the lawn and now, as a grand finale, Catherine wheels and a pair of fantastic firework fountains lit the fuse that ignited dozens of little flashing, fizzing, sparkling fireworks spelling out the words, 'Happy Anniversary Rose and Jack,' in glittering Technicolor. People cheered and clapped as the pyrotechnic good wishes burst into life.

A little way along the path, under a pergola picked out in the glow of the fairy lights that he had hung earlier, Sam stood cradling a glass. He had had way too much to drink. He knew that because when he tried to focus on the tiny pinpoints of light, they fractured into shards, the fireworks refracting and reflecting in the bulbs only making matters worse.

He'd spent a lot of the evening thinking as

well as drinking; he couldn't believe Suzie would carry on behind his back, not with Matt . . . not with anyone, if he was honest. It wasn't the kind of woman she was, it was not in her nature and there was nothing, no real hard evidence to make him believe that what Liz had said was true — except perhaps for his own terrible sense of guilt. Perhaps him behaving the way he did had changed her. Perhaps he had driven her into the arms of another man.

He winced at the image of him gathering Matt up by the neck like some Neanderthal. God, that wasn't the kind of man he was, what *had* he been thinking of? *Himself*, his conscience snapped back. Him and his ego and his outrage and his hurt and his pride.

He had been neglecting Suzie of late, that was the problem. Maybe neglect was too big a word but it was the only one Sam's vodka-addled brain could come up with that came anywhere close to what had been going on. Things had been tough at work for the last couple of years, but he knew that that wasn't really the problem. If anything, it had been his excuse for not helping out, because Sam knew in his heart that he hadn't been supporting her, he hadn't been there for her at all. And so over the course of the last few years the house had become her problem, the girls had become her problem, the dogs, the cats, the cars, the garden, the shopping, the day-to-day management of their busy, noisy, stress-filled lives — all her problem.

And where had he been? *Sulking*. Sam belched and then hiccupped. It was true, he couldn't deny it. The vodka had given him an amazing clarity of mind, if not vision, that truly surprised him.

He had been feeling neglected and resentful for a while now and he knew he had been taking it out on Suzie; he just hadn't wanted to admit it to anyone, least of all himself. One of the initial reasons had been her going off to college, and although that was back when Megan started school full time, he knew damn well that was when the rot had set in.

Since then a little worm had been slowly eating away at his brain, one tiny bite at a time. Having the children early meant that up until now he had always been the breadwinner in the family; Suzie and the girls had needed him. Knowing that gave him a sense of pride and purpose, but there was a bit of him that was anxious that perhaps one day, one dark day, one day soon, Suzie wouldn't need him any more.

The rational man in him could see how it would be nice to have more money coming in, to have a wife who was happy with a fulfilling job, but that rational man's knuckle-dragging counterpart couldn't help but look ahead to a time when he would become superfluous to requirements, and Suzie would decide that she could live without him. Given the way he had behaved recently, who could blame her?

The alcohol allowed him to consider with detachment the things he had been ashamed to admit to himself until now. When exactly had he turned into a pantomime version of his father, all moody and grumpy and uncommunicative, the things he had loathed most?

When she'd finished college Suzie had started working part time, fitting in everything around him and the girls. She had taken on designing, hands-on gardening, maintenance, and that had grown and grown until finally one day there had been the walled garden. The walled garden, her baby.

In his head Sam had planned to say 'her job', but he knew that the garden was just so much more than that to Suzie. It was a passion, a calling and it was fantastic that she had made such a success of it. He could see how much she loved it and there was a big part of Sam that was proud and delighted for her — but there was also a part of him that was horribly, horribly jealous. Not just of the hours she put in but of the joy the whole thing gave her. He was envious of how much she loved what she did. And how awful was that?

Having the garden project also meant that for the first time in years Suzie wasn't always home when he got in from work, and often when she was she was preoccupied, or on the phone, or busy planning. People rang up and dropped by and wanted to see her. He had to cook supper and do more around the house, and even though he didn't mind doing any of those things, the truth was he felt neglected. While he felt petty and childish for feeling like that, another part of him felt that she had taken her eye off the ball. The ball being *him*, and it was hard to talk rationally when one of you was sulking.

He also knew that thinking like that made him

sound like a dinosaur, and now, on top of all the stuff with Suzie and the garden, there was Hannah. He shook his head in despair.

He was getting more and more unsettled by the way Hannah was behaving. Was it his fault? Or Suzie's? Was their daughter picking up on what was going on between them? Was this her way of crying for attention and if it was, why the hell couldn't he handle it better? God, he was supposed to be the grown-up here.

Once upon a time, in what now seemed like the dim and distant past, he and the girls had got on brilliantly. He remembered sitting at the kitchen table having Hovis moments with them after work, eating supper, chatting about the day, helping them with their homework, giggling together. Looking around those faces, at Suzie and the girls, Sam remembered thinking that his life was complete, a joy, something that they had built between them that made his heart sing.

Now if it sang it was mostly thrash metal or something nasty by a band with a swear word in the title. The previous week he'd come home from work to find Suzie was out at a meeting. The dogs hadn't been fed or walked and were eating out the kitchen bin. Megan had been at the kitchen table with her iPod on, totally oblivious to his arrival, eating peanut butter sandwiches, fishing it straight from the jar onto the bread without worrying about cutting up the bread or putting it on a plate. There was a great smear of peanut butter across the tabletop which suggested this was not her first attempt. Hannah had been up in her room playing music so loud that the plates were rattling on the dresser downstairs and, short of joining Megan in her peanut butter fest, there was nothing to eat, despite Suzie having asked Hannah to put supper (which she had made before she left for work) in the oven to reheat.

When Sam had gone upstairs to ask Hannah to turn down the music and give him a hand, she had told him to get out her room. When he refused she had stormed out herself, telling him he was a Nazi. Megan caved in and gave a hand although, as she quite reasonably pointed out, it was hardly fair because she always picked up the lion's share of the work since Hannah had turned into a screaming troll.

Despite the truth behind this statement, Sam had shouted at her and sent her to her room, which meant that by the time Suzie came in no one was speaking to anyone else, supper was burnt and one of the dogs had crapped on the kitchen floor. And what had Sam done then? Rally round, help her clean up? Nip out to get a takeaway? No, he had let her take over while he went upstairs to check his email.

Oh yes, he could quite see why Suzie might leave him.

On the whole, Megan was still fine, peanut butter and outrage notwithstanding, but he didn't understand what was happening to Hannah at all. It was as if she had turned into someone else. For the first time since the girls had been babies he felt totally at a loss and frustrated by parenthood. If he asked Hannah to do something, she whined or snapped at him or stormed off in a huff, or burst into tears. Now, from his alcohol-fuelled high ground, he could see that he had passed the buck there too, complaining to Suzie because Hannah had behaved badly towards him, and accusing Suzie of taking Hannah's side.

Sam took another long pull on his drink. Only that very evening, hadn't he said in a sullen, little-boy voice, 'Oh that's it, take her side, why don't you?'

He winced.

God, wasn't he meant to be the grown-up here — just how adult did that sound? And here Sam was threatening to punch out Suzie's friends like some teenage thug.

Actually, he thought, draining the glass down to the icy dregs, he wouldn't blame Suzie if she *was* having an affair. Who in their right mind would want to share their life with a miserable, self-pitying, whining man-child?

Sam stared deep into the ice nuggets, and the fairy lights and fireworks reflected there. He really needed another drink.

* * *

It was practically dark when Sadie, Hannah and Tucker got to Sadie's house. There were lights on and music playing and people spilling out of the doorway into the garden and the lane beyond that. There were people hunched around a firepit on the lawn, sharing a cigarette, passing it backwards and forwards, and others drinking and laughing and dancing.

As Sadie opened the garden gate, a woman came running out of the house across the yard, giggling furiously and shrieking.

'Don't you dare, don't you . . . You bastard,' she yelled, hitching up her skirt and racing barefoot out onto the tangled grass, leaping over and ducking between the groups of people. She was being closely pursued by a man with dreadlocks, who was carrying a yellow plastic bucket in his hands, a cigarette clenched firmly between his teeth.

The woman swerved first left and now right to avoid him, before finally running for cover behind a little stand of old apple trees — not that it did her any good. The two of them feinted back and forth, bobbing and weaving, her shrieking and laughing, him grinning but determined. She kept it up, this game of trying to avoid him, but in the end the man was too quick for her. As the woman twisted the wrong way, he whooped triumphantly and threw the contents of the bucket over her. There wasn't that much water in it but it was enough to soak her tee-shirt and make her scream in protest. And then all of sudden the roles were reversed and the woman was chasing the man, squealing like a banshee, till at the doorway he turned again and, grabbing hold of her, hot and panting and laughing, he kissed her hard, bending her over, kissing her mouth and her neck and her shoulders, looking for all the world as if he was trying to eat her alive.

'I thought you said your mum was going out,' said Tucker.

'Me too,' said Sadie, taking another swig from the bottle she was carrying.

* * *

Back at the marquee, people were slowly drifting back inside after the fireworks. While the guests had been outside the staff had cleared away more of the tables and set chairs around the sides of the marquee.

The band was playing. Jack and Rose had made straight for the dance floor, arm in arm, looking every inch like a couple in love, despite all the ups and downs of life together. As soon as people started to dance the band upped the tempo a notch, playing something summery and light.

Suzie smiled; her parents looked as if they were having a great time. Liz meanwhile was heading for the door. Suzie's smile deepened as she noticed that Liz was carrying two glasses and had a bottle of champagne tucked under one arm. Probably her man was about to arrive or perhaps he was already there, Suzie thought, watching the way Liz was hurrying. She knew how Liz hated people to be late; she wouldn't be best pleased that the new man had missed supper. But maybe she had finally got it right. She certainly looked like a woman on a mission.

Sam was nowhere in sight. Suzie let her gaze work around the inside of the marquee, moving from face to face and group to group as she tried to spot him in the crowd. He couldn't be far away surely? Unless of course he had gone home or gone looking for Hannah. Maybe he was still outside. As she was about to go out, Suzie heard someone call her name and turned.

'Suzie?' It was Matt beckoning to her from the kitchen. 'Have you got a minute?'

'Hi, how's it going?' she said. 'The food was absolutely fabulous, we've had nothing but compliments.'

'Great, but actually it's not the food I'm worried about. I've been trying to find you. Have you seen Sam recently?'

Suzie shook her head. 'No, I'm looking for him now. Why, what's the matter?'

Matt stepped closer so they wouldn't be overheard. 'Sam tried to lay me out.'

Suzie's first reaction was to laugh. 'You are joking. I know he's had a couple but — '

'But nothing,' said Matt. 'He's had a lot more than a couple, Suzie. You really need to talk to him.' He paused. 'Sam thinks we're having an affair. For God's sake, find him and put him out of his misery, will you, before he does something he regrets?'

Suzie stared at him. 'An affair? Are you serious?'

'That's what the man said.' Matt pulled a face. 'Oh come on. Don't look like that. I'm hurt. I mean, why not? I'm not that bad, am I?'

Suzie smiled and shook her head.

'And another thing . . . ' he hesitated.

'What?'

'Hannah's friends, you know, the ones who crashed the party?'

Suzie nodded, feeling her heart sink. 'What

about them? What have they done?'

'Nothing major. They grabbed a couple of bottles of booze and buggered off. I ran after them but . . . '

Suzie groaned. 'But you couldn't catch them?'

'Unfortunately not, I'm not as quick as I used to be.' Matt put his hand on her arm. 'It's all right, it was nothing really, just a couple of bottles of the first thing they came to by the looks of it. I mean, we've all done it, maybe not quite like that, but I thought you should know that Hannah went with them.'

Suzie stared at him. 'Hannah stole booze?'

He shook his head. 'No, it was the other two but she was there and she ran off with them.'

'Oh, Matt,' sighed Suzie. 'It feels like my whole life is falling apart . . . What am I going to do?'

'Go and talk to Sam.'

'And what about Hannah?'

'She'll be fine; she's just busy being a teenager.'

'And Sam?' she asked.

Matt laughed. 'Midlife crisis? Second childhood? Go and talk to him. Set him straight before he comes back for me.' He smiled. 'I paid a lot of money for these veneers.'

* * *

Tucking the bottle of champagne up under her arm and taking a firm grip of the two glasses she had taken from one of the waitresses, Liz headed outside into the warm dark evening air.

Sometimes you just have to strike while the iron is hot.

As she made her way into the shadows, she spotted Suzie over by the kitchen area deep in conversation with Matt, which as far as Liz was concerned was more or less perfect.

Outside people were wandering around the gardens, catching up with old friends, drinking and talking in low voices, while the music rolled out into the darkness, filling in the spaces between the words. The night air was heavy with the scent of roses and honeysuckle.

Liz made her way around the different groups, making small talk here, sharing a joke there, even signing a couple more autographs. All the time she was being adored by the hoi polloi, she kept an eye out for Sam. He had to be around somewhere. Eventually she found him sitting in the shadows on a bench by the summerhouse, well away from the rest of the revellers. He was leaning forward, apparently deep in thought with his head down, forearms resting on his thighs, hands cradling an empty glass.

'Well, hello there, stranger,' she said, her tone an artful mixture of concern and seduction. 'Penny for them?'

He glanced up at her. 'What do you want? Come over to gloat, have you?'

'Oh, come off it, Sam. You know I'm not like that. I was just getting a bit of fresh air and catching up with people. It's all bit airless in the marquee. Do you fancy some company?'

He glanced up at her. 'Do I look like I want company?'

She decided to ignore that and sat down alongside him. 'I brought champagne.'

'Oh well, that's good of you,' he said. 'What are we going to celebrate? The end of my marriage? Presumably you heard about me having it out with Matt?'

Liz stared at him, and felt her stomach lurch. *So it was true?*

'Really? No . . . Oh, Sam. Are you serious? I'm so sorry . . . I didn't think when I said . . . ' She grabbed back the breath and the words, stopping right on the very edge of the abyss before admitting she had simply been making mischief. Instead she said hastily, 'What did Suzie tell you? I mean, did she tell you she's been seeing Matt?'

He stared at her. 'I thought you knew all about it? She hasn't said anything to me yet but that's mainly because I haven't spoken to her about it. I mean, what can I say? What can *she* say? I talked to Matt though. He denied anything was going on between them, but then again, he's hardly going to own up, is he? Not even man enough to tell me straight out. Slimy bastard.'

Liz waited to see if there was any more and when it became obvious that there wasn't, she handed him a champagne flute. 'There you go,' she said, topping up his glass. 'How about we drink a toast to slimy bastards everywhere?'

Sam set his empty tumbler down on the grass and looked at her. 'Did I miss something?'

'My Mr Right.'

'Slimy bastard?'

Liz nodded, surprised to feel her eyes prickle

with tears. 'Hole in one. Give that man a coconut.'

'But I thought from what Suzie said that this was *it*,' said Sam. 'The big one — Mr Right. Wedding bells and all that jazz.'

'Me too,' said Liz.

'And wasn't he coming down to meet the family tonight?' Sam continued, his expression implying he was having to search around for the thoughts.

'Uh-huh, although the emphasis there should be on *was*. He rang while everyone was getting themselves settled in to tell me that he wouldn't be coming after all because something had come up.'

'Something important?' asked Sam.

'A twenty-two-year-old lingerie model.'

'Ah,' said Sam with a nod.

Liz smiled ruefully. 'You know what they say, lucky at cards, unlucky in love.'

Sam frowned. He had obviously had a lot more to drink than Liz had first thought. 'I didn't know you played cards,' he said.

'It's an old saying.'

Sam looked none the wiser. 'About what?' he asked, brain obviously taking a while to catch up. He took another swig of champagne.

'About life,' she said. 'I'm lucky in life but not in love.'

Sam gave a miserable sigh. 'Right. Not so long ago I used to think that I was lucky in both.'

This wasn't exactly how Liz had imagined their conversation going. She moved in a little closer so they were sitting shoulder to shoulder.

'I'm really sorry that things have t
way,' she whispered, taking his h
very special man, you know that
As their fingers touched Sam
He looked surprised and slightly
he couldn't quite believe what was h
He had such lovely eyes and he was so close
that she could feel his breath on her cheek. Liz
swallowed hard, wondering what was going to happen next and if she had the nerve for it. After all, it was she who had started the ball rolling, and he *was* Suzie's husband — but then hadn't he just said that it was over between the two of them?

The problem was that, even as she thought it, Liz couldn't quite believe it. Suzie wasn't the type to be carrying on with anyone, particularly not Matt. He was way too smooth and gorgeous for someone like Suzie, surely? Although maybe that was it, maybe that was the attraction. Matt liked non-threatening women who didn't hog the limelight *or* the bathroom mirror. You never could tell, and even if it *was* true about Matt and Suzie, how much worse would it be when people found out about Liz and Sam? After all these years. She smiled as her imagination dropped into overdrive. She could practically see the front of *Heat* magazine now:

''I always loved him but he was forbidden fruit,' *Starmaker*'s top presenter tells us about her years of inner torment as she finally marries the man of her dreams.' Or, 'Sisters in tragic love triangle.'

Not quite true because she had never properly

Sam but it was good headline fodder d people eventually got over those kind of gs. Liz was imagining the repercussions and ighing up how awful Christmas would be ersus the column inches she'd get and the news coverage, when she suddenly became aware that Sam was staring at her. She wondered if she had been speaking out loud. His eyes were a little glazed and very slightly out of focus but he was most definitely staring at her.

Was this a bridge too far, or was it fate that had finally brought them together after all these years? Liz considered the thought for a moment. A bit of cliché, all that 'bridge too far' and 'fate' stuff, and she would have to think about how to phrase it for the tabloids so that it didn't sound sordid. She was thinking something along the lines of 'igniting a fire that had been smouldering untended and unintended in the background for years'. Waiting or smouldering? And could you marry your own brother-in-law? Or did they consider that incest? It would probably be worth looking up . . .

She was still thinking when Sam leant in a little closer and, for one heart-stopping moment, Liz thought that he was going to kiss her.

Instead he belched quietly and then said, 'Sorry about that. I was going to ask you how long have you known about this thing with Matt and Suzie? I don't understand why you didn't say something before. Why now? You know, I feel such a fool for not seeing it — is she going to leave me, Liz? Is that what this is about? Is she going? Is that why you said something?'

As he spoke a great big tear rolled down his cheek. 'I know I haven't been there for her just recently. And she's needed me, what with the garden and the extra work and the girls and cooking supper and everything. What are the girls going to say — do they know? God, Liz, I really love her. I really, really do. Do you think it's too late to get her back?' He let out a thick miserable sob. 'Oh God, what have I done?'

Liz stared at him in amazement and before she could help herself said, 'Never mind about what *you've* done, Sam, what has Suzie done?'

He looked up at her words, his eyes ever so slightly crossed. 'Exactly. *What has she done?* I mean, what has she definitely, *definitely* done? I've been sitting here thinking about it. What do I know for *certain*? I'm not talking about the things that my mind is making up just because I want to be the one up here on the moral high ground but the *real* things. You tell me — *what has she done, Liz*?'

Liz hesitated. Sam really was an awful lot drunker than he looked.

'Maybe Matt was telling the truth, you know?' he continued, his words crashing randomly into each other. 'Maybe there really isn't anything going on between the two of them. I don't know that much about Matt but he always seemed like a reasonable sort of guy really — bit of a wanker maybe, but not a wife stealer if you know what I mean. Maybe I'm reading this all wrong. You know, in all the years I've been with Suzie I've never thought for one single solitary moment, not ever, that she was the sort of woman who would cheat on me. Not once . . . so why now? What do you think, Liz? What do you think? You're her sister, for God's sake. I need to think . . . '

Liz stayed schtum. She was slightly concerned by the journey his alcohol-fuelled brain was making. She wondered how long it would be before Sam came full circle and realised that the seeds of doubt that he had been so carefully tending were the ones that she had planted.

22

Hannah had come to the conclusion that all the weird people who lived in Moongate Lane and possibly the whole of Crowbridge were at Sadie's mum's party. It certainly looked like it. The place was packed with people with dreads and tattoos and piercings. She squeezed her way between the party-goers in the little yard outside the door and in through the tiny crowded kitchen, all the while staying as close as she could to Sadie and Tucker, trying hard not to catch anyone's eye.

The party had obviously been going on for some time. There were empty glasses, bottles and cans all over the work-tops, in the sink and on the windowsills. The detritus of drinking was mixed with takeaway cartons, empty crisp packets, odd bowls of nibbles, and a pudding basin half full of dried-up pasta salad standing alongside an open pizza box. Someone had ground a dog end into one of the remaining slices. Sadie tore off a piece furthest away from the cigarette butt and, stuffing it into her mouth, waved them through.

'Come on,' she called over the thumping beat of the music. 'We'll go upstairs to my room, out of the way of this lot.'

Hannah took a last look back at the open door, regretting having come back to the cottage, and wishing that there was some way she could just slip away and go home. She hesitated just long enough for Sadie to notice.

'Are you coming upstairs or not?' Sadie shouted, taking a swig out of the bottle she was carrying.

Hannah nodded.

Sadie grinned. 'Come on then. Move yourself. Tucker, grab that bowl of peanuts, will you?' Both of them did as they were told.

Framed in the doorway behind Sadie was a large man leaning over a much younger, smaller woman. He had a mass of grey curly hair and a scrubby beard. His arm was resting against the wall above the young woman so that she was pinned there like one of the butterflies Hannah had once seen in a museum. The girl was small and blonde, with short spiky hair, and was wearing a minidress, cut thigh-high to reveal slender, suntanned legs. The man's tee-shirt barely covered his hairy milk-white belly and there was a damp circle of sweat under his armpit. The girl looked drunk, pale and uncomfortable, the man proprietorial and predatory.

As Hannah followed Sadie towards the stairs, the man looked up and grinned at her. 'Well, hello there, sweet thing, and where did *you* spring from?' he said, all eyes. He licked his lips. 'Do I know you? Haven't we met somewhere before?'

The miniskirted girl seized the chance to slip away.

The man stepped closer. Hannah felt like a rabbit trapped in the headlights. His smile widened wolfishly. 'No need to be shy there, honey. I don't bite. So what's your name then?'

Hannah stared at him, dry-mouthed, pulse thumping in her ears. She didn't want to tell him her name.

'Fuck off, Dexter,' snapped Sadie, grabbing her arm before Hannah could speak. 'She's with me. I've warned you before, you creep, don't letch my friends. All right?' There was a real threat in her voice.

The spell broken, the man turned towards Sadie and laughed. 'One of yours, is she? I might have bloody guessed. You still hanging around with boys, are you?' he said, eyeing up Tucker, all his remarks now squarely aimed at Sadie, who regarded the man with barely concealed contempt. 'What you need, Sadie, is a *real* man.'

Sadie snorted. 'Well, if you ever meet one, Dex, be sure to let me know, won't you? Come on, Hannah, let's get upstairs away from the pensioners.'

As Hannah tried to get past him the man made a point of brushing himself against her. The smell of him made her skin crawl.

'If you ever get bored of playing around with Little Miss Psycho up there, you come and find me,' the man said, with a big fat grin. 'My name's Dexter — everyone knows me. Would you like my card?' He made as if to reach into his pocket.

Sadie glared at him from half way up the stairs. 'I thought I told you to fuck off, Dexter.'

Hannah quickly slid past him and hurried to catch her up. 'Who the hell is he?' she hissed, as Sadie opened her bedroom door.

'Dex? He's one of mum's exes — and a total creep. I mean, *really* creepy. Used to try and watch me in the bathroom, you know, like burst in when I was having a bath and stuff.' She shuddered. 'Sicko bastard.'

For a moment Hannah wondered what it must be like to grow up like Sadie, where strange men burst into the bathroom and you could never be sure where your mum was or who she was with, and for a second or two the glamour around Sadie's life didn't seem quite so compelling. Who did Sadie have to depend on? The answer came back loud and clear — just Sadie, because there was no one else she could trust. For an instant Hannah caught a glimpse of how lonely and how vulnerable Sadie's upbringing made her.

'If he ever lays a finger on you I'll punch his lights out,' Tucker was saying, squaring his shoulders, all bravado and macho posturing now that the moment had passed.

Sadie looked at him and laughed. 'It's not his finger I was worried about,' she said, and then she began to giggle. Hannah laughed too, although she wasn't altogether sure why.

⋆ ⋆ ⋆

Back at Jack and Rose's anniversary party, Suzie had scoured the tent and then the garden searching for Sam and couldn't find him anywhere. He wasn't back at their house; she'd rung. He wasn't out in the lane. He wasn't answering his mobile. His car was still in the road. She was starting to panic — this was so out of character for Sam. No one had seen him since the fireworks had finished, and it was hard to keep up the pretence that everything was all right. People wanted to talk to her, to tell her what a lovely party it was, to talk about the walled garden, and the radio show and her parents and her oh-so-famous sister and it all seemed like distraction, pulling her away from what was really important, which was finding Sam. The other problem was that she couldn't find the girls either. It felt as if her entire family had vanished, and the sensation of loss and anxiety were growing and growing. Where the hell were they all?

She was about to head back out into the garden for another look around when a young woman touched her arm.

'Excuse me,' she said. 'Are you Suzie? You are, aren't you?' Suzie nodded but before she could say anything the woman continued, 'I'm Nina, Janet's daughter — Janet Fielding? Your mum's bridesmaid. I've been hoping to speak to you. I was wondering if I could have a word with you — '

'I'm really sorry,' said Suzie, trying very hard to be polite. 'But actually I'm looking for my husband at the moment. Maybe later.' Something about the woman's expression made Suzie stop in her tracks. 'Is everything all right? Are you okay? Did you say you're my mum's bridesmaid's daughter?'

The woman smiled. 'Yes, that's right, Dad couldn't come — and I'm absolutely fine, you go. I'll catch you later when you're not so busy.'

She sounded as if she had had to pluck up courage to talk to Suzie, which seemed odd, although Suzie kicked herself for noticing. 'If you're sure?' she said.

The woman nodded. 'Really. You go . . . '

Guilt had such a loud voice, and told Suzie that maybe if she had spent more time noticing how Sam felt and less time on strangers then she wouldn't be where she was now. Which was where exactly?

As the woman melted back into the crowd, Suzie headed out into the garden. Where the hell could Sam have got to?

* * *

'We used to come here when we were kids,' said Sam miserably as he sloped off across the recreation ground towards the swings and slides. 'Before everyone went off to college, before all that. When we were at school we used to be down here all the time.'

'I know,' sighed Liz, picking her way across the damp uneven surface in her high heels, struggling to keep up with him. She hadn't factored bark chippings into her wardrobe choice, and the grass was playing hell with her Louboutins; she was having to prise herself out of the subsoil every two or three steps and there was just bound to be a pile of dog poo lurking somewhere out there in the darkness.

'I was there, remember?' she said. 'I used to tag along too. Suzie's cute little sister?'

Head down, hands in his pockets, Sam said nothing.

Liz sighed; she might as well have been talking to herself. 'You know, Sam, I always thought you were pretty cute too . . . '

Was cute the right word to use on a straight brother-in-law from the sticks? She wasn't sure — he didn't exactly fit the metro sexual profile. Either way, Sam didn't appear to have registered her comment.

It was dark now, and she was finding it hard to see. The village hall was closed up and quiet. The football pitch and the cricket pavilion were silent, while a single lamp, a cyclops eye, kept watch in the darkness and threw a pall of light over the grassed area outside the public toilets. It was hardly Hollywood. Liz shivered, wishing they were back at the party.

The recreation ground and village playing field were bordered on two sides by the village graveyard, with the road on the third and a row of bungalows, tucked away behind the pavilion and the village hall, and a high hedge on the fourth. In the graveyard a huge Cedar of Lebanon stood sentinel against a moonlit sky. Wind played in and out of the chains on the swings. The ice-cream cone shape of the children's roundabout groaned grimly.

Liz was getting cold. Now she remembered why it was she always came up here with the others. It was way too spooky to be up there on your own, particularly at night. While going for a walk with Sam had seemed like a good idea back at the house, a way of getting him on his own, it had completely backfired. Walking down to the Rec was like a trip down memory lane . . . literally.

Sam pointed out the shelter down by the bowling green where he had kissed Suzie for the first time. 'You see *this* path,' he said, showing Liz a little break in the bushes, as if she was a total stranger who hadn't grown up alongside him and Suzie and had never been that way before. 'We used to go through there, between the bungalows and take the footpath down to the river. We got drunk there together, there — I think we'd just finished our A-levels or something, and I remember I'd biked all the way over to Crowbridge to see her. I asked my dad if I could have a bottle of wine and Suzie packed up this picnic — really nice food, you know how she likes to cook. It seemed so grown-up then . . . Anyway, next morning my old man was furious because I'd taken something that he had been saving for him and Mum. It was fizzy — not champagne or anything.' He laughed to himself, completely unaware of Liz, his gaze turned firmly inward.

Liz sighed. *Riveting*, she thought grimly. The man was totally and utterly obsessed with her sister.

'How about we go back?' Liz said brightly. 'Or we could go down the pub if you like?' *Anywhere where there was a bit of life*. However, Sam had slumped down onto one of the swings, grabbing hold of the chains to steady himself. He had the look of a gorilla that had been too long in captivity.

'You know, you're so much better than this,' Liz said, sitting down alongside him. God alone knew what was on the seats, probably chewing gum knowing her luck, but back to the matter in hand. 'I'm really worried about you, Sam.'

Even the sound of his name didn't rouse him. She fished around for platitudes to make him focus on her and realise just how kind and lovely she was, all the while wondering if it was worth the effort. Did she *really* want a man who had a mortgage, two kids, and was her sister's husband?

The reality was no, of course she didn't, but there was a part of Liz that wanted to know that if she *did* ever want Sam she could have him. Snap him up, just like that. That would be a big, big win in the sister rivalry stakes. And of course, if it worked, Sam would always know it, know that *she* had won. It would be their guilty little secret. Liz smiled; actually it would be *his* guilty little secret — so *well* worth the effort then.

She pushed her swing a little closer to his so that their knuckles just touched. 'I'm so sorry,' she murmured, stroking the back of his hand. 'You're such a good man.'

Sam stared at her and then, as if seeing her for the first time, he grinned in a leery, boozy, lopsided way. 'You're a very attractive woman, Lizzie,' he said thickly. 'I've always thought that. Always thought you were very lovely . . . beautiful . . . ' He hadn't sobered up any, and the words weren't crystal clear, but even so, this was more like it.

She smiled and turned her head to give him

the full benefit of her best side. 'That's so sweet of you, Sam. But at the moment it's *you* I'm really concerned about.'

'Really?' He hiccupped. 'You see that's the thing, Lizzie, you've got such a kind heart really.'

Really?

'Underneath all that head-girl, bossy, goodie-two-shoes thing you do, that whole Lizzie-knows-best-act, there's a heart of gold, isn't there? And you know that I've always thought that you were lovely.' He hiccupped again, and then continued. 'Really lovely.' He beckoned her closer.

This was getting better and better. Liz moved in, trying to ignore the sweet sickly smell of booze on his breath and the little smidgen of coleslaw on his lapel.

'Oh Sam,' she said in a slightly breathy voice. 'I had no idea. All these years . . . '

They were so close now that their noses were almost touching. God, he was just bound to kiss her now surely?

'So, the thing I can't work out is why can't you get yourself a decent bloke — and then hang onto him,' said Sam. 'I mean, I'm just wondering if you're trying too hard.'

Liz pulled away as if he had slapped her.

'*What?*' she growled. 'Trying too hard? What the hell is that supposed to mean?'

'Well, you have to admit, Lizzie, you're high maintenance. You're lovely but you're hard work. Trust me, no bloke wants to wait around for three or four hours for any woman to get ready, however great you think she looks. That's one of the reasons I love Suzie so much — ten minutes,' he said, hands raised to make his point. 'She pulls on a clean pair of jeans, brushes her hair, bit of lipstick and she looks like a million dollars.'

Liz stared at him. 'A million dollars,' she repeated. '*A million dollars?* You're telling me that my sister looks like a million dollars after *ten minutes?*'

At which point Sam practically leapt off the swings and hurried across the grass back the way they'd just come. 'Yes, yes you're right, God, you know, you're so absolutely right,' he called over his shoulder. He was fleet of foot for a drunk. 'Which is exactly why I need to go back and find her and tell her. Thank you, Liz — you've been absolutely brilliant, and I've been such a bloody fool. Talking to you has really helped. Now I need to go and find Suzie.'

Liz watched him vanish into the gloom and sighed. Well, that didn't go quite the way she had planned. She slid off the swing and was about to follow him back to the party when she realised just how dark it had become and how very quiet it was out there on the Rec. Sam was nowhere in sight and she was all alone in the darkness.

Liz shivered as the wind made the chains on the swings rattle and creak ominously. Right on cue from close by an owl hooted in the graveyard. She felt the hair on the back of her neck prickle and rise.

Liz considered her options for a second or two and came to the conclusion that there was no way she was going to go through the back lanes on her own. So, with a sense of resignation, she headed down towards the road and the long way home.

Why was it she couldn't find herself a man like Sam? A man who would love her just the way she was. She sniffed back a tear. Maybe Sam was right, maybe she was bossy and high maintenance, but that was only the outside. Surely the right man would understand she had had to work hard to get where she was and it didn't do to be vulnerable.

Her shoes weren't ideal for a forced march, and by the time she got to the edge of the Rec Liz's feet were killing her and she was hot and flustered, but at least she was heading in the direction of streetlights and a proper path.

Just as Liz reached the pavement, a black cab drove past very slowly, a sight as rare as a mermaid in the backwaters of rural Norfolk. Hands on hips, she watched its tail lights as it turned left into High Lane, cursing under her breath. If she had been there a second or two earlier she would have flagged the bloody thing down, whether it had had a fare or not.

Another hundred yards up the road, not caring who saw her, Liz sat down under a streetlight, eased off her shoes and rubbed her feet. The new shoes had raised blisters on her heels and rubbed the skin off the top of her toes. Even in this light and without her glasses, she could see that her spray tan had gone streaky round her ankles. She was hot and hurt and annoyed. She would never get home at this rate.

Just as Liz set about trying to put her high heels back on, the cab passed her again and this time she leapt up and stuck out her hand. She would happily pay double or treble to get a lift home. Sod's law being what it was, however, as she leant forward to wave it down, she missed her footing and lurched forward into the road, not so much flagging down the cab as throwing herself under its wheels.

The driver slowed and opened his window. There was a passenger in the back seat who had leant forward to see what was going on.

'You all right, sweetheart?' said the driver, getting out to help her to her feet.

Liz was about to nod and then decided to admit defeat. She shook her head. 'No, not really. Is there any chance you could take me home, please?'

The heel had broken on one of her new shoes, her dress was covered in grime, she was hot and sweaty, she had grazed her knee, got gravel rash on her hands where she had tried to stop herself from falling and God alone knew what her hair looked like.

The driver looked at her long and hard. 'Don't I know you?' he said, his expression suggesting he was struggling to remember where exactly he'd seen her before. Then he grinned. 'The name's on the tip of my tongue. Don't tell me, don't tell me . . . '

Liz would normally have smiled but she was in no mood to be recognised so she settled for a grimace instead. 'Look, I know you've got a fare onboard but I'll give you fifty pounds if you'll just take me home. I live just round the corner. It won't take you five minutes.'

He looked at the shoes she had in her hand. 'Not exactly dressed for a hike, are you?' He turned to look at his fare with a boy's own grin. 'We can hardly leave her here, a damsel in distress, can we? Be all right, won't it?' he said. Turning back to Liz. 'Let's get you in here; those look more like instruments of torture to me than shoes. You know you women make me laugh. You look frozen — do you want to borrow my jacket?'

Liz shook her head. 'No, I'm fine.'

Meanwhile the back door of the cab had swung open. Liz peered inside. There was a tall elderly man sitting in the back seat cradling a huge bouquet of flowers. Smartly dressed and good-looking in a rangy way, he looked harmless enough.

'Hello,' he said. 'Are you okay?'

Liz nodded. 'More or less,' she said, sliding into the seat alongside him. 'Nice flowers.'

He smiled. 'They're for my girlfriend. You took a bit of tumble back there, are you sure you're all right?'

'I'm fine, just pleased I haven't got to walk home.'

'So you're a local then?' he said.

'Yes, I live just up the road.'

'Great, in that case maybe you can help me.' He pulled a piece of paper out of his pocket and tipped it towards the streetlight in order to read what was scribbled on it. 'I'm looking for somewhere called Isaac's Cottage, Mill Lane?'

Liz stared at him. 'You *are* joking, aren't you?'
The man shook his head. 'No, why?'
'That's where I'm going.'
'Oh right,' said the man cheerfully. 'Well, that's great, you going to the party too then?'
'Actually I organised it,' said Liz.
The man's smile broadened. 'Well, that's fantastic. So you'll know Fleur?'
'She's my aunt.'
He stuck out his hand. 'Well how about that for a stroke of luck. I'm Frank Callaby — Frank to my friends.'
'Do I know you?' asked Liz, trying to pick out his features in the gloom.
'No, but I thought there was a fair chance Fleur might have mentioned me . . . ' He waited, and when Liz said nothing continued, 'Apparently not. Fleur and me, we're a bit of an item back home — well, at least we were.'
Liz raised an eyebrow. 'Were? So what, you're stalking her?'
He laughed. 'Not exactly. Place is not the same without her around.'
'So you've come God knows how many thousands of miles on the off-chance?'
'More or less.' Frank grinned. 'You know what Fleur's like, all prickle and spit — she'll probably have me slung out when we get there. Or arrested; she did that when we went to Brisbane for the weekend.' He paused. 'I really missed the old girl, so I thought I'd just nip over and surprise her — '
'Nip?' Liz said pointedly.
His good humour held. 'Figure of speech,

darlin' — Fleur and me live in the same street. I've been keeping an eye on her place while she's been away. Stroke of luck finding you though. We've been circling round for the last twenty minutes; you know, I wouldn't have thought you could get lost in a little place like this. I couldn't really ring and ask Fleur for directions without giving the game away now, could I?'

The taxi was moving off.

'It's just up here,' said Liz. 'First on the right, then just go straight up to the end of the road and turn left.'

The driver laughed. 'I don't think it is. We've already been up there a couple of times. It's a dead end.'

'Mill Lane's not signposted.'

The driver snorted. 'Well, that's handy, how's a person supposed to find anywhere round here?'

'It's a country thing,' said Liz.

'It's a crazy thing,' Frank said. 'How do you find your way around?'

The cabbie laughed. 'Ask a good-looking local?'

Frank nodded. 'I suppose you've got a point. Is that how you trap all your men?' And before Liz could say anything he winked at her and said, 'Works like a charm, I reckon you're in there, darling.'

Liz, glowing white-hot with indignation, pretended that she hadn't heard him and kept her eyes firmly on the road. 'So,' she said, attempting to deflect attention away from herself. 'What happened with you and Fleur?'

'She walked out on me,' Frank said. 'Middle of dinner.'

Liz glanced across at him. 'Maybe you should take the hint.'

'Maybe, but I never was that kind of guy. And your aunt, she's a fine woman. I thought she was worth another go . . . ' He paused. 'Maybe you're right, but you know, I had to give it one more chance, I'll know by the look on her face when she sees me if I've made a mistake.'

Liz stared at him, contemplating coming all that way, with the risk that he might simply be rejected. He grinned as if he could read her mind. 'Love's a funny thing.'

'You love Fleur?'

Frank nodded. 'Oh yes,' he said.

The cab crept slowly back up the road and into Mill Lane. They could hear the music as they drew up in front of Isaac's Cottage, even with the car windows closed.

'Looks like this is it,' said the cabbie cheerfully. 'At long last.'

Good old Frank was fleet of foot: he was out and had the cab door open before Liz had the chance to pick up her shoes. 'You get your dancing pumps on, sweetheart, and I'll sort out the fare,' Frank said, pulling his wallet out of his jacket pocket. 'And not a word to Fleur, y'hear? I don't want to spoil the surprise. Okay?'

'Okay,' said Liz. 'And good luck.'

'Thanks, sweetheart — and you too.'

Liz glanced up at the driver who had got out to assist Frank. He was nice looking in a well-worn sort of way.

'Do you need a hand to get out?' the driver asked, eyes bright with amusement. 'You're not going to try and walk in those, are you? That heel's broken.'

Liz looked down at her new shoes. 'I'll be fine,' she said, forcing her toes into them and stepping out of the car. It took her a split second to realise putting them back on had been a big mistake. It felt like she had stepped into boiling treacle, every step agony, not to mention the fact that her broken heel made her roll like a drunk.

'How much would you charge to run me to the front door?' she asked, looking up at him.

'That bad, huh?' he said, struggling to suppress a grin.

She nodded. 'Worse. I don't think I can get the damned things off.'

He laughed. 'Here, let me help you. You can have that one on the house. Have you got any more here?'

'Shoes? Yes, I've got some upstairs.'

'Okay, jump up,' he said, turning and patting his thigh.

She stared at him. 'What did you just say?'

'Jump up. I'll give you a piggyback over the front door if you want.'

Liz stared at him in amazement. 'You can't be serious?'

'Why not? I mean, you're not that heavy, are you? It's either that or a fireman's carry. You know, over one shoulder. Take your pick.'

Frank laughed and looked from one to the other. 'I'll leave you two to it, shall I?'

Liz ignored him. 'Couldn't you just carry me to the kerb?'

'What and then you'll hobble over all that gravel? Looks pretty sharp to me. Come on, hop up.'

Liz looked down at her shoes one more time. 'Hang on,' she said, and prised them off. Then she sighed and, perching on the sill of the car, she looped her arms around his neck and clambered up onto his back. He was strong, with a broad muscular back. He smelt warm and of something soft and sandlewoody. It was oddly comforting to be lifted up as if she weighed next to nothing at all.

'Here,' he said, holding up an electronic key fob. 'Can you just lock the car for me?'

Liz did as she was asked. As soon as she was settled, the cabbie carried her across the road and up the gravel driveway. It wasn't the most elegant mode of transport but it seemed like a very sweet thing for him to do. She found herself tempted to rest her cheek against his shoulder.

'Are you okay?' she said.

'I'm fine, you hardly weigh a thing. Would you like me to take you over to the house?'

Liz didn't really have chance to answer as he was already striding out cross the front lawn, before turning around so she could step down onto the front doorstep.

'There you go,' he said with a smile, offering her his hand. 'All safe and sound.'

'Thank you. Have you driven all the way up from London?' she asked.

'Uh-huh, certainly did. I'd forgotten how

much I love this drive. I used to come up here a lot when I was a kid with my dad — and then later I'd bring him.'

Under the porch light she noticed just what gorgeous eyes he had.

There was a funny little electric pause, and Liz heard herself saying, 'Why don't you come in and have a drink, grab something to eat? I'm sure we can find you something before you head home. A cup of tea maybe?' She took a long look at his hands as he shook hers in a firm presidential style handshake. No rings, nice long fingers, strong and masculine.

'That would be great,' the driver was saying. 'My name's Max. And you are?'

'Liz,' said Liz.

'It's nice to meet you,' he said. 'Whoever you are.'

She laughed. 'Come on in,' she said, stepping aside to wave him by. She had felt tiny when he had been carrying her, tiny and safe, and she couldn't help wondering if there was a Mrs Max waiting patiently at home.

23

Megan and Simon had searched all the easy places. Hannah, Sadie and Tucker weren't at Megan's house and they weren't at the Rec or in any of the bus shelters or hanging about outside the pub, so that just left Sadie's house.

'The trouble is,' said Simon, stuffing his hands into jacket pockets as they walked back from the pub, 'they might not be at Sadie's house either. I mean, they could be anywhere by now, you know, like moving around?'

Megan sighed. *Boys*. 'I'm not stupid, Simon, I do know that. But we said we'd go up there and have a look, and I'm all out of other ideas.'

Simon said nothing, which made Megan think he hadn't got any other ideas either, and then he said, 'We've got this den down by the river but we don't usually go there after dark because the gamekeeper goes down there looking for poachers, and we don't want to get shot.'

'Sounds sensible,' said Megan.

'Maybe we could go round again. To double check.'

Megan sniffed.

'Sadie's house then?' said Simon grimly.

Megan nodded; it seemed as if Simon was as reluctant as she was. She didn't think he was afraid of the dark, but then again, maybe if you were friends with Sadie, there were other things to be frightened of.

They fell into step and a companionable silence. Megan didn't really know what to say to Simon. It wasn't that she felt uncomfortable with him — it was just that she had no idea what it was that boys talked about.

They walked through the village, past the shop and the green, by the church and up and out towards the old aerodrome, the houses getting further apart and the night getting altogether darker. The turning into Moongate Lane was lit by a single streetlight. The lane wasn't tarmacked and was pitted with great ruts and puddles, and the high overgrown hedges curling from either side seemed to emphasise the dense darkness beyond. It looked and felt as if they were walking into a cave. Megan's skin felt prickly and chilled even though she was wearing her fleece.

Breaking her stride, she peered into the gloom.

Simon, as if he had sensed she was no longer alongside him, turned back towards her and laughed.

'Come on, it's not far now,' he said. 'We're nearly there. Don't look so worried. We'll be fine.'

The very fact he felt the need to say it suggested to Megan that he wasn't quite as confident as he appeared.

* * *

'There you go,' said Sadie, handing Hannah another drink. Despite her best efforts to avoid it, Hannah had drunk quite a lot of the concoction that Sadie had mixed for them.

Once they had settled in her bedroom, Sadie had slipped back downstairs to the party and returned a few minutes later with a jug half full of what she said was a proper cocktail. Hannah had no idea what cocktails should taste like but this one was sweet and heavy, and tasted and looked a lot like cough mixture, even after Sadie had poured a great deal of value lemonade into it and swished it around. The mixture split and clung to the sides like oil as she stirred it.

Hannah knew there was some of the blue alcopop in there too because she had just seen Sadie pour half a bottle into the jug and stir it around with a ruler, but she had no idea what else there might be in it. There was no way she could avoid drinking it altogether because Sadie was watching her like a hawk.

'You just need to neck it down you,' said Sadie, waving another full glass at her. Hannah hesitated long enough for Sadie to shake her head, and down hers in one with a shudder. 'Oh come on. It's supposed to be a bloody party — and if you're worried about what Mummy and Daddy might say if you roll home pissed, then you can sleep here. Text them and let them know you'll be back tomorrow. Come on, get it down.'

Hannah glanced at the brimming glass and then at Sadie. There was something nasty and threatening in the set of her face.

'We're mates, aren't we?' Sadie cajoled, nodding towards the glass in her hand. 'Come on, it won't do you any harm and then I was thinking that we could maybe go downstairs, put some decent music on and have a bit of a dance.' She waved her hands above her head, aping dance moves.

'What's the matter?' she snorted, as Hannah took a tiny sip from the glass. 'Too grown-up for you? You maybe want a little bit more lemonade with that?' she continued in a mocking baby voice.

Hannah shuddered as she swallowed a mouthful of the glass's contents. The taste and the smell of it made her stomach heave.

'Lightweight,' Tucker commented as he knocked his back, chasing it down with one of the cans of beer that Sadie had brought with her from her foray downstairs.

Sadie's bedroom was tiny, barely more than a box room, tucked up under the eaves of the cottage. It was hot and smelt biscuity and stale like a hamster cage. Here and there the wallpaper had lifted and peeled away from the damp, uneven walls. There were piles of clothes heaped on the dressing table and on top of the chest of drawers, and other piles that had tipped over and tumbled onto the floor. You couldn't see the carpet for clothes, shoes, books, magazines, DVD cases, papers, and empty plates and cans.

Behind the door was a bare single mattress, with a pile of coats, an army blanket and a brown sleeping bag piled up on top of it. The sleeping bag was curled around the coats and there was a rip in the fabric where the stuffing was spilling out. It looked for all the world as if whoever had slept there had just left, leaving behind an empty chrysalis.

Hannah sighed. She didn't want to be there, she wanted to be home. Her head ached from the booze and the music from downstairs with its heavy heartbeat of bass, forcing its way in through the walls, up through the floor and into her bones.

Trying to drown out the noise of the party, Sadie had her music on full blast, creating a counter beat that was almost as loud. The cacophony was making Hannah's head pound and her teeth ache. A flatscreen television stood balanced on a piano stool by the dressing table. Tucker was busy killing things on the Playstation 3, sitting on the only chair, his fingers working into a blur over the buttons on the controller. Every few seconds the room lit up with great flashes and flares from the TV screen and the sounds of mortar and machine-gun fire from the game cut through the music.

Across the sea of debris on the bedroom floor Hannah and Sadie were sitting at either end of a single bed, which had been tucked up under the slanting roof and was covered in a faded Indian throw. Hannah could see how this room might once have been lovely, with its floral wallpaper and pretty leaded dormer window — a tiny textbook country cottage bedroom. But it was far from lovely at the moment.

Among a mish-mash of posters, stolen road signs and pictures torn from magazines, Sadie had taken a spray can of paint to the walls and the door and added her tag and various obscenities along with symbols of peace and war and all things in between. A collection of severed dolls' heads hung by their hair from the central light shade, and for a moment Hannah caught a glimpse of what it was that her mum saw when she walked into Hannah's room, and felt the same sense of despair. How could Sadie sleep in this horrible damp dank pit? Everything smelt as if it needed washing or throwing away. Hannah swallowed hard, choking down a taste of bile and booze. She didn't want to think about being sick again.

Sadie meanwhile was propped against the wall by the window, with half an eye on the comings and goings outside in the garden, and amusing herself in between by watching Hannah.

'Another drink?' she said, leaning forward to retrieve the jug, which was standing on her bedside cabinet.

Tucker nodded and held out his glass. Hannah really had had enough in all senses.

'I've got to go the loo,' she said, getting up unsteadily and heading for the door.

'Not going to be sick again, are you?' Sadie said, her attention wandering off to something out in the garden.

'No.'

'Good,' said Sadie. 'Just don't be too long. I'll pour you another one for when you get back — and hurry, you wouldn't want to miss anything now, would you?'

Hannah, with her hand on the doorknob, hesitated. 'Why, what's going to happen?'

Sadie laughed. 'Well, first of all me and Tucker will obviously miss your scintillating company, won't we, Tucker? And also because I've got a little surprise for everyone,' she said with a grin. Even Tucker turned around to look at her, his thumbs poised above the game controller.

'I found these when I was downstairs,' Sadie said. Between her finger and thumb she was holding a little plastic bag in which there were maybe half a dozen tiny tablets. She wafted the packet to and fro and grinned. 'So what do you say? You game? You want one?'

'What are they?' asked Hannah.

Sadie rolled her eyes. 'You know, you are such a bloody wimp, Hannah. I dunno, do I? I mean, I could probably take a guess but they'll be fine — the guy I lifted them off is a dealer. He's round here all the time. Really sound guy. So how about we think of them as a little present? Except of course he doesn't know that he's given them to us yet.' She giggled.

Hannah, avoiding Sadie's eye, nodded. 'Okay sure, I'll be back in a few minutes.'

'Don't be long,' said Sadie, peeling open the packet.

Out on the landing Hannah took a deep breath, trying to quell a sense of panic, while at the same time realising exactly how drunk she was. When she had been sitting down in Sadie's bedroom she had felt fine, but now up on her feet and outside in the real world she was finding it hard to stand. She also knew that whatever happened, however bad she felt, she had to get away and get away now. The wall lurched as she put out her hand to steady herself.

There was a queue all the way along the

landing for the bathroom upstairs. Four or five women waited in a straggling line, chatting, smoking, laughing, oblivious to Hannah joining them.

'Is there another loo?' she asked the woman immediately in front of her.

The woman nodded. 'Yeah, outside apparently, but I can't find my sandals and I'm not walking around out there without them.' Giggling, she lifted up her long purple velvet skirt to reveal big bare brown feet with rings on the toes. She looked at Hannah's ballet shoes. 'You'll be okay — it's only over by the log store. It's not like it's muddy or anything.'

Hannah thanked her and made her way unsteadily past the people sitting on the stairs and crammed into the hallway. She eased her way between the party-goers packed into the kitchen, and finally out of the back door and into the cool night air.

Even though she was glad to be outside, away from the press of bodies, the music and the noise, the fresh air made her feel drunker still. It took her a few seconds to get her bearings. The outside loo had a sign above it and was across a little enclosed yard beyond the back door. There was another woman queuing outside, sucking on a roll-up as if her life depended on it.

'Hannah,' called a voice from somewhere above her. She glanced up; she had forgotten that Sadie had a view out over the garden. 'What're you doing?'

'I won't be a minute,' Hannah said, pointing towards the toilet in a pantomime gesture.

'There's a long queue upstairs.'

'Okay, well don't be long, we're waiting for you,' Sadie said in a spooky jokey voice, before pulling the bedroom window closed.

Hannah nodded and turned away. By the time she had crossed the yard the woman had gone and the toilet door was ajar. Once inside Hannah bolted the door tight, sat down and considered her options. One thing Hannah was clear about was that there was no way she was going back upstairs and take any of those tablets, but she also didn't want to have to stand up to Sadie if she could possibly avoid it.

It was so odd how things had turned around. When they had first started being friends it felt as if by having Sadie around Hannah was finally having fun, had finally arrived, and living the kind of life she had always imagined herself living.

She had loved going into town on the bus and hanging around together, or going to the pictures, or just chilling at the park or at Sadie's place, listening to music, watching DVDs or sitting around down in the woods. Looking back, it felt like they laughed a lot at people and the stupid things they said and did. But things had started to slowly change and these days there were more and more things happening that Hannah didn't like.

Hannah knew Sadie stole things from shops because she'd seen her. It hadn't been long before Sadie had wanted her to do the same, and so in the end Hannah had, just the once, just to shut her up. Even now, sitting in the toilet all on her own, thinking about it made her feel sick.

They had gone into Beloes the chemist in town. It had been at lunchtime when it was really busy and there were only two people behind the counter. While the Saturday girl was serving customers, Sadie had started asking the lady in the pharmacy about athlete's foot cream, which was so gross. But anyway, while she had been asking the woman all these questions Hannah had gone round to the make-up counter and slipped some make-up into her rucksack.

She could still feel the fear now, could still remember the way her heart had practically buzzed in her chest because it was beating so fast. She had lain awake all night waiting for the police to come round and arrest her, while worrying about what her mum and dad would say. A tube of lipstick and a navy-blue eyeliner pencil were just not worth that kind of stress and she'd never done it since. And now she hated going into town with Sadie, because Sadie was likely to steal something and Hannah knew it was only a matter of time before they got caught.

She had always known that Sadie took drugs too, not like seriously or anything, but at parties and when they were hanging out Sadie would roll a joint and hand it around. So far Hannah had managed to avoid it, despite Sadie's teasing. But pills were something else; Hannah wanted to be cool, not off her face or dead.

The idea that she had been formulating on the way downstairs was shaping up into something real. She had to get away. She would creep outside, making sure that Sadie wasn't looking, staying tucked in close to the wall. As soon as Hannah was certain Sadie hadn't seen her, she'd slip away. Although maybe not back to her grandparents' party — Hannah wasn't sure she could face her mum and dad yet. Maybe she would just go straight home. The idea of her own room and her own bed felt like heaven.

'Are you going to be long?' shouted someone from outside, banging on the toilet door. The noise made her jump.

'Won't be a minute,' Hannah called back. She washed her hands and splashed her face with cold water, hoping it might help to sober her up. There was a towel on a hook in the toilet but it was stiff and dirty, so she dried her hands and face on her cardigan instead and then very slowly opened the door. Outside a large woman and her boyfriend were deep in a loud conversation, blocking her from view as the door opened. She stole a glance up towards the bedroom window; Sadie wasn't looking.

Hurrying across the few feet of open space, Hannah slipped into the little crush of people gathered in the yard. Head down, she eased between them until she reached the far wall where she hoped Sadie wouldn't be able to see her. A moment or two later she was edging her way around the party-goers, and then out across the front garden, all the time keeping to the shadows. As she got beyond the apple trees she could see the lane and felt her tension easing. Not wanting to strike out across the lawn, Hannah stayed close to a tangle of old sheds that ran along the boundary fence. Just another few seconds and she would be clear. But as Hannah reached the last of the derelict buildings, she felt a hand drop onto her shoulder and shrieked in a mixture of surprise and fear.

Swinging round, she came face to face with Dexter, the man from the hallway. Looking into his eyes, she knew with terrifying clarity that he had followed her from the house.

'Well, hello there, baby,' Dexter purred, stepping in closer so that she had to back up into the doorway of one of the sheds to avoid touching him. It took her a split second to realise that he had her trapped.

Dexter grinned. 'Well, well, well, I wondered where you'd got to. Not thinking of going home yet, are you, eh?' he said. His eyes were as dark as coal in the moonlight. 'I was thinking maybe you and me could have a little fun — maybe a little dancing.' He moved his shoulders and hips in an obscene parody of a slow dance. She could smell the booze on his breath. Her pulse was racing as he took a step closer, backing her deeper into the filthy shed. From the corner of her eye she could see a tumble of oil drums and broken pallets, a stack of rotting sacks, piles of wood — and on the windowsill propped up against the broken empty window was a small plump naked doll. Hannah swallowed hard. She didn't want to be here. The place looked like something out of a horror movie: anything could happen here, anything at all. Fear drove the adrenaline through her veins like molten lava.

Dexter grinned. He was taller than her by a foot, and much, much bigger in every other sense. Everything about him made her nervous and his wolfish expression suggested that that was exactly the effect he was hoping for.

'Thanks but I don't want to dance,' she said. 'I've got to go home. My mum and dad are expecting me.' Her tiny little voice sounded pathetic in the gloom.

'Really,' Dexter said, closing in on her. 'So do they know where you are? Out here with our Sadie? I'm surprised that your mum and dad let a nice little thing like you mix with someone like her — or are appearances deceptive?' He was so close now that she could feel the heat of his body and smell his sweat.

'Yes . . . I mean, no,' she stammered.

Dexter was closer now, leering at her. The way he looked her up and down made her flesh creep.

'So which is it then, yes or no?' he murmured. 'Why don't you tell me, sweetpea?'

She couldn't even remember what the question was. 'Look, I really need to be going, my dad is going to be here any minute,' she stammered.

He must have sensed it was a bluff or maybe he didn't care because as Hannah tried to step past him Dexter grabbed her arm and pulled her close trying to grab her around the waist and kiss her. It was such a shock that she yelled out in terror.

'Sssssh, shut up, doesn't do to fight it, sweetie,' he said, holding her tighter. His breath was foul and he smelt of stale sweat and cheap aftershave and something dark and feral. 'It'll be fine, just you see. You'll like it, I promise — come to Dexter.' And then he pressed his body close up against hers and with drunken heavy hands made a grab for the front of her shirt.

'Get off me,' she whimpered. 'Please, you're hurting me. Stop it — stop it — ' she begged, all the while struggling to push him away. But instead of letting her go Dexter looked down and laughed, and she saw in a moment of comprehension that he was enjoying her fear and fight. The realisation lit a great flare of fury within her and a screaming banshee wail came from somewhere down deep in her chest. He looked startled by the noise.

The next few seconds seemed to take forever, seared into her retina in the brightest sharpest colours. Before the scream had time to stop Hannah had brought up her knee as hard as she could into Dexter's groin. He let out a strange strangled howl and as he crumbled forward, Hannah punched him hard in the face. She was stunned as much by her own actions as by Dexter's obvious pain and surprise.

'I said, *get off me*,' she snarled, in between great sobs of fear and fury.

Before he could recover, Hannah pushed him away, and as he stumbled she ran out of the shed, charging through the gate and exploding out into the lane, trembling, crying, her heart beating like a steam hammer in her chest, wondering how long it would take Dexter to recover. She looked left and right, mind racing. Should she try and out-run him, or head back in the house and get help — and was there anyone inside the house who would help her?

The adrenaline coursing through her was burning off the effects of the booze and leaving a great raw slew of emotions behind — how dare he think he could touch her like that, *how dare he?* She was filled with so much rage and disgust and anger that for a split second Hannah didn't notice that there were people standing out in the lane.

'Hannah?' said a voice.

She looked up, fearing it might be Sadie but at the same time knowing that it wasn't.

'Megan?' she said in amazement. Breathing hard, she stared at her little sister. 'What on earth are you doing up here?'

'I thought I ought to come and find you, I was worried about you,' Megan said. 'Simon showed me where it was. Are you all right?'

Hannah looked at the two of them. She opened her mouth to say something sharp and sarcastic, something that Sadie might say, but instead she said, 'I'm so pleased to see you, but we really need to get out of here. There is this man, he tried to grab me — '

And with that Dexter staggered out a few yards behind her, still clutching his groin. 'Come back here, you little bitch,' he shouted.

Before Hannah could say anything Megan pointed at him and bellowed, 'Fuck off, you dirty old man, before we ring the police.' Her voice cut through the night like a knife.

Dexter blinked and peered at her. A couple of men who were smoking on the lawn over by the trees turned to see what all the fuss was about, while another little group moved closer to join them.

'He tried to grab my sister,' Megan continued, still shouting but now for the benefit of the audience. 'Him.' She carried on pointing.

Simon stepped up alongside Megan. 'That's him,' he echoed, his gaze catching Hannah's. She could see the concern in his face and felt tears prickling up behind her eyes.

Dexter snorted. 'What's this, the fucking Waltons?' he growled. 'She wanted it. Little bitch was all over me like a rash.'

Simon took another step forward. 'I don't think so,' he said, squaring up to the older, bigger man. Alongside him, Megan, hands on her hips, stepped forward too.

One of the men who had been standing by the trees came over. 'Come on in, Dex,' he said, catching hold of Dexter's arm. 'Leave it, mate. Let's go back inside and grab a beer — come on. How's it going to look, you beating up a kid?'

Drunkenly Dexter squared his shoulders. 'She was all over me,' he mumbled.

'Yeah, yeah, yeah,' said the guy with obvious distaste, and then he turned to the three of them. 'I'd get out of here if I were you, we'll get him back in the house.'

Megan tugged at Hannah's sleeve. 'Come on,' she said. 'Let's go home.'

'Are you okay?' Simon said anxiously.

Hannah felt the great welter of tears bubbling up and struggled to hold them back. 'No, not really. But I will be. Come on,' she said. 'I just want to go home.'

The three of them started off down the lane towards the village. As they did, Simon caught hold of her hand and smiled, and Hannah returned the compliment by catching hold of Megan's hand and squeezing it gently. Megan looked up and grinned as they wordlessly made their way back to the village. At no point did Hannah hesitate or look back. There was nothing in Moongate Lane that she ever wanted to see again.

* * *

Back in the marquee Fleur was standing by the bar watching Peter Hudson dancing with Mary. There was no doubt that they made a handsome couple. As he twirled Mary around Peter glanced in Fleur's direction, with a smile that most definitely said, 'This could be you.'

Fleur shook her head in disbelief — the arrogance of the man was astonishing — but even so she still couldn't quite bring herself to look away.

When Peter had started talking to her about the good old days earlier on in the evening, there had been a part of her that had been flattered, and for the briefest of moments she had thought about what it was she might have missed, and smiled at those memories of her younger self. After all, it was true that all those years ago she *had* wanted Peter in a feral, lustful kind of way.

Looking back, it was easy to see how different her life would have been if she had carried on lusting after him and they had made different choices after Rose and Jack's wedding reception. And how badly wrong it could have all gone, she thought wryly, as Peter twirled Mary one more time and did a fancy little dip at the end of the sequence. The man was a manipulative bully, and she had had a lucky escape, said the sensible voice in her head.

It didn't matter what Peter told her, Fleur knew very well that this particular leopard would never have changed his spots, and all these years later, chances are she would have been the one being cheated on. Sometimes hindsight was a powerful thing, but even though Fleur was relieved that she hadn't ended up with Peter, there was a part of her that couldn't help but hanker after the good old days, the craziness of youth, all that desire and excitement, and the feeling that you would live forever and that anything and everything was possible.

Feeling tired and old and lonely, Fleur waved the barmaid over to refill her glass. She looked up at the banner above the top table and sighed. Forty years on, what had she got to show for life?

When her phone started to ring again Fleur was very tempted to ignore it. She didn't want to speak to anyone, didn't want to tell Frank her address or admit just how much she missed him, or how very sad she felt being here all on her own, but it kept on ringing and so eventually Fleur took it out. It said Frank again on the caller display, which came as no surprise.

'Hello?' she said. 'You still there?'

He laughed. 'Oh yes. Flowers for Fleur Halliday?'

Fleur laughed in spite of herself. 'You already told me that, Frank — and I'm touched and I promise that just as soon as the flowers get here I'll text you and let you know. You sound drunk.'

'And you look beautiful,' he said, which took her by complete surprise.

'Really?' she said. 'And how would you . . . ' The word *know* lingered on her lips unspoken. Something about the way Frank said *beautiful*, something about the warmth and conviction in his voice made her look up, and as she did she caught sight of a familiar figure standing by the entrance to the marquee, carrying a huge bouquet of roses.

'Frank, is that you?' she said into the phone.

He laughed and waved. 'It most certainly is. I thought you might be lonely over here all on your own.'

Still talking into the phone, Fleur climbed down from her bar stool and hurried over towards him. 'You know that I hate flowers, don't you?' she said, smiling, as she eased her way between the people.

'Yup, although the good news is these ones aren't real — they're silk or something, and the woman in the shop said all you've got to do to keep them looking good is give them a real good shake once in a while.'

She was nearly there now.

'I'd like to give you a damn good shake, having me on like that,' she said, purring now.

'You'd rather I hadn't come?' he said.

Fleur beamed. 'You took the words right out of my mouth.'

'Well, hello there, gorgeous,' Frank said, still with the phone to his ear. 'You know, about ten minutes after your flight left I realised just how much I was going to miss you being around, bossing me about, telling me what to do. I didn't think I'd be able to manage without you telling me what to wear and why I shouldn't eat — well, you know, whatever it is that I shouldn't be eating.'

'Really?' Fleur said. 'But I didn't think . . . ' she began, her eyes bright with tears, as she finally switched off her phone.

'What was it you didn't think, eh? That I cared? Or that I loved you?'

Fleur felt her jaw drop. '*You love me?*' she gasped. 'Are you serious?'

He grinned. 'Never more so. In fact I love you so much I've just paid a bloody fortune to have that mangy stray you've been feeding for months taken off to the vet and neutered while I'm away.'

She laughed. 'You're all heart, Frank Callaby.'

'I couldn't wait three weeks to see you again, Fleur, and I couldn't let you come over here thinking — well, I don't really know exactly what you were thinking, but my guess is that I didn't come out of it well.'

She looked at him, for once totally at a loss for words. 'Oh Frank,' she murmured, realising just how much she had missed him.

'Anyway, before you pull yourself together and tear me off a strip, there's something I wanted to ask you.' He paused.

'What?' said Fleur. 'Don't tell me, you want to

borrow the cab fare? What is it? Come on.'

He grinned. 'You're always so bloody impatient. I want to ask if you'll marry me.'

She stared at him, all the bravado and bluster entirely blown away. She had heard the words clearly enough but couldn't find any to answer him with. It seemed like an age before he said, 'So what do you reckon then? Is it a goer? Or do you want to phone a friend?'

'Oh Frank . . . ' Fleur said, finally finding her voice. 'Yes, yes.'

He grinned. 'Yes, yes?'

'Yes, yes, I'll marry you — of course I will.'

And with that Frank took her in his arms and kissed her long and hard. As he pulled away he said, 'Oh bloody hell, I almost forgot I bought you something else as well.' And from his pocket he produced a tiny padded box. 'I know you don't like flowers very much but I'm hoping you don't feel the same way about diamonds.'

Inside the box was a white gold engagement ring set with a solitaire diamond that caught and reflected the light in the marquee.

'Oh Frank, I love it,' she whispered. 'It's absolutely beautiful.'

He smiled. 'I was hoping you'd say that. Here, let's see if it fits — '

She held out her hand and very gently he slipped the ring onto her finger. It fitted perfectly. Fleur wriggled her fingers. 'It fits like it was made for me. How on earth did you manage that?' she asked in amazement.

'You remember when Lola the head waitress at your place got engaged last year and you told me you tried on her ring?'

'That's right. It was a tiny bit too big, but that girl was determined that I try on the damn thing. I was worried it would slip off down the cracks in the deck.'

'Uh-huh, and you said that you'd read somewhere that statistically women over forty had more chance of being murdered than married?'

She laughed. 'That'd be me.'

'Well, I took Lola down to Lake Street before I left Cairns and we got her finger measured up and I bought a half size smaller.'

Fleur stared at him. 'Seriously?'

He nodded.

'So all the staff know about this as well?'

'Oh Christ, yes,' said Frank. 'The staff and all your regulars and your neighbours, and that weird little guy with the dodgy moustache who runs the crystal healing place next door — it's them that sent you the flowers.'

And with that Frank leant forward and kissed her and she never wanted that feeling, welling up like champagne bubbles in a glass, to ever end.

Finally, breathless and weak-kneed, Fleur pulled away and grinned. 'Oh Frank,' she said, through tears of joy. 'Come and meet my family.'

* * *

If Fleur had looked up at that particular moment she would have seen the look of shock and amazement on Peter Hudson's face as Mary, fresh from the dance floor and breathing hard, leant in close to tell him that she was sick to death of him, had met someone else and wanted a divorce. ASAP.

* * *

Out in the back garden, Suzie was beside herself with worry. As she moved between the groups of party-goers it was getting harder and harder to keep up the appearance that there was nothing wrong. Despite searching high and low, ringing home, and ringing their mobiles, there was still no sign of the girls or Sam. This was crazy. They had to be somewhere. Suzie was beginning to panic.

She had looked everywhere she could think of, and was just taking another look around the back of the summerhouse before walking home to check on the house, when she heard the back gate creak open and swing shut. As she turned she saw Sam heading across the grass. He looked like a man on a mission.

'Sam!' His name came out in a rush of relief and tears.

'Suzie?' He looked up at the sound of her voice. 'What are you doing round here?

'God, I'm so glad I've found you. I've been looking for you everywhere — you and the girls. I can't find them anywhere.' She stopped. 'Oh Sam, I was really worried about you, are you okay?'

'Me? I'm fine,' he said, sheepishly. She couldn't remember him looking so ill at ease. 'We really need to talk, Suzie.'

'I know. I heard about you and Matt,' she said. 'He said you tried to punch him and I wanted to tell you — '

But Sam held up his finger to her lips. 'No, I want to talk. I've been a complete idiot, Suzie, I wanted to tell you that I'm sorry — '

'No, most of this feels like it's my fault,' Suzie said. 'I've been trying to find a way to tell you about me and Matt for weeks but I just didn't know where to start.'

Even before she had finished speaking Suzie saw Sam's face fall as surely as if she had slapped him and an instant later realised what she had just said and how it must sound.

'Oh God,' Sam said. 'So it's true then. You're leaving me, aren't you?'

Something tightened like a fist in her chest. 'No, of course not, God, no Sam. No, I'm not leaving you. No, it's that Matt and I have been offered this fabulous opportunity; a production company want to make a TV programme about his restaurant and the walled garden. We're going to talk to them next week to sort out the details and go through the contract.'

'We?'

'Matt and I, He's worked with them before.'

'So it's a done deal?'

'Well, more or less.'

Sam stared at her. 'Bloody hell, a TV show? Really? That's amazing.'

Suzie nodded. 'It is, isn't it? And it's such a brilliant opportunity, and the money's good and it'll mean we can do loads of the things we'd planned down there. The greenhouse, the big cold frames, sort out the sheds and maybe do something to the old gardener's cottage — there's so much we could do if we had the money. And it'll be good for us too — you and me and the girls. I wanted to talk to you about it and discuss it and I wanted you to be pleased about it, but . . . ' Suzie stopped and stared at Sam anxiously, not quite sure how to go on.

'But you weren't sure that I would be pleased?'

Suzie nodded. 'No, or how you'd feel about it. We don't seem to have had much time for each other recently. And I know a lot of it's been my fault, I've been so busy. I should have found the time. But . . . ' She stopped and looked up at him. 'Sam, I hate this. What on earth happened to us? We've always been so good together and now we just seem so far apart. Is it my fault?'

Sam looked into her eyes, his own bright with tears. 'God, no, Suzie. It's not you at all, I think it's me. I've been a complete waste of space the last couple of years. Life just seems to have been changing so fast, what with the girls growing up and you out at work.' He stopped, voice crackling with emotion. 'It's crazy but even saying this aloud I feel like some kind of nineteen-thirties throwback. I don't know how else to explain it really — I suppose I've been feeling left out and neglected.' He laughed grimly. 'I mean how grown up does that sound? Great big grown-up man that I am, I've been sulking.' He smiled at her. 'And I know I've been grumpy. I'm so sorry, so very sorry. Can you forgive me? I've been an idiot.'

'Oh Sam,' she murmured. The man smiling down at her was the man she knew, the man she had loved since she was barely out of her teens. 'I've missed you,' she whispered.

He leant close. 'Suzie,' he said softly. 'I've missed you too. I've been so worried. We just stopped noticing and talking and we've both been letting things slide. I think we've been in this relationship so long that we've taken *us* for granted.'

She was about to take his hand when Sam said, 'So where exactly does Matt fit into all this?'

'I'm not sure what you mean, what about Matt?'

'You and him.'

Suzie shook her head and laughed. 'There is no *me and him* in the way you mean it. He's helping to set up the TV deal, or at least the initial contacts — and we'll be working together to plan the planting so that next year we'll be growing things that he can cook. And there's a book planned for the series that they've asked me to write. It's one of the reasons why we need to introduce some animals and look at other farmers and growers in the area. Matt's partner, Rory, is going to help us source ingredients. He's got this fantastic organic farm over at Fallham Bulbeck — besides meat, they're making butter, cheese and yoghurt over there.'

'His partner? You mean business partner?'

Suzie shook her head. 'No, Rory and Matt are a couple, they've been together for years.' Suzie glanced up at him, watching the penny drop.

'So you're not . . . ' The words faltered and stalled. 'You and him,' Sam continued lamely. 'I thought that you were — '

'You thought we were having an affair.'

He ran his hand back through his hair. 'I hadn't really given it that much thought until tonight.' He stared at her. 'I don't know why but all of a sudden it seemed so obvious when I thought about it and then the thought just wouldn't go away. You and Matt have been spending so much time together and you seem so comfortable in his company.' He paused. 'And I've been such a pig.'

'We've been really busy. There has been so much to talk about.'

'I know — I didn't want to believe that you and him were having an affair, but then I started to think about how things have been between us, how I've been treating you, and there was a part of me that would have almost understood if you had been seeing someone else.' He looked at her. 'Part of me thought I deserved it.' He stopped and took hold of her hands. 'I thought I'd lost you, Suzie — I really did, and I realised that I couldn't bear to live without you. You're my life.' His voice cracked and broke.

Suzie's eyes filled with tears. 'Oh Sam. I've only been spending so much time with Matt because there has just been so much to do, and to be honest, I've needed someone to talk it all through with — all this is new territory to me.'

'And you couldn't talk to me?' Sam sounded deflated.

'You didn't seem interested; you've been so

distant recently. I thought there was something wrong at work. Or that maybe . . .' She paused, reluctant to say the words aloud. 'I was worried that maybe you didn't want to talk to me any more. That you'd gone off me.' It sounded childish when she said it out loud but it was the thing that Suzie had feared the most. 'I'm so sorry.'

'We can put it right though, can't we?' he said in a low even voice. 'Or are you telling me that it's over; is this it?'

'Oh Sam, of course it isn't *it*. It never occurred to me in a million years that this was the end — more like a new beginning. But you are right. We can't go on like this, not all moody and silent and distant or there's no point. I just wish we talked about it earlier; it's kind of crept up, this not talking to each other thing. We used to talk all the time.' She paused. 'And at least half the fault is mine.'

'Okay, how about we talk about how we're going to put it right tomorrow?'

'You mean it?'

He nodded. 'Uh-huh — practical ways to sort it out. How about we go out to lunch, just you and me and talk about us?'

Suzie was about to protest that there was just too much to do and so many things that needed sorting out, but the words died in her mouth; wasn't that exactly how they had got to this point in the first place?

'I'd love to,' she said.

Gently he bent down and kissed her, slipping his arms around her, and for a second the music from the marquee seemed to bubble up and catch them like a tide and Sam slowly began to dance with her. She giggled, forgetting everything except how good it felt to be with him and to be in his arms, and how good it had always felt. He pulled her close up against his chest and they began to dance around the lawn.

'You're drunk,' she teased.

He kissed her neck. 'I know, but I'd do this whether I was drunk or not. We should do more of it. A lot more of it. You know I love you with all my heart, Suzie, don't you? I thought for one awful moment that I'd lost you. It's so good to be back.'

'What about the girls?'

He pulled her closer. 'They're bound to be here somewhere. We'll look for them together.'

And all the tension and the fear she had been feeling over the last few days and weeks and months ebbed away as his arms closed tight around her, and she let the music lead them through the shadows, into the soft warm darkness behind the marquee.

24

Inside the marquee Rose needed a breather from all the dancing. She hadn't danced so much in years, and the long, long day was beginning to take its toll. While Jack went off to fetch them both a drink she sat down and took the time to catch her breath and look around the faces of the people gathered to help celebrate all the years they had spent together.

When it came down to it, just exactly how many years wasn't the point, surely? They had loved each other through thick and thin, bad times and good. Love could have so many faces and be so many things in a lifetime. Being *in love* was different from loving someone, and both were very different from falling in love. She and Jack had done all these and more over the years they had been together.

Out on the dance floor, in the garden, gathered around the tables were their friends, neighbours, relatives, work colleagues, and as Rose put names to faces, she smiled to herself and thought how lucky they had been to get this far surrounded by so many good people.

'Penny for them,' said a woman standing beside her.

Rose looked up. 'Oh Janet, how lovely to see you,' she said, getting up to give her a hug. 'We were looking for you earlier to come and have your photo taken with the rest of the crew.' Rose laughed. 'The girls were desperate for us to re-do the original wedding photos. You're looking good.'

Janet slipped into the seat alongside her. 'I'm sorry I missed it, I've only just arrived. I hope you don't mind me showing up late, but Tony and I have been over in the States to stay with his sister for the last two weeks and we only got back last night.'

'Is he here?' said Rose glancing around.

'No, he's exhausted. In fact, I wasn't sure I'd be able to make it either. I've booked into a little B&B just up the road. I'm hoping I can get a cab later.'

'You can always stay at ours if you get stuck. There's plenty of room.'

Janet smiled. 'Still the same old Rose, I see. You know, it's really good to see you again. I was trying to think how many years it's been since I've seen you — anyway, you look fantastic too.'

Rose smiled. 'Thank you. I don't feel it, I'm absolutely shattered, but it's lovely of you to say so . . . Obviously life up north suits you.' She looked over towards the bar. 'Jack will be back in a minute; he's just gone to get a drink. Would you like something to eat? I'm sure we can rustle you something up if you're hungry?'

'No, I've already eaten, thank you,' said Janet, holding up her hands to decline the offer.

There was a tiny but weighty and rather uncomfortable silence between them, and then both women began to talk at once. 'The girls don't know, we didn't tell them — ' Rose began, just as Janet said, 'I was a bit surprised to be invited to be honest — '

And then they looked at each other, woman to woman, and Rose smiled and said, 'I'm glad they did ask you, it really is good to see you, Janet, but I have to tell you that Suzie and Liz, they have no idea who you are.' Rose was aware that she sounded defensive. 'Peter Hudson told them about Jack and me being divorced tonight — just before the party.'

Janet stared at her. 'Really? Oh my God. Trust Peter.'

'I know, I wish it hadn't come out like that, and before you say anything I know we should have said something before.'

'Did he say anything about me?'

Rose shook her head. 'No — he didn't get that far.'

'Well, that certainly explains why they invited me.'

'We just never got around to telling them.'

'What, none of it?' Janet asked incredulously. She laughed. 'Oh God, that is just so like you, Rose — '

'Stop saying that,' said Rose. 'Jack's as bad.'

'No, he's worse. Anything for a quiet life.'

'You make him sound weak,' protested Rose.

Janet smiled gently. 'Well, we both know he isn't weak, don't we? Just too kind sometimes, that's all. He was always a good man, Rose, trouble is he just doesn't know when it's better to be cruel.' She paused. 'I hadn't realised that Suzie and Liz didn't know. I wanted to say thank you for letting me be here tonight. It really is nice to see you again. Even after all these years and all the things that have happened there are times when I still think about the good old days and what good friends we were. I miss you . . . '

Rose felt her eyes prickle with tears. 'Me too, although I'm not sure it would have worked out any other way.'

'No, me neither. I know Tony couldn't have dealt with it if we had stayed around here. It's one of the reasons he didn't want to be here tonight.'

'He didn't mind you coming?'

'I don't think he was that keen but he's another good man, Rose.'

Rose nodded. 'The girls didn't have any idea when they invited the two of you.'

And then Jack was there with their drinks. There was a moment when Rose could see that he was totally wrong-footed, and then finally he said, 'Janet, glad you could make it. How are you?' He leant in to peck her on the cheek. 'You're looking well.'

'You too, and what a great turn out,' she said, looking around the room. 'Congratulations. Forty years give or take is no mean feat.'

Rose and Jack exchanged glances, and then Rose said. 'The party was a complete surprise, we had no idea, you know.' And they talked about the food and the marquee and going to the gardens with Fleur and somewhere in among the pleasantries the tension between them gradually eased.

'Let me go and get you a drink, Janet,' said Jack. 'What would you like?'

Janet grinned. 'I'm very tempted to say the

usual but I'm not sure how good your memory is after all these years, so how about we settle on a glass of white wine and call it quits?'

Jack nodded. 'Right you are,' he said. 'Tell you what, why don't you take mine? I'll just go and get another,' and with that he headed back towards the bar.

Janet laughed at his retreating back. 'Running away.'

'I don't think so,' said Rose. 'I'm sure he was as surprised as I was to see you. Let's sit down, shall we?' said Rose, indicating the seats.

'Don't mind if I do for a few minutes and then I really ought to go and find the girls,' said Janet. 'You know of course that technically I was married to Jack for almost twice as long as you were.'

Rose smiled grimly. 'I know, but no one else here does.'

'So did you and Jack get married again?'

Rose shook her head. 'No — once bitten twice shy. Don't get me wrong there's never been anyone else and I love Jack more than — well, I don't need to tell you, but I felt so trapped before, it felt claustrophobic. He asked me on and off over the years.' She paused. 'Maybe one day, but not now. I'm happy as we are.'

Janet lifted her glass and clinked it against Rose's. 'Our secret.'

Rose raised her eyebrows. *But probably not for long*, she thought as she took a sip of wine.

* * *

'So where do you think the girls have got to?' Sam asked Suzie, as they made their way around to the front of the marquee.

Suzie looked up at him. 'I had been hoping that you would be able to tell me.' Suzie's voice caught in her throat. 'For a while there it felt like I'd lost my whole family.'

Sam took hold of her hand. 'Well, you haven't. Come on, they've got to be around here somewhere. Have you tried ringing the house?'

'There isn't anywhere I haven't tried. I've rung, I've texted — nothing.' Although I suppose if they are at home it doesn't mean they'd answer the phone. Maybe they're watching TV or up in their rooms. I was just about to walk back there when I found you.'

'Okay, we'll take one last look around here and then I suggest we head home to check. Chances are Hannah thinks she is in trouble,' said Sam, walking back towards the cottage. 'The last time I saw her she was running out of the back gate with that girl she's been hanging about with, the one with the blue hair, and a couple of bottles of booze.'

Suzie stared at him. 'Sadie?'

Sam nodded. 'That's the one.'

'Was Megan with them?'

'No, just Hannah, Sadie and some boy.'

'And you didn't go after them?' said Suzie in amazement.

Sam shook his head miserably. 'No, I'm not proud of this but I was too drunk. And I deserve that look. I'd just threatened to punch Matt out — I was in no state to go anywhere. Matt and a waitress went. By that stage he was a lot quicker than me. I don't know whether he managed to catch them up. Look, I'm sorry, Suzie,' Sam said, looking horribly contrite, 'but I wasn't in any fit state to go anywhere. My mind was on other things. And I can't remember the last time Hannah spoke to me without us ending up having an argument. I assumed she'd just come back as soon as we were out of sight. You know what she's been like the last few months.'

Suzie nodded. 'Hannah, and how we handle her, is something else that we really need to talk about, Sam.'

'I know, so let's take one more look around the marquee and the garden, and then we'll go home and see if the two of them are there.' He paused. 'Don't worry. I'm sure they'll be all right. Hannah is a big girl — and Megan is sensible.'

Suzie nodded. 'It's not Megan I'm worried about,' she said.

They did one more circuit. As they made their way around the marquee, Suzie saw the young woman who had spoken to her earlier deep in conversation with a couple of other people. Suzie made an effort not to catch her eye or draw attention to herself: she wanted to find her girls, not be drawn into helping someone else.

'Suzie? Suzie, *over here*.' Still trying hard to be invisible, Suzie winced as Fleur called to her and waved madly from the far side of the tent. Fleur shouldered her way between the revellers. It took Suzie a moment or two to realise that Fleur was hand in hand with a tall, good-looking, tanned man, who looked to be around the same age as her aunt. Probably someone from the good old days, thought Suzie, to judge from the expression of sheer delight on Fleur's face.

'Suzie, Sam, there you are, I wondered where you'd got to. I'd like you to meet Frank. Frank's my neighbour or at least he was. We're going to get married!' she squealed, wriggling her left hand excitedly under Suzie's nose. 'I've got a ring and everything.'

Alongside her Frank was grinning from ear to ear, looking for all the world like the dog who had got the doughnut.

* * *

At Suzie and Sam's house Hannah was fighting her way into the kitchen where Sam had shut the dogs earlier.

'Get back, get back, go!' said Hannah firmly to the posse of wet noses and wagging tails that greeted them as she pushed open the kitchen door. The two family dogs, a big blonde mongrel and a small hairy crossbreed terrier called Pip and Squeak, were delighted that she, Megan and Simon had decided to come home, taking their arrival as a personal triumph.

The family cats, Sid and Harry, tried very hard to look hard done by and miffed, but in the end couldn't resist and trotted over in a show of synchronised neediness, purring and mewing for attention.

Hannah looked around the cosy familiar interior of the family kitchen. It felt as if she had been away for months rather than a few hours.

Home now, she finally let out a long breath as the back door closed and the tension eased out of her shoulders.

Simon meanwhile had crouched down to stroke everyone who came within reach.

'Wow, they are just so cool,' he said, with a big cheesy grin as Pip started licking his ears and Squeak leapt into his lap, while the cats tried very hard to wind themselves into a perfect clove hitch around his ankles.

Hannah and Megan's eyes met and they both burst out laughing. The relief of stepping in through the kitchen door and being greeted by the dogs and cats was so great and so special that Hannah could hardly hold back the tears and for a moment she felt almost overwhelmed by the simple joy of just being home with people she knew and cared for — even Simon came under that umbrella at that moment.

'I'm really hungry,' said Megan, making a show of normality. 'Anyone else fancy pizza?'

Simon nodded. 'Sounds good to me. I'm starving. Do you want a hand to sort it out?'

* * *

'I'm just going to go upstairs and have a quick shower,' said Hannah. 'If you want to watch TV or something, Simon, I won't be long.'

'It's okay, I'll switch it on for you if you like,' said Megan briskly. 'Only Dad's really picky about who plays with his toys. Unless of course you want to play a boardgame or something. Are you any good at Monopoly? Or we've got

Scrabble if you like. I'm allowed to use the dictionary because I'm littler than everyone else,' said Megan, looking anything but. 'You fancy a game?'

'You going to be all right?' Simon asked Hannah as Megan selected a pizza from the freezer.

Hannah nodded. 'I'm fine. I just need to go and get cleaned up.' She didn't plan to tell him that she felt dirty and spoilt and more than anything else she wanted to wash Dexter's pawprints and the smell of Sadie's house out of her hair and off her body.

'Pizza in twenty minutes,' said Megan conversationally. 'You want a hot chocolate or a can of Coke or something with it? Or we could have chocolate spread sandwiches.'

Hannah laughed as her little sister fussed around the kitchen. 'Mother hen.'

Megan shrugged. 'Please yourself, you don't have to have one if you don't want.'

'I'd really like a hot chocolate,' said Hannah. 'With marshmallows.'

Simon nodded. 'Me too. Come on, I'll give you a hand.' And gently moving the dogs to one side, he bobbed down to switch on the oven for Megan.

Hannah could hear them talking from the landing, chatting about whether they all should go back to the party once they'd eaten or maybe stay in and play Monopoly. Megan was telling Simon how good she was at it and how he'd have a job to beat her. She could hear him laughing. Hannah smiled with a heady mixture of relief and pure joy.

In the bathroom she slipped out of her clothes and dropped every last thing into the laundry basket before stepping into the hot shower, letting the water course down over her head and shoulders, relishing the sensation of the hot water on her hair and her skin, waiting a long time before she finally picked up the shampoo and soap. It felt so very good to be home, to be safe and warm. By the time she stepped out and wrapped herself up in her bathrobe, she felt shiny and new and ready to start over.

⋆ ⋆ ⋆

Back at the party, way across the garden, Max, her taxi-driver-cum-knight in shining armour handed Liz a glass of fizzy water and then sat down alongside her on the garden bench.

'It's a great party. You said that you arranged it?' he said, sipping his mug of tea.

Liz nodded. 'That's right, for my mum and dad. It was for their fortieth wedding anniversary . . . or so we thought,' she said wryly.

He smiled, not picking up on the last part of the sentence. 'That's great. So you're close to them, your mum and dad?'

Liz nodded. 'Yes — I love them very much. We have our ups and downs like most families, but yes, we're close.'

'And you've got brothers and sisters?'

'Just the one sister. It's a family tradition. My mum's got one sister, called Fleur, and I've got a sister, her name's Suzie, and she's got two girls too. Our family tree is pruned into a neat, regular pattern. In every generation, going back as far as the eye can see, every branch has had two daughters on it, one is bright and clever and goes on to do marvellous things, while the other bright and clever one stays home and brings up the next generation.'

Max laughed. 'So from that I'm assuming you're the bright and clever one that's gone on to do marvellous things? What do you do exactly?'

Liz stared at him, trying to work out if he was being serious. 'Do you watch TV?' she said, when it became obvious he was.

'No, I'm afraid not. I haven't got one — I'm more of a Radio 4 man.'

'Really?' she said incredulously.

'Uh-huh, cross my heart,' he said.

'What about newspapers?'

'Sometimes. The *Independent* occasionally — oh, and I read books.'

'Okay . . . well, I'm on a TV show . . . '

He looked surprised. 'Really? Wow, that *is* amazing. I'm impressed. So what do you do on it?'

'I'm one of the comperes — you know, hosting it. I used to be a real live journalist before that, but then this came up . . . ' The words dried up. Liz wanted him to think well of her, and not be caught up in the whole TV fluff and glamour thing. To her relief he didn't seem in the least bit fazed.

'And what about your husband, is he here with you tonight?' he said, glancing around as if there was some chance they might spot him.

Liz shook her head. 'No, no husband, no boyfriend, no significant other. As long as you discount a designer wardrobe and a pathological addiction to shoes.'

He frowned. 'I'm even more amazed by that, but then again I'd hope that any man worth his salt wouldn't have let you wander around in the dark barefoot and miles from anywhere.'

Liz laughed. 'Hardly miles, but, no, there's no one. I think I've more of less given up on the whole idea of romance or maybe it's given up on me. I'm not great with relationships.'

He grinned. 'Why? Oh come on. A fabulous-looking woman like you should be beating the beefcake off with a stick.'

Liz took a sip of water. 'You'd like to think so, wouldn't you, but actually I think people — men — are freaked out by successful bossy women.'

'You're bossy?'

'Oh God yes,' she said. 'Can't you tell? Bossy, stroppy, hard work and a total control freak.'

He nodded. 'You know why you do it, don't you? You know, behave that way?'

She looked at him.

'Because you're afraid of being let down, afraid that if you let your guard down and let anyone in — let go by one iota and let that control slip — that you'll let the chaos in, that you'll get hurt and you'll lose control, lose yourself. You think that the only person who really knows how to look after you, when it comes right down to it, is you.'

Liz stared at him in amazement. 'And you

know that *because*?'

'Because I've seen it before. I had a great job, great salary, fabulous car and then one day I looked at it and wondered exactly what it was I'd really got. I had a show flat not a home, I was never there to enjoy it because the fantastic job I was so proud of kept me away from it all hours that God sends, and if you weren't there someone would try to shaft you — half the guys over thirty had ulcers or high blood pressure and anyone under thirty was clawing their way up the greasy pole to try and get a big slice of what you had — preferably your job, your office, your desk. Some people thrive on that sort of lifestyle but I was going into work one morning and suddenly realised that I didn't want to be there. I was lonely and lost — angry.'

'And so what? You dropped out and bought a cab?'

It was his turn to laugh. 'Something like that. Actually I took my money, rented out my flat, bought a cottage and a smallholding — '

'You should talk to my sister,' said Liz, with a little edge to her voice.

'But I don't want to talk to your sister, Liz. I want to talk to you,' Max said. And something about the way he said it made her believe him.

'So this rural idyll . . . ' she continued.

'Uh-huh.'

'How come you're driving a taxi if life in the country is so wonderful?'

'Because I want to. I've always liked driving so I do a couple of nights a week. Makes sure I don't become too insular. And it gets me out, gives me some shape to my week. Works for me — and now I love what I do.'

'And all this joy and contentment, does it include a good woman and a dog?' Liz asked, almost afraid to hear the answer.

Max nodded. 'Funnily enough, yes.'

Liz sighed; she might have known. He had to be too good to be true. 'And so where is she tonight, your perfect woman, presumably at home warming your slippers by the Aga?'

Max rolled the mug around slowly between his long fingers and shook his head. 'Sadly not, well, not any more. We had ten great years together and then four years ago she was diagnosed with cancer. She died two years ago. Her name was Julie.'

Liz felt her heart lurch. 'Oh God, I'm so sorry . . . I didn't mean to — '

Max held up his hand to stop the apology. 'You didn't do anything. I loved her very much. She was the most amazing woman and I wouldn't have missed the time we had together for all the world.' He laughed. 'She was really bossy too — stroppy, hard work . . . '

Liz looked at him, eyes prickling with unshed tears. 'God, I'm sorry. It must have been awful,' she said and then winced. 'To lose her, I mean, not her being bossy.'

'Worst thing I've ever had to deal with, but you know what? She taught me that you can't control anything — chaos comes whether you're ready or not. Love, death, you think you can hold it back but actually you can't, and if you're not careful you can miss an awful lot by trying to protect yourself too hard. You end up beating off the good things along with the bad.' He pointed to her glass. 'Now do you fancy another designer water or would you like a glass of champagne? Celebrate being a bossy, stroppy woman?'

* * *

'And then he asked me to marry him,' said Fleur, her expression ecstatic. 'Isn't that just amazing? I mean, who would have believed it? Flying all this way to come and see me.' Alongside her, Frank, who was holding her hand, beamed. It must have been the fourth or fifth time Fleur had told Suzie.

'That's wonderful,' said Suzie, hugging her aunt, while part of her attention was on the crowd behind them, trying to pick out Hannah or Megan's faces among the others. 'I'm really pleased for you.'

'Have you set the date yet?' asked Sam conversationally.

Fleur laughed. 'Some time soon before he comes to his senses would be my call.'

Frank smiled down at Fleur. 'She's right but for the wrong reasons. Obviously we all need to talk about when. We'd like everyone to fly over if possible.'

'We couldn't be more pleased for you, Fleur, but we really ought to go and find the girls,' said Suzie, gently tugging on Sam's arm. 'You haven't seen them, have you?'

Fleur shook her head. 'I'm afraid not — we

were just going to go and find Rose and Jack and tell them the good news. If we see them we'll tell them you're looking for them.' And with that she and Frank were gone.

* * *

Back at Suzie and Sam's house, Hannah had slipped on a pair of jeans and a cami top and, with her hair still wet, headed downstairs into the sitting room where Megan and Simon were busy sorting out the Scrabble.

'You're going to play, aren't you, Han?' said Megan as she set a plate of pizza slices down alongside the Scrabble board.

Hannah nodded and wordlessly sat down on the sofa next to Simon. The dogs were asleep on the floor, the cats on the back of the chair. Someone had put a saucer over the top of her mug of hot chocolate so that it wouldn't get cold. When she peeled it off, the marshmallows had melted into a sweet sticky layer over the top. Nothing could beat this.

They were two or three rounds into the game when the dogs sat up and then leapt to their feet barking as the back door opened. Her mum and dad were inside the sitting room before any of them had the chance to move.

'So this is where you've got to!' said Suzie, staring at the coffee table with the wreckage of their impromptu supper on it. 'Why didn't you answer the house phone or your mobile? We've been looking all over for you.'

'We didn't hear it,' Megan began. 'We haven't been back long.'

'Your mother's been worried sick,' said Sam. 'Why didn't you tell us that you were going home?'

Hannah stood up. 'I'm really sorry,' she said. 'This is all my fault. I was bored.'

Suzie stared at her. 'So you stole a bottle of booze and ran off?'

Hannah dropped her head; putting things right was the only thing she cared about, even if it did mean she was in big trouble. This trouble was so much easier than the trouble she could see ahead for Sadie.

'That wasn't me, Mum, honestly. It was Sadie and I know it was stupid but I didn't take it and I only ran away because she did. And I'm really, really sorry — about everything.' She didn't mean to cry but there was a little quiver in her voice. 'It was such a brainless thing to do, and you're right about Sadie, she is horrible — and cruel,' Hannah said, feeling the tears building up inside. 'I do know that, but I just didn't want to admit it. I thought that she was really cool and that it would be good to be her friend . . . '

She stopped and bit her lip. Suzie stepped closer. 'Do you want to tell me what happened?'

Hannah shook her head. 'No, not really.' She looked up into her mum's face and hoped that it would be enough.

'Whatever it is, you know you can tell us if you want to, don't you?'

Hannah nodded, trying hard to keep the tears

in check. 'I know, it was nothing really but sometimes you just know things from what might have happened, do you know what I mean?'

'Yes, I do,' said Suzie. 'And it's good if you can spot those things.' She put an arm around Hannah. 'You know that we love you, don't you?'

'Even when I've been so horrible.'

'Even then.'

'Oh Mum,' she snuffled. 'I don't think anyone loves Sadie, not enough to give her rules and make her feel like they care about her — not anyone, and that's why she wants to get people to do things.'

Suzie looked at her and waited.

'So I thought I'd come back,' Hannah said. 'And then I met Megan and Simon and we thought we'd all come back together.'

Suzie nodded to acknowledge Simon, who smiled back nervously.

Just for a moment Hannah was worried that Megan might say something to Suzie about her being drunk and about the man in the shed but instead Megan said, 'Do you want some hot chocolate? Only the kettle just boiled and there are some more marshmallows left in the jar if you want some.'

And it was her dad who said, 'Yes, that would be great and then I think we should all go back to the party — just for half an hour to say goodnight to Grandma and Granddad. Then if you want to come back here you can.'

Which was the kind of thing he used to say

before Sadie had shown up and everything had gone wrong.

* * *

Back at the party, as the evening unwound and the night darkened, the band had slowed the music down to match the increasingly mellow mood. People drifted away into the garden and to the tables to drink and chatter, while others made their way onto the dance floor, getting close, enjoying the softer sounds and the warmth of the summer night.

Fleur and Frank danced cheek to cheek, gracefully moving around to something soulful and romantic, while a few feet away Liz was enjoying her first dance with Max. For the first time all evening she was really enjoying herself, and thinking how very lucky she was that Grant hadn't showed up after all. She wouldn't have relaxed if he had been there, she would have been worried about what he was thinking, about the judgements he was making about her family and her roots. Certainly he wouldn't have been at all happy with something so homespun, not unless Liz had managed to whip up some big name to entertain them, and enough Class As to keep the party humming.

No, this was much, much easier and felt so much nicer. Max's strong arms held her tight but not too tight, he looked rakish and piratey in his jeans and creamy-white cotton shirt, which highlighted his tan, and the five o'clock shadow he was sporting made a lot of his cheekbones and those humorous bright eyes. She could feel her imagination struggling to invent all kinds of endings and ideas and possibilities but she kept it firmly in check. Tonight for once she was going to do this one step at time. Enjoy it for what it was, not what it might be or could be or could be shoe-horned into, although it was hard to resist the headline: *TV's top girl falls in love with gorgeous country farmer*.

Suzie meanwhile had her head on Sam's shoulder, delighted to be back in his arms, delighted that they had begun to clear the air between them. There was still a lot to talk about, a lot of things to do and a lot of things to get to the bottom of: the girls, the TV show, the garden, his job, and how they would make sure that they didn't end up back in this mess again. But she knew now that they were talking they could get it back on track. There was still the matter of her parents not exactly making forty years of happy married life . . . but that could wait a while longer.

Across the dance floor in a quiet corner away from the pack she could see Simon and Hannah experimenting with the first, uneasy, self-conscious fumblings of dancing for real with someone you cared about. It made her smile. Simon seemed like a really nice boy. Close by, Megan was dancing with her granddad Jack, who was swinging his hands from side to side, dancing in a circle. As her eyes met Suzie's, Megan waved and giggled and Jack gave her the thumbs-up and did a little granddad-dance-wiggle that made Megan roll her eyes and then fall into another fit of giggling. Suzie smiled, the tension easing. Tonight, for the first time in a very long time, everything felt all right.

Over by the kitchen she could see that Rory had arrived to give Matt a hand with the last of the clearing away, and both were singing along with the chorus of some mushy old love song, grinning at each other as they wheeled the last of the boxes outside.

Over by one of the tables, Suzie caught sight of Rose deep in conversation with a little group of women. There was something familiar about all of them. She was sure that one was the woman who had been trying to talk to her earlier in the evening, and as the music faded, Suzie decided to make her way over, something drawing her towards the little huddle.

'Do you want a drink?' asked Sam, as she slipped out of his arms and made her way across the marquee. 'I thought I'd get the kids something too.'

'Great idea,' said Suzie. 'I'm just going to see if Mum's all right.'

'And how about you?' he said, catching hold of her hand. 'Are you okay?'

She smiled at him. 'Never better.'

Sam grinned. 'You know that I love you, don't you?'

And for the first time in months she said, 'Yes and I love you too. I'll be over there.'

Sam nodded. 'Do you think your mum wants anything?'

Suzie shrugged.

'I'll ask,' he said.

The women gathered around the table didn't take much notice of Suzie or Sam's arrival.

'Hi Mum,' Suzie said. 'Everything okay?'

Rose nodded but Suzie wasn't totally convinced and hung on in there.

'I'm just going to the bar,' said Sam, looking from face to face. 'Anyone else here want a drink?'

Rose took a breath and then said, 'No, I'm fine thank you. Suzie, Sam — this is Janet. Janet Fielding. Janet, this is my eldest daughter and Sam, her husband.'

Suzie smiled. 'Pleased to meet you.'

'Janet was our bridesmaid.'

'Oh right,' said Suzie, holding out her hand. 'I remember the name now. We were looking for you earlier to come and have your photo taken with the rest of the gang. I'm sorry that we couldn't find you.'

Janet smiled graciously. 'It should be me apologising. I wasn't sure that I'd be able to make it tonight so I gave the girls my invitation.'

'Oh well, that's fine,' said Suzie, glancing at the other two younger women. It seemed like a rather bizarre solution, she thought, but given the night's events, it felt as if anything was possible. Both of them looked like a younger version of their mother.

'Helen and Nina. They're twins,' Janet said proudly. 'Non-identical obviously. Helen's a school teacher and Nina is training to be a nurse.'

Nina laughed. 'Like people need to know that, Mum.' She spoke with a soft Scottish accent.

'Well, some people do,' protested Janet.

'We met earlier, didn't we?' Suzie said to Nina as she shook their hands.

'This is my sister, Helen,' said Nina.

'Pleased to meet you.'

'It's lovely to meet you at long last, I've often wondered what you were all like,' said Helen brightly, which struck Suzie as an odd thing to say.

'So, drinks then,' said Sam. 'What's everyone having?

Helen laughed. 'We were thinking champagne, weren't we, Mum? After all, it's a real night to remember.'

'I don't know, I'm not sure if — ' Janet began, sounding slightly embarrassed.

Sam smiled. 'Don't you worry, I'm sure we've got some tucked away somewhere.'

At which point Liz came over, hand in hand with a tall good-looking man. 'Hi, there you all are — you okay?' she asked, glancing from face to face, her gaze finally settling on her mum. Obviously there must be something in the air if even Liz picked up on it, thought Suzie.

Rose laughed. 'What is it with everyone? I'm fine. Really.' She looked at the man with Liz and smiled. 'Hello, pleased to meet you. I'm so glad you finally turned up, Liz has been looking for you all night, you must be Mr Right.'

'Max,' said the man, leaning in close to kiss her on both cheeks. 'And you must be Liz's mum.'

'Call me Rose,' she said with a big smile.

'My pleasure,' said Max.

'We've heard a lot about you.'

Max laughed. 'Really?' he said, throwing a sideways glance at Liz, who blushed crimson.

But there was something else. Suzie could feel it bubbling just below the surface. Noticing the little look that passed between Janet and Rose, she couldn't help herself.

'What is it?' she asked. 'What is going on?'

'Nothing, not really . . . well, not at all.' Rose smiled nervously. 'There is something we need to talk about and there's really no easy way to explain all this,' she said, taking a deep breath. 'I just wish we had said something to you years ago.'

Janet nodded. 'You really should have said something, Rose, you really should have.'

Rose sighed testily. 'Hindsight's all very well, Janet, but it's not helping me now, is it? Suzie, Liz — Helen and Nina are your sisters. Well, your half-sisters anyway.'

'And they're twins,' said Janet, in case they hadn't caught it the first time.

As Suzie stared at the two of them, the first thought that came into her head was, *no wonder they look so familiar*. It was as if her brain had taken a second or two to catch on and realise exactly what Rose had said. Then it felt as if every thought she had ever had was blown out of her head, leaving a great empty void. A second later, the thoughts crashed back in like a tidal wave to fill it up. Questions clamoured for answers, stray thoughts careered round like stray bullets, so many that she had no idea where to begin or what to say.

Instead she simply stared at the three of them.

Nina was the one who spoke first. 'I know it must be a bit of a shock for you. We weren't sure if you knew or what you knew or what exactly you'd been told about us, so that's why I wanted to talk to you earlier — you know, kind of feel the way.'

'How long have you known about Liz and me?' Suzie stammered.

The two women looked at each other. 'Well, we've always known,' said Nina. 'Since we were little.'

Suzie glanced at Liz. Her mouth had fallen open and she looked like someone had just punched her.

'I can't deal with this,' Liz stammered, holding up her hands in shock. 'First of all I find out that my parents aren't married and now this? Have you any idea what the papers are going to make of it all? They'll have a field day. They'll rip us to shreds.'

Suzie watched the words register on Sam's face but before he could say anything, Nina smiled and said, 'We always watch you on TV — don't we, Helen?'

Liz glared at her. 'And say what?'

'Well, that we're proud of you, obviously,' said Nina, without a shred of malice. 'And we are. Really proud.'

'I don't understand, how on earth can we have sisters that we don't know about?' asked Suzie, looking at Rose. 'How come you never said anything, Mum?'

'Keep your voice down,' snapped Liz. 'People

can hear what you're saying, you know.'

'It's a long story,' Rose began, looking uncomfortable.

'It better be a good one,' said Liz.

'Why didn't you tell us, Mum?' Suzie pressed again.

Rose sighed. 'We should have. It was a mistake, I know that now, but at the time it seemed so much easier for everyone if we kept it to ourselves.'

Suzie stared at her. 'But we're your family, your children. Why didn't you tell us about Janet and the twins?'

'We talked about it — me and Rose and Jack,' Janet said.

Liz glared at her. 'You obviously did a lot more than talk.'

Rose held up a hand to quieten her. 'Liz, please, this is not Janet's fault. It's not really anybody's fault — in fact, to be fair, if it's anyone's really, it's mine. When we first got married your dad worked away a lot and before you two were born we always used to travel to places together, and then when I got pregnant with Suzie we decided to move back to Crowbridge. Our families and friends were here and it made sense. Things were okay to begin with, but we were both young and I was a bit fierier back then and we used to argue quite a lot and then make up, and it would all be fine again for a while.'

'Well, everybody does that,' said Liz. 'It hardly explains — ' she glanced at Helen and Nina — 'how we ended up with a whole family we knew nothing about.'

'I know,' countered Rose. 'I'll explain if you just let me. When I got pregnant again I was quite poorly and started to feel neglected and trapped all at the same time.' She sighed. 'Hormones do peculiar things to your brain. Your dad was away and it felt like I'd been abandoned. The more I needed him to be there, the further away he was. Looking back now, I should have said something — he would have been home like a shot. But I didn't, in fact, the more he tried to help me, the more distant and snappy I got. I just felt sorry for myself and hard done by and he felt like it was all his fault. Then I had you, Liz, and Suzie was little . . . it was a lot of things combined but I felt dull and tired and neglected and the long and short of it is I asked your dad to leave.' She smiled grimly. 'Actually I told him not to come back.'

Liz nodded. 'So you said before, but you didn't say anything about — about . . . ' She stared at the two other women. 'There being more sisters,' she eventually managed to say.

Rose nodded. 'I know. When I asked him to leave, your dad had got nowhere to go. So . . . ' She glanced nervously at Janet.

'So,' said Janet, taking up the story. 'Jack rang me up and asked if I knew anyone who'd got a room he could use while he was home. He wanted to see you both and see Rose to try and put things right and he needed somewhere to stay if he was going to do that. We'd all been friends for years,' she smiled. 'And I'd always had a bit of a thing for Jack.'

‘So we can see,’ snapped Liz.

Suzie shot her a sharp look, but Janet was oblivious. ‘Anyway I’d just split up with my boyfriend. He was in the RAF. I wanted to settle down and he didn’t — he said we were too young and he had things to do, and a wife and family weren’t really part of the equation. I was devastated. Anyway, I was sharing a house in Ely at the time and there was a spare room. Jack worked away for a lot of the time, so I didn’t think it would change things and to be honest I didn’t think that he’d stay that long. I thought he and your mum would sort it . . . But meanwhile, like I said, he’d be close enough to see you all. And he loved you two so much.’ Janet paused, eyes brightening with tears. ‘And Rose too. We all knew that. He was devastated when she said she wanted him to leave.’

Rose bit her lip. ‘These things happen, and it all seems so long ago now. Like another lifetime.’

‘Anyway,’ said Janet. ‘One night Jack and I started to talk and one thing led to another — we were both lonely, both liked each other, both been dumped by our respective partners, and it just seemed right, like sort of a natural progression really. We’d always got along very well. Although looking back now it was madness, but at the time it just seemed like the right thing to do — like fate.’ Janet laughed and shook her head. ‘We started going out together, first of all just to cheer each other up. Rose wanted a divorce, I hadn’t heard from my boyfriend since he left, and so as soon as Jack’s divorce came through we got married.’

'Just like that?' said Suzie in a whisper.

Janet nodded. 'I know it sounds mad now, but looking back on it that is exactly how it seems. I can't even remember now if he asked me. I mean, we must have talked about it but I don't remember much about it at all. One minute Jack was on my doorstep with his suitcase, broken-hearted and angry, and the next thing we're at the registry office. It was totally crazy, but we were both on the rebound, both hurt — probably if I'm honest, both trying to prove a point to the people who'd left us. And there we were, married.'

'And it took us about a week to realise that we'd both made the most terrible mistake,' said a male voice behind her.

Suzie turned and looked up to see her dad standing alongside her. Both Janet and Rose smiled at him.

'Janet and I had always been friends, but marriage — well, it wasn't right for us. To be honest, I think both of us knew that before the ink was dry on the certificate. I'd been seeing Rose every weekend, and we both regretted splitting up but I didn't want to let Janet down, even though we both knew it was never going to work. And then one night Janet's ex, Tony, turned up.'

Janet laughed. 'God, that was so awful. You wouldn't believe . . . We'd split up because Tony had said he wasn't ready to settle down but being apart had made him rethink and realise what he'd thrown away. He came round to see if I'd take him back, and there I was married to one of his best friends. He was stunned. Poor Tony — I'll never forget the look on his face. He'd turned up at the house with this big bunch of flowers saying he'd made the most terrible mistake, and I said that I had too.'

Jack nodded. 'When I got home Janet told me about Tony and said they had spent the afternoon talking — that they still loved each other and they both thought that they had a chance together, and that seeing Tony made Janet realise how much she loved him. And we both agreed that we'd just been foolish.'

'*Foolish?*' hissed Liz. 'How can you say that? Foolish? You make it sound trivial.'

'It wasn't like that at all. Don't tell me you've never done something foolish or something you've regretted, Liz? Janet and I were lonely and lost and great friends. We should have left it at that. We made one mistake, that was all — why compound it by making another? Janet had a second chance to be with the man she loved . . . '

'And Rose had already told Jack that she wanted him back. He was trying to find a way to tell me but was afraid of letting me down. I often think that if Tony hadn't shown up we might both have carried on — both unhappy . . . but anyway,' said Janet. 'We didn't. Jack moved back in with Rose and Tony moved in with me. It was all a bit up and down at the time and I'd been feeling terrible for weeks. Anyway I went to the doctor's, thinking it might be my nerves, and he told me that I was pregnant. Talk about a surprise. And given how far along I was, it was obvious the baby couldn't have been Tony's.'

Suzie looked from face to face. 'God . . . ' she whispered.

'How could you?' gasped Liz, looking first at Jack and then at Janet.

'They were married,' said Rose defensively.

Janet nodded. 'And of course when I went to the hospital they told me they thought we were having twins. Tony was brilliant about it. He said fine — we'd start over, just me and him and the babies. Move away. So we did, we moved up to Scotland. He was wonderful.' She smiled fondly. 'He still is.'

Suzie looked at her dad, who sighed. 'It was a hard place for all of us to be in. We were young and — well, to be honest I would really have liked to have seen the girls, and for you to have known them and spent some time with them, but I had to respect what Tony wanted. He wanted them all to have a fresh start and I can't blame him for that. He didn't want me to support them or pay for them — as far as he was concerned he wanted to be their dad.'

Helen nodded. 'It's true, and he's been the most brilliant dad.'

Nina laughed. 'The best. We've always known that he chose us.'

Janet smiled. 'We couldn't have any more children — after all that, Tony found out that he had a problem, and so in a funny way we owe the wonderful family we have got to this mess. Ironic, isn't it?'

Suzie looked from face to face, trying to imagine what it must have felt like to have been in the middle of it all. 'Was he upset that you were coming here tonight?' asked Suzie.

'Tony? Well, yes and no,' said Helen. 'I think he understood why we wanted to come but there was a wee bit of him worried that we might look at Jack and wish he'd been our dad — or something like that — but we don't know anything else. As far as we're concerned he's the only dad we've known and that's the end of it.' She grinned. 'We love him and we aren't planning to swap him any time soon.'

'I wish he was here,' said Janet wistfully. 'So he could see. What you imagine is often so much worse than the real thing.'

And to Suzie's surprise it was Rose who hugged Janet. 'You should bring him down to visit if you want to — whenever you want.'

'It's been too long since we've seen you,' said Jack.

Suzie thought of all the times they had spent together as a family, the brilliant, shiny, warm, loving man that her dad was, and realised how hard it must have been for him to have turned his back on his other two girls, who — now she knew about their parentage — she could see shared some of Jack's features. He must have seen it as his way of making life right for all of them.

'I wish you'd told us before,' Suzie said quietly.

'I know, we talked about this earlier upstairs, me and your mum, but it was so tricky,' said Jack. 'First of all, it was a different time back then. And if we'd told you I can see that we'd have felt you should meet, and that would have been hard for everyone — for Tony especially.'

'But not impossible,' said Rose gently, touching his hand. 'I do see that now, but it all seemed so complicated at the time, and I think we all thought there was very little to be gained.'

'And perhaps a lot to be lost?' asked Suzie.

Liz sighed. 'And so what we're saying is that if we hadn't had this party and if we hadn't tried to recreate your wedding reception, we'd never have known about any of this?'

Rose reddened. 'I don't know. I suppose we would have had to tell you eventually.'

Liz stared at her. 'Eventually?'

Janet smiled. 'I have to say when I got the invitation I thought you must know. An invitation sent from both of you, it felt like an olive branch, a call to come in from the cold. Whatever else we were, your mum and me, we were always great friends.'

Suzie looked across at her mum.

'It's true,' said Rose, in answer to the unspoken question. 'Janet came round when she and Jack were first thinking about getting together to ask how I felt about it — to say that if I was unhappy with it then she would put a stop to it. And I know she would have done, and I said no, that I was really happy for them. They were both lovely people. And you know what?' she said, looking first at Janet and then up at Jack. 'They still are.'

A tear ran down Suzie's cheek. 'Oh Mum,' she said. 'It must have been really hard for you . . . for all of you.'

'How about I go and see if I can get that champagne?' said Jack.

'I'll give you a hand,' said Sam. 'You coming Max?'

The women all looked at each other.

And then Helen smiled. 'You know how much I always wanted older sisters?' she said with a warm grin. 'I've been dying to meet you for years. We've got so much catching up to do.'

At which point Megan rolled up with Hannah and Simon in tow, and then Fleur came over with her arm through Frank's.

'We've just asked the band if they could pick up the pace a bit,' said Fleur. 'I asked them to play something with a bit of a beat, you know, cheer the place up.' She looked around the faces and smiled. 'For God's sake, come on,' she said. 'It's meant to be a party. Oh Janet, there you are — we were wondering where you'd got to — and are these your girls? Come on, they're going to play some rock and roll, come and dance, you can talk later.'

Epilogue

'And that brings us to the end of our programme,' said Suzie, who was leaning casually up against a potting bench, dressed in jeans, tee-shirt and a snug fleece. 'Next week we'll be taking a look at the old gardener's cottage and planning the planting for the courtyard, as well as looking at what Matt's got in store for the inside. And I'll be off to look at some of the stunning gardens in the Scilly Isles. So join us if you can here at Crowbridge, same time, same place.'

In the sitting room of their house, as the titles began to roll, Suzie leant over and pressed the off-switch on the DVD remote. She sat back. 'So,' she said. 'There we have it. What do you think?'

Megan, who had been sitting on the floor in front of the fire, leapt up and burst into a spontaneous round of applause, quickly joined by Simon and Hannah, who added in a couple of whoops for good measure.

'It's really good, Mum,' said Hannah sagely. 'I really liked it.'

It was late afternoon on Christmas Eve. Outside it was almost dark and they were all curled up around the fire to watch the pilot of Suzie and Matt's TV show.

'Ace,' said Simon approvingly.

'Fantastic,' said Megan.

Liz shook her head. 'I hate to say this, but it's brilliant: make-overs, cookery, grow your own, gardening tips, travel ideas — damn it, Suzie, you've managed to include every saleable trend from the last decade,' Liz said as she raised her glass of designer water. 'How about a toast? Here's to the famous fabulous television sisters and your programme being a roaring success.'

Suzie blushed furiously.

'Hear! Hear!' seconded Sam and Max.

'I think we should maybe break out the champagne,' said Sam, heading toward the kitchen.

'I'll clear a space for the glasses,' said Suzie, tidying the coffee table.

'You know I'm helping out down there part time now,' said Sam conversationally as he came back in. 'And I'm loving every minute of it.'

Liz raised her eyebrows. 'Really? At the gardens?'

Sam nodded.

'What about the factory?'

'I'm taking voluntary redundancy in the New Year. It'll give us a decent lump sum and Suzie and Matt really need someone at the gardens to sort out the business, the logistics, marketing, staff, the whole shebang really, so I'm starting there in January as general manager.'

'Working together?' said Liz incredulously.

'Don't say it like that. Sam and I make a great team,' said Suzie, grinning at Sam. 'We always have and given the choice between taking on an unknown quantity and taking on Sam, I'd be mad not to grab him with both hands. He's got all the expertise we'll need to help grow the business.'

Sam laughed. 'Not to mention being cheap.'

Suzie slapped him playfully before turning to Hannah. 'Hannah, would you please go and get the champagne flutes? Oh, and while you're there, get yourself and Simon another can of Coke if you want one.'

Hannah nodded. 'Is it all right if I have some crisps?'

Suzie nodded. 'Sure, there are some in the pantry. Oh and some Christmas cake too if you'd like some.'

'I'll give you a hand,' said Simon, getting to his feet.

Suzie watched Simon follow Hannah out. Between them Suzie and Sam had sorted out an awful lot of things since the anniversary party: the first being making the time and the effort to start talking to each other again — and not just about what they were doing, but how they felt.

Hannah had settled down and was doing well at school again, and although she wasn't always easy, she was a million times better than she had been. Sadie and Tucker seemed to have faded out of her life and Simon, gangly and funny and lovely to have around, had crept in and it didn't take a genius to see that he was a good influence.

Megan had grown two inches since the summer and was changing fast from little girl into little woman, but so far was cannily avoiding the pitfalls that had beset her older sister.

Suzie and Sam were still working life out, both realising that they had been horribly close to throwing away something very special. And now Sam was going to join Suzie in her grand passion. When Suzie and Matt decided they needed someone full time and hands-on to make the most of what they'd got down at the garden, it had been Matt who had suggested Sam for the job. Once he had, it seemed like a natural choice and Suzie had backed the decision all the way.

'Mum's hoping that we'll all go to the midnight carol service with her tonight,' said Suzie, ejecting the DVD and popping it back into its case.

Max got up to throw another log on the fire. 'You know, it looks like it's going to snow,' he said, peering out of the window.

'It'll be lovely if it does,' said Suzie. 'We can all walk to church.'

'Wouldn't it be nice to be snowed in?' Liz said dreamily.

'Not with you it wouldn't,' said Sam, topping up their glasses. 'Bloody hell, we have enough trouble getting into the bathroom as it is.'

It was almost exactly a year since they had sat around the fire and planned Jack and Rose's surprise party. No one could have guessed what an impact it would have, nor how much things would have changed since then.

Suzie glanced up at the mantelpiece as Sam opened the champagne. This year there were cards from her new sisters, Nina and Helen, in pride of place, and a bright newsy letter about Helen's engagement and how Nina's new job was going. There was also one from Janet and

Tony and alongside that another card in the shape of a palm tree hung with baubles from Fleur and Frank, standing beside an invitation to their wedding.

Sam made his way over to the sofa where Max and Liz were sitting. Liz held her hand over the top of her glass. 'Not for me.'

'Oh come on,' said Sam. 'One's not going to hurt you. You've been on water all day. It's not because of your famous dermatologist guy we've all been reading about in the papers, is it?'

As he said it, Suzie caught the look that passed between Liz and Max and felt her jaw drop.

'No?' Suzie whispered in surprise and delight. 'You're kidding me?'

Sam looked bemused. 'What is it? What did I say?'

'Not you,' said Suzie, waving towards the sofa where Max and Liz were sitting. 'Those two. Tell me I'm wrong.'

Liz threw back her head and laughed. 'Trust you to guess. We were going to keep it a secret and tell everyone tomorrow at lunch.' She paused and took a deep breath. 'Yes, we're going to have a baby. There I've said it now. Isn't it brilliant?'

'Oh my God,' said Suzie. 'I can't believe it, that's the most wonderful news.' Then she pulled a face. 'What about the big white wedding you always told me you were going to have?'

'Give me a break, I was six,' protested Liz.

'How did you know?' asked Sam in amazement.

Suzie grinned. 'It's something to do with being sisters.'

'So are you going to get married?' asked Sam.

Liz smiled as Max said, 'Actually we already are, we nipped off as soon as we found out about the baby. But before you get all upset about it, Liz thought we'd have a big white blessing next year, once the baby's here and we've had a chance to plan.'

'And invite everybody,' said Liz. 'I'm already trying to arrange it. I was thinking maybe we should try and talk Mum and Dad into getting married too — it's high time Dad made an honest woman of her.'

Suzie groaned. 'Remember what happened last time we tried to organise a party?'

Liz looked fondly at her husband. 'I found Max,' she said.

'So will your big white blessing be included in *Hello!* magazine?' Suzie said. 'If so, I'm thinking we're probably going to need a bigger marquee.'

Liz shook her head. 'No. We were thinking just family and friends — *all of them*,' she said, nodding towards the Christmas cards. 'Time Nina and Helen got to know what their big sisters are like.'

'Well, I couldn't be more pleased for you,' said Sam. He handed her a champagne flute. 'You can have one glass, surely?'

Liz glanced at Max. 'Maybe just a little one.'

'I can't wait to be an auntie. It's the most wonderful news,' said Suzie.

'It certainly is,' said Max, eyes bright, as he

took Liz's hand. 'And you know what? We're having a boy.'

Suzie looked at him incredulously. 'No. That can't be right? No one in our family ever has a boy.'

Liz giggled as she gently stroked her stomach. 'Well, we're going to start a new trend.'

Other titles published by
The House of Ulverscroft:

BEYOND THE STORM

Thompson

The fiercest storm in living memory pounds the shores of nineteenth century Cornwall, wrecking ships and bringing death and destruction to seafarers and coastal communities. When a young girl is found, washed up among the rocks of a remote North Cornish cove, she is barely alive. However her arrival, and the mystery surrounding her background, will affect the lives of those who come to know her — and, for Alice Kilpeck in particular, nothing will ever be the same again.

JAMRACH'S MENAGERIE

Carol Birch

1857. Jaffy Brown is running along a street in London's East End when he comes face to face with an escaped circus animal. Plucked from the jaws of death by Mr Jamrach — explorer, entrepreneur and collector of the world's strangest creatures — the two strike up a friendship. Before he knows it, Jaffy finds himself on board a ship bound for the Dutch East Indies, on an unusual commission for Mr Jamrach. His journey — if he survives it — will push faith, love and friendship to their utmost limits.

AFTER YOU

Julie Buxbaum

Ellie's life is turned upside down when her best friend, Lucy, is murdered. She drops everything to travel to London to pick up the pieces, desperate to help Lucy's traumatized child, who has simply stopped speaking. Ellie turns to the book that gave her comfort as a child — *The Secret Garden*. And while its story of hurt, magic and healing blooms around them, so too do the secrets Lucy kept hidden, even from her best friend. As Ellie peels back the layers of her friend's life, she's forced to confront her own as well. Suddenly her carefully constructed existence spins out of control in a chain of events that will transform her life — and the lives of those around her — for ever.

BLEAKLY HALL

Elaine Di Rollo

Old friends Monty and Ada worked together on the front line in Belgium: Monty was a nurse; Ada drove ambulances. Now, Bleakly Hall Hydropathic has brought them together again. Monty has arrived to look after the gouty residents taking the Hall's curative waters, via nozzle, douche and jet — and Ada is the maid and driver. For all those at Bleakly, the end of the Great War has brought changes — not all of them good. Monty has a score to settle with Captain Foxley; Ada misses her wartime sense of purpose and the Blackwood brothers must reinvigorate Bleakly for a new era. But with the crumbling, rumbling hydropathic threatening to blow its top, what will become of the folk thrown together in its bilious embrace?

THE COINCIDENCE ENGINE

Sam Leith

A hurricane sweeps off the Gulf of Mexico and in the back-country of Alabama, assembles a passenger jet out of old bean-cans and junkyard waste. An eccentric mathematician vanishes in the French Pyrenees. And the thuggish operatives of a multinational arms conglomerate close in on Alex Smart — a harmless Cambridge postgraduate who has set off to ask his American girlfriend to marry him. At the Directorate of the Extremely Improbable — an organisation so secret, many of its operatives aren't a hundred per cent sure it exists — Red Queen takes an interest. What ensues is a chaotic chase across an imaginary America, haunted by madness, murder, mistaken identity, and vast amounts of unhealthy but delicious snacks. The Coincidence Engine exists. And it has started to work.

THE SPOILER

Annalena McAfee

In January 1997, during the dying days of John Major's government, newspapers fight for a dwindling readership and they plunge downmarket amid rumours that the internet is about to change the world for ever. Two women journalists meet for the first time: Honor Tait (b. 1917), is a renowned journalist and veteran war correspondent. She is haunted by her past; Tamara Sim (b. 1970), is a writer of celebrity gossip for *Psst!*, the weekend entertainment supplement of *The Monitor*. She is struggling to secure her future, at any cost, in an increasingly precarious industry. When Sim is sent to interview Tait, their mutual incomprehension generates a rich seam of dark comedy. But when their different worlds finally collide, the consequences are devastating.